THE SHEPHERDS OF SHADOWS

THE SHEPHERDS
OF SHADOWS

HARRY MARK PETRAKIS
WITH A FOREWORD BY PETER BIEN

SOUTHERN ILLINOIS UNIVERSITY PRESS / CARBONDALE

11   10   09   08   4   3   2   1

Library of Congress Cataloging-in-Publication Data
Petrakis, Harry Mark.
  The shepherds of shadows / Harry Mark Petrakis ;
with a foreword by Peter Bien.
      p. cm.
  ISBN-13: 978-0-8093-2863-5 (alk. paper)
  ISBN-10: 0-8093-2863-1 (alk. paper)
  1. Greece—History—War of Independence, 1821–
1829—Fiction. I. Title.
  PS3566.E78S54 2008
  813'.54—dc22   2008012093

Printed on recycled paper. ♻
The paper used in this publication meets the minimum
requirements of American National Standard for Information Sciences—Permanence of Paper for Printed
Library Materials, ANSI Z39.48-1992. ♾

For the Cretan Nikos Kazantzakis,
greatest of the modern Greeks
(and his beloved wife, Eleni),
whose life and work have nurtured and inspired me

S S I A

SEA OF AZOV

CRIMEA

THE OTTOMAN EMPIRE
AT THE TIME OF
THE GRECIAN WAR OF
INDEPENDENCE

0   MILES   200

GREECE

Lamia

PINDUS MTS.

Thermopylae ✕

MT. PARNASSUS
BOEOTIA   EUBOEA

Missolonghi
(DESTROYED 1826)

Itea
Kravasaras   • Levadia

• Petra

Patras   Egion   GULF OF
CORINTH

Plataea
✕

ATTICA   Marathon
✕

Kalavryta

Aghia Lavra
(MONASTERY)

Lambi •

ARCADIA

Corinth

Athens

SALAMIS   Piraeus

Langadia

• M O R E A
(PELOPONNESUS)

Mills of Lerna
Kariterna •   • Tripolitza
(DESTROYED 1821)

Megalopolis

Epidaurus •

Nauplion •   ARGOLIS

Poros

HYDRA

SPETZIA

Navarino
(MAJOR
SEA BATTLE,
1827)

Kalamata   • Sparta
Mistra

Methone

Kardamyli

Tsimova •
MANI

Monemvasia •

N

0   MILES   30

CONTENTS

FOREWORD

PETER BIEN

❦I happened to be reading the typescript of *The Shepherds of Shadows* on the Fourth of July. As soon as darkness fell, I heard the muffled puffs of the fireworks going off in our distant village. That prompted me to remember the parade I had witnessed in Rethymnon, Crete, on the most recent March 25—Greek "independence day," the equivalent of our Independence Day. What a joy it was! Instead of the usual tanks, rifles, bayonets, and ranked soldiers, along came the city's *nurses* as most important, followed by firefighters, athletes, children from each of the primary and secondary schools, and only a few infantrymen at the end. Nationalism here was obviously less bellicose than usual. This made me think of George Orwell's piquant definition of nationalism as "the habit of assuming . . . that whole blocks of . . . people can be confidently labelled 'good' or 'bad'; . . . the habit of identifying oneself with a single nation . . . and recognising no other duty than that of advancing its interests." He opposes this to patriotism, by which he means "devotion to a particular place and a particular way of life, which one believes to be the best in the world but has no wish to force upon other people. Patriotism is . . . defensive, both militarily and culturally. Nationalism, on the other hand, is inseparable from the desire for power."[1]

Happily, Harry Mark Petrakis has given us an account of the Greek War of Independence that is patriotic rather than nationalistic. Of course, many of the conflict's "patriotic heroes," as depicted here, are extraordinarily nationalistic, because their primary objective is self-aggrandizement, the desire for power overruling everything else. Indeed, Petrakis's aim is to portray the truth of this (and presumably every) "crusade for freedom," honoring its motives yet refusing to label all Greeks "good" and all Turks "bad." This is brave. Arnold Toynbee was pilloried for reporting that Greeks as well as Turks had committed atrocities in Asia Minor in the conflict that ended (from the Greek point of view) as the disaster of 1922. The historian Nikos Svoronos was stripped of his Greek citizenship, his offense being a "slim volume offering a Marxist interpretation of the modern history of Greece."[2] *The Shepherds of Shadows* is not Marxist; it is simply an honest account of the horrors of any war and in this case of factionalism among the Greeks, who were fighting each other when all groups were meant to be fighting a foreign enemy. The novel attests to atrocities perpetrated by both sides, yet it celebrates the miracle whereby on occasion a squad of ill-trained Greek farmers, armed with primitive rifles that needed to be reloaded after each shot, could somehow withstand the sultan's professionalized cavalry and infantry.

We do not get the full story of the war, because the book's action goes only from the spring of 1823 until the summer of 1825, whereas Greece's definitive victory did not occur until the naval battle at Navarino on October 20, 1827. But we do get Lord Byron's arrival, his failure to lead a campaign owing to the obstreperousness of his Suliot troops, and his death; the horrible massacre of the Greeks on the island of Psara; the arrival of Ibrahim Pasha; General Yannis Makriyannis's successful defense of Navplion against Ibrahim's Egyptian army. And, of course, we hear about Markos Botsaris, Alexander Mavrokordatos, and the Maniot primates, who eventually assassinated Ioannes Kapodistrias, Greece's first president. But the chief characters, some of whom appeared as well in *The Hour of the Bell*, Petrakis's 1976 novel treating the period from autumn 1820 until summer 1821, are the compassionate Father Markos, the young soldier Manolis Kitsos, Theodoros Kolokotronis's scribe Xanthos, and Kolokotronis himself. There are love stories here, very tenderly treated; a marvelously described Greek wedding; the desperation of a storm at sea; all the gruesomeness of the *Iliad* in a prolonged description of hand-to-hand fighting.

What is Petrakis really trying to say about Greece through this patriotic rather than nationalistic reenactment of its struggle for freedom? His strange title provides part of the answer. Shepherds need constantly to protect their sheep against wolves. But the enemies of freedom are not as easily identifiable as wolves—they are sometimes one's supposed friends rather than one's enemies; nor are the sheep always so identifiable either. Thus the Greeks are shepherds of *shadows*. And they function in this way not just during their nineteenth-century War of Independence. Petrakis says it best in his epilogue: "From the time of the Persian invasions, through centuries of Roman and Ottoman rule, through two world wars, two Balkan wars, an Italian invasion, and German occupation in World War II . . . , [Greece] has managed to endure and survive." What *The Shepherds of Shadows* will teach its readers is that a nation deserves to endure and survive if it is devoted to a particular place and a particular way of life but has no wish to force those admired attributes upon other nations, knowing as it does that every absolute valuation of "good" and "bad" is merely another elusive shadow.

NOTES

1. "Notes on Nationalism," in *England Your England, and Other Essays* (London: Secker & Warburg, 1953), 41–42. Reprinted in *Collected Essays* (London: Secker & Warburg, 1961), 281–82.

2. Richard Clogg, "Lives and Times: New Opportunities for Truth in Greece," *Times Literary Supplement*, June 22, 2007, 7.

PRINCIPAL CHARACTERS

AHMED BAJAKI	Wealthy Turkish farmer of Kravasaras
ALEXANDER MAVROKORDATOS	From the Phanar region of Turkey who became the first provisional president of Greece
ALEXANDER IPSILANTIS	Prince from the Phanar, commanding Greek forces invading Moldavia and Walachia
ALI PASHA	Ruler of Ioannina who revolted against Sultan Mahmud II
ANAGNOSTARAS	Revolutionary leader
ANDREAS MAKRAKIS	Youth of Crete
ANDREAS MIAOULIS	Greek admiral from Hydra
ARCHBISHOP GERMANOS	Metropolitan of Patras, reputed to have begun the revolution
ATHANASIOS DIAKOS	Greek captain, spitted and burned by the Turks in April 1821
BALALAS	Veteran soldier from the Mani
BOUBOULINA	A famed Greek woman privateer
BOUKOUVALAS	Legendary old warrior from Suli
BROTHER APOSTOLOS	Monk at the monastery of Aghios Vasilios
COSMATOS	Cretan captain from Sphakia
DEMETRIOS IPSILANTIS	Commander of Greek forces
DEMETRIOS PAPANIKOLIS	Sea captain from Psara

ELIAS MAVROMICHALIS	Son of Prince Petrobey Mavromichalis
ELMAS BEY	Captain of Albanian mercenaries
ELIAS KARNEZIS	Comrade to Xanthos
FATHER MARKOS	Priest of Kravasaras
GHIOURIS	Second-in-command to Vorogrivas
KATERINA MAVROMICHALIS	Wife to Prince Petrobey Mavromichalis
KHURSHID PASHA	Turkish military commander
KONSTANTINE KANARIS	Greek admiral from Psara
LAMBROS KASANDONIS	Cretan captain
LASCARINA	Woman fighter of the klepht band
LEONIDAS KONTOS	Sea captain from Psara
LEONTIS MAKRIS	Mayor of Kravasaras
MANOLIS KITSOS	Youth of Kravasaras who joins klepht band
MATINA VROUVAS	Beloved to Xanthos
NIKETARAS	Greek revolutionary leader
PAPALIKOS	Renegade monk-soldier
PETROBEY MAVROMICHALIS	Prince of the Mani, commander of Greek forces
PETROS BACTAS	Seaman sailing with Leonidas Kontos
SKYLOS YARKAS	First mate to Leonidas Kontos
THEODOROS KOLOKOTRONIS	Revolutinary leader returned from exile to lead the Greek armies
VOROGRIVAS	Leader of klepht band on Parnassus
VOULA PSYCHOUNDAKIS	Young girl of Crete
XANTHOS	Historian from Zante and scribe to Kolokotronis
YANNIS MAKRIYANNIS	captain of Greek forces at the Mills of Lerna
ZARKAS	Lieutenant to Vorogrivas

CALENDAR OF THE GREEK
WAR OF INDEPENDENCE

1821

FEBRUARY: Prince Alexander Ipsilantis invades the Danubian provinces and proclaims the revolution.

MARCH: Archon and clerics meet to discuss the revolution under Metropolitan Germanos at the monastery of Aghia Lavra.

MARCH: Revolt breaks out across Greece.

APRIL: Kalamata falls to Petrobey Mavromichalis.

APRIL: The Greek patriarch is hanged in Constantinople, and thousands of Christians are massacred in Asia Minor.

MAY: Islands of Spetsia, Psara, and Hydra join the revolt.

SEPTEMBER: Tripolitza is destroyed, and Turkish inhabitants are massacred.

DECEMBER: The First National Assembly of Greek leaders meets at Epidaurus.

1822

MARCH: Chios is destroyed, and the Greek islanders are massacred.

OCTOBER: The Turkish flagship is attacked near Tenedos by the fireship of Konstantine Kanaris of Psara.

1823

MAY: Theodoros Kolokotronis is elected vice-president of the Executive Committee.

AUGUST: Markos Botsaris leads raids against the tents of the pashas. Botsaris is killed in the battle.

AUGUST: Lord Byron joins the Greeks at Missolonghi.
SEPTEMBER: First civil war breaks out in Greece.

1824

APRIL: Lord Byron dies at Missolonghi.
JUNE: Psara is destroyed, and the islanders are massacred.
JULY: Second civil war begins in Greece. Kolokotronis is imprisoned on Hydra.

1825

FEBRUARY: Egyptians make their first landing under Ibrahim Pasha at Methone.
MAY: Navarino surrenders to Ibrahim Pasha, who begins ravaging the Peloponnesus.
JUNE: Kolokotronis is released from prison to lead the Greek forces against Ibrahim Pasha.
JUNE: Ibrahim Pasha captures Kalamata; is defeated by Makriyannis at the Mills of Lema.
DECEMBER: Armies of Ibrahim Pasha join the Turks besieging Missolonghi.

1826

APRIL: Missolonghi falls, and the massacre or enslavement of Greeks follows.
JULY: The attempted invasion of Samos by the Turks is foiled by the Greek fleet.
JULY: The Maniots are victorious against Ibrahim Pasha at Politsaravon.

1827

JUNE: In London, England, France, and Russia sign an agreement on the Greek question.
OCTOBER: During the naval battle of Navarino, units of English, French, and Russian fleets sink the Egyptian-Turkish fleet of eighty ships, a turning point in the war.

1828

JANUARY: Ioannes Kapodistrias arrives as president of
Greece.

APRIL: Russia declares war on Turkey.

AUGUST: French troops land in the Morea to evacuate
Egyptian-Turkish forces.

1829

MARCH: England and France sign agreement on fixing the
frontiers of the proposed Greek state and its independence from the sultan.

SEPTEMBER: Greeks are victorious against the Turkish forces
at Petra in Boeotia. This is the last battle of the
Greek Revolution.

1831

FEBRUARY: The Maniots revolt against the government of
Kapodistrias.

OCTOBER: Ioannes Kapodistrias is assassinated.

1832

JULY: Russia, France, and England sign the final treaty
on the establishment of the new Greek state.

1833

FEBRUARY: Prince Otho, son of King Ludwig of Bavaria, is
installed as king of Greece.

THE SHEPHERDS OF SHADOWS

CHAPTER
ONE

That Sunday morning in March of 1823, the third year of the great war that the Greeks were fighting for their liberation from the Turkish sultan, spring came suddenly to the village of Kravasaras on the lower slopes of the great mountain of Parnassus. Within the span of a few days, pale-green stalks sprang up around the sheepfolds and cheesemakers' huts on the mountain. Tiny lizards emerged from the shelter of crevices to thaw their scaled bodies on the sun-warmed boulders. The chilled earth, for months barren and dark gray, lightened to silver, and the jagged rocks gleamed golden with reflections of the intensifying sun.

When Father Markos, the priest of Kravasaras, woke that morning in March, he glimpsed a faint daylight entering his house through the solitary window. He gratefully accepted the stronger light as a sign that he had survived another winter. Still in bed, he began his morning ritual, gingerly flexing his arms and legs to loosen his joints from the stiffness that had set in during the night. Pushing himself to rise, he groaned at the dagger of pain that stabbed his right shoulder, the arrow of pain that seared his right hip. Slumped on the edge of his bed, he gloomily echoed the lament of Euripides on how old age weighed on a man, heavier than the rock of Etna.

His house near the outskirts of the village was a single large room with his bed along one wall, a wooden table and several chairs in the center of the room, and a large stone fireplace in the corner. A small grate above the smoke-blackened hearth provided a means to make tea, heat soup, and boil pots of greens and herbs. During the cold nights of winter, the fireplace also warmed the room. In the corner closest to the fireplace, one small cabinet held a few pots, tin plates, and porcelain mugs, and beside his bed, a shelf on the wall held his treasured books. Besides copies of the Old and New Testaments inherited from his father, the books included the *Lives of the Church Fathers,* the *History of the Saints,* a handcopied manuscript of the Psalms, and his beloved Hesiod's *Works and Days.*

He walked stiffly on stockinged feet (he slept with his stockings on for warmth) and opened the door. In the moist dawn air, he inhaled the scents of spring, although he understood it did not portend any renewal in his own aging carcass.

Another spring would not mend the destruction in the village caused by the burning of the Turkish houses when the revolt broke out in March of 1821. The years since then were marked by roofs collapsing, stone walls crumbling, blackened beams falling. The rubble and debris, no longer fit for human habitation, had become the haven of stringy chickens and gaunt dogs. Repairs to the crumbled structures were almost impossible because most of the able-bodied men of the village and many of the younger women were away in the armies fighting the Turks. All that remained in Kravasaras was a population of about a hundred souls, mostly old men and old women and a covey of lean-boned and rag-tail children, grown unruly in the absence of their parents.

After Father Markos splashed cold water on his cheeks and dressed, stifling the pangs of hunger gnawing at his belly, he left his house and set out through the village toward the church for his Sunday morning service. To keep from reviving his despair, he avoided gazing at the ruins of houses. Yet, he could not escape a pang of sadness at the burned-out debris of the mosque, because of its former size and prominence in the village. Now, only piles of rubble remained of that resplendent temple, whose golden dome and graceful minaret once ascended into the sky above Kravasaras like a passageway to the stars. As he passed the ruins, his shoes scuffed across the dark stains of blood embedded in the stones, blemishes that two years of wind, sun, and rain had been unable to wash away.

On that historic day in March of 1821, the Christians of Kravasaras joined the revolt that had broken out in various parts of the country and slaughtered their Turkish neighbors. To that time, the Christians and Muslims had lived together for decades at least in harmony, if not as equals. Father Markos's closest friend in the village had been the Turkish farmer Ahmed Bajaki. The priest had found his friend's body among the corpses of the slain Turkish villagers who had been piled onto a heap and burned. Ahmed Bajaki's robe had been torn off his limbs, and his fez and white hair were matted with blood. In the cradle of his arm, as if his final struggle had been a vain effort at protection, was Ahmed's only son, Hassan, the beloved boy's slender throat slashed open by the knife of a vengeful Greek. For as long as he drew breath on God's earth, Father Markos would not forget the horror and grief he felt then.

He came to the ramshackle dwelling of Kyra, one of the older widows in the village. Father Markos knocked on her door each day to make sure the aged lady, who lived alone, hadn't fallen or expired in her sleep. That morning, as if she sensed his presence, before he had a chance to knock, the old woman jerked open her door. In the misted light of dawn, she resembled an apparition—lank, stringy hair and dark eyes burning in the skull of her face.

"Spare your knuckles, Father Markos!" she cried in a robust voice that belied her appearance and age. "The old dragon still lives!"

Father Markos marveled at the durability and spirit of the woman whose husband's death in a rockslide fifty years earlier had left her a young widow. In the second year after the revolt began, her only son had been killed in the mountains of Thessaly while fighting the Turks. Each time Father Markos considered the unfair burden of grief the poor woman had endured, he drew upon St. Paul for reassurance: "Shall the mortal vessel say to him that formed it, why hast thou made me thus? Hath not the potter power over the clay to make what design he wishes?"

"God be praised, Kyra," Father Markos spoke loudly because the old woman was nearly deaf. "We've both survived another night." As he waved good-by, he called, "I'll see you in church."

He continued walking through the narrow, cobblestone village streets, and beyond the tiled roofs of the houses, he glimpsed the colossus of the mountain looming above Kravasaras. A series of massive ridges and cliffs ascending to a snow-crowned peak, the majestic summit glowed brilliantly in sunlight. Under a starry night sky, Parnassus reflected a lustrous silver. What couldn't be seen from the village at night were the mountain's luxuriant forests of spruce, fir, and balsam, the air within the trees sweet and cold.

Father Markos gazed with pleasure and awe at the mountain's grandeur and imagined shepherds waking beside their flocks and stretching their winter-cramped limbs under the sun. At that moment, a flock of wild crows took flight, their black-plumed wings sweeping along the open face of the rock.

He could not imagine any village in all of Greece placed any more providentially beneath the sanctuary of the mountain, once the sacred domain of the legendary gods. Kalovouno, the villagers called Parnassus, the Good Mountain that embodied the history of their land from ancient times when the armies of the Persian kings, Darius and Xerxes, descended from the North. From that period through the Dark Ages, successive waves of invaders had followed—Byzantine adventurers, Frankish crusaders, and Venetian traders, all laboring to cross those peaks. Finally, the Turks had succeeded and enslaved the land.

But the mountain never lost its place as a sanctuary of freedom. During the centuries of Turkish occupation, it had been home for the staunch warrior bands of klepht, or guerilla fighters. Any invading army had to travel the mountain's precipitous passes and cross hazardous ravines where small bands of brave men could hold them at bay for weeks. No matter how many lowland villages the Muslims ravaged and burned or how many forts they leveled, as long as the klepht held those mountain battlements, the whole of Greece could never be defeated.

At the outskirts of the village, Father Markos came to his beloved church of Saint Athanasios, a whitewashed, stone structure with a red-tiled dome whose peak offered up a small, golden cross. Next to the dome arose the bell tower enclosing the great ornate bell that could be heard for miles across the countryside.

The original church of Saint Athanasios had been built in Kravasaras during the reign of the last Byzantine Emperor, Constantine XI Palaeologus, who reigned until Constantinople fell to the Turks in 1453. By 1710, eroded by time and weakened by earthquakes, the church in Kravasaras collapsed.

Greece had been under Muslim rule then for several centuries, and the villagers petitioned the pasha of the province for permission to rebuild the structure. In granting them a dispensation to erect their church, he imposed brutal restrictions. They were not allowed to labor more than a total of five hours a week and those hours confined to darkness, so that the eyes of the Muslim faithful might not be offended by the sight of the infidel's church.

Working by moonlight and torchlight, the Christian men, women, and children of Kravasaras worked no more than the five hours a week. For ten years, the church grew slowly, the old people grieving when their time came to die because they would not see it completed. Finally finished, the last stone mortared in the autumn of 1720, the Greeks of Kravasaras joined with Christians from neighboring villages in a solemn thanksgiving for the consecration of the church. All that remained was to install the magnificent bell brought by ship from the artisans in Italy into the church bell tower.

The guileful pasha, who had never expected to see the church completed, delivered his final edict. He ordered that the bell be buried in the cemetery of Kravasaras. There it would ring for the bones of the infidels as a reminder of the benevolence of their masters even unto death. Stories passed from grandmothers and grandfathers and recalled and whispered to children told of hearing the bell tolling from the cemetery on those nights when the wind wailed from the mountain across the plains.

In the spring of 1821, when the Greek villagers of Kravasaras joined the revolt breaking out across Greece and after killing the Turkish villagers, the bell had been excavated and hung in the bell tower of the church. The first time Father Markos heard it ring, he wept with thankfulness because the bell his grandfather and father had never heard was finally pealing its litany of freedom. He also grieved because the terrible price paid for the bell's resurrection had been the slaughter of their Turkish neighbors.

Father Markos pushed open the creaking door of the church and stepped into the damp shadows. As his eyes grew accustomed to the dark, the saints, stern and vigilant sentries of the church, beckoned from their icons. He made his sign of the cross and sent them a silent greeting.

After lighting the wicks of the oil lamps hanging before the icons, he prepared for the morning liturgy, pouring a cup of wine into the chalice and trimming the dried crusts of bread into tiny pieces. He slipped carefully into his faded and worn vestments. After the outbreak of the revolt, wandering peddlers no longer brought in cloth and brocade, and Father Markos didn't know what he would do for another vestment when the old one finally fell apart.

As he finished preparing the communion, Panfelio, his sexton, a wizened grasshopper of a man, appeared, anxiously awaiting the priest's permission to ring the bell summoning the faithful to church. Father Markos nodded assent, and the old man scurried to his task. A moment later, the pristine sound of the bell of Saint Athanasios pealed across the village and the countryside. The bell seemed the only part of the village undamaged by the ravages of war and time. In some ways, it seemed to the priest, the century of entombment had strengthened the bell's resonance, which year by year, grew even purer and stronger.

As Father Markos waited at the altar table, the first villagers entered the church. They walked forward slowly to stand with folded hands before the sanctuary. Grizzled old men, tattered clothing covering their lean frames, stood beside wiry-bodied old women, gaunt from years of labor and scavenging for food. In the flickering light from the oil lamps, their faces appeared impassive, drained of emotion. Only when they bent to speak in whispers to the children who held their hands or clutched at their clothing did a warmth enter their cheeks and a sweetness inflect their voices.

The priest began the liturgy, his chants carrying in hollow echoes through the church. Almost every man and woman who survived in Kravasaras had lost a brother or husband, a daughter or a son, in the years of fighting. Father Markos prayed for those who had died. He prayed for the living as well, even as he understood his prayers were of meager comfort. For every man and woman, suffering was as solitary an experience as dying. He knew suffering and death prevailed across all of Greece. Fulfilling old prophecies, smoke stained with blood rose from countless fires, and a mist of tears covered the stars. Brutalities and catastrophes followed one another.

In the second year of the war, Father Markos had learned the dreadful tidings about the island of Chios, destroyed by marauding

Turks who had slaughtered the men and sold the women and children into slavery. He also heard of the destruction that befell the Turkish inhabitants of the city of Tripolitza in the first year of the war when it surrendered to the Greek armies besieging its walls. A band of Greek soldiers who had been among those who attacked Tripolitza after its surrender had passed Kravasaras on their way home. They spoke proudly of the slaughter and the loot they had collected when that city fell.

"We crushed the vermin like roaches!" one man boasted. "That garbage heap of Turkish bodies made it so hard for my horse to trot along the street, the poor creature nearly collapsed!"

When Father Markos considered all these barbarities, he thought sadly that, however noble the cause, war unleashed a ferocity from which no one escaped. So in his liturgy, he prayed for both Christians and Muslims that when their struggle finally ended, they would be able to live together in peace. Despite all the cruelty and bloodshed, no one could be certain whether in the end the Greeks would be victorious, or whether this revolt, as with those insurrections in past centuries, would end again in failure.

Yet, Father Markos found it an agony to believe a merciful God would allow His people to fight so long and suffer so much and still deny them freedom. So that Sunday morning, the priest offered his fervent prayers once more for their tormented and war-torn land to be liberated. His parishioners walked forward to take communion, and he gave them each a tiny spoonful of wine from the chalice. He bent to offer communion to the children, their great, dark eyes staring up at him as if imploring him to redeem them from hunger and sorrow.

After the service, the worshipers dispersed, and Father Markos removed his vestments while Panfelio extinguished the wicks of the oil lamps. Before walking to the square where the villagers gathered each Sunday for a communal lunch, the priest rested for a while on a bench in the cemetery adjacent to the church. Each year, the markers and stones, shaded by tall cypress trees, grew more numerous. His beloved grandmother occupied one of the graves beside his grandfather, who had been a priest in Kravasaras and one of the builders of the church. The graves included Father Markos's father, also a priest in the village, as well as his mother and his sister. The cemetery held his dear wife, Antonia, who had died of illness at nineteen, three years after their marriage. Father Markos lamented the brief span of her life, and he grieved because their union had only produced one child, stillborn, before her death. He had been denied a daughter to console his old age and a son who might also have become a priest to serve the village after he was gone.

But his beloved family did not lack for companionship in death. In addition to the old men and women buried there, the cemetery held the graves of young men and women who had languished under slavery and died of heartsickness and despair. There were young mothers who had died in childbirth and children who had perished of illness. In the end, the bodies of young and old were joined in dust, their skeletons linked in the ancient and eternal fraternity of the dead.

The priest finished his prayers for the souls of those who were deceased, and as he walked from the graveyard, powder from stalks of asphodel drifted eerily across the flowers. The petals rustled and trembled, as though the inhabitants of the graves were bidding him farewell.

On Sundays following church, the villagers assembled in the square for their lunch, each family contributing what meager fare they could muster—a few pots of lentils and wild greens, cooked with snails and herbs, chunks of creamy, white cheese, and herdsman's bread so hard it had to be soaked in water before it could be eaten. As a special treat that Sunday, Varkelis, the shepherd, contributed a basket of wild, sweet grapes he had brought down from the mountain.

The priest blessed the frugal meal, and the villagers ate as they had grown accustomed to eating in that period of deprivation, less with pleasure than for sheer survival. They spoke very little, saving their breath, hoarding their energy for the food. The great, sad eyes of the children having skewered his appetite, Father Markos refused the larger portions several of the villagers pushed upon him.

"Eat, in the name of God, Father!" Leontis Makris, the church elder who served as mayor of the village, said. He was, at seventy-seven, just a few years older than Father Markos, a wiry, vigorous old man with thick, white hair and bushy, black eyebrows. "God help us if you grow weak and ill, and we lose you!"

"You won't lose me that easy, Leontis," the priest patted his midriff hidden beneath his cassock. "You may not be able to see my girth, but I still have ample fat to sustain me."

As the old man moved away, the priest motioned to a pair of pale-cheeked children and offered them a portion of his lunch. He kept a slice of bread and some herbs for himself. Despite his reassurances to Leontis, he did not wish to fall ill and be of little help to his flock.

After the meal, the children, who were the only ones who had eaten enough to replenish their energy, shrieked and ran in the village square, while their grandparents felt their own hungers soothed as they watched the children play.

Later that afternoon, as the women were cleaning up, and the men sat under the plane tree smoking their chibouks, a ragged party of Greek refugees straggled into Kravasaras. Father Markos had seen such bands before, survivors from one of the villages on the other side of the mountain. Without the protection the mountain and its freedom fighters afforded them, these villages were attacked and pillaged by Turks or looted by gangs of renegade Greeks without allegiance to any cause but their own greed.

In the first year after the outbreak of the revolt, the villagers of Kravasaras had greeted these refugees with compassion, sharing their bread, offering them refuge in their houses. As the bands became more numerous, they also grew more desperate and rapacious, stealing chickens or a sheep and even breaking into the houses. Now, when such refugees appeared, the villagers greeted them warily.

This band consisted of about thirty to forty men and women, most of the men and women older, with a few younger women, and about a dozen children, lean and tense as wolf cubs. One of the women, trailing some distance behind the others, carried a small, blanketed bundle. Because the woman wore a ragged shawl over her head, Father Markos could not tell her age or whether the bundle she carried was a baby.

The leader of the band was a swarthy man in his sixties, skin drawn tight as a drum across his cheekbones, his eyes deep, black pits under his brows. With apprehension, Father Markos noticed a bone-handled pistol jammed into the sash around the man's waist.

"Welcome to our village," the priest spoke quietly, trying to keep his voice reassuring. "If you're in need of food, we have little ourselves, but we'll be glad to share what we have."

"God knows we can use any help you can give us, Father," the man's voice was hoarse and rough as his face. "I'm Akragas from the village of Mertina, on the other side of the mountain. When the cursed Turks first attacked us a year ago, they stripped us bare, looted whatever grain we had stored, and even carried off a few of our women. Some of us managed to escape into the woods to wait until they left, and then we returned to our village, thankful we were still alive."

He paused, and then, bunching his body, he spit violently at the ground. "A month ago, the bloody savages struck us again, took whatever they hadn't stolen before, and, because they thought we were hiding provisions, burned our village to the ground!" Rage made his voice shrill. "We had only the clothes on our back and not a solitary roof to shield our heads. So we took off, crossing the mountain, living on animals we killed or on wild herbs and whatever else we could beg from each village we passed."

"God's mercy be upon you," Father Markos said. He spoke solicitously, trying to soften the sullen faces of the women and the tense faces of the men. "Come to the tables, and our villagers will offer you whatever we have."

In the following hour, in response to the pleas of the priest, the villagers carried a few loaves of hard bread and boiled herbs to the square. The refugees ate ravenously, several arguments breaking out among those who felt they were being deprived a fair share. The hungry children whined and tugged at the skirts of their mothers. The ragged woman with the bundle on her knees sat on a bench a short distance separated from the others. No one moved to take her any food.

Feeling a twinge of pity for the woman, the priest carried her a chunk of wheat bread and some cheese. As he came closer, he saw that the open blanket she cradled on her knees held a tiny, naked baby she was trying to clean with a piece of cloth. Father Markos noticed the soft dark tangle of the baby's hair, its skin tinted brown as if it had been burned by the sun. When his shadow fell across the woman and child, she looked up in terror, clutching the baby tightly.

"Don't be afraid," the priest spoke reassuringly. "I've brought you a little food."

The woman was disheveled, her dark hair tangled about her cheeks, her shawl a rag. Yet, through the soiled and shabby disarray, she had a lovely face with fine, delicate cheekbones and large, raven-black, almost-Oriental eyes.

She held the baby tightly on her lap as she bent to kiss the priest's hand. Afterwards, shyly and awkwardly, she took the bread and cheese he had brought.

"Thank you, Father," she whispered.

As she raised one hand to brush her long, thick strands of hair away from her cheeks, he saw a large, ugly, crimson bruise on her forehead.

"Have you been injured?" Father Markos asked with concern. "Our village midwife can bring you a poultice."

"It's all right," the young woman said quickly. "It's healing now."

Father Markos gestured toward the infant.

"What is the child's name?"

The young woman hesitated and lowered her head. "He hasn't been baptized." Her voice trembled as though she were ashamed of her admission. She fell silent again, her hand holding the bread and cheese, waiting for him to leave before she ate.

After a moment, Father Markos murmured, "God bless you both, my child." As he started to walk away, the woman tore hungrily at the chunk of bread.

When the priest returned to the group of refugees, one of the old women hissed, "Don't waste your time on that one!" She spoke harshly, "May she and her bastard burn in hell!"

"Our savior teaches us to have compassion for all," the priest said reprovingly.

At that moment, Akragas, the leader of the band, who was nearby, interrupted. "Is this all the food you can provide us?" he asked sternly. "We're not beggars or gypsies, you know. We're Greeks driven from our homes by the bloody Turks!"

"We have so little ourselves," Father Markos said. "Look around at our village, and you can witness our own poverty."

"I can see you've got roofs over your heads to protect you from the rain and cold," Akragas said, envy and resentment spitting the words from between his teeth, "You've got goats for milk, and you've got chickens!"

"We have had to kill most of the chickens for food," Father Markos said. "We keep the ones that are left for the eggs to feed our children."

He paused. "Believe me, my friend, we'd be pleased to share more if we had more."

The man's dark face seethed with an effort to suppress his anger.

"Well then, for God's sake, how about breaking out some of that wine you serve up for communion? You've got thirsty, hungry people here, and I'm sure God would prefer they be taken care of first before you worry about saving souls!"

"I have so little wine left that I dole it out for communion in drops," the priest said. He did have a few small flasks stored away in a cellar that he was tempted to provide as evidence of his good faith, but he feared the wine might only aggravate their anger and hostility.

For the remainder of the afternoon, the refugees remained huddled together. Akragas squatted on the ground under the shade of a plane tree, his arms folded, legs stretched out in front of him. Despite the man's sullen immobility, Father Markos felt the threat of his presence.

Later, as the priest walked to the house of an ailing villager, he passed a group of the refugee children. They had snared a rock pigeon, and one of the larger boys pried the bird's beak open until it broke. While the other children shrieked in approval, he savagely squeezed the downy head of the pigeon between his fingers, crushing its skull. The bird's wings fluttered with a final spasm and then went limp.

"For shame!" the priest said sternly. "That poor creature had done nothing to you!"

"He won't go to waste, your holiness," the boy smirked. "We'll roast and eat him, bones and all."

The priest turned away with a shudder, grieving at how the brutality of their elders bred cruelty in the children.

As the shadows of late afternoon slanted across Kravasaras, the lanes and houses receding into twilight, intimations of danger grew stronger. Fearing the arrival of darkness, many of the villagers retreated into their houses and barred their doors. About a dozen men and women, seeking the reassuring presence of their neighbors, gathered with Father Markos in the church. Meanwhile, the only one of the refugees who joined them in the church was the young mother who stood in the shadows in a corner, her baby clasped in her arms.

Stavroula, one of the old village women, bent closer to the priest.

"Be on your guard, Father," she whispered hoarsely. "They could have sent that one in to spy on us."

"I don't think so," the priest said. There was something vulnerable and innocent about the woman and infant that elicited pity and not suspicion. He walked to the corner where she stood, and when she raised her head, he saw the paleness of her cheeks and the intensity of her dark eyes. He was struck once again by her beauty.

"Do you want me to leave, Father?" she asked in a thin, nervous voice.

"Stay as long as you wish, my child. If you'd like to sit a while, there is a bench in the alcove."

"If it's all right," she said quickly, "I'll just stand here."

At that moment, the door opened, and Leontis entered with his wife, Dafni, and granddaughter. He motioned the priest to one side.

"That band is turning ugly, Father," he said in a low, concerned voice. "They're arguing amongst themselves like buzzards over the spoils. I hope to God they're not trying to decide whether to attack us."

"They may be hungry but they're Greeks and Christians," Father Markos spoke as much to hearten himself as to encourage Leontis. He knew there was little he or any of his parishioners could do to prevent an attack. He returned to the holy altar and with the other villagers knelt and prayed for the safety of their village.

While they were still at their prayers, his sexton, Panfelio, hurried into the church.

"Father Markos!" he said shrilly, "There are horsemen coming!"

"God help us!" the priest exclaimed. If the horsemen were Turks who had somehow made their way across the mountains, villagers and refugees alike would be in peril. He hurried to the door and peered out, the sexton and villagers huddled behind him, one of the old women praying in a terrified voice.

When the horsemen came nearer, Father Markos saw there were two men riding along the trail toward the church, the hooves of their horses clanging noisily on the stones. The men were armed with muskets and pistols, bulky cartridge belts strapped across their chests. Although their leisurely pace suggested they were not Turks intent on doing the villagers harm, Father Markos waited anxiously—they

still presented an unknown danger. Before the church, the younger
of the two riders, a strapping, young giant, dismounted. He was
strikingly handsome, with strong, distinct features and blue eyes the
priest found strangely familiar.

The young man stepped forward and reached down to grasp and
kiss the priest's hand. When he straightened up, he smiled, his teeth
flashing white in the sun-bronzed circles of his face.

"Don't you recognize me, Father Markos?"

"I'm sorry, my son," the priest shook his head in bewilderment.
"Forgive my memory and body, both racing to see which fails first."

"I am Manolis Kitsos," the man said. "I'm from this village, from
Kravasaras."

"God be blessed!" the priest exclaimed. He could hardly believe
this stalwart warrior was the same stripling youth Manolis who had
left the village two years earlier at the outbreak of the revolt to join
the klepht band of the chieftain Vorogrivas. The last time Father
Markos had seen the young man was a year earlier at the funeral of
his mother, Ephrosene.

When the priest fervently embraced Manolis, he felt the pressure of
his cartridge belt and pistol at his waist. A scent of mountain thyme
rose from the young man's clothing.

"Forgive me for not recognizing you, my son!" the priest said. "You
seem so changed from the last time I saw you."

"Time and war do that to a man, Father," Manolis smiled. He
gestured to his companion. "This is my comrade, Zarkas, from the
village of Anochorion."

Zarkas was a weather-beaten warrior with frosty cheeks and black
eyes that held the wary glint of a man who lived close to animals and
the weather. He bent and brusquely kissed the priest's hand.

"Manolis talks often about you and his village, Father," Zarkas
said.

"God bless you both!" the priest said, and his voice trembled with
relief because they were allies and not enemies. "We welcome you
heartily! I am only sorry we have so little to offer you. Our village
has been decimated by the war."

"We aren't looking for anything, Father Markos," Manolis said.
"We have brought provisions in our saddlebags for you."

He motioned toward the refugees still gathered in the square under the plane trees.

"We found that band trekking across the mountain several days ago," he said. "We gave them food and blankets, and, after a couple of days, they continued on their way. They claim they're on the way to relatives in a village farther south. They're a desperate lot, and that man who leads them is a real rogue. Knowing Kravasaras was in their path I thought it best Zarkas and I ride down to make sure they didn't do you any harm."

"We gave them what food we could spare," the priest said. "I'm afraid that wasn't very much. One must pity them for they've lost everything. The Turks looted and burned their village."

"As they've looted and burned a hundred other villages across Greece," Zarkas spit vehemently. "Those bloody butchers are most courageous when they fall on a settlement of women and children!"

The villagers peered out from within the church and seeing the horsemen conversing amiably with Father Markos grew emboldened and came outside to join them. When they discovered one of their visitors was Manolis Kitsos, they greeted him with jubilation.

"Your mother, bless her soul, was my closest friend!" one woman cried.

"She and I took communion together!" another woman said enthusiastically.

"When you were a child, I carried you in my arms!" old Barba Nikos fumbled to clasp the hand of Manolis.

Their pleasure in greeting the young warrior was the first evidence of joy Father Markos had witnessed among the villagers in a long time. Manolis greeted them warmly, pleasing a number of them by recalling their names.

"We've brought fruit, cheese and some boiled potatoes for you," Manolis said. "We'll also send some food over to those refugees. Zarkas and I will keep an eye on them as well and make sure they're on their way in the morning."

Zarkas unpacked the saddlebags on the horses. While Manolis distributed the provisions to the villagers, Zarkas carried bread and cheese to the refugees. When Zarkas returned, he spoke in a voice so low only Manolis and the priest could hear.

"Like tossing scraps to a pack of starving wolves to keep them at bay," he said somberly. "That leader is a real cutthroat. I warned them, but if there's trouble, he'll be the one to light the fuse."

As night fell, the presence of the two mountain fighters reassured the villagers and rekindled the custom of hospitality among them. A number of families offered the refugee women and children shelter for the night in their houses. Remembering the young woman and her baby, the priest asked Leontis if he would provide them shelter.

"We'll be glad to share our house with them," Leontis said gravely. His wife, Dafni, nodded in agreement.

After everyone had been settled, and the refugee men bedded on their blankets in the square, the priest led Manolis and Zarkas into his house. He lit the tiny wick floating in a saucer of oil, producing a faint light that dispelled the lengthening shadows.

"Every family in the village would be blessed to offer you their hospitality," the priest said, "I'd count it an honor to have you both sleep here." He spoke to Manolis. "It would also please me, my son, if you accepted my bed."

"I've slept on rocky, barren ground for years now, and my body no longer abides a bed," Manolis laughed. "A roof over our heads is bounty enough. Don't worry about us, Father. Zarkas and I will toss our saddle blankets here by the fireplace."

With kindling and logs from the small woodpile outside the house, Zarkas lit a fire in the fireplace. He tugged off his cartridge belts and hung them on a nearby hook and laid his musket and pistol on the floor close to his blanket. In a few moments, the fire warmed the chilled air and brightened the room.

"Hot as midsummer in here now," Zarkas said. He tugged off his jacket, lowered himself to his blanket, and sprawled on his back. "God be praised for letting this worthless Greek survive another day." He finished his brief prayer with a fervent "Amen!" In an instant, the klepht was fast asleep, his breath erupting from his lips in a low, hoarse snore.

Outside, the village had grown quieter. From one of the goat pens, a dog barked, and among the refugees settled in the square, someone played a reed flute, the sound carrying in plaintive echoes across the night. Manolis sat on his blanket before the fire, his booted legs stretched out, and stared silently into the flames. The priest sat in a chair close to him and recalled the day, two years earlier, when Manolis had left the village to join the guerilla band in the mountains. The youth had asked his mother, Ephrosene, to plant a carnation and a rose to mark his departure. As long as they bloomed, he told her, she could be sure he was well. If they withered, she'd know her son fighting to free Greece was dead, and she should have the priest say a last Mass for his soul.

For the next year, even as winter mantled the land, both flowers miraculously survived, their blooms intact. Then, with the second winter, an early cold spell struck the village. While the rose held its bloom, the carnation withered. In terror and rejecting the warnings of the villagers, Ephrosene Kitsos fled from the village to search for her son she was sure was dying or already dead. She lost her way in the mountains, and several days later, shepherds leading their flock to higher ground found her body and brought her back to the village. She had fallen to her death in a ravine.

Father Markos sent two villagers into the mountains to seek out the band and notify Manolis. A day later Manolis and half a dozen men appeared to join the priest and the villagers for the funeral. Afterwards, they buried Ephrosene in the cemetery beside the church. Father Markos understood with a strange sadness that the withering of the carnation had not been an omen of her son's death but of her own.

As if Manolis had divined the priest's thoughts, he spoke, his voice low and melancholy in the silence.

"In this last year, I've meant a number of times to return to Kravasaras so we could hold a memorial service for my mother," Manolis said. "but it seemed if we weren't fighting a battle, we were planning one."

"Each time I recite the liturgy, I pray for those who have passed on," the priest said. "I always remember your dear mother."

"Thank you, Father."

"How soon will you have to start back up the mountain?"

"We'll stay long enough in the morning to make sure those refugees get on their way," Manolis said. "Then we'll have to leave. Vorogrivas will need us."

"How is your captain?"

"Slashed and shot more times than any other mortal could sustain," Manolis said. "By some miracle, he survives to keep leading us. I think his strength comes from the mountain itself. He knows every pass and ravine, every rock and tree. We'd go on fighting without him, I know, but if we lost him, I'm sure we'd lose more battles and many more men."

"How large is your band now?"

"Somewhere between sixty and seventy palikars," Manolis said.

"It's only been a couple of years since the revolt broke out," he said quietly. He clasped his hands behind his head and continued staring into the fire. "But it seems to me we've spent a lifetime fighting. We harass the Turkish garrisons and attack their supply and ammunition trains. We've buried some fine palikars among the mountain rocks. They are replaced by other good men. Every village the Turks burn brings us new recruits. They are farmers and herdsmen we have to train to be mountain fighters."

"Is there any news about the fighting in other parts of Greece?" the priest asked. "We are ignorant here in our village about what is happening elsewhere. Sometimes a few soldiers homesick and weary of fighting come by on their way to their families. They tell us of a battle being fought in one place or another. In that way, we learned that the Greek volunteers captured the Turkish fortress of Tripolitza. We also heard that the Turks massacred and enslaved every Christian on the island of Chios. Do you know if those events are true?"

"We've heard news of Tripolitza and Chios as well," Manolis said. "Mostly there are only whispers and rumors carried by bands of refugees like those out there. We hear of battles won and lost and of killing and butchering. We also hear about fighting at sea between the ships of our islands and the Turkish fleet. There is some talk about different factions calling themselves the government of Greece. But until the land is liberated, there isn't much to govern. One thing we can know for certain. Now that spring melts the snows and opens the passes, the Turks will be on us in force again."

As Manolis fell silent, Zarkas grunted hoarsely in his sleep and shifted his body. One of his booted feet bumped a kettle beside the fireplace. As the sound clattered through the room, the klepht burst instantly awake, grasping swiftly for his gun.

"Steady, comrade," Manolis grinned. "Your enemy is a fearful bucket."

Zarkas mumbled a low curse and turned on his side. In another moment, he was snoring again.

"I remember you as a boy, Manolis," Father Markos said pensively. "You were always running and jumping, leading other children in some reckless foray. I remember the way you sang as well. You had a fine voice."

"There's little to sing about now," Manolis said. "As for childhood, why that seems a lifetime away." He paused. "I have seen things in these last few years, Father. . . . I have done things . . ."

"You're fighting in a noble cause, my son, to free our land and our people," the priest said.

"In the heat of war, a man doesn't think about the noble reasons he is fighting," Manolis said. "There are simply battles in which you kill so you will not be killed." He paused. "And, sometimes, there are things worse than killing. Last year, on one of our raids, just north of Kerasia, we found about twenty wounded and dying Greeks from another klepht band who'd been ambushed by a troop of Turks. The Turks had pulled out the men's teeth and then scooped out their eyes and shoved them into their mouths. When we cleared the eyeballs from the throats of those poor devils who were still alive, they pleaded for us to kill them . . ."

The priest felt a shudder sweep his body.

"We tracked the Turks who had done it, and, when we caught them, our men went crazy," Manolis said. His words echoed starkly from the hidden corners of the room. "If Vorogrivas or I had tried to stop them, I think they would have killed us. They formed a cordon around those Turks, beat them to the ground with their muskets, and then, with their boots kicked them in the head and in the gut, kept on kicking them until their bodies were raw, battered meat with not a bone unbroken. They didn't stop until the ground was littered with eyeballs and teeth, crushed livers and bloody hearts kicked out of the Turkish bodies."

"God relieve your burden, my son," the priest struggled for words to console the young man.

"I think sometimes God has turned away from us all," Manolis said, the flames glinting across his dark, tight cheeks. "He no longer accepts us as created in his image. We have become murderous strangers to him now."

Manolis fell silent then and closed his eyes. After a moment, the priest rose from his chair and walked wearily to his bed. He slipped off his cassock and shoes and lay down on the quilt. He watched the fire burn down slowly, the shadows again lengthening across the walls. From time to time, Zarkas let loose a rasping snore. The priest thought of what Manolis had told him about the brutalities of war. When peace finally came, would the men who had seen comrades killed and who had killed other men be able to return to the tasks of peace? Would they be able to plant crops and tend sheep again and look after the groves of olives? Or would the violence and slaughter they had known sow a bitter harvest that would forever poison their lives?

He did not know how long he slept when a piercing cry shattered his sleep. He woke to shouts and shrieks from outside his house and to the wild barking of the dogs guarding the goat pens. By the time the priest had cleared the web of sleep and scrambled from his bed, Manolis and Zarkas had already left the house. With his heart flailing, Father Markos fumbled into his shoes and cassock and went outside.

A short way down the street, a crowd was gathered within a ring of torches, and angry voices were raised in a loud clamor. The priest hurried toward the torches. At the outskirts of the crowd, he clasped a villager by the arm.

"What is happening, Sotiris?"

"That refugee leader, the thug with the gun, he tried to rob Cleon Pitsas!" Sotiris said excitedly. "Broke into his house and threatened to kill him! Cleon's wife, Katerina, managed to get out and started shrieking."

When Father Markos had pressed into the center of the mass of people, he saw the refugee leader, Akragas, backed against the stone wall of a house, his gun in his hand. The man's face held the ferocity of a wolf at bay, and he waved the gun, threatening anyone who came near him. Manolis confronted him, Zarkas close beside him.

"He tried to rob me!" Pitsas, standing among the men, cried, his voice shaking with outrage. "Broke in and threatened to kill my wife and me if we did not give him food and money!"

"You black-hearted bastard!" Zarkas spit. "I warned you!"

"You go burn in hell!" Akragas cried, frantically waving the gun, pointing first at Manolis and then at Zarkas.

"Man, listen to me now," Manolis spoke quietly but his voice carried a vein of iron. "If you put down that gun, you may save your life."

"You have no right to tell me what to do!" the man cried. "We deserve to share the things these people have! Why should they have sheep and chickens and a roof over their heads, when we have nothing! We're not Turks, we're Greeks, too!"

"Give me the gun," Manolis said. "We can talk later, but first, give me the gun."

The man trembled, and the gun wavered in his hand. His face teemed with terror and rage, and the priest understood Akragas was a breath away from murder. Fearing suddenly for the young warrior's life, Father Markos pushed forward to partially shield Manolis. His limbs trembled so violently, he wondered if he'd be able to speak.

"I beg you to put down that gun," Father Markos pleaded. "We'll talk afterwards, I promise, and share whatever we have with you. But now, in God's name, put down that gun."

The man let loose a choked curse and swung the gun to aim at the priest. Manolis moved quickly to protect the priest, the man swivelled the gun back toward him, and instantly Zarkas leaped the short distance separating them and slapped the gun to the ground. As Akragas scurried frantically to retrieve it, Zarkas struck him a savage blow across his head that sent him sprawling. In a flash, Zarkas straddled him, his own gun drawn, the muzzle poised against the man's temple.

"I'll finish him!" Zarkas hissed. "The bastard isn't worth keeping alive."

The priest saw the klepht's face drained of any mercy or compassion.

"In God's name, Zarkas, don't kill him," the priest pleaded.

For a moment, Zarkas stared grimly at the priest. Finally, he lowered his gun. He swung off the man's chest and then pulled Akragas roughly to his feet.

"Bring some rope," Zarkas motioned to the villagers. "Tie the bastard up. We'll keep him secure in one of the sheds until morning and then decide what to do with him."

He released the man with a slight shove. Akragas stumbled back a step. As Zarkas turned contemptuously away, the refugee bent and swiftly drew a knife concealed in his boot. He raised his arm to swing at Zarkas's back. A shot exploded like a clap of thunder across the night. Manolis held a smoking gun, as Akragas tumbled to the ground. By the graceless way he fell, one arm flapping from his side as if it were a limb severed from a tree, the priest knew the man was dead.

Zarkas looked down contemptuously at the body. "Give a snake a second chance, and he'll try to bite you again." He turned away.

In the shocked silence that followed the shooting, one of the other men from the refugee band stepped forward. He tugged off his cap and appealed to the priest and Manolis.

"Don't blame us for what he did, comrades," he said, his voice trembling. "He's been like a wild animal in our midst for weeks now. He had the only gun, and we were afraid for our lives. You won't have any trouble from us, I promise, and in the morning, we'll be on our way."

He looked at the other refugees around him, and several of them nodded, mumbling in agreement.

"All right then," Manolis said sternly. "but God pity the first man who makes a wrong move. Now let's get this body out of here, and we'll bury him tomorrow. The rest of you, go back to your houses."

Several men brought a sheet and wrapped it around the body of Akragas. They carried him to a stone shed behind one of the houses.

Father Markos turned aside, a nausea sweeping his belly, a coating of sweat broken out across his flesh. The man's demise was the first violent death he had experienced since the massacre of the Turkish villagers two years earlier. As if Manolis sensed his emotions, he clasped the priest's shoulder in reassurance.

"Go and rest now, Father Markos," he said quietly. "Zarkas and I are awake, and it will be daylight soon. I don't think we'll have any more trouble and, in the morning, we'll make sure the band leaves Kravasaras."

The priest walked wearily back to his house to wait out the balance of the night. He lay across his bed without removing his cassock or shoes. In the darkness of the room, only a fragment of ember still glowing in the fireplace, he recalled the stern faces of Zarkas and

Manolis in the torchlight. He reproached himself for not having made a greater effort to convince Akragas to give up his gun. If Father Markos had been quicker and more courageous, the man might still be alive. Instead, the man had died a violent death in a strange village in the night, his death as unmourned as the death of a bird fallen behind a bush or a dog dying behind a rock.

When the first tracings of dawn lightened his window, Father Markos rose wearily from bed and washed. On his way to church for his morning liturgy, he stopped in the shed where they had carried the body of Akragas.

The narrow enclosure, lit by a row of candles, had the smell and presence of death. Several women from the dead man's village were washing his naked body. They worked quickly and silently, swabbing wet cloths across the man's torso and legs, afterwards, anointing him with oil. In one corner of the shed, an old woman squatted on a stool, her gray head rocking back and forth, while she intoned a lament in a low, thin voice, filling the shed with the chants of mourning.

Father Markos gazed sadly at the corpse. Below his sun-darkened face and neck, the man's flesh was pale and unblemished. Save for the wound over his heart from the bullet that had killed him, his strong-limbed, sturdy body seemed strangely unsuited for death. His passive, untroubled face, no longer held the harshness and fury he displayed when he first entered the village. In death, his more tranquil countenance suggested the man he might once have been before war and the brutality of other men inflamed him and brought about his death.

As the priest turned to leave, the keening woman's voice rose in shriller tones of anguish.

"Early death was his destiny!" she wailed. "While he was still in his mother's womb, while he played as a child, as he grew into manhood, so was his fate decreed. Now, he has eaten his last bread, drunk his last wine, his days on earth ended. God forgive his sins and may the All Holy Virgin grant him peace for eternity."

Long after he'd left the shed, Father Markos could hear the old woman's shrill dirge echoing in his ears.

At the church, the villagers and refugees gathered in the courtyard greeted him. Manolis bent and kissed his hand.

"Good morning to you, Father Markos," the young man said, his voice brisk and cheerful.

"Good morning, Manolis."

The priest vainly searched the young man's face for any sign of remorse about the killing that had transpired during the night.

"We're grateful to be able to start the day with a prayer, Father," Manolis said. "It's been a long time since Zarkas and I've taken communion."

"If I were a younger, more valorous man," Father Markos said pensively, "I would join you and the other palikars up in the mountains so you could partake of communion every day."

"Better to have you lodged here in the village, Father," Zarkas said sternly. "In the mountains, a stray Turkish bullet might catch you in the middle of a prayer, and then no one would ever hear your blessings again."

Before entering the church, Father Markos spoke to Leontis and several other elders about holding a funeral for the dead man later that day.

"I'd as soon throw him to the buzzards," Elias, a weather-beaten, old farmer, scowled. "If Manolis hadn't killed the beast, he would have killed one or more of us for sure."

"Whatever he did, Elias," the priest said, "he is still a Greek who suffered the hardship of war. It will not harm us to say a prayer over his body. That would be the Christian thing to do."

"What about his burial?" Panayotis, another elder, asked. "I don't think he should be interred among our own blessed dead. Let's bury the wretch somewhere outside the village."

"The dead cannot taint one another," the priest said firmly. "Once they breathe their last, all mortals are linked in eternity."

"Father Markos is right," Leontis said gravely. "Devil or saint, hero or coward, every man who leaves this world of pain and tears deserves a prayer and a patch of land in which to hold his bones. Since the poor devil died in our village, let him be buried here."

As the priest left the elders, and entered the church, the refugee who had spoken to him the night before approached him, hat in hand.

"With your permission, Father," the man said in a low, nervous voice. "My name is Angelides, and the others have chosen me to speak for them. If you and your parishioners don't mind having us in church, we'd be thankful to share your prayers."

"You are all most welcome in our church," Father Markos said earnestly. He motioned to his sexton. "Panfelio, ring the bell."

Panfelio moved in a quick, lopsided gait into the church. Moments later, as daylight cast brighter streamers of light over the mountain and the village, the bell of Saint Athanasios pealed its melodious ring across the clear morning air. The villagers and refugees—men, women, and children—assembled in the church with Manolis and Zarkas standing guard.

Panfelio lit the oil wicks and the candles while Father Markos mixed the fragments of bread and wine in the chalice. Seeing the church crowded with worshipers reminded him of what the liturgy had been like before the war. Sometimes, three generations worshiped together, from the grandparents to the young married sons and daughters with their children, sometimes newborn babies, their cries echoing through the church.

That morning, Father Markos was gratified to see villagers and refugees mingling without animosity, all the initial wariness and hostility vanished. In a strange way, the death of Akragas had relieved the tension and bonded the families.

In his liturgy that morning, he prayed for the safety and salvation of the villagers and of the refugees. As the men, women, and children came forward to receive communion, Father Markos blessed each one, in his heart wishing them well. At the end of the liturgy, Father Markos offered a memorial prayer for Ephrosene Kitsos and all the brave men and women fighting for freedom who had died in battle.

As the parishioners filed slowly from the church, and Father Markos was removing his vestments, Leontis came forward with the refugee leader, Angelides.

"My wife and I and some neighbors were talking this morning, Father," Leontis said. "We told Angelides here that if his people wanted to leave their children and the women with us, we'd look after them as well as we could, sharing whatever we have. It would be better if they were kept warm and dry with a roof over their heads then have them wandering in the rain and cold up and down the mountain. If the group gets settled safely, someone can come back for them."

"God knows, we'd be grateful for that kindness," Angelides said earnestly. "Maybe the war will end soon, and we can return to rebuild our village . . . " He paused, fighting the tears that threatened to break from his eyes.

As the two men left the church to discuss with villagers and refugees the lodging of the women and children who would remain, Father Markos noticed the solitary figure of the young woman with her baby. He walked to where she stood in the rear of the church.

"How are you and your son today, my child?" the priest asked gently.

"We're all right, Father," she said, her head down and her voice so low he could barely make out her words. She hesitated. "Before we leave today, Father, do you think . . . could you, perhaps, baptize my son?"

"I'll be glad to, my child," Father Markos said. "Do you have a friend or family member from your village, someone to act as the baby's godparent?"

The young woman stared at him in silence. After a long, awkward moment, she shook her head.

"Both my parents were killed in the attack on our village," she said quietly. "I have no one else."

"I'm sorry," Father Markos paused. "Perhaps another relative or a friend?"

In the shadows of the church, the girl's eyes glistened in the paleness of her face.

"No one," she said, a somber finality in her voice.

The priest struggled for a way to explain to the young woman that a godparent was absolutely necessary. A godparent created a sacred bond with the baby that extended to all the relatives on either side of the families, a link as binding as those united by blood.

Father Markos had not seen Manolis approach, until the young man spoke.

"Next week or in the weeks to come, a battle may end my life," Manolis said, "but if the mother is willing to accept me, I'll be godfather to her child."

The young woman raised her head to look at Manolis and, for a moment, the almost unearthly beauty of her face shone in the faint light. As if he were seeing her clearly for the first time, Manolis stared at the girl as if he were transfixed. The priest felt an uneasy tremor through his body.

"Thank you," the young woman's voice was barely a whisper.

He called to Panfelio to heat a pot of water for the font. Afterwards he sent him to fetch Thea Pipitsa, the village midwife, to assist in the baptism. While they waited, Manolis left the young woman and her baby and came to speak to Father Markos.

"I volunteered because she has no one, Father," he said in a low voice. "The refugees despise her and her baby. She's been traveling with them because she had nowhere else to go."

"I find it hard to believe she hasn't a single friend or relative among all the villagers," the priest said. "What could the poor girl have done?"

Manolis stared at him for a moment in silence.

"The baby was born after the girl was raped by a Turk during the first attack on their village," Manolis said, his voice trembling with an effort to contain his rage. "In the beginning, she tried to abort the child, but the seed hung on. When the baby was finally born, the villagers wanted to kill it. But the mother refused and protected the infant. Some of the women beat her and even threatened to kill them both."

Even as the horror of what the young mother had endured swept over him, the priest felt a welling up of compassion and affection for the mother and her baby. He imagined her ordeal facing the scorn and fury of the villagers, the abuse and the beatings in which mother and baby might have been killed.

"Poor child," the priest said. "She's being punished even though the sin isn't hers."

"It's not safe for her to travel any farther with the baby," Manolis said. "One of the villagers may still kill the baby and her as well, or a band of rogue Greeks or Turks may find her, and she'll go through that hell again." He paused, a naked plea entering his voice. "Do you think, Father, you might find a merciful family in Kravasaras that would take her in?"

The priest understood it would be a daunting challenge to convince any of the villagers to take the girl and the spawn of a Turk into their house.

"I'll try, Manolis," he said. "I'll speak to a few families that I know as good people. I promise I'll make every effort."

"Thank you, Father," Manolis said. He looked across the church at the young woman and her baby. "Turning the two of them away would be like setting a lamb and a ewe loose among wolves." ✓

Clustered around the small baptismal font at the side of the sanctuary, in addition to the young woman, Maria, her baby, and Father Markos were Manolis, Zarkas, Panfelio, and Thea Pipitsa, who had participated in the delivery of scores of babies in her eighty years. She deftly stripped off the baby's ragged clothing and held him securely in a sheet. Panfelio poured the bucket of heated water into the base of the baptismal font, mixing it with cooler water to moderate the temperature.

Father Markos began to chant the baptismal liturgy, his voice resonating through the near-empty church. At a point in the ceremony, Thea handed him the naked baby. The priest held the tiny infant aloft and then lowered him gently into the water. He raised and lowered the child into the water twice more and swung him lightly to the right and to the left. The baby, body and head soaked and dripping water, squirmed in the priest's hands but did not cry. After Father Markos had dabbed the infant with oil, Thea quickly dried and dressed the infant in clean clothing donated by one of the village families.

When it came time for the godfather to hold the baby, Manolis took him gingerly, as if fearing the baby might fall or break. The priest found the sight of the young warrior holding the tiny infant intensely moving. The young mother watched, her eyes moist and shining. Around them, the church was heavy with the fumes of incense and the heat of the candles.

"What name have you chosen for the baby?" the priest asked.

"Lefteris," Manolis said, looking toward the baby's mother, who nodded. "The word for freedom. God grant Lefteris grows to his manhood in a Greece that is free once again."

"Lefteris," the priest repeated the name. He blessed the child and blessed the mother and Manolis.

After the baptismal service, they moved into the sunlight outside the church, Manolis holding the baby in his arms.

"A brave little warrior," Zarkas said gruffly. "Dunked like that under the water and never uttered a peep. I wager he'll grow up to be a captain."

Manolis handed the baby to Maria, reached into his pocket, and brought out a tiny cross on a slender gold chain.

"For Lefteris," he said quietly. "This was given to me by my own godfather when I was baptized a long time ago. It will keep my godson safe until I see him again."

The young woman took the chain gratefully and murmured her thanks.

Manolis looked pensively at the priest.

"There should be a celebration to follow the baptism," he said to Father Marcos. "But I don't think any of them," he pointed toward the refugees, "would want to join us."

"Not many of the villagers either, I'd wager," Zarkas said.

"What matters is that the child has been baptized," Father Markos sought to reassure them.

"Father Markos," Manolis spoke in a low voice as he drew the priest aside. "Remember, I'm depending on you to find Maria and my godson a home."

"I pledge I will, Manolis." The priest spoke with more assurance than he felt.

As the priest watched, the young warrior gently took the tiny baby into his arms and held him close. Seeing them in that moment, the girl and her son who had come into the village as strangers, now bonded to Manolis by the ritual of baptism, caused the priest to make his cross.

"O Lord," he murmured, "Thy ways are a mystery beyond human understanding."

Although Manolis and Zarkas had planned to leave that day, leading the refugees for a number of kilometers to make sure they were safely on their way, they decided to remain longer.

"There is work on a few of the houses that Zarkas and I can do," Manolis told the priest. "There are also some fences to mend. We'll get the best of the men from the village and refugee band to join us. A few strong hands and strong backs for one more day won't hurt."

"Everyone will be grateful for your help," Father Markos said.

For the balance of the day, Manolis and Zarkas diligently led a group of refugees and villagers in clearing away piles of debris and rebuilding a broken fence enclosure for the goats. The animals were led into it, their horns clanking and their shaggy flanks bumping into one another. A small opening left at one end allowed the shepherd to seize each female goat as she came through and milk her.

Late in the day was the brief funeral service for Akragas. A cluster of the refugees from the dead man's village gathered for the rites, a few lackluster children at their sides. The old woman who had mourned while his body was being prepared for burial continued her lament in a low chant during the burial service. Akragas was buried in a corner of the village cemetery.

That evening, weary from their day of hard labor, everyone gathered around the fires for their last meal and evening together. Manolis joined Maria and Lefteris just beyond the circle of campfires, and for the first time the priest heard the girl laugh, a soft, shy ripple of mirth that echoed strangely in the twilight.

Father Markos was suddenly seized by a suspicion that the reason Manolis had decided to remain another day was less a matter of the work to be done than because of the young woman. As soon as the duplicitous thought possessed him, he banished his skepticism as unchristian.

During the day, Father Markos had asked half a dozen village families whether they'd be willing to take in the mother and her child. For various reasons, all refused.

"I lost my son, Gianni, in the fighting against the Turks in Thessaly last year, Father," the blacksmith Carfares told him. "Taking the filthy spawn of a Turk into my house would dishonor his memory. As a Christian I'd like to do it, but my heart will not consent."

The priest was suddenly struck by an audacious thought. He'd take the baby and young mother into his own house. His initial elation was quickly tempered by an anxiety that his decision had been born of his own selfishness, using Maria and her baby as surrogates to solace his own childless life, but he swept it aside. If they were in his house, everyone in the village would understand they were under his protection. They'd eat their evening meals together, and he'd be able to help the mother with the child. Slowly, the village would come to accept them.

In that moment, he became aware of the stars and the moon shining upon the roofs of the houses and the aromas of thyme and sage. He was suddenly returned to a buoyant memory of his boyhood when, young and agile, he leaped from rock to rock as fleet-footed as an ibex. There were often nights while tending the sheep in the mountains when he slept under the stars, wrapped in a goat-hair cape. He'd lie on his back, staring at the heavens, marveling at the vastness of the starry firmament above him. He saw the sky as the night pasture of God, and he was possessed with awe at the mystery and beauty of life. Now, seized once again with wonder at the ways the Lord crafted His intricate design, he hurried towards Manolis and Maria, eager to tell them that the young woman and her baby would come and live with him in his house.

CHAPTER
TWO

When Manolis woke beneath the plane tree where he and Zarkas slept, the village was still mantled in darkness. Savoring the warmth of his body beneath the blanket and reluctant to disturb the stillness, for a few moments he did not move. In that final hour before dawn, the cicadas had ceased their shrilling, and the earth was hushed. Above the foliage of the shielding tree, a sickle of moon was receding in the night sky. A tranquility hung over the earth, and he imagined this was how it might feel to wake in a land without war.

In the next moment, Zarkas woke. Lurching to his knees, he passed a deafening tornado of wind that shattered the night's serenity.

"That will wake every dog in the village," Manolis laughed.

"I don't care if it wakes the hounds of hell," Zarkas grunted. "Those stringy fibers of goat I chewed on last night fostered an earthquake in my gut that's been laboring to storm out of me all night."

As they walked to a well to wash, a lean, vagrant cat emerged from the shadows, its sinewy form visible for an instant before it was lost again.

"Returning, I wager, from a midnight orgy," Zarkas snickered.

As they finished washing, tracings of dawn rimmed the sky. The mountain looming above the village bristled like a great beast, pine and fir forests emerging from the shadows of the slopes.

The first light roused the refugee men from where they slept beneath the trees. The women came from the houses to gather branches and twigs for the fires in the ovens. Within minutes, the flames were hissing, and sparks were leaping into the sky. The square grew crowded and noisy with people, and the smell of roasting meat seeped across the air. Sarantis the farmer brought a basket of juice-heavy melons that were sliced open and eaten from the tip of long knives. Kyra Margari brought Manolis and Zarkas copper plates of greens sprinkled with olive oil to enhance their flavor.

"Thank you, mother," Manolis said.

"My husband and son are fighting in the north," the woman said somberly. "This morning, I pray to God some good soul carries them a morsel of food."

After Manolis and Zarkas finished eating, they walked to their horses. The dogs in the sheep pen began barking shrilly, their yelps echoing loudly in the still morning air.

"They've caught the scent of a prowling wolf," Zarkas said.

As they saddled their mounts, Father Markos joined them. The old priest's white hair cascaded from beneath his black cap, and his white beard was disheveled. Beneath his long cassock, he wore a woolen sweater that made his body appear bulky and misshapen.

"We've packed baskets with provisions for you onto a donkey," he said. "I'm afraid it isn't much, but you'll have some food to start you on your journey."

"You have our thanks, Father," Manolis said.

Father Markos tightly clasped Zarkas's hand in both his palms.

"I'll pray for your safety every day," he said earnestly to the burly klepht.

"No offense, Father," Zarkas said, "but don't waste your prayers on a foul-tongued, bad-tempered, worthless old sinner like me."

"If the fall of a sparrow is precious in the sight of the Lord, Zarkas," the priest said, "do you think he'd forsake a warrior risking his life to bring freedom to our people?"

Father Markos reached awkwardly to embrace Manolis, who inhaled the scents of incense and candles on the old priest's cassock.

"Come back to us soon, my son," the priest said, his voice husky with emotion. "Seeing you is a tonic for our battered spirits."

"As soon as I can, Father." Manolis paused. "How did Maria and Lefteris pass their first night in your house?"

"We hung a quilt across the center of the room for their privacy," the priest said. "Hard as I tried to convince her, the poor girl would not accept my bed but slept with her child on a pallet before the fire. During the night, she seemed restless, but the baby slept soundly."

"A good beginning," Manolis smiled. "Bless you, Father, for your kindness in taking them into your home."

"I have lived alone for almost a lifetime, Manolis," the priest said pensively. "To have other human beings close in the night is a blessing."

A short while later, villagers and refugees gathered in the square with Father Markos. The priest crossed himself and began a prayer.

"Lord, in your mercy, please carry these souls safely on their journeys," his voice echoed in the morning stillness, "and bring them safely back to their loved ones here in Kravasaras. Also, Lord, we beseech you to keep our valorous palikaria, Manolis and Zarkas, safe as they struggle to liberate our anguished land. Amen."

As Manolis and Zarkas mounted their horses, the villagers clustered around to bid them farewell. Leontis gently stroked the flank of Manolis's horse.

"A magnificent animal, Manolis."

"His sire was a pureblood stallion from some land in Arabia," Manolis said. "Before Axios became mine, he lodged in the royal stable of a pasha."

"We dispatched that pasha, with his throat cut," Zarkas laughed. "He'll have no need for a horse in hell."

Manolis lightly tapped Axios with the reins, and they started from the village at a slow gait. Behind them, one of the refugees led a donkey with the baskets of food lashed to its side, while a procession of about twenty of the refugee men followed. For a while, the women and children they were leaving in the village walked alongside the column.

"God go with you," a woman holding a child cried.

"Don't worry, Stathis, I'll look after little Vasili," another woman called.

"Come back soon, Paulo, so you can watch your grandchild grow taller and stronger!"

"In God's name, don't forget us!" another woman said, her voice breaking.

"Good-by . . . good-by . . . "

As women and children straggled back from the departing men, their final farewells were carried in plaintive echoes by the wind.

At the outskirts of the village, as the band passed the priest's house, Manolis saw the young mother Maria in the doorway. Unable to see her clearly in the shadows, he conjured a vision of her sad and lovely face. He waved, and the girl raised her hand and waved back, a flutter of her fingers in a mute farewell.

As the band traveled through the morning, the sun rose higher in the sky, the shadow of tall eucalyptus trees diminishing along the trail. A light wind rose and shook the horse's manes. In the distance, small, whitewashed chapels glimmered on the slopes of the mountain.

A woman trudged toward them on the trail, her black-clad body bent almost double under a load of kindling she carried on her back. Straining under her burden, she did not look at the men as they passed.

At midday, they reached the Matumi fork. From that junction, Manolis and Zarkas would turn to ascend the mountain, while the refugee band continued along the trail to the south.

They rested for a while under a canopy of fir branches beside a small mountain stream that had begun its spring thaw. The men drank and washed their faces in the trickle of water running down between the rocks. Before resuming their journeys, they ate some of the bread and cheese they'd carried from the village. Several men approached Manolis and Zarkas where they sat on the ground, their legs outstretched, their backs braced against the stunted trunk of a dead tree.

"We didn't want to speak up back in the village so the women would hear and wail like women," a grizzled oldster said earnestly. "But we've spoken among ourselves and decided that we'd like to join your band." He sighed. "Now, the hard truth is that our moldering bones don't let us move the way we did once, but give us guns, Manolis. I vow we'll kill our share of Turks."

"In this war, every patriot, whatever his age, is sorely needed," Manolis said quietly. "But war in the mountains is war on the run. We ambush the Turk, and before his force can assemble to fight back, we're gone. Then we strike them again somewhere else. If you can't move quick and quiet as a fox, you endanger your own life and put the band at risk. For those reasons, comrades, I'm sorry but we cannot take you with us."

They did consent to take one of the refugees, a wiry old man named Sarantis with a hooked nose and teeth stained by tobacco. The man swore that his knowledge of horses would be invaluable to them.

"I grew up with horses!" Sarantis said eagerly. "I know at least a hundred dried herb remedies for all their ailments! And, believe me, I'm stronger than I look. I can cut and carry acres of grass for their feed!"

"If you're lying, by God, you'll regret it," Zarkas scowled. "Before we toss you out, you'll feel my boot in your bony ass!"

"I'm not lying!" Sarantis protested. As if to confirm his ability, he approached Manolis's horse tethered nearby and briskly felt its knee joints, tapped the animal's tendons, and squeezed the bone above the fetlocks.

"A fine, sturdy animal," he said. "He will never let you down. Give me a chance, comrades, and Sarantis vows he will help put all your other animals in the same fine shape!"

After exchanging their farewells at the stream, the refugee band started south, and Manolis and Zarkas with Sarantis riding the donkey turned west to ascend the mountain. Within a few hours, they had left behind the fields of scrawny pine on the lower slopes and entered a grove of trees where the foliage was denser and greener and the air colder. Huddled on the back of the donkey, Sarantis shivered.

"What's the matter, you lowland bumpkin," Zarkas laughed. "Your blood too thin for this bracing air?"

"I'll get used to it, comrade," Sarantis said quickly.

As they crossed a mountain ridge, they passed a small, drab village abandoned by the inhabitants. An eerie stillness hung over the deserted houses that time and neglect had caused to fall into ruin.

"Another village abandoned to ghosts and the wind," Manolis said. "The young men and young women leave to join the war, and the villages die."

"What happens to the old men and old women they leave behind?" Sarantis asked.

"They wander off into some mountain cave to die, too," Zarkas said grimly.

At dusk, they camped in a glen of wild fruit trees.

"Start showing us how useful you are by gathering some brush for a fire," Zarkas said to Sarantis, who scurried off. In a few moments, he had returned with wood, and the warmth and light of a cackling fire held the night at bay. They ate greens and chunks of hard bread while Sarantis babbled a flurry of village gossip.

"In the village of Pentaki next to our village," Sarantis said, "there was a widow who owned six fields and thirty olive trees that produced the best oil in the district. Believe me, she wasn't a beauty, but she took a fancy to me. I swear, comrades, if I'd moved quickly, I could have married her and never had to work another day in my life. But a man with an ugly wife sees only darkness when he lights the evening lamp and, trying to make up my mind, a lout from the village of Agrapha stole her instead. A night doesn't pass when I don't mourn my loss."

Zarkas cut him off brusquely. "In God's name, you're worse than an old woman!" he growled. "When you're among fighters in the mountains, you'll find they don't waste time in foolish chatter."

Sarantis retired into an injured silence.

After they'd eaten, they stripped off their cartridge belts. Keeping their pistols beside them, they wrapped themselves in blankets. Within minutes, Zarkas snored in a heavy slumber while, in his sleep, Sarantis emitted a low moaning. After a while, the rasping of cicadas drowned out the sounds of the sleeping men.

With the fire burnt down and the embers glowing in scarlet ash, Manolis lay gazing up at the sickle of moon. As the night grew darker, the stars resembled a great web with myriad specks of light. From the rocks nearby, he heard the sound of night creatures scurrying from crevice to ledge, and from a hidden peak came the plaintive howl of a wolf.

Hard as Manolis tried to sleep, a vision of the young mother invaded his thoughts. If he and Zarkas had not followed the refugee band to the village, he would never have met the girl and wouldn't have become godfather to her infant. When he considered the Turkish brutes who had violated her, a rage for vengeance wracked his soul. Yet, from that savage assault, the undefiled baby had been born. He wondered if there existed in the child's blood any awareness of the violent attack that had brought him into the world.

He thought about what his own life might have been like if the war for liberation had not begun. Living in Kravasaras, he'd have married some village girl. They would have had children and spent their days as other families. Even as he tried to imagine the peacefulness of such a life, Manolis did not regret that loss of tranquility and family because their children would have been born slaves in an imprisoned land. They were fighting now so that his godchild, Lefteris, and the other children in their anguished country would grow up to live someday as free men and women.

Yet, through days and nights of fighting and war, he had moments of longing for the tenderness that loving a woman might bring. He wondered how it would feel to embrace a woman's naked body, an intimacy he had never known. He recalled once again the beauty of the young mother—her fine, olive-tinted complexion, her hair black as a raven's wing, and her great dark eyes with their burden of sorrow. He allowed himself the brazen thought of Maria as his wife, sharing a bed, rising in the morning to share their day.

Even as he considered being married to Maria, he found it hard to imagine her laboring from dawn until dark like other village women, washing and cooking for her family, growing weary and old bent in torturous labor in some village field. In Kravasaras, he had witnessed how quickly village women aged, how swiftly they were transformed from the buoyance of girlhood to the resignation and drudgery of wife and mother.

He twisted restlessly in his blanket, the night dragging, his thoughts woven restlessly around women and love. In the years he had spent with the band in the mountains, during the interludes between raids, men betrothed to a girl or those with wives sometimes journeyed home for brief reunions. They returned gloating and cheerful, relating outlandish stories about their sexual prowess.

"My sweetheart, Anthoula, and I never left our bed for three days," Manolis remembered a young palikar boasting. "By the time I was ready to leave, the poor girl was so exhausted, she was barely able to stand!"

During the intervals between battles, those men who were not married or betrothed visited the renegade towns that had sprung up high in the mountains. These ragged, teeming settlements were inhabited by refugees and deserters, Gypsies peddling charms, musicians playing for pennies, monks whom the Turks had driven from their cloisters selling small icons to ward off the evil eye, and, finally, cutthroats without loyalty to any cause.

There were also women in those settlements willing to sell their bodies to whoever would pay. Some women did it out of desperation because they had lost their husbands in the war and had to feed hungry children or aging parents. Other women needed money just to survive. Whatever the reasons, men never hesitated to take advantage of them.

"A man can't worry about why a woman plays the harlot," Katsikas, a member of the klepht band, put it bluntly to Manolis. "He needs to empty his sacs, or his health will fail." He nodded sagely. "Believe me, thrusting one's bone into a woman's pouch is good for the jaw, the brain, the stomach. Impaling a woman will cure fever, mountain sickness, scurvy, boils, and melancholy!"

Manolis sometimes joined the men on their visits to these settlements, but he could never muster the bravado to take his turn with any of the women. He was restrained by his pride, which resisted having to pay a woman for sex. He also was dissuaded by a vision of what true love might someday be like. Yet, there were times he had been tempted.

A few months earlier, in one of those renegade towns, he had watched a circle of lusting men stalk a Gypsy harlot. She had a slender body, long glistening dark hair, and below the graceful curve of her throat, the low cut of her frock displayed the swell of her pale, soft breasts. Like rams in heat, the men milled restlessly around her. Meanwhile, her body weaving in a slow and sensual dance, the woman teased and taunted the men, turning flirtatiously from one to another.

Although he did not join the chorus of obscene proposals the men were calling to the woman, Manolis could not resist pushing through the crowd to get closer to her. Standing near the center of the circle, he saw the sheen of moisture across her forehead and cheeks, inhaled the scents that carried from her body, caught glimpses of her slender, bare feet below the fringed hem of her frock.

As her bold eyes surveyed the men, her gaze came to rest on Manolis. She studied him for a moment and then raised her hand to her lips, slowly, erotically, licking her fingers and revealing the pink tip of her tongue. Her gesture was so brazen an invitation that Manolis felt the blood pounding in his head and his body scalded with a thunderclap of desire. He was also filled with a rage at the other men he saw as drunken and boorish rivals. Fearing he'd be unable to control his anger, he wrenched himself away. His final sight of the woman was her face mocking him, and then she whirled away from the grasping hands, flouncing her hips seductively toward the crowd in a shameless gesture that set the men to howling. As he strode toward his horse, Manolis, still trembling with the effort to contain his desire and rage, marveled at the power of a woman over men.

These interludes when men could leave the band were rare. Most of their time was spent fighting in the mountains, planning raids, attacking or being attacked, resting wearily, and recovering from their wounds. During those periods of abstinence, men had no other recourse but to relieve themselves. Manolis knew by the grunts and hoarse moans of men in their blankets around him in the night that they were indulging these rituals without pleasure but merely to release the pestering pressure in their loins that interfered with their need to fight and kill. There were times when Manolis also relieved himself in that way, but he found the kneading of his genitals a poor, joyless substitute for what he imagined love with a woman to be.

He felt he had just fallen asleep when Zarkas woke him. They brewed strong coffee over a small fire and ate some melon and cheese. As they resumed their journey toward the higher ridges of the mountain, the eye of the sun brought a brighter light to the fir and pine forests. Manolis swayed lightly in the saddle, his body adjusting seamlessly to the gait and rhythm of his horse. Zarkas rode beside him, while Sarantis, on the shorter-gaited donkey, trailed some distance behind them.

"I've never asked you before, Zarkas," Manolis said. "Have you ever married?"

"I was married once," the klepht said somberly. "That was years ago back in Rumeli. When the war started, our village was right in the path of the Turks."

"What happened?"

"The Turks attacked our village, and our people scattered. Some fled into the mountains to hide, and others like myself joined the klepht. I was gone about a year, and when I returned to the village, some of my neighbors had returned to the homes the Turks had not demolished. A friend told me my wife was among those who had returned and that she had bedded another man and was living in his house. I gave them both a sound beating and left her for good."

"She might have thought you were dead," Manolis said. "Can you blame her for turning to someone else?"

"Penelope waited on that rascal, Odysseus, for ten years, while he coupled with assorted nymphs and sirens," Zarkas growled. "That's the kind of loyalty a man expects from a Greek woman. After only a year, my wife put a cuckold's horns on my head. She was lucky I didn't kill her."

At mid-morning, they were spotted by one of the camp sentries in the rocks above them. Zarkas waved his musket in the air and shouted a greeting. The sentry fired a single musket shot to alert the camp. As they rode into the midst of tents and lean-tos and the cluster of men, they were greeted boisterously with taunts and coarse jests. Zarkas responded with quick parries of his own.

"Did you bring me back a present, Zarkas?" a brawny klepht named Aris asked with a grin.

"A turd from a Turkish filly," Zarkas said.

"How many Turks did you kill?" another klepht asked.

"As many as you have warts on your scurvy balls!"

The men scoffed at the sight of the scruffy peasant, Sarantis, astride the donkey.

"Is this oaf on an ass all the booty you brought back?" tall, lean Doulos smirked.

"I thought he'd make a fine bridegroom for your sister," Zarkas grinned.

When they reached the center of the camp, Vorogrivas, the leader of the band, emerged from the shelter of his cave to greet them. As the men dismounted, he reached out and clasped their hands in his own. When their palms and fingers touched, Manolis felt the reassuring strength of the chieftain's strong grasp.

"Welcome, comrades," Vorogrivas smiled. "It's good to have you back. How did things go in the village?"

"As we suspected, that refugee leader did cause trouble," Manolis said. "We had to kill him."

"I feared it might come to that," Vorogrivas said. "Before the war, he would have lived quietly, tending his crops, loving his family. But war and its cruelties turn some men brutal, and then they are lost." He paused. "What became of the others?"

"The women and children stayed on in Kravasaras while the men traveled south to find relatives and friends," Manolis said. "We rode with them to see them safely on their way."

"Get some rest now and something to eat," Vorogrivas said. "At twilight, we'll be riding to raid the garrison at Biskika. Early this morning, Stomas brought word the Vinnitsa Pass has begun to thaw. He thinks a band of horsemen would be able to get through. The Turks in the garrison may not have that news yet, and we'll have a chance to surprise them. Manolis, stay with me to make some plans."

Manolis and the chieftain rested under the shade of a plane tree. Vorogrivas poured raki from a flask into cups and handed one to Manolis. For a little while, they sat and drank in silence.

Manolis was grateful to be back in the reassuring sanctuary of the camp. Above them were the ramparts of the mountain, a landscape of stony ridges and precipitous peaks creating an impregnable fortress. In the camp below, men sharpened their knives on whetstones and cleaned and oiled their muskets. Others lit fires to cook their meals.

"How did you find the old priest in your village?" Vorogrivas asked.

"He has aged since I last saw him," Manolis said, "but he is still the heart and spirit of the village. They look to him for guidance as well as prayer."

As they spoke of the events that had transpired during the journey to Kravasaras, Manolis could not resist telling Vorogrivas about the girl and her child and how he had become a godfather. The chieftain listened intently, and when Manolis had finished, for a few moments Vorogrivas did not respond.

"That may have been a merciful act for the poor woman and her infant but not a wise one, Manolis," Vorogrivas said. "You know our life here and to stay alive you must think of nothing but your comrades and your survival. This girl and her child . . . you will worry whether they are safe . . . it will be a distraction."

"No one else would baptize the child," Manolis said, distressed by the captain's reprimand. "And the girl was so despised they might have killed her if not for my becoming godparent to her infant. No one will harm them now for what I did and because that good priest took them into his house." He paused. "Captain, I'm sorry to have displeased you, but I could not forsake them."

For a reflective moment, Vorogrivas gazed at the stony peaks above them. Finally, he turned back to Manolis.

"You have not displeased me, my comrade," he said quietly. "You acted honorably to protect a helpless woman and her child who were in danger. I would not have expected any less of you. So now we'll put it to rest."

Both men fell silent. From the camp, a klepht played a reed flute, and several men joined him to sing a mountain ballad that celebrated a young hero killed in battle. As the voices of the men faded, as if sensing they would be going into battle, the restless horses snorted and pawed the rocky earth of the corrals.

After they'd discussed strategy for the impending raid and drunk the cups of raki, Vorogrivas leaned wearily back against the rock and closed his eyes. The descending afternoon sun burnished his cheeks with a crimson hue.

While the chieftain was awake, his eyes, fierce and compelling, dominated anyone in his presence. A man could not sustain the power of that unflinching gaze and was forced to look away. Only in those moments when Vorogrivas slept, those mesmerizing eyes concealed, could one gaze upon his face.

As he studied the captain's visage, Manolis marked again the changes the years of war had wrought on Vorogrivas. The chieftain's hair that had once been long and dark with the sheen of the blackest night had become streaked with strands of gray. The wind and sun had so darkened his flesh that it resembled the hard, crusted bark of a tree. Around the great mustache, furrows and creases were etched sharply in his cheeks. One of his temples bore the scab of a wound that hadn't healed properly, and a powder explosion had left a patch of scar tissue at his throat. Concealed beneath his long mane of hair was what remained of an ear partially severed by a Turkish scimitar.

Manolis also bore scars of battles they had fought. His wounds were superficial compared to the lacerations Vorogrivas carried on his body. Seeing him stripped to the waist as he washed, Manolis found it painful to look upon the knife and sword scars across the chieftain's shoulders and chest. Injuries had left him with a stiffened left arm and when he grew weary, a slight limp. Yet, in spite of these afflictions, Manolis marveled at how the captain remained the swiftest and strongest among the men of the band.

Vorogrivas had told the men that if a battle ended his life, Manolis was to be their leader. Although Manolis understood that in the mountain wars few fighters would ever die of old age, even as heroic a figure as the chieftain, he dreaded a time when Vorogrivas would not be there to lead them. No man knew the mountains as he knew them, every crevice and crag, every valley and summit. Nor could Manolis imagine any other man imbuing these fighters with the valor and spirit Vorogrivas instilled in them. It might have been such loyalty and devotion that the young king Alexander produced in his men as he led them to conquer most of the known world.

Yet, through the years they fought side by side, there were other subtle changes Manolis had noted in Vorogrivas. At times, the chieftain reflected a melancholy as if he were laboring under burdens no other man could see. On occasion Manolis caught the chieftain watching him, a gaze that confirmed their staunch friendship and yet one that also contained a pervasive sadness.

Manolis closed his eyes and napped briefly. When he wakened, Vorogrivas had joined the men at the fire. He motioned for Manolis to join them. The Spartan Batsakis squatted on his heels, tended the fire, and then slowly turned the spit impaling the carcass of a lamb, its glistening skin crackling above the logs. Meanwhile, Tinos swabbed the lamb's flanks with a sponge full of grease. When the skin was browned and crisp, several men used their long knives to slice off savory chunks they passed around. They also brought out flagons of wine stolen the week before from the caravan of a Turkish tax collector. The men drank and laughed and exchanged lewd jokes. As Doulos moved to open a third flagon of the wine, Vorogrivas spoke sharply.

"No more than a cup apiece," he warned. "I want no drunken fighter falling off his horse."

Manolis ate and drank with the others, bolstered by the friendship and loyalty he felt for these comrades. They had fought many battles, defended one another, saved one another's lives. There wasn't one of the band of brothers he would not have trusted with his own life.

Yet, even as he enjoyed the boisterous banter of the men, his thoughts returned to the young mother in the village. He imagined her preparing broth or greens at the hearth in the priest's house or sitting by the fire with the baby clasped in her arms. He envisioned the glow of the flames across her shimmering, black hair. Although immersed in his reverie, he was conscious of being watched, and when he looked up, he saw Vorogrivas gazing at him. He could not meet the captain's eyes and quickly looked away.

At twilight, the men assembled for the raid and saddled their horses. Each klepht bristled with weapons, a pair of pistols as well as twin knives inserted into each waistband. Cartridge belts dangled across their chests. The curved yataghan swords and long Albanian muskets were strapped to their saddles.

As they began their descent from the mountain hideout, their noisy passage roused flocks of birds cackling from the hidden cliffs above them. Along the trail, leaves on the trees shook as they passed, and small mountain creatures scurried aside to escape the hooves of the horses. Just as the scout had reported, the pass had thawed sufficiently so that riding in single file through the slushy remnants of the snow, the men were able to make the crossing.

Darkness found the band gathered upon a ridge above the Turkish garrison. Perhaps feeling reassured that the mountain corridor was still impassable, the garrison had not posted sentries. In the camp, Muslim troopers lounged around their fires, smoking their chibouks. Other Turks strolled lazily around the compound. Snatches of voices and laughter carried up into the rocks where the band waited.

Vorogrivas motioned Manolis to lead one group in an attack on the camp from the left flank while he led a second group from the right. The signal to attack would be Vorogrivas firing a single pistol shot. About a score of fighters followed Manolis along the rocky slope. They held the reins of their horses tightly to keep them moving as quietly as possible. Manolis felt the tension and excitement that possessed him before an impending battle, every limb and muscle tensed as if on the blade of a knife.

From the ridge where Vorogrivas held his men, a solitary shot pierced the night like a clap of thunder. An instant later, the men with Manolis released roars that rumbled across the mountain. They spurred their horses and raced down the slope.

The Turkish troopers were caught by total surprise. Some scurried for their muskets and pistols, while others stood transfixed as the horsemen burst out of the darkness. As Manolis charged toward the compound, a Turkish trooper fumbled to point a pistol at him. Manolis ran him down, the man tumbling awkwardly on the ground. As the Turk struggled to rise, another klepht swung at him with his yataghan, the blade slicing the Turk's arm off at the shoulder like a branch severed from a tree.

All across the garrison, the wild tumult of battle erupted. Men shrieked and shouted amid the cracklings of muskets and pistols. Manolis saw men fall and knew they were dead by the way they sprawled on the ground. Only a bullet or the slash of a yataghan separated a living mortal from a man drained of life.

Manolis led his men through the garrison gates into the center of the compound and confronted Turkish soldiers running from the barracks while aiming their muskets at the attackers or brandishing their swords. The klephts slaughtered them and rode across their fallen bodies. Before the entrance to the main barracks building, Manolis dismounted and, followed by Zarkas and Tinos, rushed into the foyer and hacked down several troopers in their path. Pistols and yataghans in hand, they raced up the stairs, kicking in the doors. Amid the shots and shouts of battling men, Manolis heard Zarkas bellowing.

At the end of the hallway, Manolis kicked open a door and was startled to see a bedroom. Standing beside the bed was a half-dressed Turkish officer, perhaps the camp's commander, his face torn between surprise and rage. Hs shirt flapped about his naked legs as he gripped a scimitar that he waved toward Manolis. In the bed beside him was a half-naked girl, her dark hair matted about her forehead, her cheeks frozen with shock. Manolis realized he had interrupted the pair making love.

The Turk lunged toward him with his scimitar. Manolis aimed his pistol and fired, his shot striking the Turk in the forehead. The man's face seemed to explode, eyes and nose blown apart, blood and bone splattering across the bed. The girl screamed, a piercing cry that spiraled from the room. Her dark beauty reminded Manolis of Maria, and he felt a surge of pity for her, wondering if she was the commander's wife. Hearing the clamor of fighting from the hallway, he turned away.

An intuitive sense of danger made him twist back, and he saw the girl gripping a pistol in both her hands aimed at him. In the next instant, she fired, and a bolt of lightning struck his body. He had never known such pain before, and he dropped like a slaughtered animal to his knees, the room whirling, the ceiling visible for an instant, and then vanishing as his body struck the floor. He was conscious of Zarkas entering the room, lunging to the bed, swinging his yataghan at the girl. The last thing Manolis remembered was the way her dark-haired head flew like a severed melon off her body.

What followed were blurs and snatches of sound and movement. Overwhelming everything was the scorching pain. He felt himself being lifted, and he gasped at how any move sharpened his agony. When he tried to speak, his mouth and throat seemed clogged with blood. He lost consciousness for an instant. A sliver of awareness returned, and his body was braced against the chest of someone holding him in the saddle. Each step the horse took ravaged Manolis with renewed pain and a gush of blood from his mouth. All thoughts of bravery fled, and he tried to scream, believing it was the last sound he would utter on this earth.

He woke later on a pallet inside what he imagined was a cave, his muscles and bones on fire, blood still clogging his mouth. He tried to spit to force past his lips the thick fluid threatening to choke him. He heard a low, shrill moaning, a sound such as a mortally wounded animal might make, and realized it was coming from him. He was aware of movement, voices coming to him from a great distance. As warm poultices were applied and then removed from his throat and chest, faces of men were blurred images he could not recognize. The only human he could distinguish was the voice of Vorogrivas. And always the dreadful pain. At one point with strong arms holding him so he could not kick and thrash, the pain became unbearable, and he understood they were cutting the bullet from somewhere near his throat.

He entered an endless span of time when he seemed to be burning. He imagined he had died and been consigned to the fires of hell. He remembered dead comrades and wondered if they'd be reunited in those eternal fires.

That burning passed as well, and a moment came when, for the first time, he saw more clearly the image of Vorogrivas kneeling beside him. Manolis tried to speak, his tongue twisting to form words but only a guttural babble emerged.

"Don't try to talk, Manolis. Rest now . . . rest and sleep . . . "

Reassured by the captain's presence, Manolis drifted into sleep again and endured nightmares beset by multiheaded demons. The only innocent image in that array of monsters was the face of the girl Maria. Then he saw her head severed brutally like the head of the girl in the garrison bedroom.

Drifting in and out of delirium, he was again aware of Vorogrivas, now hovering above him. The captain held a cup of warm liquid to Manolis's lips. He tried to swallow and gagged.

"Slowly, Manolis. A little at a time. Slowly, my comrade, slowly."

He became conscious of others tending him. He recognized the great head of Zarkas. The burly klepht looked down at him and smiled, his teeth flashing like pearls within his beard.

"By God, it's time you came back from the dead," Zarkas said, his rough voice unusually gentle. "Half a dozen times, we swore you were gone, and then some part of your carcass moved to prove you still held a thread to life."

Manolis felt a word struggling to form within his mouth and then cross his dry, crusted lips. "Zarkas . . . " But even uttering that name did not sound as if it were being spoken by his voice but by the voice of a stranger.

"He knows me!" Zarkas let loose a jubilant roar. "By God, the first word from his lips is my name!" He called exultantly to men nearby, and they came excitedly to surround Manolis, who recognized Tinos, Tsoumas, and Vasilakos. Then, among them, he saw Vorogrivas, and remembered how often he had seen the chieftain's face flow in and out of his fever.

"God be praised. Manolis," Vorogrivas said. He motioned to one of the men. "Bring some chamomile tea—"

"How about a chunk of lamb and some savory greens?" Zarkas grinned.

As if they were greeting someone returned from Hades, the men crowded closer. Vorogrivas sternly waved them away.

"Clear out now," he said brusquely. "If he is seeing us for the first time, don't smother him all at once."

The men departed the cave, and Manolis was left alone with Vorogrivas. Someone brought tea, and the chieftain held the mug to Manolis's lips. The liquid lingered in his mouth and burned as he tried to swallow.

"A score of times we swore we'd lost you." Vorogrivas's voice trembled. "But I knew you were battling death as you battled our enemies in life. I never lost faith."

Beyond the captain's shoulder, Manolis saw daylight at the entrance to the cave.

"Is it morning?" His question hung weakly in the air.

"It is a morning in early May, my friend," Vorogrivas said. "You have been hovering between life and death for almost two months now. Summer is here . . . The mountains are bursting with flowers. Soon now we'll take you outside so you can see for yourself. . . . Soon now, my comrade, my friend."

One morning a few days after he'd spoken the name of Zarkas for the first time, several burly klephts carried Manolis carefully from the cave into the sunlight. Even with his face shielded by the brim of a hat, the stunning brightness of the sun scorched his eyes. He felt as if he had been buried for years inside some subterranean darkness and, for the first time, was emerging into the light.

He was aware of the mountain's beauty, smelled the air laden with the scents of mid-spring, saw the wild fruit trees dropping their pools of shade across the rocks. He heard as if for the first time, sweeping above the promontory, the cawing of small gray rooks. In an eruption of almost blinding color, he absorbed the great scarlet bougainvillea radiating the luminescence of the sun. He wept then with gratefulness for the salvaging of his life.

His comrades marveled at his survival. Zarkas kept boasting that his name was the first word Manolis had spoken.

"I've seen mortally wounded men wrestle the devil on the threshing floor of death," Manolis heard Zarkas tell a group of the men. "But I've never seen a battle such as the one this young warrior fought. Each time the devil had him pinned, he'd leap back up. I tell you, it's a bloody miracle we've witnessed now."

When Manolis was able to comprehend how serious his wound had been, he learned the bullet had struck just to the side of his throat, which caused blood to bubble up when he attempted to speak. If the bullet had struck two centimeters to the left, it would have pierced his jugular. A few more centimeters lower, the bullet would have pierced his heart. But he was not unscathed. The injuries had left his speech impaired. The words from his lips did not emerge in his own voice but were altered in tone with a hoarseness that sounded as if it were the voice of a stranger. Even as he began to swallow fluids and eat more-solid food, simple actions that exhausted him, he was overwhelmed with despair. He could not imagine ever regaining his strength, being able to stand and ride, let alone fight once more. He recalled the fate of the great old warrior Boukouvalas, grown weak and frail, enduring his last days as an invalid in the camp.

Vorogrivas sought to console his concern.

"You're young and vigorous, Manolis, and while your wounds have weakened you, they will not prevent you becoming strong again," the captain said. "This war will go on a long time, and there will be many battles to fight. Be patient, and time will do its healing."

"What battles has the band fought since the attack on the garrison?" Manolis asked.

"We have been on a score of raids and have had some fierce battles," Vorogrivas said. "Several times strong Turkish forces tried to cross the Makrinoros Pass. We fought them off and killed scores of them, their bodies piled in the canyons to rot. But we have paid a price and lost good men. Anastis died in a battle at Kerasovo in April, and in early May, we lost Tzimas and Ioannides at Bakrina."

For a pensive moment, Manolis recalled the faces of the lost men, stalwart palikaria who would never fight or laugh again. "What about the war elsewhere?"

"Rumors and whispers," Vorogrivas said, "but we have no reliable way of knowing how the overall fighting is going. From time to time, a deserter or refugee stumbles into our camp and tells of some massacre or a battle won or lost. But here in the mountains, we live like a pack of wolves in our own secluded sanctuary, ignorant of what is taking place elsewhere."

"Has anyone visited my village?"

Vorogrivas understood the reason for his concern. "Zarkas and several of the men have checked on the village several times. The old priest is alive and well and still tends his flock." He paused. "The girl and your godson are also well. Zarkas said the child is growing like a weed." The captain's voice was low and reassuring. "Father Markos and the young mother send you their blessings and their prayers."

Vorogrivas was right in that Manolis mended quickly. By the end of May, he was able to walk on his own. At first, he tottered on unstable legs. As his muscles firmed and grew stronger, he was able to walk without the aid of a crutch. Meanwhile, Vorogrivas and members of the band were diligent in helping him recover, working with him daily, assisting him to flex his arms and legs, having him lift increasingly larger rocks to build back his strength. While most of the men were careful in their assistance, Zarkas drove him mercilessly.

"Come on, man!" Zarkas growled. "Faster! Lift! Push!"

"Damn you, Zarkas!" Manolis cried angrily. "You torment me as if I were an unruly horse that needed to be broken!"

"You're worse than a horse!" Zarkas grumbled. "A horse doesn't have a loud mouth to talk back to his rider! I'm only pressing you so you don't slacken your efforts and decide it's more comfortable to stay sprawled on your ass!"

By the middle of June, Manolis was able to mount his horse for the first time, swaying precariously in the saddle and feeling suspended from a great height. When he felt his body trembling and feared he might tumble off, Zarkas reached up quickly with a strong arm to steady him.

"Don't fall off now, in the name of God," Zarkas warned. "If I had the burden of nursing you all over again, I might desert the band!"

In late June, one of the sentries spotted a trio of riders crossing the ridge on the trail to the camp. A half-dozen armed men quickly rode out to determine if the trio was hostile and discovered the men were Greeks seeking a meeting. The klephts led them to Vorogrivas. Shortly afterwards, the captain sent for Manolis to join them. He found the captain and the strangers sitting under the shade of a plane tree.

"This is Manolis Kitsos, my lieutenant," Vorogrivas said. "He's recovering now from a serious battle injury but, in my absence, he commands our band. I want him to hear your news."

He pointed to a lean, older man with graying hair and a sensitive face. "This traveler is Xanthos," Vorogrivas said to Manolis. "Since the early months of the war, he has been an aide to General Theodoros Kolokotronis and to Prince Petrobey Mavromichalis of the Mani. Xanthos was with them in the early battles at Karytena and at the siege of Tripolitza. He is now acting as an emissary for the general." He pointed to the other two men who sat cross-legged on the ground.

"These two stalwarts are Selim and Notis from the northern mountains of Suli," Vorogrivas said. "They travel as escorts to assure the safety of Xanthos."

The bodyguards were strongly built warriors, bristling with knives and guns. They had dark skin, curled mustaches, and eyes that bore the glint of fighters who thrived on war. The front part of each man's head was shaved clean of hair, a ritual among the warriors of Suli, as it had been with the Macedonian soldiers of Alexander the Great. The purpose was to prevent an enemy getting a grip on their hair in hand-to-hand combat.

The Suliots who lived in the mountain fortress of a land on a plateau three thousand feet above the river of Acheros were the most renowned fighters in Greece. The great warrior chieftain Boukouvalas, who had led the klephts before Vorogrivas and who had died in battle shortly after Manolis first joined the band, had been a Suliot. Boukouvalas had told them the tale of the Suliot women and children fleeing the Turks of Ali Pasha of Ioannina, who, having reached a final ridge on the mountain of Zalongou, had sung and danced and then, one by one, holding their children in their arms, had jumped to their death.

"Xanthos brings us unhappy news of what is happening with the war in the south," Vorogrivas said. "We'll keep these dark tidings to ourselves for now."

After Manolis sat down, Xanthos resumed his recital of the events taking place in other parts of Greece. For a few moments, Manolis thought the man was speaking in a strange foreign dialect until he understood it was the way Xanthos fashioned his words and sentences. He spoke with a flowing ease and eloquence of language that Manolis had never heard before. From time to time, Xanthos also used words Manolis couldn't understand.

Xanthos told them of the conflicting councils that had been set up in different parts of Greece.

"Each one claims to represent the government of the revolution," Xanthos said, "but only our council includes warrior leaders such as General Kolokotronis and Prince Petrobey Mavromichalis of the Mani. They launched the first battles of the revolt and achieved some of the first victories."

He paused to sip from a cup of raki.

"Another group, now allied with Kolokotronis and Petrobey is led by a Greek Phanariot, a man named Alexander Mavrokordatos, born of an old Constantinople family. He is respected as a patriot. His problem is that he also fancies himself as a general capable of leading an army."

"One decisive defeat in a battle should teach him a lesson about playing the general," Vorogrivas said grimly.

"As if these divisions in western Greece weren't problem enough," Xanthos said. "In the eastern part of the country, another self-styled leader named Theodore Negris has convened an assembly he calls the Areopagus, whose purpose, he claims, is to coordinate the war and political effort."

Xanthos shook his head gravely. "Mavrokordatos may delude himself about his military prowess, but there isn't any question he is a patriot. I fear that isn't true of Negris. He is considered an unscrupulous and ambitious politician, and the Areopagus is nothing more than an instrument to help him achieve his own selfish ends."

He paused in his recital.

"If there is one man who can unify the factions in this conflict, it is General Kolokotronis," Xanthos said. "He is respected, and he has proven his abilities in war. The mission he has assigned to me is to recruit mountain fighters to join the army he is assembling near

Corinth to face the forces of Reshid Pasha, who is moving into the Peloponnesus. They say Reshid's army numbers forty thousand regulars with cavalry and artillery. The orders he carries from his sultan is to destroy the rebellion using any force required. That means he will scorch the earth, burning villages and attacking whatever fortresses still remain in Greek hands."

"To meet such a threat, our people must be united in a single, powerful force," Vorogrivas said. "These quarrels and petty ambitions are a curse."

"That is true," Xanthos said. "It is also true that as our race breeds patriots and heroes, it also spawns men driven by vain dreams of personal glory, men who once they acquire power abuse that power."

"That does not speak well for the success of our rebellion," Vorogrivas said.

"Despite all these rivalries and dissensions," Xanthos said, "there are also hopeful auguries. We've achieved great victories at sea with our fleets commanded by Admirals Konstantine Kanaris and Andreas Miaoulis. Their exploits have captured the imagination of noted citizens such as Lord Byron, the great poet in England, who, from everything I've been told, is a truly noble man. He had visited Greece nearly a decade ago. Since the outbreak of our revolt, this Lord Byron has written impassioned poetry about the Greek struggle for freedom that has made the nations of Europe more supportive of our struggle. He has also inspired hundreds of young men from Germany, France, and Italy to come to Greece to fight for our cause. I have heard that this English nobleman plans to travel to Greece later this year himself to join our battle."

An afternoon breeze carried the scent of mountain flowers across the encampment. Manolis sat entranced listening to the voice and words of Xanthos.

"The tragedy of these internal conflicts is that sometimes it isn't even politics that divide the leaders," Xanthos said, "but simply one Greek unwilling to accept the authority of another. Yet, by not unifying under leaders like Kolokotronis and Petrobey, to fight the Muslim invaders, they endanger the revolution itself." He paused, his quiet voice revealing a tremor of emotion. "I'm sorry to have to say there are plots to imprison or even to kill Kolokotronis."

Vorogrivas's eyes flashed, and an oath burst from his lips.

"That would be a calamity!" he cried angrily. "Our greatest general and a patriot who helped launch the revolt and fought the first battles! And there are traitors among us who seek to destroy him!"

"Fortunately, he remains protected by men who have fought beside him and know his worth," Xanthos said.

"By God, he'll have our help as well!" Vorogrivas said, his voice still hoarse with anger. "I have stalwart palikars in our band, veterans of many battles with the hearts of lions!" He paused. "I will lead them to join the general. We'll leave a small force here to fight off any Turkish attempts to cross the Makrinoros Pass."

"Let me ride with you!" Manolis said, his voice an urgent plea.

"Be patient, Manolis," Vorogrivas spoke quietly in reassurance. "Wait and regain your strength. If you cannot join this battle, there will be other battles."

"You can be certain of that," Xanthos said. "We have been fighting for almost three years now, and God only knows how many more years of struggle we still have before us."

The evening, after they had eaten, Manolis sat with a group around a fire and listened to Xanthos. Drawn by his voice and his eloquence, men singly and then in small groups left their fires to join him.

In the primitive environs of the mountain villages, boys learned rudimentary reading and writing through the secret schools conducted at night. The history of their enslaved country was transmitted to them through stories and poems about the heroes of earlier revolts. They learned of patriots like Rhigas Pheraios, put to death by the Turks in 1798. The words of his famous war hymn were passed on from generation to generation, retold by grandparents and parents to their children. As a boy, Manolis had memorized the poem of the legendary patriot and martyr.

> How long, my heroes, shall we live in bondage,
> alone like lions, on ridges, on peaks?
> Living in caves, seeing our children
> Turned from the land in bitter enslavement.
> Losing our land, brothers and parents,
> our friends, our children, and all our relations?

And the final impassioned lines.

> Better an hour of life that is free,
> than forty years of slavery!

Now, that evening, listening to the scholarly Xanthos, for the first time Manolis learned the history of how the enslavement of Greece began. The story Xanthos told started with the great Byzantine city on the shores of the Bosphorus—Constantinople, a city that had existed for a thousand years and that fell to the Ottoman Turks under Sultan Mehmed II in May 1453.

"It was a glorious and cosmopolitan city," Xanthos told the men sitting around the fire, "built by the Emperor Constantine I on the nine-hundred-year-old site of a Greek city-state named Byzantium, as the eastern capital of the Roman Empire. It was a city of great splendor with a fine library and scholars that preserved the great literature of the past from Homer to Aristotle. It was also a city of incomparable beauty."

As Xanthos spoke, Vorogrivas took a place nearby and appeared as captivated as Manolis and the others by the narrative.

"It was also a city that possessed one of the most beautiful churches in the world, the great cathedral of Aghia Sophia," Xanthos said. "The walls and ceilings held golden mosaics of Christ and his saints, images of the emperors and empresses of Byzantium who had ruled the city. When prayers were held in its vast interior, it sparkled with a thousand candles and resounded with a thousand voices offering prayers and thanksgiving."

Xanthos paused, and for a moment, the air hung still. A man coughed and cleared his throat. The booted foot of another klepht scraped against a rock.

"This city had been looted in the past by the Christian soldiers of fortune of the Roman Church, who stripped the gold from the icons and holy artifacts," Xanthos said. "They attacked with brutality and greed, but still the city survived. After these crusades, however, it became the obsession of the Sultan Mehmed II, who had earned the name of the Conqueror through his bloody conquests. His ambition was to accomplish what had eluded his predecessors—to conquer Constantinople, that queen of cities. He believed that Byzantium was the root of evil that fought against Islam, that the city held within its walls the enemies of God and of his prophet Muhammad, and that it had to be utterly destroyed, root and branch and tree."

The chill of the night grew sharper. One of the klephts, moving as quietly as he could, added more wood to the fire. Several men sitting on the outskirts of the circle moved closer to the fire for warmth and to be nearer to Xanthos.

"Mehmed assembled an army of eighty thousand soldiers. He commissioned an engineer from Hungary, one of the nations in Europe, to construct a gigantic cannon that he boasted 'would blast the walls of Babylon itself.' The length of the cannon's barrel was twenty-six feet, and the cannon balls weighed twelve hundredweight. They brought it to the outskirts of Constantinople drawn by sixty oxen and two hundred men marching alongside the huge gun carriage to hold it steady."

No man stirred, the only sound in the clear night air the calm, precise voice of Xanthos. Even the usually noisy birds seemed hushed by the narrative.

"Day by day, the monster cannon was moved closer to the city that was surviving the siege only because of Greek ships that carried them provisions. The sultan was so enraged at his admiral for failing to prevent the Greek ships slipping in and out of the port that he stripped him of his command, bastinadoed his feet so he was forever crippled and sent him to die in exile."

A night wind rose, causing the flames to flare higher. From the darkness above their heads came the hoarse screech of a hawk, perhaps snatching a smaller bird as prey. Manolis felt his body chilled as he imagined the despair of the city's inhabitants.

"After weeks of bombardment from the monstrous cannon, the walls of Constantinople were breached in three places. By the end of May of that year, it was clear the holy city of Christendom could not survive."

Some of the men made their cross as if joining the prayers of the besieged inhabitants.

"As the plight of the citizens within the city became more desperate," Xanthos said, "the bells of the churches rang, icons were borne upon the shoulders of the defenders, everyone sang hymns and chanted the Kyrie Eleison. Their emperor Constantine sought to reassure them by reminding them they were the descendants of ancient Greek heroes, and, with God's help, they would survive. But anticipating their fate, the citizens embraced and prayed, as men and women expected to die.

In one corner of the sky from behind the clouds, a full moon appeared, its light illuminating the ridges of the mountain.

"On that day of the final battle, wave after wave of Muslim troops attacked the city. First, Mehmed sent in his irregulars, raw and poorly trained recruits he chose to sacrifice in order to exhaust the Greek fire. And then he dispatched his Janissaries, fresh and vigorous, men regarded as fierce and invincible. Armored and merciless as wolves, they stormed the city, tore down the stockade, and overran the final resistance.

A rise in the wind whirling down from the peak caused the fire to flare.

"The Greeks fought valiantly," Xanthos said, "street by street, house by house, but they could not prevent the city being brutalized and looted. The sultan had promised his troops three days of pillage and looting, and his soldiers joyfully obeyed that edict. The Church of Saint Mary came to be known as the church of blood because of the blood that flowed from its nave on the heights of Petra toward the sea. The savage killing went on and on. The historian Phrantzes later wrote that 'in many places the earth could no longer be seen but only the piles of dead bodies.'"

A bitter hissing rose from among the men. A few uttered angry oaths.

"So fell the greatest city of Christendom," Xanthos said. "Afterwards, region after region of Greece, island after island, fell to the advancing Ottomans. And so began those centuries when our land was enslaved, centuries of bondage, centuries of hopelessness, centuries in which children born slaves grew to adulthood as slaves and died as old men and old women, still grieving as slaves."

Xanthos bent his head, and when he raised it again, his voice was somber and elegiac. "Many Greeks today still believe that the Emperor Constantine was not killed by Turkish soldiers at the entrance to the Romanus gate. Legend tells us that he had been carried away by an angel to a secret cave near the Golden Gate where he once led his imperial processions into the city. The story passed from generation to generation tells us the emperor waits there, disguised as a marble statue, until that day when the great city is liberated. Then, another angel, sent by God, will bring him back to life and restore him to his throne."

Xanthos paused again, and the circle of men waited tensely for the words to follow. When they understood that the narrative was finished, they rose silently and left the fire. As if the long recital had exhausted him, for a few moments Xanthos did not move. Vorogrivas approached him and whispered a few words to him before the men dispersed to sleep.

Manolis walked slowly to his own blanket. He lay wearily on the ground and covered himself with a wooly shepherd's cape. For a long time, beneath a bright, full moon, he was unable to sleep. He seemed to hear the mountain whispering, retelling the story Xanthos had related.

His thoughts seethed, and his heart felt unsettled. He could not banish the images Xanthos had fashioned, the flames of the great fires that consumed the splendor of the city, and the shrieks of the inhabitants being butchered. Above all, the presence of the last great Byzantine emperor, frozen in marble, waiting through the centuries for the city to be liberated, so he might return to life and once again lead his people.

And in that moon-bright summer night, Manolis felt he had been allowed to survive his wounds in order to avenge the centuries of brutality and bondage his people had suffered. In that moment, he renewed his vow to fight for the liberation of their suffering and anguished land.

Yet, his final thoughts before falling into welcome sleep were not about vengeance and wars or his vow to liberate their land. Instead, he was overwhelmed by a vision of Maria and his godson sleeping under that same bursting moon.

He felt his heart aching with a longing to be reunited with them someday.

CHAPTER
THREE

🌸In the morning as Xanthos and his Suliot guards prepared to leave the camp, he met for a final time with Vorogrivas.

"There are other klepht bands in these mountains you might convince to join your general," Vorogrivas said. "Remember, these bands are not always led by patriots and honorable men. Some as skilled at evil as Turks live by preying on the villagers in the lowlands who pay them tribute to assure their safety. These bandits have no loyalty except to their own greed. But among them, you'll find patriots as well, men who understand what it means for our people to be free. To help you separate patriot from scoundrel, I'm sending Zarkas and Tinos with you. The klepht captains know them and will understand their presence means you have my support."

The two men clasped hands in farewell. Xanthos understood that in Vorogrivas, he had found one of those honorable patriots the revolution sorely needed. Xanthos also said good-by to Manolis, in whom, even now, his handsome face drawn, his cheeks pale, his tall, strong body ravaged by the assault upon his strength, one sensed the resolute spirit of a battle-hardened fighter. Had he lived in ancient times, Xanthos thought, Manolis might have been a hero such as Hector or Achilles.

"I haven't given up hope, Xanthos, that I'll be able to join you soon," Manolis said. "I'll make every effort to get ready for the battles to be fought by your general Kolokotronis."

"First, rest and regain your strength," Xanthos said. "There will be many battles still to be fought before we can be liberated."

When their small group departed the camp that morning, in addition to Xanthos and the two Suliots, they were accompanied by the burly Zarkas and the Rumeliot fighter Tinos, a tall, wiry man with black hair he wore braided to his shoulders. The men of the band waved their farewells.

"Take care now, teacher," a grizzled klepht called to Xanthos. "Make sure Zarkas and Tinos and those Suliot tigers protect you from wolves and Turks so you can keep telling your stories."

They rode through the morning, their journey carrying them higher up the mountain. The jagged trail ran alongside enormous gray rocks that formed natural fortresses against any invading army.

As if he had sensed what Xanthos was thinking, Zarkas said, "A few fighters lodged in these rocks could hold off an enemy force for weeks."

"The way Leonidas and his three hundred Spartans held off the Persians at Thermopylae," Xanthos said.

"I've heard those palikars fought to the last man," Zarkas said. "That's a noble way for warriors to die. If I'm fortunate, maybe my end will come in that way."

"You might also survive to reap the fruits of freedom and victory," Xanthos said. "You could marry again, bear children, and tend your field like a good farmer."

"That's another one of your stories, teacher," Zarkas shrugged. "I don't think my life will end in that peaceful way. Every month, the bloody swords and bullets seem to be coming closer. Someday, I suspect, one will arrive bearing the name of Zarkas."

As the hoofs of their horses trampled clumps of brush and flowers, the air grew fragrant with the scents of heather, thyme, and sage. The ascent became steeper, the trail rougher and more inaccessible. At times, the path narrowed into a passage only wide enough for a single horseman to tread at a time. Zarkas rode ahead of Xanthos with Tinos following a short way back. One of the Suliot guards, Selim, rode some distance ahead of their group to make sure the trail would provide the horses a durable footing while the other Suliot, Notis, tracked a short distance behind.

Ever since they'd begun their journey, Xanthos had grown more impressed with the strength and endurance of the two Suliot warriors. They were as fierce as a pair of mountain lions bred from birth for war and survival. They were superb marksmen, never appeared weary, and subsisted on a minimum of sleep. Except for a few brief exchanges about where they should make camp and what trail to follow, Xanthos hadn't been able to coax a dozen words from either one about what they were thinking or how they felt. At times, he saw them speaking in low tones to one another and wondered what confidences they shared, but their thoughts and emotions remained concealed from him.

When the mountain path widened once again, Zarkas reined his horse back alongside Xanthos.

"You know these mountains have harbored klepht bands for centuries," Zarkas said, gesturing at the bulwark of rocks. "All those years when the land was in bondage to the Turks, free men held these ridges and peaks. Now the truth is that they weren't always thinking about liberating Greece but only about making life hell for the Mussulmen. They ambushed the Turkish tax collector, slit his throat and the throats of his bodyguards. They raided supply lines and looted the depots where the Turks stored their arms. After a battle, they'd celebrate by returning to their mountain hideouts to drink, dance, and sing the rest of the night. They were a wild, swaggering bunch of palikars, but they kept the mountains a sanctuary for freedom."

The trail narrowed again along the precipitous edge of a deep chasm. Once more, the men rode in single file and held on carefully to the reins of their horses. A single misstep by one of the horse's hoofs would have sent horse and rider tumbling over the edge.

"Tread carefully, teacher," Zarkas called a warning to Xanthos. "If I lose you, the captain will have my head."

Xanthos did not wish to reveal his nervousness to the others. When the trail widened, he felt his heartbeat return to a normal rhythm, and he spurred his horse forward to ride alongside Zarkas.

"How did the Turks respond to those attacks by the klepht bands?" Xanthos asked.

"They sent troops into the mountains to find them but those regulars didn't know the terrain and were often ambushed and butchered," Zarkas said. "So the Turks recruited a militia made up of Greeks who knew the mountains. They were known as *armatoloi*, armed men without allegiance to any cause except to whoever paid them. Sometimes, they took Turkish money and fought the bands of mountain fighters, and sometimes they took Turkish money and then joined the bands. The worst of these renegade Greeks were as rapacious as Turks. They'd raid a village, steal the chickens and sheep, and even carry off the women."

"Barbarians preying upon their own people," Xanthos said.

"That they were, teacher," Zarkas said grimly, "and may their worthless souls plunder one another in hell for eternity."

They rode in silence for a while. As they crossed a bluff, the crags above them seemed to disappear into the clouds. Xanthos recalled a passage from Aristophanes about clouds that resembled the shape of a centaur, a leopard, a bull. He was roused from his reverie by the voice of Zarkas.

"This klepht encampment we'll be coming to later this afternoon, teacher," Zarkas said, "the captain is a brigand called Barbelas. I know he's taken money from the Turks, but I also know he has no love for them. He has a large band, bigger than our own, perhaps as many as a hundred men. You'll see they live differently than our men do." He uttered a sardonic laugh. "Vorogrivas believes in keeping us lean and a little hungry. He thinks men too well fed grow lazy and lose their zeal for combat."

"Can Barbelas be trusted?"

"That depends on what's in it for him," Zarkas shrugged. "His trust goes that far and no farther."

"We have such selfish, untrustworthy men in the governing councils in the Peloponnesus as well," Xanthos said. "Men who harbor their own ambitions while claiming to be united in the battle for freedom."

"These fighters of Barbelas might be scoundrels, but they are also seasoned veterans," Zarkas said. "Any one of them who joins your army is worth ten farmers who take up arms against the Turks. Speak to them, teacher, as eloquently as you spoke to us, and you may find them willing to join your cause." He shook his head gravely. "Last night around the fire, you had the men hanging on your every word."

"The trouble with words is they are like snowflakes," Xanthos said. "Often they melt before they settle on the ground."

The men rode in silence through the early afternoon, their heads bent against the brightness of the sun. The valley was thousands of feet below. The fields gleamed like distant lakes in the sun, and here and there a small cluster of white blocks marked the houses of a village. At one point on the mountainside above them, they spotted wild ibexes, the animals ascending a sheer surface of rock as fleetly as if they had wings instead of hoofs. At a mountain stream, they led their horses to the water's edge, the animals drinking thirstily and tossing their manes to ward off the flies. The men rested and ate the fruit and cheese they carried in their saddlebags.

Resuming their journey, they climbed still higher up the vast, stunning mountain, its rocky crags glimmering yellow in the afternoon light. Later in the day, the Suliot Selim, scouting ahead of them, brought his horse trotting back to tell them that on one of the ridges he had spotted the sun reflected off the barrel of a musket.

"Must be a sentry from the camp of Barbelas," Zarkas said. "I'll send Tinos up to alert them we're coming."

Tinos spurred his horse forward. A short while later, he returned.

"As long as we're coming in peace, we're welcome," he said.

"Fair enough," Zarkas said. "All I want is peace enough to feed my belly and rest my ass."

When they rode into the encampment, Xanthos noticed at once the differences in the way this klepht band lived in contrast to the one led by Vorogrivas. Their houses were better-built structures of logs and stone, and their campfires were set within rocky enclosures to protect them from the wind and rain. The saddles hanging on the fences of the corral were more ornate than those owned by the men of Vorogrivas, the cradles of leather beautifully inlaid with gold and silver. When Xanthos caught glimpses of women in the camp, he asked Zarkas if they were fighters, as well.

"I'll wager they do most of their fighting on their backs," Zarkas grinned. "But I'm sure, like she-wolves, they could also tear a man to bits. I've heard sometimes Barbelas turns them loose on a captive Turk they're trying to get to talk. A woman can devise more devilish ways to torture than any man. They rub their breasts against his body until the poor devil, who can't help himself, gets an erection. Then they use a knife to clip off his foreskin inch by inch. If that doesn't do the trick, they start making incisions in his balls." He shrugged. "I guess that manner of cruelty is bred in women from the time Eve and the snake conspired to get that poor bastard Adam thrown out of Eden."

"Men can be equally cruel," Xanthos said. "That is true for Greeks as well as Turks. When Tripolitza fell to the Greek armies, the blood of Turkish women and children ran like water in the streets."

"I wasn't at that slaughter," Zarkas said grimly. "It's hard to know just what I would have done. When war boils a man's blood, then the devil takes over his soul."

At the center of the camp, Barbelas emerged from one of the larger dwellings and swaggered forward to meet them. Unlike the tower-ing, muscular Vorogrivas, Barbelas was a short, stocky, dark-skinned, and bearded fighter. Within the tangle of hair tumbling around his cheeks, his small, dark eyes were cold and cunning. Around his waist, he wore a brightly beaded sash that held a pearl-handled dagger and two silver-handled pistols.

"Welcome to our camp," he said. He gestured derisively at Zarkas. "I'm surprised you're still alive," he laughed hoarsely. "I thought a Turkish bullet would have dispatched your ugly, oversize carcass to hell a long time ago."

"I've always feared you'd show up there," Zarkas grinned. "That keeps me eager to stay alive."

The Suliots tethered their horses to a nearby tree. Xanthos, Tinos, and Zarkas joined Barbelas at one of the campfires. A pair of women with greasy, black hair brought them flagons of fine wine and plates of savory noodles, large, tangy yellow beans, crisp-crusted bread, and creamy, white cheese.

"You're still eating well, I see," Zarkas said between vigorously chewing the food and consuming ample quantities of the wine.

"As long as there is decent food and drink anywhere within fifty kilometers of us, we'll eat well," Barbelas boasted.

After they had eaten, Xanthos explained his mission of recruiting men for the armies of Kolokotronis and the provisional government. Barbelas continued to drink long, noisy swigs of wine. Finally, wip-ing his wine-stained beard with the back of his hand, he cut Xanthos off impatiently.

"Save this jabbering of patriotism and liberation for schoolchildren," he said harshly. "I know what's going on with your patriots in the Peloponnesus, every man fighting for influence and power and to feather his own nest. If my men and I join the struggle against these Turks, it won't be for any of the high-flown reasons you're babbling about. We want our share of whatever booty your army takes." He fixed his sharp, crafty eyes on Xanthos. "I warn you, if we don't get what we feel we deserve, we'll take it, anyway."

"I'm sure General Kolokotronis will make sure each fighter is properly compensated," Xanthos said. "But I can't promise how much you'll receive."

"And I can't promise you how much we'll fight," Barbelas smirked. "When will these battles you anticipate take place?"

"Before I left headquarters, we had word that Khurshid Pasha is leading an army up from Kalamata. Another strong Turkish force is raiding villages and burning towns south of Astros. Our leaders are fairly certain their goal is to attack Navplion, where the Greek leaders have set up a government of free Greece. The plan is for one of our armies to challenge Khurshid Pasha and another to confront Dramalis somewhere between Astros and Dhervenakia. We must prevent the two armies from uniting. A major battle is probably a matter of no more than a couple of months away."

"Before we ride anywhere, we have to make a social call on a wealthy Greek in Antirion," Barbelas said. "The scurvy swine lives like a king, with a dozen lackeys to wait on him. After the raid, I'll decide whether my band of palikars will join you."

"You're attacking Greeks now, are you?" Zarkas asked, his voice thick with sarcasm. "Aren't there enough Turks to suit your needs?"

"This sack of shit is a *kodja bashee*, a collaborator," Barbelas scowled. "The only way a Greek becomes that wealthy is by working with the Turks. That makes him fair game. We'll relieve him of some of his prized possessions, and perhaps he'll think twice about who his friends are." He winked and laughed. "If we slit his throat, we might even make a dead patriot out of him."

Sated with food and wine, Barbelas retired to sleep soon afterwards. One of his men showed Xanthos and the others a lean-to where they spread their blankets. Xanthos lay down on his pallet and covered himself with his sheepskin cape. The moon had begun to wane but still cast bright beams across the encampment. Outside the lean-to gleamed the ash of the chibouk being smoked by one of the Suliot sentries. Whether in the midst of enemies or among apparent friends, the two warriors never relaxed their vigilance and never slept at the same time.

When Xanthos lay down to rest, the wounds he had sustained at Tripolitza rose to plague him. The scar at his shoulder from the hunchback's knife burned and, from time to time, he felt a searing pain in his groin. He recalled his months of convalescence at the monastery, the pleasure he had taken teaching the orphaned children, his reluctance to leave the peacefulness of the cloisters. But as the war raged on, he could not sit idly by. When he felt well enough to ride, he left the monastery to join Kolokotronis once again.

Thinking of the intrigues and bitter wrangling rampant among the leaders of the governing council at Navplion made him reflect as well on the greed and selfishness of the klepht captain Barbelas. Xanthos considered sadly how little Greeks had changed since ancient times. The history of their small, often-suffering country had proved that when Greeks joined their forces and united their energies, they were capable of developing flourishing civilizations such as that created by Pericles in the Golden Age. That unity also produced great military victories such as the one won by Miltiades over the Persian Emperor Darius at Marathon and the one by Themistocles over Xerxes, the son of Darius, at the sea battle of Salamis.

Yet, that rapport and harmony were often dismembered by the hatreds and rivalries among the Greeks that led to the terrible twenty-seven-year Peloponnesian War between the city-states of Athens and Sparta. While it ended with Sparta the apparent winner, it exhausted both states and destroyed the military and political supremacy of the Hellenes. Their influence and power passed to the Dorian kings of Macedonia, Philip II and his son, Alexander, until that ambitious young king foundered in the vast recesses of the eastern lands he sought to conquer. The historian Herodotus summed up the tragic history of Greece: 'It was the custom of the gods to bring low all things of surpassing greatness.'"

In reading the history of the ancient civilizations from Thucydides to Tacitus, Xanthos had learned that the decadence and collapse of a society that once bestrode the earth like a colossus weren't the fate of

Greece alone. Other great civilizations were swept away by the flaws of mortals and the flow of time. Few of the rulers and potentates seemed to understand that in the relentless passage of centuries, even the wealthiest and most powerful kings and emperors succumbed to decay and death, their ultimate fate defined in the somber lines of a Persian poet, "Spiders spin their webs in the palaces of Caesar."

After departing the camp of Barbelas the next morning, Zarkas led Xanthos into two more klepht camps secluded in mountain hideouts. One of the captains they met named Asimakis, a rock-faced fighter from Trikala, with a band of about fifty fighters, solemnly vowed to lead his band to join Kolokotronis.

"That captain is a true patriot!" Xanthos told Zarkas fervently as they were riding out of the camp. "He offered his help and asked for nothing!"

"You've already seen fighters as different as Vorogrivas and Barbelas," Zarkas said. "Asimakis is also among the honorable men. But, believe me, teacher, you'll meet others more like Barbelas."

That proved true in the next camp, situated under rocky crags in the western ridges of the mountain. The captain, Mavroulis, a swarthy man with sharp, cruel features, brusquely dismissed Xanthos and his appeals.

"These mountains are my country and my sanctuary," he told Xanthos. "My father fought and died here before me. I was born here, fight from here, and, someday, when my arm and eye falter, I'll die and be buried here. Then my sons will fight on after I am gone. This is the domain my clan rules no matter whether Greek or Turk holds the lowlands. Their battles don't concern me."

"That captain speaks a hard but honest truth," Zarkas said grimly to Xanthos as they rode away from the camp. "After a lifetime of living in the mountains, the valleys become alien patches of land, and the villages like prisons."

On the fourth day after leaving the camp of Vorogrivas, the group parted company at the fork of Rentina. Zarkas and Tinos were to return to their camp, Xanthos and the Suliots to travel on to Navplion. Xanthos had grown fond of Zarkas, and he bade farewell to him sadly.

"I'll miss your company and your tart tongue, Zarkas," Xanthos told him with affection.

"I'll miss you, too, teacher," Zarkas grinned. "But, God willing, we'll meet again when the armies assemble for battle. If we survive, I want to hear more of your stories. Next time tell us the one about the Greeks who sailed to Troy to fight for a harlot who put horns on her husband's head. And how, as long as they were there, they were crafty enough to loot the treasury of that rich city as well. I like the way that story ends better than the one you told us about in the camp."

Zarkas braced his hand on his horse's withers and swung lithely up into the saddle. With a final wave, he and Tinos rode off at a swinging trot.

Xanthos and the Suliots began their descent of the mountain to pick up the road for Corinth on the way to Navplion. Away from the coolness of the mountain, the air of the lowlands grew hotter and dryer, the landscape more barren. The hoofs of their horses rang loudly on the stone-strewn earth. When they came to a small olive grove with stunted, gnarled trees that shielded a patch of ground from the summer sun, they paused to rest.

Xanthos lay down on a thick bed of moss beside the tangled roots of one of the trees. He fell asleep and dreamed of his homeland, Zante. Whether in dream or daylight fantasy, each time he envisioned that blessed island, he saw the faces of his dead parents and the sun-bright house on the sea where he had lived his childhood. Thoughts of his island also blended into a vision of the young girl Chryseis, who had been a student in his history class at the university. She was half his age, a lovely girl with pale, reddish hair and a complexion like the bloom of an orange. He had understood the impropriety of the relationship between teacher and student, but she seemed attracted to him, and he did not have the strength of character to resist his own longing. For a brief, idyllic summer, they were lovers. Yet, lovers with their roles strangely reversed, she seeming the mature woman and he the nervous student. Part of his awkwardness came about because of his amazement that she should have accepted his own lean, ungainly frame against the consummate loveliness of her body.

When the noisy snorting of one of the horses woke him, he accepted pensively that the dream of ever seeing Chryseis again was a futile fantasy. They had been separated now for the five years that he'd been in Greece. She'd probably married and might even have borne children. He'd have to be content with the nurturing memory of the love they had so briefly shared.

He and the Suliots resumed their journey. In early afternoon, the fields along their path shimmered in the sunlight, and every stone gleamed as if on fire. They rode for several hours without seeing a house or human being until they came to a small field where the figure of a man could be seen bent over a pale-green patch of potato plants. The man rose from his crouch as they approached. He was wizened, his nose hooked and his beard stained by tobacco. His shirt and trousers were soiled and tattered, and he wore a band of damp, dirty cloth tied around his wrinkled, sun-baked temples. His sharp, black eyes stared up at them without a trace of fear.

"We offer you our greetings," Xanthos said. "We're travelers on our way to Corinth."

"Where you're going is your own business," the old man said brusquely.

"What village are you from?" Xanthos asked.

"I have no village," the man scowled. He gestured toward a small grove some distance away where a shabby hut was visible within the trees. "I live there alone."

"Is there a village nearby?"

The old man stared silently at him for a moment. Tensing his weather-scarred body, he spit scornfully at the ground. "There is a cesspool named Garolimi about twelve kilometers ahead," he said. "I'd stay away from the place if I were you."

"Why?"

"There is a Turkish garrison, another ten kilometers beyond the village," the man said, "and the villagers live by serving the soldiers. There isn't a man among them who doesn't soil his pants when a Turkish shithead rides into the village. The only reason the Turks don't slaughter every worthless creature in the place is because they milk them like goats and shear them like sheep."

"Aren't you afraid of having Turkish troops so close to you?" Xanthos asked.

The old man's mouth twisted into a virulent sneer. "I've lived three score and ten years," he said bluntly. "There's little enough of my life left to take, so why should I be afraid? Let those gutless shits in Garolimi be afraid."

"Are there any younger men in the village who might be recruited as fighters for the revolution?" Xanthos asked.

"Didn't you understand what I just told you?" the farmer snapped impatiently. "You'll find no fighters there." As if dismissing any further dialogue with Xanthos as useless, he crouched once more over his potatoes.

Xanthos decided that despite the danger of encountering Turkish soldiers, they'd chance stopping in the village to obtain provisions and fresh water for their flasks. They'd enter it warily, on the lookout for Turkish troopers.

In mid-afternoon, they spotted the bell tower of the church in Garolimi rising above the cluster of houses. When they rode into the village, the dusty streets were deserted except for the embers of a fire that still burned in an outdoor oven. The houses looked shabby and in need of repair. A little farther along the street, a crudely built wooden enclosure held a mangy donkey and two scrawny sheep. A shaggy dog drowsing in one corner of the enclosure raised its head slowly for a moment as they rode past and then lethargically curled its body back into a ball.

Riding past the shuttered houses, Xanthos felt their passage being watched by people hidden inside. Selim and Notis were wary and held their muskets waist-level in their hands, each man carefully watching opposite sides of the street.

At the end of the main street was a small, shabby coffeehouse with a dilapidated terrace holding several empty tables and chairs. Selim dismounted and with musket in his hand ascended the steps and entered the coffeehouse. A few moments later, he emerged.

"Old men smoking and drinking," Selim said tersely. "They said the Turks don't come into the village until tonight." He pointed farther up the street to the small church with the bell tower. "The priest is at the church."

The grounds of the church reflected the general seediness of the village. Some of the bell-tower stones had crumbled. The frames around the windowpanes were rotted, and the outside stucco walls needed repainting. A few sunflowers and hibiscus brought a patch of color to a weed-strewn and neglected garden.

Selim brusquely pushed open the wooden door and entered the church. When he returned, he came out with a small, frail-bodied middle-aged priest wearing a black cassock that fell to his ankles. His sandals were visible below the cassock's hem, and his dirty, bare feet with long toes appeared too large for his body.

He cringed when he saw Xanthos and Notis, and his thin, pinched face went ashen with fear. A stench of sweat reeled from his trembling body.

"My name is Xanthos, Father. My companions and I are on our way to Navplion," Xanthos said quietly to allay the priest's fears.

"I am Father Cleon, the priest here in Garolimi." His voice low and shaken. "We are a poor village living at the mercy of the Muslims." He peered nervously at Xanthos. "What is it you want from us?"

"We'd like to purchase any provisions you can spare," Xanthos said, "and we need fresh water."

The priest looked nervously at the heavily armed Suliots.

"We have little enough ourselves," he said, "but we'll give you water and what food we can." He paused. "You should know that Turkish troopers are stationed in a garrison not far from here. At nightfall, they come into the village to drink and eat. If they find you here, there will be bloodshed." His hand fluttered from his side in a nervous gesture of entreaty. "They might accuse us of sheltering you and punish us. Our people have suffered enough already." He looked beseechingly at Xanthos. "I beg you to have mercy on us and leave as soon as you can."

"My mission is to recruit men for the armies of the new provisional government that has been set up in Navplion," Xanthos said. "Are there any young men in the village who might wish to join us?"

"Our young men and young women are either dead or have gone into hiding," the priest said. "Only old men and old women and some children are left in Garolimi."

He peered anxiously into the sky, as if assessing the descent of the sun and how soon night would fall.

"Sometimes a few Turk soldiers come in early," he said, "If they find you here . . . " His voice trailed away weakly.

The Suliots stared scornfully at the trembling, frightened cleric.

"We'll leave as soon as we get provisions and water, Father," Xanthos said. "Is there some place away from the Turkish garrison where we might camp safely for the night?"

"There are the ruins of an old monastery about three kilometers east of here," the priest said. "You could find shelter there. In the morning, you could travel the valley path that bypasses the Turkish garrison, and that will put you back on the road to Livadia. That will take you to the gulf."

"Thank you, Father," Xanthos said. "Now if you can provide us bread and some fresh water, we'll be on our way."

The priest, walking with short, quick steps, led them to fill their flasks from a well behind the church. He brought them several loaves of bread and a small container of olives. When Xanthos offered to pay him, the priest shook his head.

"I want no money," he said. "All I ask is that you leave now as quickly as you can. God help us all if the Turks come to the village early."

"Aren't the villagers here in Garolimi aware there is a revolution in progress?" Xanthos asked. "All across Greece, armies are fighting to liberate our land. Don't the people here have any desire to be free?"

"We are just a poor, helpless village," the priest mumbled again. "We have no part in any revolution, and we have no choice but to remain loyal subjects of the sultan, or they'll burn us to the ground as they have burned so many other villages." He stared at his feet and continued in a low, mournful voice. "God help us, all we want is to be left alone."

He turned then and with quick, nervous steps disappeared back into the church.

A massing of clouds drifted across the sky, arching shadows across the houses. As Xanthos and the Suliots rode the narrow street from the village, someone peered out at them behind the shutters of one of the houses. Before another house, an old man emerged, but when he saw them, he hastily reentered the house and closed the door.

Xanthos knew that at one time, strangers entering any village in Greece would have been met with unwavering hospitality. The war had disrupted that tradition and instilled fear and distrust of strangers in its place. Xanthos was also aware that nowhere in the village had they heard the voices of children. Perhaps the adults had hidden them.

He realized sadly that any human longing for liberation had been bred out of the inhabitants of Garolimi, draining from them any feelings except those linked to their terror and to their need to survive.

When they rode past the enclosure that held the donkey and the sheep, the drowsing dog did not bother to lift its head and mark their passage.

They traveled through the waning afternoon light toward the monastery, the clouds grown denser and darker. The wind rose, whipping a cooler breeze against their faces and ruffling the manes of the horses. As they crossed a ridge, the monastery suddenly appeared in a mist before them. A main building linked to several smaller ones, all in ruins—the walls crumbling, the roofs collapsed, the windows shattered. A broken shutter dangled from a window ledge, the wind arching it slowly back and forth, a rusty hinge making a grating sound. Beside the monastery, a solitary and misshapen cypress tree swept gaunt tentacles against the sky.

They tethered their horses in a shed under the cypress tree. In the main monastery building, they found it divided into a series of miniature cells where the monks had once lived and slept. There were also the remnants of a large fireplace in a room that might have been where the monks ate their meals. A worn stone plaque embedded in a wall showed a barely legible date of 1547, revealing the monastery had been in existence for several centuries before its collapse.

Another room appeared to have been a chapel, because it still contained a musty smell of incense and wax. Sections of walls on either side of the altar reflected a lighter shading of where icons, probably stolen, might have been.

Behind the altar, Xanthos found a smaller table on which a score of human skulls were lined up in neat rows. The skulls, all that remained of the monks who had once occupied the cloisters, were of varying sizes, but all were bleached white by time and the ravages of weather. Staring at the rows of skulls, Xanthos imagined them resting there, decade after decade, untouched except for lizards darting through the bones and the wind sweeping about the hollow sockets of the eyes and nose. If not disturbed, such skulls might endure for a millennium. He felt suddenly chilled by an eerie feeling that the ruins were still inhabited by the ghosts of men who had once lived and prayed there.

In one of the alcoves shielded from the wind by a wall and a still-intact portion of a roof, they built a small fire of twigs on which they heated a barley broth. Through the partially shattered roof, the full moon emerged from the masses of clouds to shine its light briefly across the ruins. Moments later, the landscape darkened once again.

While Notis stood watch in the perimeter of darkness outside the monastery, Selim and Xanthos ate chunks of wheaten bread and drank the broth. Afterwards, Selim picked up his musket and went to relieve Notis who came into the enclosure to eat.

Sitting with his back braced against a wall and listening to the wind sweeping through the empty cells that surrounded them, Xanthos grew drowsy. Notis, his head bent slightly, his body relaxed, sat cross-legged on the opposite side of the small fire, which had burned down to glowing embers. A moment later, their tranquility was shattered when Selim suddenly came running into the enclosure. He made a quick, wordless gesture to Notis who leaped up and swiftly ground out the glowing embers beneath his booted feet. A few faint tendrils of smoke drifted off into the darkness.

Xanthos was bewildered at what was happening, until, in the next instant, Selim grasped his arm and tugged him to his feet. The Suliot pulled him deeper into the cloisters and then pressed him roughly against the wall in one of the cells.

"What is it, Selim?" Xanthos's low, shaken voice echoed strangely in his ears.

"Horsemen!" Selim whispered harshly. "Wait here!"

He slipped soundlessly into the darkness, leaving Xanthos trembling in the corner, his heart flailing in his chest. He drew his pistol from his belt and held it tightly in his hand. As he strained to listen for sounds he could identify, he heard only the wind blowing through the ruins. When the wind subsided, he heard the droning of cicadas and far out in the night the barking of a dog.

Through the shattered remnants of the monastery roof, the moon suddenly appeared gliding soundlessly from the sheathing of clouds. With the landscape illuminated, a single musket shot shattered the night. That solitary shot was followed by a clamorous volley of musket

fire that set off a series of strident echoes. When the moon slipped
behind the clouds once again, the shooting slowly trailed away. Into
that silence, a voice shouted what seemed a command, words in Turkish, garbled and incoherent to Xanthos.

He realized they were being attacked by Turks but he hadn't any
idea how many there were of the enemy. Long tense minutes passed
while he waited, all his senses on edge. Each time the moon emerged
from the cluster of clouds, and the landscape was illuminated, the
volleys of musket fire erupted once again. The clouds then shielded
the moonlight, and the darkness and silence returned.

Xanthos felt his legs grow cramped and his back ache. He waited
and listened, nervously brushing away the moths flitting about his
head. After what seemed an endless period of time, a man's startled
shriek cut the darkness and was suddenly choked off.

Xanthos knew the Suliots were considered to have the eyes of cats in
the night. He had an image of Selim and Notis prowling the darkness,
the hunters who had attacked them becoming the hunted. He wanted
to rise and help in whatever battle was taking place, but since he was
unable to see, he could only be an obstacle to the Suliots. Or, was it
fear that kept his legs rooted to the earth? While he deliberated, he
did nothing, remaining crouched in the corner, seeing menace and
threat in every phantom shape the night fashioned before his eyes.

Twice more, the shrieks of men pierced the night, each time followed by a volley of musket fire being discharged in the dark. When
the barrage ended, a man's voice erupted in shrill, frantic cries that
swelled in volume and then ended. A horse snorted, the sound loud
and discordant across the night. Then the silence returned until, as
if playing a capricious game, the moon emerged and again set off a
flurry of shouts and shots. A shriek pierced the night unlike any sound
Xanthos had heard since the battle of Karitena when the Turkish
cavalry had routed the Greek forces. He recognized it as a cry not
made by any human voice but the death scream of a horse.

He did not know how long he huddled in that corner of the cell,
darkness and moonlight coalescing into weird shapes around him.
Each time he swung his pistol toward the phantoms, they vanished.
For a while, as hard as he listened, all he heard was the wind. As the
gusts subsided, he felt the pounding of his heart. His fingers grew
numb and sweaty gripping the handle of his gun.

Finally, from the darkness beyond the monastery ruins rose a clatter of hoofbeats—the rumble of galloping horses receding into the night. Whatever force had attacked had given up and taken flight.

Moments later, a shape took form in the doorway, and as Xanthos frantically raised his gun in defense. Selim called, "Xanthos" and came to the corner where Xanthos crouched. The Suliot smelled of blood and death.

"The priest betrayed us," Selim said in a low, toneless voice.

Xanthos walked with Selim to the shed where they had sheltered their horses. Only two animals were tethered, and he wondered about Notis. As if he understood, Selim said quietly, "Notis will come."

They led their horses away from the ruins. The capricious moon emerged once again. In the eerie light that illuminated the landscape around the monastery, Xanthos witnessed the debris and carnage of the nightlong battle. A dead horse lay in the open field, one of its hoofs suspended stiffly and awkwardly upward, the iron horseshoe reflecting the moonlight that also exposed the animal's bloodstained flanks. Also visible in that ghostly light were the bodies of men Xanthos recognized as Turkish soldiers. They lay on the ground in grotesque heaps, on their backs or on their bellies, the moonlight making them appear weird growths spawned by the earth itself. He counted at least eight bodies and imagined the terrifying and stealthy warfare that had gone on through the night with the Suliots stalking the soldiers. They led the horses among the fallen bodies. Agitated by the scents of blood, the animals snorted nervously and tugged at the reins.

When they passed a Turkish soldier's body lying face down against the earth, the man's booted foot quivered. In an instant, Selim had straddled the man's back, grasped him roughly by the hair, and jerked back his head. The soldier moaned, his booted feet suddenly kicking and twisting, as if trying to dig into the earth. Selim's knife slashed an arc across his throat. The Turk's moan became a hoarse rattle of expiring breath. The booted feet were still.

Xanthos's body chilled at the swiftness of the kill. He recalled stories of the ferocity of the Suliots, merciless in war against their enemies and equally merciless in their own society. A Suliot stealing from a neighbor would have his hands severed at the wrists. A Suliot woman found guilty of adultery was encased still alive in a sack and hurled over the cliffs onto the boulders of the Black River flowing below Suli.

At the edge of the field, Xanthos and Selim mounted their horses and started at a quick trot from the monastery toward the road that bypassed the Turkish fort. They left behind the monastery ruins, the neat rows of skulls behind the altar, and a field strewn with the bodies of the newly dead.

They rode on at a quick trot as the first tracings of dawn lightened the horizon, and the rough, stony earth became visible. The corona of the sun appeared, bringing a flush of warmth and light to dispel the shades of night. The tense and sleepless night had exhausted Xanthos. Each time his horse's hooves struck the earth, the rocking jarred his weary body.

The sun was higher in the sky when they heard the approach of a galloping rider behind them. It was Notis. The flanks of his horse were flecked with foam from its hard ride. He said nothing but reined in his horse's gait to match the stride of their own mounts. The three of them rode on in silence.

At a fork in the trail, Xanthos looked back towards Garolimi. In the distance, he observed the spire of the church rising higher than the houses of the village. Above that spire, he saw swirling into the sky the plumes of fire and of black smoke. And he understood why Notis had returned to Garolimi.

For an anguished moment, he hoped the Suliot had only burned the church and not killed the poor terrified priest who had betrayed them.

By late afternoon, as they came nearer the Gulf of Corinth on the journey to Navplion, they encountered a stream of refugees in flight from villages in the path of Turks attacking from the south. A long, ragged column of straggling men, women, and children stretched back along the road as far as the eye could see. A few men led donkeys laden with children or a few belongings; others tugged carts holding parents and grandparents.

Xanthos's heart was torn by pity for the wretchedness of the refugees. He saw young women clutching babies in their arms, frightened, crying children stumbling along clutching their clothing, men shouting across the column. When Xanthos and the Suliots approached, a shrill wailing of terror rose from the column, and a group of armed men surged toward them. Xanthos called out that he and the Suliots were Greeks, and the words of reassurance traveled swiftly across the straggling refugees. But the pace of their frantic, terrified flight did not falter.

"Where are you from?" Xanthos asked a ragged, old man carrying an ancient musket on his shoulder.

"From the village of Sikion," the old man wheezed. He gestured with his arm back to the south. "There are more poor wretches behind us from the mainland seeking to cross the gulf." He paused. "It's the cursed Turks burning the villages! They're crucifying men and chopping the heads off babies! You had best flee, too!"

Several women approached them and raised babies in their arms, imploring Xanthos and the Suliots to carry their children to safety. Their pleas were frantic and shrill.

"We're crossing the Gulf to the south," Xanthos tried to explain, but the hysterical women would not listen, continuing to beg them to save the children.

"They are butchering and burning!" one woman screamed.

"Help us!" another woman pleaded. "In God's name, take our children to safety!"

Heartsick because he was unable to offer them any aid, Xanthos spurred his mount away from the wailing women. As they rode back along the length of the column, he witnessed other sights of horror and despair. A frantic farmer ran alongside the column, calling out the names of his family, each name rising in a wail. A son or grandson carried a frail woman like a sack on his back. The kerchief slipped from the old woman's gray head, which flopped back and forth like a puppet on a string. Not far behind them, a burly father struggled with three small children clinging to his neck and arms. He wasn't walking as much as staggering, his chest heaving with the effort to carry his load. Some of the refugees stared up with apprehension at Xanthos and the Suliots, but most kept their eyes on the road, stumbling along in a collective terror.

The closer to the harbor, the more numerous were the columns of refugees streaming from the cities and villages and stumbling on the heels of one another in their flight. A number of men and women, mostly those who were older, had fallen exhausted by the roadside. They sprawled on the ground, arms raised, pleading for assistance no one paused to offer. After a while, Xanthos could no longer bear to look at them but kept his gaze on the mane of his horse.

The city of Anthousa on the water was jammed on every street with people. A few armed men tried to apportion order, but their shouted commands were ignored, and they gave up. At the harbor, a ferry from the southern coast of the Gulf was unloading more people, some stumbling or slipping as they crossed the gangplank from the boat to the dock. A woman and her child were being pulled from the water. A second ferry, emptied of its passengers, was just pushing away from the dock.

"Come back for us!" Xanthos cried to the ferryman. "We'll ride across with you!"

"Go to hell!" the ferryman snarled. "When I get to the other side, I'll only have time for one more load before the Turks strike!"

Xanthos knew the man's concern was not compassion but greed, taking from the refugees whatever they could pay to ferry them across the water. In a flash, Selim spurred his horse forward into the surf, and, at the last moment, before both were submerged, he leaped into the water. In several long, strong strokes, he reached the ferry and vaulted himself onto the deck. Selim caught the startled ferryman by the scruff of his collar and with a savage heave flung him off the deck into the water. The Suliot turned menacingly toward the seaman holding the tiller, who bleated in terror and frantically swung the tiller to turn the ferry back to shore. When he brought the boat to the dock, he scurried to lower the gangplank. Xanthos and Notis rode their horses onto the ferry while Selim retrieved his horse, which had splashed back to shore, and joined them. The seaman turned the boat's bow back to the south, with the ferryman floundering in the water and waving his hands and cursing them. When Notis pointed his musket at him, the man swiveled in the water and swam desperately toward shore.

When the ferry reached Likoporia on the south side of the gulf, they found pandemonium. There seemed no organized plan of resistance or retreat. The soldiers milled with the refugees.

"Who is your captain?" he asked one of the soldiers.

"We have no captain," he said. He gestured at Xanthos and the Suliots. "Who is *your* captain?"

"My commander is General Kolokotronis," Xanthos said. "The duly elected vice-president of the executive committee of the Greek government in Navplion."

"To hell with your committees and governments," the man sneered as he spurred his horse away. "All I know is the Turkish bastards with cannon and cavalry are hot on our heels!"

Xanthos and the Suliots made their way through the terrified mob, left the city, and turned east towards Navplion. When they looked back, they saw the endless columns, ragged and disordered, streaming up from the south toward the sanctuary of the gulf.

Each time he approached the outskirts of Navplion, Xanthos marveled anew at the beauty of the old town set within a ring of three fortresses that had been a major Greek port since the Bronze Age. The principal fortress was the towering Palamidi, whose ramparts overlooked the sea. The smaller fortresses were Akronafplia and the diminutive bastion of Bourtzi on an islet some distance from the town but visible from the harbor.

The main streets held the remnants of elegant Venetian houses, many of them commandeered by captains and primates as their headquarters. Bands of armed men drank outside the tavernas and argued in the streets. At one corner, a half-dozen soldiers were interrogating several farmers loudly proclaiming their innocence. As Xanthos and the Suliots passed, one of the soldiers struck a farmer savagely across his head with the barrel of his musket. The man collapsed like a slaughtered animal. At the outskirts of the town, Xanthos and the Suliots arrived at the headquarters Kolokotronis had established in one of the large neoclassical mansions. Notis and Selim led the horses toward a barracks in the rear of the compound while Xanthos entered the house.

In one of the anterooms, men were scribbling and making entries at their desks. In a corner, two burly, fully armed men sat with muskets across their knees. An officious clerk, a spindly necked man with charcoal-shaded cheeks, brusquely told Xanthos he'd have to make an appointment to see the general.

"His schedule all afternoon is filled with important people," the clerk said.

"What I have to tell him is important."

"Everybody's message is important," the clerk said impatiently. "I am under strict orders from the general that people must wait their turn."

"Will you let him know I'm here?" Xanthos asked.

"In due time, in due time," the clerk said and gestured at one of his associates. "Take this man's name, and put him on the list to see the general later today."

"My name is Xanthos."

The man bent over his pen, repeating the name.

As Xanthos turned to leave, the door of the inner office opened, and Kolokotronis emerged. His powerful body and imposing presence seemed suddenly to fill the room. He waved a sheaf of papers at the clerk, his harsh voice offering some instruction, when he spotted Xanthos.

"Xanthos!" he cried. "Where are you going? Why didn't you let me know you'd returned?"

"We have made an appointment for him to see you this afternoon, general," the clerk said.

"Take your appointments with you to hell!" Kolokotronis roared. The clerk cringed, his face suddenly pale. Kolokotronis ignored his distress and came eagerly toward Xanthos, embracing him roughly in his great arms.

"Come in! Come in!" he cried. Tugging Xanthos by an arm, he dragged him into the inner office and kicked the door shut with his booted foot.

"I'd begun to worry about you," he said. "We hear rumors daily of what is happening to armies in the field, but it is impossible to know how much is true. There are militias assembled by self-styled leaders fighting in one place or another and we haven't any idea what they're doing." He shook his head in frustration. "Chaos!" he said. "The only word is chaos!" He paused. "Never mind that now. How did your mission go? Can we count on some good men for the coming battles?"

"Perhaps no more than a few hundred," Xanthos said, "but they are warriors. Several of the captains pledged to meet us here in Navplion within the next few months."

"Good!" Kolokotronis said. "One of those battle-hardened veterans is worth a dozen ordinary soldiers." He sat down wearily at his desk.

The years of warfare had aged the heroic general. His hair, which flowed to his shoulders, held thicker strands of gray, and wrinkles were more deeply carved in his cheeks and beneath his eyes. It was less the battlefield that had worn the stalwart general down than the relentless political quarrels.

"Before crossing the gulf, we encountered columns of refugees fleeing from villages that had been attacked and burned," Xanthos said. "There were thousands and they seemed without any order or destination except flight."

"There are a dozen battles going on in various parts of the Peloponnesus," Kolokotronis said somberly. "We know the bastard Dramalis is moving north to retake Tripolitza with only the army of Odysseus in his path. Meanwhile, our forces are laying siege to several Turkish fortresses. I have instructed the officers in command to offer safe passage to any Turks who surrender."

"That was the same promise the Greeks made and broke at Monemvasia, Navarino, and Corinth," Xanthos said.

"God help us, that's true," Kolokotronis said. "The only reason the same mass extermination did not take place when the Acropolis fell to Odysseus was the intervention of the French admiral who escorted those Turkish inhabitants who remained to safety. Most of them were the sick and wounded. When I condemned the slaughter to Odysseus, he blamed renegades among his own men." Kolokotronis released a great sigh of anguish. "These massacres shame us before the world. They make us appear to be tribes of savages, unfit to rule ourselves."

He walked slowly toward the windows looking out across the courtyard.

"Yet the worst of these was the butchering our men did at Tripolitza in the first year of the war," he said, his voice low and despairing. "You were there, my friend, and were sorely wounded so you did not witness the full extent of what took place. When I entered the city, from the rampart walls to the Pasha's seraglio, my horse's hooves trod upon the butchered bodies of Turkish men, women, and children. God blind me before I see a sight like that again."

"The siege of the city had lasted so long, general," Xanthos said. "Some captains had been bartering with the wealthier Turks, taking their jewels in exchange for bread. The common soldier felt he'd been cheated of a share of any spoils, and, when the city fell, he was bent on vengeance."

Kolokotronis nodded, his face grave and reflective.

"In Tripolitza, I was shown a plane tree in the marketplace from which Greeks had been hung for centuries," he said. "I thought then how many of my own family, my own race, had been hung on that cursed tree. I ordered it cut down and felt less remorseful about the way our men had slaughtered all the Turks."

There was a timorous knock on the door, and then it opened. The nervous face of the clerk appeared. Before the man could open his mouth, Kolokotronis roared.

"Not now!"

The clerk hurriedly shut the door.

Kolokotronis paced the office, restless as an animal in a cage.

"Put aside concerns about humanity and mercy," he said. "From a military standpoint, it makes sense to spare our enemies who surrender. If the inhabitants of a town or a fortress once understand our assurances of safety are worthless, they will fight to the death. As a result, many of our own brave palikaria will die needlessly."

Once again, there was a knock on the door, and when it opened, the clerk's face appeared for a second time, his anxiety bordering on panic.

"Forgive me, general," his voice quaked. "His Excellency, President Mavrokordatos is here!" He hesitated. "His guards are with him, and our guards wish them to disarm."

Kolokotronis went quickly past the clerk to the outer office where his guards were confronting those accompanying Mavrokordatos. A threat of violence hung across the room.

Surrounded by the stalwart guards was the slightly built, dark-clad figure of Alexander Mavrokordatos, the elected president of the senate.

"Welcome, President Mavrokordatos," Kolokotronis said brusquely. "Is this a visit or an attack?"

"A visit, of course, general," Mavrokordatos hesitated. "But you know I have had threats against my life. My men are reluctant to put down their arms."

"My guards remain armed because there are also men who wish me dead," Kolokotronis said gravely. "Let the armed men wait here, and I invite you into my office. You know you have nothing to fear from me."

Kolokotronis turned and walked back into his office and Mavrokordatos followed. He peered nervously at Xanthos through his horn-rimmed glasses.

"This is my trusted aide, Xanthos," Kolokotronis said. "Nothing I do or say need be hidden from him."

Mavrokordatos had come to power as a result of a national assembly that had been convened in February that year near Astros in an orange grove beside a stream. Xanthos suspected the site had been selected because the stream could be used to divide the warring factions.

Petrobey Mavromichalis, prince of the Mani, had been elected president of the executive committee. Allied to Petrobey, Kolokotronis was a logical choice to join the executive, but fearing that would add to his already considerable power and influence, the committee members present did not elect Kolokotronis to any position. He became incensed at what he felt to be a slight and insisted on being designated vice-president. The council submitted to his wishes, but to counterbalance his power, they chose Mavrokordatos as president of the senate. That did not end the bickering and feuding, nor did it discourage the shifting alliances and disputes.

Seeing the two men together, Xanthos could not help making a comparison. Kolokotronis was above-average height and built like a bull. Mavrokordatos was small-boned and short in stature, and his dark suit fitted him poorly, its large collar and cravat encircling his throat like a noose. His bushy, black hair and abundant whiskers were augmented by a huge mustache that curled up from his cheeks to his ears. Xanthos knew Mavrokordatos had grown the mustache because it resembled the bold swashbuckling mustaches that adorned some of the more noted warriors of the war. Besides the mustache, however, nothing else about the man's uninspiring presence suggested the warrior he longed to be.

"Have you had any word from Odysseus or Anagnostaras?" Mavrokordatos asked. "This lack of news is deplorable. We must know what is happening in the Peloponnesus so we can plan what action to take."

"There's no word from either of them yet," Kolokotronis said. "Xanthos here, who has just returned, tells me of refugees streaming north from Sparta to cross the gulf. That means the forces of Dramalis are coming closer."

Mavrokordatos turned his earnest dark eyes on Xanthos. "Did you see any sign of Turkish troops?"

"We saw only refugees in panicked flight," Xanthos said.

Mavrokordatos turned again to Kolokotronis. "Against the advice of others, general," he said, "I have come directly to you. This bickering and dissension must stop. We must coordinate our actions." His voice trembled slightly. "In order to do so, we must be informed about the movement of armies so we might take charge and plan a strategy." He paused, seeking to make his voice more resolute. "We must exercise central authority, general, or others will do it for us."

"I agree with what you say, President Alexander," Kolokotronis said. "I know we both have the welfare of our long-suffering land at heart."

Mavrokordatos seemed about to say something more. Then he turned on his heels, and walking with his curious, awkward waddle left the office, closing the door behind him. For a few moments, the bodyguards were heard loudly hurling insults at one another, and then there was silence.

"I believe Mavrokordatos to be a bright and decent man," Kolokotronis sighed. "But he is not a soldier. You remember last year, hoping the campaign would give him the military prestige he so badly needed, he led his men and the foreign regiments into the disaster at Peta." A harshness and outrage entered his voice. "In any other country, he would have been sent into exile for that catastrophe. Instead, our distinguished senate appoints him president."

Xanthos had recorded in his history of the war the details of that bitter defeat suffered by Mavrokordatos the previous year. In response to the invasion of Thessaly by the Turkish general Reshid Pasha, Mavrokordatos had led a Greek force of three regiments from Missolonghi to confront him. One of the regiments comprising mainly Italian and French volunteers was commanded by a flamboyant Italian colonel called Dania. A second regiment comprising mainly German soldiers was commanded by a Swiss officer named Chevalier. These two volunteer regiments were joined by a third contingent, the regiment Tarella, with about five hundred Greek troops commanded by Mavrokordatos.

The regiments of Philhellenes, who entered into battle with the zeal of crusaders, were organized like a Napoleonic army, quartermasters, paymasters, standard-bearers, a medical corps, and a drum major. The problem confronting them was that the war wasn't being fought by conventional armies lined up in neat columns on a field. The battles were being fought across a rocky, mountainous terrain ideally suited to ambushes and guerilla tactics.

After a minor skirmish that repulsed an advance guard of Turks, the Philhellene and Greek regiments took up defensive positions at the small town of Peta, a short distance from the strongly fortified Turkish city of Arta.

As they prepared for battle, Mavrokordatos showed his military inexperience. His troops were tired after their long march from Missolonghi, and their supplies had not yet arrived. The hungry men sorely needed food and rest before they would be fit for battle. In addition, despite being warned that the klepht chieftain Gogos Bakolas, who had joined the Greek forces with several hundred men, could not be trusted, Mavrokordatos assigned Bakolas the crucial responsibility of protecting the mountain pass that led to the rear of the Greek forces. Mavrokordatos further weakened his force by sending two hundred men to Ioannina to aid the Suliots who were being besieged.

On July 8, 1822, the Turkish army under Reshid Pasha attacked the regiments of Philhellenes and the weary and hungry regiment of Greeks at Peta. Any chance the Greek regiments had of victory was rendered hopeless when, at the last minute, Gogos Bakolas, whether because he feared defeat or simply as an act of treachery, abandoned his position protecting the pass. His flight left the rear of the Greek forces unprotected, and the ensuing battle was brief and deadly. The Turks defeated the regiments of Philhellenes as well as the force under Mavrokordatos.

The survivors straggled back to Missolonghi. Dania, Tarella, and Chevalier, the Philhellene leaders, had been killed, and the regiments they commanded had been almost totally destroyed. The losses suffered by the Greek regiment were equally severe. So ended one of the darkest days the Greek armies had to endure since the beginning of the revolution.

In his journal, Xanthos had transcribed the words of Kolokotronis when he assessed the battle at Peta and the role of Mavrokordatos: "The tragedy of his leadership was that he neither knew what he ought to do nor what he ought to leave undone, so that his disastrous military operations were generally determined by accident."

Kolokotronis interrupted his reverie. "You look as if you have not slept in a week," he said. "Go and rest a while now, my friend. Return here later this evening, and we'll have dinner with a group of my officers and friends. Then, tomorrow, we need to talk. Perhaps you can help me bring some order to the confusion taking place around us."

With his arm flung around the shoulders of Xanthos, the two men walked to the outer office. They were met by the nervous clerk.

"General," he said, his voice trembling. "Your appointments have fallen behind . . ."

"I told you before to take those appointments with you to hell!" Kolokotronis bellowed. Xanthos pitied the poor clerk, who flinched as if the warrior's powerful voice had been a whip across his skinny frame.

"And furthermore," Kolokotronis shouted, "this man you see with me here has access to me whenever he wishes! I don't care if I'm meeting with a prince or a king! He has been my comrade since this war began and will always take precedence over anyone else! Do you understand?"

The terrified clerk shook his head in a nervous, flustered assent.

Xanthos left the headquarters of Kolokotronis and went to his room behind the barracks. Spartan as it was, with a chair, oil lamp, small desk, and cot with pallet for a bed, he was grateful for the privacy. After washing at one of the wells the soldiers also used, he returned to his room to fall into exhausted sleep riddled with fitful dreams. There were fragments of the sights he had witnessed in the past few weeks, the meetings with the klepht in the mountains, the faces and voices of the captains, in turn, greedy, arrogant, bold, courageous. When he woke, his room shrouded in darkness, the final images he carried from sleep were the ragged columns of refugees streaming north to escape the Turks.

Xanthos joined Kolokotronis and about a dozen other men for dinner that evening at a long table set up in the courtyard of the general's headquarters on the ramparts above the city overlooking the sea. Torches and lanterns had been set up around the perimeter of the table. In the harbor, several brigs lay at anchor with a score of smaller fishing boats moored around them. Beyond the ships, lights flickered on the islet of Bourtzi.

As the men took seats at the table, the summer night around them was fragrant with the profusion of flowers. When a slight breeze spiraled from the sea up to the ramparts, it carried a rumble of voices from the harbor where the soldiers gathered.

Among those at dinner were half a dozen Greek officers in the general's forces, Father Nikita, a bearded, black-cassocked priest from a parish in the town, and several Philhellenes, professional soldiers who had joined Kolokotronis several months earlier. Two were Italian artillery officers, who spoke only their own language and communicated with the Greeks by animated gestures, and the third was an English officer named Eric Wyndham, a tall, handsome soldier with reddish hair. Xanthos knew that Kolokotronis respected and trusted the soldier who had commanded one of Wellington's regiments at Waterloo, the battle the famed English general had fought against the Frenchman Napoleon Bonaparte. After the epic conflict that ended the dream of Napoleon to replicate his earlier victories and regain his prestige, Wyndham had wandered across Europe, joining the many soldiers of fortune orphaned by the end of the Napoleonic Wars. These men were unqualified for any other trade but war, and many of them, driven by hopes of glory and wealth, had come to Greece to join the revolution. They offered their services as mercenaries to whatever captain would pay them. Wyndham's long association with the Greeks had gained him a fluency in speaking Greek that gave him an advantage over the other foreign soldiers. His valor in battle had been brought to the attention of Kolokotronis, who enlisted the English officer into his service.

Also at dinner that evening was a youth no more than sixteen or seventeen years of age named Lukas Chalandritsanos, who had joined Kolokotronis a few months earlier. The youth was of a noble family who had once befriended Kolokotronis, and he had promised Lukas's family that he would take the young man into his service and under his protection.

"I know that since his arrival, I spoil the youth much as his mother and sisters spoiled him back in his home," Kolokotronis had confided to Xanthos not long after Lukas arrived in Navplion, "but he is a bright and well-meaning young man intent on finding his place in the world. It's not his fault that his mother and sisters constantly let him have his way." The general paused with a wry smile. "God help me, Xanthos, I also find a pleasure in having him around so I can look at him, finding it almost as great a delight as I find in looking at a beautiful woman. If I were one of those men inclined to take their pleasure with younger boys, he would not be safe in my presence. I fear there are men who might kill so they could possess him."

Xanthos conceded there was about the youth a haunting and uncommon beauty. He had a pale, flawless complexion and great, dark eyes. His nose and ears were small and well formed, and his lips sensuous and full. His body was slender and gave an impression of being both lithe and strong, despite his young age. But Xanthos found the young man petulant and arrogant, which was confirmed at dinner that evening. Lukas sat beside one of the Italian Philhellenes and looked restless and bored. He displayed a peevishness with the servants serving the dinner, brusquely sending back a bowl of soup he felt hadn't been heated properly. For most of the meal, he ate slowly, his expression sullen, ignoring the energetic efforts of the Italian officer to engage him in conversation.

During the dinner, several of Kolokotronis's officers who were drinking too much wine began a strident argument that threatened to bring the men to blows.

"In God's name, save your bellicosity for the battlefield," Kolokotronis cried, his voice impatient and harsh. "If we cannot maintain peace and a congenial dialogue among ourselves, what chance do we have of defeating our enemies?"

As if to distract the combatants, Kolokotronis asked Wyndham to recount something of his experience at Waterloo. "That general of yours, the English Lord who vanquished Napoleon," Kolokotronis asked, "what was he like?"

"Lord Wellington is a general in the tradition of great English generals," Wyndham replied. "He was able to inspire unwavering trust in his soldiers. He had a disdain for melodrama and carried about him a quiet confidence in ultimate victory that transmitted itself to the men who served under him."

Relishing being the center of attention, Wyndham took a sip from his glass if wine. "At the beginning of the battle, I was much less confident about the outcome than the general. My command was the Twenty-seventh Regiment, the Inniskillings. We had been on the march for most of the day and had several skirmishes with French cavalry harrying us in an effort to slow us down. Later that day at a site called Mont-Saint-Jean, we were finally allowed a few hours of sleep. When we were wakened, the main battle had begun. Our regiment was given the order to advance quickly to support a weak part of the line. The timing of the advance was ill planned, and in the following four hours of fighting, over 450 of our 750 officers and men were killed and wounded."

Kolokotronis shook his head grimly. "Even in a victory as great as Waterloo, one forgets the fearful cost in lives."

"Most of those wounded and killed were brought down by the fire of cannon placed several hundred yards away from us," Wyndham said, "or by the musketry of French snipers."

"By God, in spite of the losses, I would have given ten years of my life to have fought there!" a strongly built Greek officer named Skilizis said.

"I am also grateful now to have been part of that major battle," Wyndham said, his voice level and grave, his pronunciation of Greek slow and precise. "But once the fighting began, every man among us was only intent on whether he and his comrades fighting beside him would survive. Ask me what I know of the battle of Waterloo—it is of a patch of ground where I fought alongside my men and where many of my comrades were wounded or killed."

"And Wellington?" Kolokotronis asked. "Where was he during the course of the battle?"

"He was with the staff officers at their headquarters, and I never saw him. But I was told by other British officers who were with him during the battle, he remained confident of victory, despite the heavy losses we were incurring."

"Whatever the cost in human lives, that glorious battle will go down in military history!" Niketaras, another of the Greek captains, exclaimed. "If Napoleon had not been defeated, the history of Europe would have been changed."

"First, there are the battles where men fight and die," Kolokotronis said, "and then there is history."

"We didn't learn the significance of the battle we had fought until we returned home to England," Wyndham said. "For the first time in the history of the British army, each veteran of the battle was awarded a commemorative medal. Every soldier who fought that day was known as a Waterloo man, and that single day of service on June 18, 1815, was to count as two years toward his pension." Wyndham smiled wryly. "They did everything they could to convince even the lowliest soldier that he had participated in and survived an extraordinary event."

Later, the conversation turned to the financing of war. All of the chieftains of various factions, including Kolokotronis, had been excited by rumors sweeping across Greece that a London Greek Committee had been formed in England that would be sending large sums of money to aid the Greek cause. The first installment of the cash along with letters of credit would be carried to Greece by a famous personage—the English poet Lord Byron.

"He is among the most celebrated of my countrymen," Wyndham said. "Personally, I find his affectations and melodramatic posturing distasteful. But I must admit that along with his foppish poems about love won and love lost, he has also written stirring verses about the struggle of the Greeks for freedom. Many of the soldiers from Germany, Italy, and France who came to fight in Greece were inspired to do so by Byron's poetry."

"We owe this English poet a debt of gratitude for his devotion to our cause," Kolokotronis said. "And if he truly brings us a substantial sum of money, we'll owe him an even greater debt. Wars cannot be fought without money to buy arms and supplies and funds to pay the troops."

It seemed to Xanthos that as they spoke of the poet who would be carrying a large sum of money to aid the Greek cause, Kolokotronis grew animated, his eyes glowing and his cheeks flushed.

By the end of that evening, several Greek officers had passed out and slumped in their chairs. A few others had stumbled away from the table and fallen asleep in drunken stupors under the trees. Father Nikitas, who had also drunk too much, was asleep in his chair, his head slumped toward his chest, his thick beard fluttering in the current of air raised by his sibilant snores. The Italian Philhellenes had gone down to the harbor to seek more diversified excitements. Wyndham had departed and the young Lukas Chalandritsanos had slipped away, as well.

The servants had begun clearing the remains of the dinner. Kolokotronis rose and joined Xanthos sitting under the trees. With a sigh, the general rested his back against a tree. The night was tranquil, the scents of summer flowers carried on the breezes from the sea. From the city below them, the rumble of voices from the harbor taverns had grown quieter. The moon, a white, elusive crescent, slipped in and out of a cluster of clouds.

For a while, the two men sat in silence, Xanthos waiting for Kolokotronis to speak. Although the general had been drinking as much as any of the others, neither his movements nor his demeanor gave the slightest hint of drunkenness. He sat now without moving, seeming to Xanthos to be immersed deeply in thought.

"If it is true that this English poet will bring a large sum of money to Greece," Kolokotronis finally said, "the various captains and primates, including Mavrokordatos, will swarm around him like bees around a flower. They will flatter him shamelessly. I don't know what this Byron is like or who among our leaders will prove most successful in leeching money from him, but, by God, Xanthos, it would be disastrous if that money fell into the wrong hands."

"Perhaps when he arrives in Greece, you should travel to meet him yourself, General," Xanthos said.

Kolokotronis shook his head in dissent. "We are assembling our army here to do battle, and I have no time or the stomach for political intrigues. But I must have people to send as my envoys to this poet, people I can trust to plead our cause. Without our share of that money, I don't know how our armies in the field will survive. We have already had the sorry spectacle of the sailors in the fleet of Admiral Miaoulis deserting him when he could no longer pay their wages. What the Turks were unable to accomplish in battle was achieved by the shameful Greek retreat."

Kolokotronis reached down to loosen the sash around his waist and bent to tug off his boots. When Xanthos tried to help him, the general waved him brusquely away.

"Don't spoil me, scribe," he said. "When I can no longer remove my own boots, it will be time for me to give up leading an army and find a flock of sheep to look after instead."

With his boots off, Kolokotronis stretched out his legs and again rested his back wearily against the tree trunk. He closed his eyes, and in that moment of repose, his strong, hawk-featured face appeared pale in the moonlight like the immobile head of a corpse, and Xanthos felt a chill down his back. He feared what might happen to the revolution if Kolokotronis were lost.

After a while, the general opened his eyes. When he spoke, his voice was low and somber. "Xanthos, wherever in Greece this poet Byron chooses to reside, I want you to travel as my emissary to meet him."

"I will go where you wish, General," Xanthos said, "and to the best of my ability will perform whatever task you assign me."

"Good," Kolokotronis said. "But I will not send you alone. I will also send that officer Eric Wyndham with you. He is an experienced veteran of war, and we can trust his military advice to Byron will be sound. With your knowledge of Hellenic history and the Englishman's knowledge of war, you will make a formidable team to plead our cause."

Kolokotronis paused once again. In the light from the torches that still burned a short distance away, Xanthos saw the chieftain's piercing eyes. "But I will also send someone else with you and the English officer," Kolokotronis said quietly. "I have heard tales of this poet's rampant lust when it comes to women. It is rumored that several English ladies killed themselves out of despair because he spurned them. But I have also heard that this Englishman favors boys of great beauty. So, in addition to you, scribe, and a soldier who knows war, I will send along Lukas Chalandritsanos." He paused and then sighed from deep within. "I confess to some shame for playing upon the weakness of another human being, but we must fight with every weapon at our disposal, including the beauty of a young man. If what they say about this Byron proves true, then, by the gods, what the counsel of men who understand history and men who know war cannot accomplish might be achieved by the more tender yearning of the human need for love."

CHAPTER
FOUR

That summer of 1823, Xanthos spent hours each day composing dispatches for Kolokotronis. These requests carried by couriers to various captains were pleas for alliances, for amity among warring factions, and for unified action against a common enemy. The erratic and cursory reports that returned informed them of armed forces that were engaging the enemy and on the verge of victory. Other dispatches contradicted that. Their forces were not in contact with the enemy, and if they were, the battle hadn't ended in victory but in defeat. Kolokotronis lamented the disorder.

"There have been other revolutions before our own," he said in frustration to Xanthos. "The revolution in far-off America and the one in France that overthrew the decadent monarchy! I cannot believe either of these suffered from the confusion, chaos, and bloated egos we face in our own struggle now!"

When he wasn't composing letters, Xanthos screened the petitioners who crowded into the general's headquarters. One man sought to sell horses to Kolokotronis, and another volunteered a detailed strategy on where the next crucial battle against the Turks should be fought. One distraught farmer with four daughters of marriageable age inquired plaintively whether any of the general's captains might be seeking a good wife. At the end of a frenzied, fifteen-hour day, Xanthos collapsed onto his cot, every bone and muscle crying for rest. Despite his weariness, he had trouble sleeping, the faces and voices of the day dredging through his dreams.

What little time Xanthos was able to allot for himself, he spent reading the work of philosophers and poets who had lived through earlier periods of turmoil. Among the books he read that summer were the writings of Seneca. A singular theme recurring throughout the work of that stoic Roman poet was how frail and wretched a creature was man and how vulnerable his life was to the whims of fortune.

There were reminders of the validity of Seneca's philosophy in the meetings between Kolokotronis and various primates and captains. When the loud, belligerent advice these leaders offered was ignored, they erupted into fits of shouting and anger. Kolokotronis himself could from time to time fly into a rage. His voice exploded into the outer office like a peal of thunder, causing the pale-faced clerk a fit of trembling.

As he listened to those angry exchanges, men blustering and attempting to outshout one another, Xanthos wished he could muster the boldness to offer the combatants Seneca's counsel.

> If we are sprinkled with cold water, our body gives us no choice but to shiver. If fingers are flicked over our eyes, we have to blink. But anger does not belong in the category of involuntary movement, it can only break out if man chooses to release that most brutal part of his nature. In anger, man is capable of calling down death on his own children, ruin on his home, destruction of his country. Anger is the greatest of ills, one that surpasses all other vices.

Yet, there were reasons for Kolokotronis to be angry. Despite his efforts to work amicably with others in establishing the authority of the executive committee, rivalries and intrigues among the Greek leaders flourished in an orgy of jealousy and greed. There were even rumors of possible assassinations being planned by opposing factions, and despite the assertions of Kolokotronis that he wasn't afraid, Xanthos increased the number of guards around the general's headquarters. Xanthos's anxieties were given added credence when, fearing for his life, Mavrokordatos decided to abandon Navplion, traveling to find refuge with his compatriots and sympathizers at Trikorfo in the Peloponnesus. But he carried dissension with him. Xanthos received reports that in Trikorfo, Mavrokordatos was in bitter disagreement with another revolutionary leader, Demetrios Ipsilantis.

Meanwhile, the war dragged on, bands of Greeks laying siege to Turkish towns. If the siege dragged on too long, many of the Greeks, growing impatient, would give up and go home. The same lack of discipline existed within the Greek fleet. When the ships commanded by the admirals Andreas Miaoulis and Konstantine Kanaris were at sea, they effectively pursued the larger Turkish frigates. Although their ships were armed with larger cannon, the Turks feared the lighter, faster Greek brigs and the superior seamanship of the men who sailed them. They were especially terrified of Greek fire, the packing of a brig with combustibles soaked in turpentine and then, under cover of darkness, sailing it to ram against a Turkish frigate. At the last minute, the Greek sailors escaped in a small boat moored to the stern of the fire ship. Despite these occasional victories over the Turkish fleet, if wages for the Greek sailors weren't paid on time, they refused to engage the enemy and sailed for their home islands. The islanders themselves were just as contentious as the mainlanders, jealousies having caused Hydra and Spetsia to feud and actually fire cannon at one another. Later, the two islands formed an alliance against the island of Psara.

Admiral Miaoulis sailed his brig into Navplion to meet with Kolokotronis and expressed his despair.

"Has this ever happened in the fleet of any other country?" the admiral lamented. "To our everlasting shame, we not only witness sailors abandoning their ships and returning home because they haven't been paid but our own islands battling against one another! Meanwhile, our quarreling allows the Turkish fleet freedom to block the mainland wherever it can do the most damage."

Meanwhile, in the northern provinces of Greece, law had ceased to mean anything. Whether Greeks or Turks were victorious, the victors often massacred the defeated. When there were no battles to be fought, robbery and murder flourished. Dead bodies became so numerous that they were left unburied to rot in the streets of towns and villages or to be eaten by bands of wild dogs that roamed the countryside. These decaying corpses produced virulent outbreaks of the plague that had first developed after the slaughter of the Turkish inhabitants of Tripolitza in 1821, the first year of the war, and that ever since threatened to depopulate the country.

One of the great losses the Greeks sustained that year was the death of the hero Markos Botsaris. The famed leader was killed at Karpenisi in 1823 while leading a few hundred Suliot fighters against a Turkish force estimated at almost fifteen thousand men. Despite being sorely wounded, Botsaris continued to rally his men against the Turks until a bullet ended his life. His untimely death further adorned the legend of his heroic life. Afterwards, his grieving companions carried his body to Missolonghi for a magnificent funeral. For several days after learning the news, Kolokotronis remained secluded in his quarters, shielding from others the intensity of his mourning. When he finally emerged and spoke of the death of Marko Botsaris to Xanthos, his grief was still evident.

"Botsaris was not only a superb military leader," Kolokotronis said sadly to Xanthos, "but an honorable man as well. The two do not always go together. His death is a great loss for our revolution."

Kolokotronis ordered that a memorial service be held for Botsaris in Navplion. The service was conducted in the largest of the town's churches, and on that Sunday, crowds filled the church and packed the square around the cloister. Xanthos attended and heard the singers eulogizing the hero's death.

> There is great mourning at Missolonghi
> Marko is taken to the church, Marko is taken to
> The grave.
> Sixty priests go in front and ten bishops behind
> The women follow dressed in black, chanting
> Their grief.
> Behind them walks the wife of Marko, holding his
> Son by the hand,
> The son who will someday avenge his murdered
> father.

Numerous captains and primates aspired to replace the fallen hero. Among those traveling to Navplion that summer to meet with Kolokotronis was Andreas Zaimis, primate of Kalavryta, and his ally Andreas Londos, primate of Eyio. Kolokotronis referred to both men, who were members of the executive committee, as "the two crafty Andreases."

They made a strange pair. Andreas Zaimis was endowed with political talents, good sense, and eloquence. He was gracious to his inferiors, beloved and respected by the people of his province. Reports about

Andreas Londos were that he possessed an abundance of courage but that he was debauched, rapacious, and oppressive. There was also a striking contrast in the appearances of the two men: Zaimis, tall, well built, and handsome, and Londos, dwarfish, almost deformed. When Zaimis and Londos arrived in Navplion to meet with Kolokotronis, the alliances they projected and the strategies they outlined did not convince the general. The two men left Navplion frustrated and disappointed at how little they had achieved.

"They make a strangely mismatched pair," Kolokotronis described them to Xanthos. "I believe Zaimis is upright in his dealings, true to his word, and a man to be trusted but his faults are ambition, overweening pride, and timidity in the field when boldness is required." He paused. "As for Londos, that dwarfish body of his conceals a mind like fire. He is teeming with assorted schemes, but I believe they have less to do with winning the war than with gaining power for himself."

Another chieftain who visited Kolokotronis that summer was the brigand leader Odysseus Androutsos. His partisans described the chieftain as having a flawless character and a heart as valorous as his sword; others depicted him as deceitful and vindictive as the most bloodthirsty Turk. To these vices, still others said, were added avarice and a ferocious cruelty. Androutsos had been born on the island of Ithaca, which was also the island of Odysseus, and had provided the brigand leader his Homeric name. In his teens, he had been one of the pageboys in the court of the venal Ali Pasha of Ioannina and later had become a captain in Ali Pasha's army. After the old tyrant was killed by Turkish forces in retaliation for his rebellion against the sultan, Odysseus envisioned himself another Ali Pasha. His men told flattering stories of his physical strength and athletic skill, how he was able to leap across seven horses standing side by side. Those who opposed him scoffed that he exhibited his physical prowess in one memorable battle in which his troops were defeated by the Turks and Androutsos was said to have run away faster and farther than anyone else.

Whatever the truth about the character or ability of Androutsos, Xanthos found the chieftain's physical presence imposing. With his black, flowing locks, handsome face, and swirling mustache, his strong frame adorned with twin cartridge belts strapped across his chest, pearl-handled pistols, and an ornately jeweled dagger in his sash, he looked every inch the hero.

"I think Androutsos is vain and fancies himself a greater leader than he really is," Kolokotronis said to Xanthos after the chieftain had departed Navplion, "but if he is flawed, he is also courageous and capable and, I believe, dedicated to the success of the revolution."

The captain who impressed the general and Xanthos the most that summer was a Rumeliot chieftain named Yannis Makriyannis, who had distinguished himself in battle with the Turks. A tall, sturdy peasant with handsome features, his presence reflected dignity and strength. Makriyannis had been among the early champions of the revolt, a member of the Society of Friends, the secret organization formed to prepare for the revolt. In Patras, when the revolution broke out, Makriyannis traveled north to Arta to carry the news to members of the Society of Friends in that city. In Arta, he was betrayed by an unknown enemy and arrested. He was accused of being an enemy of the sultan and imprisoned. The details of his imprisonment that he related to Xanthos and Kolokotronis were brutal and chilling.

"Within the first week of my imprisonment, twenty-five of my fellow prisoners accused of sedition were hanged," Makriyannis said, his voice quiet but his words conveying emotion and force. "There were about two hundred of us still alive, locked in a single large cell in the tomb of the pasha's palace. Penned in like animals, we had to empty our bowels on the floor, and the filth and stink I will not get out of my nostrils for as long as I live. We took turns pressing our noses against the keyhole of the door to get a single breath of fresh air. And, each day, they chose from among us at random prisoners they would beat and torture. As a result of the beatings, my body swelled up and became inflamed, and I felt near death."

Makriyannis and several other prisoners were saved when they were able to bribe a guard to let them out to see a doctor. Of the two hundred prisoners, Makriyannis and a handful of others were the only ones who survived. Since his escape, he had been one of the boldest and most successful of the Greek captains, leading his men to victories in a series of encounters with Turkish troops.

But it was not only his bravery that distinguished Makriyannis as different from the other captains. In one of the meetings with

Kolokotronis and half a dozen of the captains when Xanthos was present, following a loud and bitter argument among several of the leaders, Makriyannis rose to speak. In a quiet but commanding voice, he reprimanded the gathering.

"The world has no handles for one man, however strong he might be, to walk off with it over his shoulder," Makriyannis said sternly. "When any single person is too weak for the job, he gets others to help him. And when it comes to answering for what has been done, let not the word *I* come to this man's tongue but *we*. If we are to achieve our liberation, we must all have our shoulders to the load, not just one man."

The captains sat somber and silent, their anger muted by the good sense of his words. Kolokotronis glanced at Xanthos and nodded in approval.

"Will you believe that Makriyannis can neither read nor write?" Kolokotronis marveled to Xanthos after the Rumeliot chieftain had left Navplion. "Yet, he has a clearer vision of what we need to accomplish our goals than men with an abundance of learning."

Along with the captains, a motley group of farmers and villagers had streamed into Navplion to join the army Kolokotronis was assembling. As distrustful of one another as they were of the Turks, they were also resistant to discipline and hard to control. The general assigned some of his veterans to drill the new men and instruct them in organized warfare. In the first few weeks, a dozen recruits were injured in fights and mishaps caused by indolence or inexperience.

"This is what happens when the Greek peasant turns soldier," Kolokotronis said to Xanthos. "He cannot abide orders and objects to anyone telling him what to do! If there are twenty Greeks taking up arms, all twenty believe they deserve to be captain. Yet, when the fainthearts and the weaklings have been winnowed out, these peasant soldiers, the bone and sinew of any army, become some of the most valorous fighting men in the world."

In September, word reached Navplion that the English poet Lord Byron had finally arrived in July in Greece, bringing with him the first installment of the funds from the London Greek Committee. He had planned to establish his headquarters on the island of Zante, one of the Ionian Islands under British mandate. When he learned that various factions were sending representatives there to meet him, Byron chose Cephalonia, another Ionian island. He would later make a decision as to where to settle his more permanent headquarters in Greece.

"That decision to bypass Zante with the horde of petitioners waiting for him speaks well for the common sense of this Byron," Kolokotronis said. "If he had landed as planned at Zante, he would have found waiting for him every petty brigand, self-appointed captain, senator, pirate, and renegade, all obsessed with getting whatever money they could at the expense of the others. Instead of hurling himself into the midst of these plotters, Byron chose wisely to settle in a neutral area. He will learn something of what is happening in Greece before the vultures descend on him again."

"Is it still your wish to have Wyndham, Lukas, and me go to meet Byron as your envoys?" Xanthos asked.

"As much as I would like to have you go and plead our cause with Byron," Kolokotronis said, "the hard truth is that I cannot spare you now. You are not only a trusted friend but also my advisor, Xanthos, and I need your good sense and your knowledge of history with me here as we plan our battles. What I will do now, however, is send Wyndham—and young Lukas—to Cephalonia. I will provide them letters of introduction to this Byron. Let them cultivate an association with him to whatever degree possible. When the Englishman decides where he'll finally settle in Greece, then I will send you to aid Wyndham and Lukas."

When told of the general's wishes, Wyndham readily agreed and prepared for the journey. But the youth Lukas resisted, pleading tearfully with Kolokotronis not to send him away. It was as if Lukas understood the nefarious purpose to which Kolokotronis planned to use his beauty. Gently but firmly, Kolokotronis told Lukas that the revolution took precedence over any human concerns. In the end, the youth had no choice but to submit to the general's edict.

In late September, Lukas and Wyndham left Navplion on the brig *Hermes*, captained by Papayannis, a close friend of Kolokotronis, for the journey to Cephalonia.

By the time of Byron's arrival in Greece, the dissension and friction among the various factions had grown more intense, rivalries and tempers more passionate. Those areas of the country in Greek hands

were divided and controlled by various chieftains. Some of the leaders, stressing the religious nature of their struggle, were urging the
creation of a monarchy. The great land primates, despite desiring
an independent nation, saw their opportunity to acquire properties
formerly held by the Turks that would add to their wealth and authority. Paying lip service to the new government, many of the captains
resisted relinquishing any of the power or influence they held in their
own districts to the control of a centralized authority.

Even Kolokotronis himself, Xanthos noted in his journal, in union
with Petrobey, the prince of the Mani, and with Odysseus Androutsos
as an ally, maintained his control over portions of the Peloponnesus.
The situation became so acrimonious that as Greek forces attacked
other Greeks, civil war threatened the revolution.

Adding to the confrontation between factions were the Philhellenes
who allied themselves with various captains, as Eric Wyndham had
joined Kolokotronis. Many of them came from a Europe swarming
with disbanded army officers and professional soldiers, men unsuited
for any other trade but war. The prospect of conflict and joining the
revolution in Greece incited their dreams of profit and glory. One of
the most prominent of the foreigners in Greece was Colonel Charles
Napier, the English governor of Cephalonia, who was urging the
forming of a national army that Lord Byron would command with
Napier as his chief of staff.

Demetrios Ipsilantis, the Phanariot aristocrat from Constantinople
and a favorite with the monarchs of Europe, also envisioned himself
assuming command of a national army. He had vowed that after
liberating Greece, he would lead that army to the gates of Constantinople and retake that gilded city from the Turks. When these reports
reached Navplion, Kolokotronis was scornful in his appraisal of Ipsilantis: "The man suffers from megalomania. He fancies himself a
great liberator and, I vow, conceives of himself as someday becoming
king of Greece!"

Kolokotronis and Petrobey accepted that a well-trained army in
the Western style might be a more efficient way of winning the war.
But they had no desire to replace the domination of Greece by Turks
to Phanariots such as Ipsilantis, whose reign would be enforced by
such an army.

"It would be like replacing a bear with a hyena," Kolokotronis said. "We'd be exchanging slavery for tyranny."

The brig *Hermes* returned to Navplion with word that Wyndham and Lukas had landed safely on Cephalonia.

"That Englishman is a stalwart soldier and took to the sea like an old salt," Captain Papayannis told Kolokotronis and Xanthos at dinner. "But that youth, Lukas, spent the voyage either on deck heaving his guts over starboard or port or huddled and moaning in his bunk."

"The poor boy didn't wish to make the journey," Kolokotronis said, "but I pressed him to go."

"Poor boy, indeed," the ship's captain muttered to Xanthos when the two of them were alone. "If I had him on my ship as a cabin boy, I'd put the sniveling pup in irons until he shaped up into a man."

Each day that passed, Kolokotronis impatiently awaited word from Wyndham on how events in Cephalonia were progressing. The first letter from the English officer finally arrived about six weeks after he had departed with Lukas for Cephalonia. When the courier brought the letter to their headquarters, Xanthos carried it immediately to Kolokotronis.

"God be praised!" the general exclaimed. "Since you'll read it faster and with fewer errors than I would make, Xanthos, read it to me, please!"

Xanthos opened the envelope.

My dear General:

I hope my letter finds you healthy and your plans for the coming campaign in good order. Our trip to Cephalonia was uneventful except for a severe gale that struck us off the coast of Navarino. The ship took a pounding, but Captain Papayannis is a superb seaman and guided us safely through the storm. Our only mishap was that for much of the journey Lukas was ill with the seasickness and was mostly confined to his bunk in extreme wretchedness.

We landed at Cephalonia and, as you predicted, found the island a hornet's nest of intrigue. Mavrokordatos and a number of the other captains and primates, including Andreas

Londos and Andreas Zaimis, who had been waiting for Byron on Zante, have now made haste to come here, each of them seeking to impress Byron with their importance. The day following our arrival on the island, I carried your letters of introduction to Lord Byron at his headquarters, but despite my assertions that your orders were to deliver them personally to Byron, I had to leave them with an aide.

Byron has within his headquarters a swarm of Suliot bodyguards, as scurvy a band of cutthroats as I've ever seen. If I had persisted in my pleas to deliver the orders to Byron personally, I might have found myself in physical conflict with those rogues. So I was forced to leave the letters and then waited anxiously three days for a response inviting us to a meeting. I was relieved when word finally arrived. and taking Lukas with me, we went to meet with the great English poet.

Byron has established his headquarters and living quarters in one of the most palatial of the island's homes. We found him holding court that day as if he were a pagan king instead of simply the emissary of a committee in London. He was dressed in the warrior regalia of a Tartar, festooned with a bright-red tunic and sash, and wearing a long saber that appeared ostentatious on a man who has had no military experience. Even in his meetings, he is surrounded by the Suliot bodyguards. (Although I have not seen them for myself, I've been told that each morning, he rides out for his morning canter accompanied by half a hundred of these Suliots. They must make an impressive although pretentious spectacle.)

I had heard stories about Byron's handsomeness, but the reality of his appearance is starkly different. Despite his being only in his middle thirties, I found him lacking in any physical attractiveness, his curly hair wispy, thin and graying, his teeth beginning to rot. For reasons of vanity, he may have been dieting, but the effect is to have his grand uniform hanging loosely on his frame. I found it hard to look at the man and conceive of him as a passionate lover.

He received us cordially enough, telling us he had read your letters and sent you his greetings and best wishes. He told us he admired your abilities and your devoted service in the cause of Greek freedom. I offered him the full resource of my military experience, and he accepted saying he would welcome my counsel. But beneath his surface civility, one sensed that he had already wearied of petitions and pleas. I think ours would have gone the way of many others, but, as you had foreseen, he seemed especially taken with Lukas. During the course of our conversation, he became most animated while conversing with the young man, asking him detailed questions about his family and his homeland. It came as no surprise to me when, at the conclusion of our interview, he asked if Lukas would like to join him as a member of his retinue. Lukas was nervously hesitant and seemed on the verge of refusing, when I quickly suggested that we be allowed a night to discuss Byron's gracious invitation.

Back in our quarters that evening, Lukas threw a fit of unseemly temper, insisting to the point of tears that he would not attach himself to Byron's court. I talked to him calmly but also as forcefully as I could, stressing upon him the importance of the opportunity he was being provided to place us in close contact with Byron. I told him how pleased you would be if he accepted and how unhappy if he refused. In the end, despite his obvious frustration, he reluctantly agreed. This event transpired about a week ago, and Lukas has since taken up residence in Byron's quarters.

I will close for now, General, but assure you that I will proceed with the instructions you have given me and provide my military services to Byron in whatever capacity he desires. We will also continue to stress to him the importance of having your endeavors on behalf of the revolution properly financed. I would hope that he will respond favorably to our petition.

Yours respectfully,
Eric Wyndham

After asking Xanthos to read the letter to him a second time, a melancholy descended upon Kolokotronis.

"I am grateful that Wyndham has made contact with Byron," he said quietly, "but I grieve that this connection had to come to fruition through Lukas. I regret having to use the boy in this profane way. But such feelings must not intrude in any way upon our ultimate goal, the liberation of our enslaved land."

In October of that year, Prince Petrobey came by ship from the Mani with a contingent of five hundred Maniot fighters. These forces were joined to the five hundred men that were already lodged and training in Navplion.

From the beginning, the Maniots were scornful of the peasants. Both sides kept to themselves, grouped around their campfires in tribal factions, avoiding those they regarded as strangers. As a result of old feuds and antagonisms, rancorous fights broke out between the Maniots and the peasants.

"Perhaps when it comes time for them to face the Turks, they will forget their feuds and stand together," Kolokotronis said wearily to Xanthos, his voice suggesting he had faint hope for such concord.

The following week, the combined force of Maniots and peasants, under the command of Kolokotronis and Petrobey, marched from Navplion to join Niketaras fighting the Turks at Aghia Lavra. In addition to a thousand foot soldiers, they had six small cannon and about fifty horsemen. When Xanthos asked to accompany the force, Kolokotronis instructed him to remain in Navplion.

"You can be of greater help to me by overseeing what is happening here," Kolokotronis said. "If dispatches of importance come in, relay them to me by courier at once."

Within ten days, the small army returned to Navplion. From the courtyard, Xanthos witnessed them straggling into the encampment, a sad, exhausted procession, a sorry remnant of the swaggering and confident force that had departed Navplion. One man had a flap of skin hanging from his cheek, which had been slashed open to his throat, revealing the blood and bone. Another man, one leg blackened with clotted blood, limped along, using his musket as a crutch. Those who could walk helped carry wounded comrades. Xanthos noted that in the courtyard, Kolokotronis and Petrobey parted without speaking or showing any civility toward one another.

"There is much to tell you about, scribe," Kolokotronis said wearily when they had returned to his headquarters. "But, God help me, first I must remove this crust that covers my body. My skin has not felt soap and water since we left Navplion. Meanwhile, make sure the wounded men are properly taken care of and the soldiers provided food."

After the general had bathed and dressed, Xanthos accompanied him as he visited the wounded, who lay on pallets in twin rows on the floor of one of the barracks. Kolokotronis spoke quietly and reassuringly to each man, and Xanthos was surprised by how many of their names he knew.

The general paused beside one of the wounded men where the doctor was preparing to amputate his leg. The bloody calf hung to the knee by a few tendons.

"I cannot bear it," the soldier cried. "I beg you, general, let me die!"

"Hold on, man!" Kolokotronis said sternly, breathing his own courage into the man's body. He held the man's hand tightly until the leg was off and the doctor had stemmed the flow of blood and then bandaged the stump.

Kolokotronis bent closer to the soldier whose face was ashen, his lips trembling. "Do you see now?" Kolokotronis said, and his voice was choked. "You had all that courage within you."

They moved on to another gravely wounded soldier. The doctor shook his head.

"This man is in a coma," he said, "and will die at any moment."

Kolokotronis knelt beside the man, whispering softly into his ear. A shiver swept the soldier's body, and then, as if some final spark of life had been roused from within, he opened his eyes. When he recognized the general, his lips trembling, he made a mighty effort to speak.

"Help me, general." The soldier's voice was hoarse and weak. "Don't let me die . . . "

Kolokotronis clasped the man's hand and held it tightly. The soldier closed his eyes again, and for several moments, general and soldier remained linked. Almost imperceptibly, the soldier's features altered, his countenance grown ashen, the rigidity of death altering his face.

Kolokotronis gently released the man's hand and rose. He stood for a moment gazing down in brooding silence at the dead soldier. When he spoke in a low, sorrowing voice, only Xanthos heard his words.

"The greatest king and conqueror in the world hasn't the power to save even one poor soldier from death."

Back in their quarters, Kolokotronis sat with Xanthos before the fire and smoked his chibouk. When he finally spoke, his voice reflected his despair.

"If you were to ask me whether we were victorious or defeated, Xanthos," he said, "in God's name, I'd have to say I don't know. Our war is snarled by such webs of rivalry and mistrust that we cannot know who to fear most . . . our allies or our enemies."

He sighed.

"We joined Niketaras in the battle against a detachment from the army of Khurshid Pasha. At first, we seemed to be driving them back and causing them heavy losses. We counted at least a hundred Turkish bodies as we advanced. Then word came that we were being attacked from the rear. One of the flanks of our force had given way, and the enemy had poured in. Our men fought valiantly, but in the end, we had to abandon our position and retreat, giving up all the ground we had fought so hard to capture."

He puffed slowly on the chibouk.

"Who was to blame? Petrobey swore it was Niketaras, whose men were supposed to have bolstered that flank, and Niketaras swore it was Petrobey. The two fell into bitter quarreling. We were forced to leave the field with nothing decided. There were only the dead on both sides and those poor devils we visited tonight."

"Every man I lose is a wound in my heart," he said, staring gloomily into the fire. "What hurts me as much is that I feel my men have lost faith in me. My alliance with the new government hasn't strengthened my position or influence but weakened it. The soldiers regard me less as the general who led his men to victory at the battle of Dhervenakia but simply as another politician. If I resign my position in the executive, then I might once again be seen as a general whose only concern is to fight and win the war."

But in the days that followed, the general retained his position as vice-president of the Executive. Xanthos knew that Kolokotronis did not resign because he feared losing any influence in the new government.

By November, the small army of Kolokotronis and Petrobey in Navplion had been reinforced by the arrival of several of the brigand bands

Xanthos had contacted on his journey to Parnassus. Among them was the brigand leader, Vorogrivas, with forty of his sturdy warriors. Xanthos felt his own spirits lifted at the sight of the strong mountain fighter with the commanding presence and his band of veterans.

"I'm pleased to see you again, scribe," Vorogrivas said at their first meeting, a smile brightening his sun-bronzed face. "After you left, my men and I missed your stories."

"Stories are easy to relate, captain," Xanthos said. "Fighting battles is much harder."

When Vorogrivas and Kolokotronis met for the first time, it was like they were a pair of bulls. Xanthos could feel the two leaders quickly and sharply appraising one another. He left them alone so their conversation could be private. An hour later, Vorogrivas emerged.

"Is there anything I can do for you, captain?" Xanthos asked.

"I'll join my men in our quarters now, friend," Vorogrivas said, "I'll see you again later in the day."

Xanthos entered the office of Kolokotronis, the general sat in thoughtful silence.

"He is a remarkable man," Kolokotronis said quietly. "In his character and in the sound way he assesses the strengths and weaknesses of men and the strategies of war, he reminds me of blessed Marko Botsaris. If I had a hundred like Botsaris and this mountain fighter, I swear before God we'd drive every last cursed Turk from Greece!"

Among the men Vorogrivas had brought was the grizzled warrior Zarkas.

"I'm glad to see your sad, blessed face again, teacher!" Zarkas embraced Xanthos roughly. "I heard your journey from Parnassus had a few misadventures, but those Suliots saved your skin. I'm pleased you escaped harm."

"I'm delighted to see you as well, Zarkas," Xanthos smiled. "And pleased that you, too, have avoided harm. I wanted to ask the captain, but he was busy with the general, so let me ask you. How was Manolis when you left the mountains?"

"The young warrior has grown stronger with each week and now shares our battles again," Zarkas said. "His living to fight once more is one of God's miracles. He was disappointed he could not come with us for this battle, but the captain left him in charge of our men back at the camp. Since you left, we have fought half a dozen hard battles in the mountain passes with the Turks. I tell you, scribe, Manolis is every bit the warrior he was before he was wounded."

"And what of his godson, Lefteris, in Kravasaras?" Xanthos asked. "Has Manolis been back to see the child?"

A glimmer of a sardonic smile creased the warrior's cheeks. "That is another story, teacher," Zarkas said with a wink. "Manolis has returned to Kravasaras several times. But my suspicion, which, of course, Manolis will not admit, is that he travels to the village as much for that pretty mother as for the child." Zarkas shrugged, his tone turning more serious. "I understand how a young buck needs to feel the bond of love. But in our lives, every day we survive is a bounty we may lose the following day."

"Perhaps they will both survive the war and make a life for themselves together," Xanthos said wistfully.

"Such things do happen, teacher," Zarkas said gravely. "But I suspect more often in stories than in life."

When the next group of peasants and villagers came to Navplion to join Kolokotronis, this time the general placed Zarkas and his men in charge of training fighting skills and developing discipline in the recruits. As before with other newcomers, these men did not take kindly to orders or direction by the rough, brusque mountain fighters. Xanthos was present when several farmers refused to obey an order given to them by Zarkas.

"Who appointed you general?" a farmer, taller by several inches than Zarkas, sneered. "I haven't seen clothing as ragged as yours since the scarecrows we put up in our field to frighten off the crows."

"You might be captain of chickens and sheep up in the mountains," another farmer chimed in, "but here we do things our own way."

Zarkas tendered both men a benign smile. "First of all, my friends," he said, his voice quiet and genial, "I have been assigned this task by your own general. He is weary of seeing you shooting one another because you can't get your deployments straight."

The guileful smile still lurking upon his face, he stepped closer to the tall farmer.

"But there is a second, even better reason for you to listen to me," Zarkas said. He placed both his hands in a friendly gesture on the taller man's shoulders. "It is to save you from pain."

"What pain?" the farmer asked.

The words had barely cleared the farmer's lips when Zarkas's hands flew from the man's shoulders to roughly clasp his head. He jerked down the farmer's head and at the same time swiftly swung up his knee. Head and knee collided with a sound like an ax striking a cord of wood. The man gasped and plummeted to the ground.

Zarkas swiftly grabbed the second farmer. He whirled him around and delivered a thunderous kick to the man's behind, a barreling blast that propelled the man forward for what seemed a kilometer before he, too, arms and legs flailing, sprawled on the ground.

Zarkas glared fiercely at the surrounding men. "Any other questions about my leadership?"

The men stared at the two farmers on the ground, one still squirming and holding his rocking head, the other trying to pick himself up from the dirt. No one else moved or uttered a word.

"Good," Zarkas said, the smile returned to his face. "Now let's get down to some shooting practice so in the battles to come you can kill Turks instead of one another."

In early December, the couriers brought word to Navplion that Khurshid Pasha with his force assessed at twenty-five thousand to thirty thousand men, with a thousand cavalry and numerous cannon, had arrived in Volos on the Pagasitic Gulf. From there Khurshid would begin his march south into Boeotia and, if his advance was not halted, continue south to devastate the Peloponnesus.

"God help us, this is the major battle we have been preparing ourselves for," Kolokotronis said to Xanthos. "Any force we muster will be much smaller than the Turkish army, but we must fight with what we have. Odysseus is coming with twenty-five hundred men, and Makriyannis has pledged to join us. So, we will march north as soon as our force here can be assembled."

"Do you want me to go with you?"

"I have other plans for you, my friend," the general shook his head. "The same couriers that brought us word about Khurshid Pasha have brought us the news that the Englishman Byron will travel soon from Cephalonia to Missolonghi. He'll make that godforsaken marshland his headquarters, although for the life of me I can't understand why. My wish, now, is that you go to Missolonghi to join Wyndham and Lukas in their entreaties to Byron. Wyndham will see that you meet him, and you will also carry letters of introduction from me." He paused and when he spoke again, his voice was grave. "I want you to know your mission is as important as anything our army accomplishes in battle against Khurshid Pasha. Without money, troops cannot be paid, and arms cannot be bought. Try to convince Byron that the most sensible use of the funds he brings is to be allotted to our forces. Explain to him that our alliance—Petrobey, Odysseus, Makriyannis, and myself—is the one most capable of driving the Turks from Greece."

At the start of the following week, the army in Navplion prepared to break camp and begin their march north. The men understood this would not simply be a skirmish but a major battle in which many would lose their lives.

The forces of Odysseus Androutsos and Yannis Makriyannis arrived, adding almost four thousand men to the army. The familiar sounds of the encampment at night, the babble of voices, the rattle of cooking pots, and fragments of music and song became more clamorous. But, on the eve of battle, there was also a growing sense of tension and danger. Bringing the superstitions of their villages with them, men marked the cycles of the moon, gauged the flight of birds, and listened to the sound of thunder, all as auguries of impending victory or omens of defeat. The horses in the corrals inhaled the scents of danger and snorted and pawed the earth restlessly. As the army prepared to depart, Xanthos packed his belongings and prepared to leave as well. Because of the Turkish ships off the coast of Monemvasia, it was deemed too dangerous for Captain Papayannis to bring the *Hermes* to Navplion, so he planned to pick up Xanthos at Corinth instead. From there, they'd sail through the gulf to Missolonghi.

On the morning of his departure, as Xanthos was strapping on his saddlebags containing clothing, food, water, and several of his books and journals, Zarkas came to bid him farewell.

"Don't tell me you're traveling alone," Zarkas frowned. "Where are those Suliot tigers who guarded you when you came to us on the mountain?"

"The general wanted Selim and Notis to ride with me, at least as far as Corinth," Xanthos said, "but I reassured him I did not need them. Those warriors will be needed for the battle you face now. It would be a shame to waste their prowess protecting the skinny shanks of a single, aging scribe."

"Even though I'd feel better if they were looking after you, teacher," Zarkas said, "what you say makes sense. If fortune deems it our time, a bullet can find us in the midst of an army."

Later that morning, the commotion and turmoil of the army preparing to march from Navplion overshadowing his own departure, Xanthos began his journey to Corinth. Riding north along the coast, he passed through several small villages. The silent, sullen villagers marked his passage with wary faces, mumbling barely audible responses to his greetings. Where once the villagers proffered unquestioned hospitality to any stranger, in the atmosphere of war, every stranger, whether Greek or not, had to be regarded as an enemy.

Closer to the water, the air turned cooler with clouds drifting across the sky. The only evidence of war Xanthos saw were spirals of smoke rising from a fort or village burning in the distance. In Corinth, the port teeming with refugees, he found the *Hermes* at anchor and Captain Papayannis awaiting him impatiently.

"We are already sailing too late," the captain told him, his craggy, weather-beaten face set in tense lines. "We had word that several Turkish ships have been sighted near Galaxidi. If we encounter them, we've eaten our last meal. But we'll skirt the southern coast until we're through the gulf and pray to God that we avoid them."

They rode in the longboat to the *Hermes* at anchor and climbed the rope ladder to the deck. Within minutes, Captain Pappayanis shouted the orders. "Stand by the capstan! Hands aloft and loose topsails!"

Xanthos watched the agile seamen climbing up the shrouds and along the swaying yards, their bodies small figures against the sky. As the canvas thundered loose from the yards, the ship lurched in the water.

From forward came the strident cry, "Anchors aweigh!"

The *Hermes* tilted to starboard, and, with more and more canvas lengthening from her yards, the brig veered off into the wind. Moments later, the ship glided past several other brigs and a scatter of fishing boats that bobbed in their wake. In a few moments, they left the port and moved into the open waters of the Gulf of Corinth.

Xanthos occupied his time on the voyage making entries in his journal. Captain Papayannis and his sailors remained watchful for any sign of Turkish ships. In the evening, Xanthos joined the captain and his first mate for a dinner of herbs and fruit. On the morning of their third day, they sailed through the passage at Antirion, where the Gulf narrowed so that land was visible off both the starboard and port sides of their vessel.

"God guided our journey," Captain Pappayanis told Xanthos. "Those Turkish ships are off creating havoc elsewhere, and we have been spared."

"Perhaps they know your cargo is one skinny scribe of little consequence, Captain," Xanthos said.

Approaching Missolonghi, Xanthos, on deck watching for the first sign of land, saw over the bow a narrow line of muddy dunes and beyond them, a wide, seemingly endless marsh. As they sailed slowly through the channel, the water of the gulf, which had been blue, became thick and brown, mud swirling in the ship's wake. For what seemed hours to Xanthos, the channel ran through a muddy, miasmic swamp until it opened into a large harbor. That was the first glimpse Xanthos had of Missolonghi, a town built on a marshy plain beside a large lagoon.

"Of all the patches of earth in Greece, the Englishman might have made his headquarters, he had to be mad to choose this spot," the captain said. "The stink, fog, and foul air rising from these swamps make this city unfit habitation for man or beast. If you are not killed by the sword of an enemy, then fever and pestilence will do you in."

Eager to avoid remaining anchored in the harbor any longer than necessary, Papayannis ordered a longboat lowered to carry Xanthos to the shore and bid him a hasty good-by. "God speed you in your mission," he said as Xanthos descended the rope ladder into the longboat. "When you see Wyndham, carry him my good wishes. As for that sniveling pup, Lukas, give him a kick in the ass for me."

After disembarking in the port and making inquiries at a tavern, Xanthos heard that Byron and his entourage had arrived in Missolonghi just the week before. At the lodgings of a former comrade of Kolokotronis whose name the general had provided him, he learned that Wyndham and Lukas had arrived with Byron from Cephalonia.

"Came right off the ship with the Englishman!" Mitsakis, the old soldier, told him. Amiable as his host was and as warmly as he greeted Xanthos, the man's stocky, unkempt frame emitted an odor suggesting he had not washed since the midwife who delivered him swabbed the mucus off his body.

Mitsakis showed Xanthos his room and then hurried off to carry word to Wyndham. Even after he'd departed, the room retained the strong odors he'd left behind. Xanthos opened his bedroom windows and breathed deeply of the breeze that came off the sea, but that did little to dispel the stench in his nostrils.

Within the hour, the English officer came to meet him.

"I'm delighted to have you here, Xanthos!" Wyndham said. "I'm only a poor soldier and all this political maneuvering is beyond me. I'll be damned grateful for your help."

He pointed apologetically to the uniform he wore, neat, blue jacket buttoned to his throat, braid and ribbons of decoration on his chest.

"Lord Byron likes those of us around him dressed in our martial trappings," Wyndham said. "It creates the sense of a military headquarters and not some decadent royal court."

"I was surprised to learn that Byron had already arrived," Xanthos said. "We thought his plans were to travel here much later."

"In Cephalonia, he made up his mind suddenly to come to Missolonghi and asked us to travel with him," Wyndham said. "We traveled in two ships. I was on the larger of the two ships, the one carrying his Lordship's aide, Pietro Gamba, a half-dozen servants, horses, some cannon, and a great mass of luggage. Byron sailed on a smaller, faster vessel that carried, besides the captain and the crew, Dr. Bruno, Byron's medical attendant, his valet, Fletcher, and his Lordship's Newfoundland dog, Lyon." Wyndham's paused. "Lukas traveled on that ship with him as well."

"So the general was right," Xanthos said quietly.

"There isn't any question that Byron is smitten with Lukas," Wyndham said, "Everyone knows it, and yet they all remain discreetly silent. We had a stormy voyage and once sighted a pair of Turkish frigates. I heard afterwards from the valet, Fletcher, that Byron was less frightened for his own safety than he was terrified about Lukas falling into the hands of the Turks." Wyndham face revealed his distress. "Whatever feelings Byron has for the youth, I must tell you that Lukas has no warmth or affection of any kind for Byron. He is most unhappy and, when he sees me, complains constantly. I have urged him to at least be civil to the Englishman. I fear if Byron finds out how the youth really feels about him, any chance we have of achieving our goals will be lost."

"Is Lukas lodging with you?"

"Lukas lives in his house with Byron, along with Byron's servants, a groom, and a band of Suliots. He's been waiting anxiously for your arrival. I sent him word that you had landed, and I don't doubt he'll be here to see you soon. I know he hopes you bring him word that the general will allow him to return to Navplion."

"By now Kolokotronis and his army have ridden off to a major battle with Khurshid Pasha," Xanthos said. "I carry no instructions for Lukas except that he should remain where he is."

"Losing that final hope will make the poor young devil even unhappier than he is now," Wyndham said. "But there's no denying that he sits in a privileged position, as close to Byron as anyone can get." He shrugged. "I have heard from Dr. Bruno, who is Byron's close friend in addition to being his doctor, that Byron has written poetry for the youth. The doctor is concerned that Lukas is a distraction, obsessing Byron emotionally at a time when he is facing an onslaught of petitioners seeking his aid. By God, Xanthos, they are all after him, like hounds after a fox. Mavrokordatos, Zaimis, Londos, all pressing their requests. They fawn and flatter Byron and make it hard for anyone else to get close. It is only as a military advisor that I manage to see him from time to time, and we only discuss strategy for the battles to come."

In the following hour, Wyndham poured out a torrent of news that Xanthos struggled to absorb.

"You would not believe our arrival on this squalid shore," Wyndham said. "Byron's ship landed shortly before ours. He was greeted by a raucous multitude, the firing of cannon, and a volley of smaller musketry. Prince Mavrokordatos as president of the senate was there in his full, formal regalia to greet us as well as a cluster of dignitaries, a bishop, and half a dozen priests in their colorful vestments, a dozen swaggering captains, sabers dangling from their belts, some foreign officers in their dress uniforms, and several hundred boisterous Suliots. Behind them was a mob of townspeople. It was a welcome one might have expected not for a poet, even a wealthy one, but for a king. I suspected much of the clamorous cheering and celebration wasn't because they regarded him as a famous poet but because they felt he was rich."

They drank a carafe of wine, and the landlord, carrying his load of oppressive odors, brought them another. Xanthos felt his senses reeling until Wyndham's voice returned him to the room. He was astonished that the English officer didn't seem conscious of the odors. He asked Wyndham why he didn't seem affected.

"The poor devil can't help himself," Wyndham laughed. "That is the smell of the swamps and marshes of Missolonghi everyone living here acquires. Since you have no other choice, you'll become resigned to it after you've been here a while."

They returned to the subject of Byron's arrival on the island.

"While I cannot claim to understand all his thinking," Wyndham said, "I believe Byron has come here dreaming of leading an army into battle. Pressing on that aspiration, Mavrokordatos and the others have convinced him that what makes sense is for him now to launch an attack on the fort of Oxia, not far from here, a bastion that overlooks the channel of Lepanto."

"I can understand why," Xanthos said. "Lepanto was the site of the naval action in 1571 when the Christian states of Europe defeated the Turks."

"That first major victory saw over two hundred Turkish galleys destroyed and fifteen thousand galley slaves set free," Wyndham said. "They are telling Byron that if he commands a force and wins a second battle of Lepanto, it would be a stunning start to his military career. They assure him the capture promises to be easy. The town is garrisoned mainly by Albanians, who have indicated they'd surrender for a reasonable payment of monies. All they ask is that an army make a token attack on them so they might save their honor by offering some manner of defense."

"Do you believe victory would be that easy?"

"I have seen too much war to assume any such thing as an easy victory," Wyndham replied. "When men start to battle, a certain grim joy in killing takes over that upsets the plans of even the most crafty generals." For a moment, he fell silent. "During these last weeks in Cephalonia, I have gained credence with Byron, but I am not his only military advisor. He respects the experience of war I bring to any discussion of strategy, but he has other voices hammering at him. He suffers from indecision and exhausts himself in planning, postponing, suffering bouts of either confidence or apprehension. In the end, he does nothing. I have told him that before he launches any kind of campaign, he needs a battery of field artillery—light and fit for mountain service and men who know how to fire them. Secondly, an ample supply of gunpowder. And, thirdly, hospital and medical stores."

"Is he listening to you?"

"I cannot be sure," Wyndham said. "He is beleaguered on all sides. Those bloody Suliots cling to his heels day and night like a pack of jackals, and he stands at bay like a harried fox. Much of his energy is spent resisting their exorbitant demands for money."

"Have you had a chance to speak to him about the monies for Kolokotronis and his alliance?"

"I have brought it up on several occasions," Wyndham said. "He listens to me politely enough, but my petition is one among many. I must confess to you, Xanthos, that as time goes on, my opinion of this eccentric Lord Byron grows better and better. Despite all the surface trappings and the man being driven by obsessions he cannot control, there is something strangely noble about him and his sense of mission. He doesn't only meet chieftains but he also visits with common people who bring him their disputes about land and quarrels with their neighbors. He listens to their problems with sympathy and even makes an effort to aid them. I don't doubt that he truly loves Greece and wishes to see her free. He also seems to understand the tortuous politics of the Greeks—how they can say one thing and mean another—and still wishes to help them. He told me once that there is no single truth in Greece but multiple truths. As for my relationship with him, he listens to my counsel on military matters and accepts me as a representative of Kolokotronis, but I perceive that in his sympathies, he leans toward Mavrokordatos. Part of this, I think, is because Mavrokordatos is so skilled at praising him. He calls Byron a 'savior' and a 'liberator' and tells him that the destiny of Greece is in his hands. That must please Byron, but he also sees Mavrokordatos as a stabilizing force among the various factions."

"How soon can you arrange for me to see him?"

"I have already informed him that you were coming as the representative of General Kolokotronis, and he indicated his willingness to see you. First thing tomorrow, I'll try to get word to him that you've arrived. Meanwhile, you'd best prepare yourself to deal with Lukas."

"I'm sorry I don't have better news for the youth," Xanthos said. "If it were my decision to make, I'd send him home."

A little later that evening, as Wyndham and Xanthos were finishing dinner, Lukas arrived. When he entered the room and removed his cloak, Xanthos saw the youth was splendidly dressed in the colorful trappings of a court squire or page. He wore a jacket made of dark-red silk, blue silk trousers, and fine velvet slippers. Despite the finery in which he was clad, his countenance revealed his anguish.

"I wish to speak to Xanthos alone," he said brusquely to Wyndham.

The English officer left the room. For a moment, the youth remained silent, as if trying to muster the eloquence to plead his cause. When he finally spoke, his words emerged as the simple, stark plea of a child.

"I want to go home!"

"I understand that, Lukas."

"Do you understand!?" Lukas asked, his voice shaken and rising. "Do you really understand during all those months in Cephalonia and now here in Missolonghi how I am suffering! If the general understood how much I want to leave this pesthole and go home, in God's name, he'd let me leave!"

"The general is leading our troops into a major battle, Lukas," Xanthos said. "He hasn't time now to consider anything else. This battle could mean victory for us or could destroy his army and leave the path open for Khurshid Pasha to devastate the Peloponnesus. You know what cruelty and suffering that would produce."

For a moment, Lukas stared at him, and Xanthos noted again the young man's uncommon beauty. The flawless complexion, the ears small as a girl's, his lips full and sensual, glistening as though he'd just bitten on a grape or sipped from a glass of wine. Yet, the most striking thing about his countenance in that moment was the despair in his pale-blue eyes.

"I cannot abide the man!" Lukas said, the words burst shrilly from his lips. "He keeps me with him for hours at a time. At least once a day, he sends me almonds and sugared sherbet. He has made me his confidant and pours out his heart to me, telling me stories of his life, his loves, his dreams. He rambles on and on, like a man drunk not on spirits but on words, telling me how he longs to do something more for mankind than write verses." A cold scorn hardened the young man's voice. "I tell you, Xanthos, I don't care a damn what he does or anything about his fears or his dreams!" He took a breath and then, his voice carrying the urgency of a prayer, pleaded, "I want to go home!"

Xanthos struggled to provide him a reassurance he had no right to offer.

"On the voyage from Cephalonia, we sailed into a dreadful storm." Lukas said, resuming his litany of complaint. "Since I cannot swim, he vowed he was strong enough to save us both. He boasted that in imitation of the legendary swimmer Leander, he once swam the Hellespont. I didn't tell him that I was so unhappy, I'd rather he let me drown."

"Has he forced himself on you, Lukas?" Xanthos asked hesitantly.

"He has not physically attacked me," Lukas said. "But his every gesture and every word indicates to me what he is after. I also have to endure the whispers and smirks of others around us who suspect there are unspeakable things going on during those hours Byron and I spend alone. They cannot understand that when I see him clad in his garish garments and limping across the room, when he speaks to me with a soft, endearing voice, when I smell the scents with which he covers himself, I am sickened." He drew a labored breath. "He also babbles on about his superstitions and how he does not expect to survive this war. A fortune-teller warned him in his youth to beware his thirty-sixth year. That is the age he will reach now." He sighed in despair. "Xanthos, if you only knew how I have been praying for your arrival," the words came in anguish from his lips, "praying that you'd bring me word that I might go home!"

"There is no home for any of us now, Lukas." Xanthos understood the futility of his words to offer Lukas any solace. "If it were up to me, I'd send you away from here tomorrow. But men are fighting and dying now in the cause of Greece. The general feels you can help us by remaining here, by staying close to Byron."

The youth stared at him, his great eyes haunted with misery.

"If we can once convince Byron to allocate a substantial portion of the monies he brings from London to the general and his allies," Xanthos said, "then we might all leave Missolonghi. Wyndham, you, and I. But until that time, each of us must fight on as best we can."

For a moment longer, Lukas stared at him, and then, as if comprehending that any further pleas were useless, he walked slowly toward the door. He picked up his cloak and turned to Xanthos.

"Other men are asked to fight for our country's freedom as soldiers," Lukas said, and bitterness shredded his voice. "I am asked to fight for our country's freedom as Byron's whore."

That night, the odors from the marshes and the raucous sounds of revelry from the taverns in the port making it difficult to sleep, Xanthos, in bed in the darkness, thought of Byron's desire for the love of Lukas. He recalled his own anxiety when he first became aware that he loved his student Chryseis. Her exquisite face framed by her shimmering, pale-reddish hair and her soft voice assailed his thoughts during the day and seared his dreams at night. When he considered his own frailties and imperfections against her grace and beauty, he despaired of ever gaining her love. Yet, that miracle had come to pass when she responded to his entreaties. He recalled his matchless joy on the night they first made love, a memory he'd recalled a thousand times since then, savoring the vision of her naked body gleaming with an erotic loveliness in the moonlight. It was spring, and in the gardens, the almond trees were budding, and delicate lilies were sprouting from the awakening earth. He felt as if their night of love was the reason he had been born.

In the nostalgic recall of his own happiness and despite his sympathy for Lukas, he could not help feeling compassion for the unrequited longing being suffered by Byron. The English poet had come to Greece, clad in all his martial finery and seeking glory. He found his favor coveted by so many, and, yet, he was denied the affection he desired himself.

Xanthos waited anxiously all the following day for word from Byron. Meanwhile, the foulness of the air caused an upheaval in his stomach and suppressed any appetite for food. He tried to read and walked along the harbor until the stench of the marshes drove him back to his room. That evening, his anxiety growing and as he was about to send Mitsakis to contact Wyndham, a young Suliot soldier brought word from Wyndham that Byron would see him the following morning.

All that night, Xanthos tossed restlessly, dreaming in fits and starts until he rose at dawn. Mitsakis had already risen to light a fire. He poured Xanthos a mug of strong black coffee and afterwards saddled a horse for him and told him in which direction to ride.

Byron's headquarters in Missolonghi was a rambling two-story dwelling west of the town that looked out over the lagoon. Several small boats were beached up against the house. When Xanthos approached the building, he saw the cluster of Suliot guards, sprawled around indolently, some smoking and others playing games with pebbles and sticks.

When he rode up and dismounted, several dark-visaged, fierce-eyed, longhaired men waved their muskets at him menacingly. Although they spoke in Greek, their snarling Albanian dialect left him unable to comprehend what they were saying, but their threats were clear. He was trying to explain that he had been summoned when Wyndham emerged from the main building and spoke brusquely to the Suliots, telling them Xanthos was Lord Byron's guest. That quieted their clamor, and one of them took his horse. Xanthos followed Wyndham into the compound's large central courtyard leading to the house. That was also filled by a horde of Suliots.

"What do they do all day?" Xanthos asked.

Wyndham answered with a sardonic smile. "The unruly wretches play their dangerous games that often end in brawls and wait to get paid."

They ascended the stairs to the second level. An outer reception area was staffed by several clerks, and two Suliot guards lounged against a wall, muskets held loosely in their hands. A handful of townspeople, apparently waiting for an audience with Byron, sat stiffly and silently in a row of chairs.

Ignoring the disapproving faces of the clerks and the annoyed countenances of the petitioners, Wyndham led Xanthos directly to the main door, knocked, and then opened it. He led Xanthos into the inner office. The first impression Xanthos had of the room and its furnishings was its resemblance to a military museum. The walls were decorated with assorted weaponry, carbines, muskets, pistols, and sabers. In one corner were two plumed Homeric helmets that might have adorned the head of a warrior in the *Iliad*.

Byron sat behind a large desk in one corner, and he rose quickly and came around the desk to greet them. What first struck Xanthos was Byron's limp, which made him rock slightly as he walked. Afterwards, he noticed Byron's apparel, a dark-green jacket with rough black cuffs and collar and a profusion of black trim resembling the formal jackets of some of the more illustrious cavalry regiments. As Byron came nearer, extending his hand, Xanthos was conscious of the poet's pale face, faintly hollowed cheeks, and large, luminous blue eyes that appeared both sensitive and probing. There were streaks of gray through his curly auburn hair, and he sported a mustachio so pale in color it appeared to be nearly white.

Xanthos bowed slightly in a gesture of courtesy and deference.

Byron grasped Xanthos's hand warmly in both his own.

"I am most pleased to meet you, sir!" Byron said, his voice strong and well modulated. "Major Wyndham has spoken of you with great admiration! And I'm also delighted to learn from him that in addition to your fluency in Greek, Italian, and French, you also speak English. If you'd be good enough to assist me, it would relieve my good interpreter, Andreas Zantachi, who is now forced to spend most of the day and many of the nights with me. I can't tell you what tribulations I endure having to translate words back and forth every time I speak."

"I'd be honored to assist you in any way I can," Xanthos said. "I also thank you for receiving me on behalf of General Kolokotronis. I bring you his letters concerning my visit."

"I look forward to reading them," Byron said. "How was the general when you left him?"

"By now he is leading an army to confront Khurshid Pasha," Xanthos said. "He commands a smaller force than the Muslims but it comprises veteran soldiers led by Captain Makriyannis and Prince Petrobey Mavromichalis."

"I have heard of their remarkable exploits," Byron said earnestly. "And I wish them and their army Godspeed." He shook his head. "Although I might be more of a hindrance than a help because of my lack of military experience, as I have told Major Wyndham, I wish to God I were with our forces in the field instead of in this office receiving endless petitions!"

He led Xanthos into a small alcove containing several upholstered sofas and chairs.

"I'll leave your Lordship and Xanthos alone," Wyndham said, starting for the door.

"Thank you, Major. Would you also be kind enough to ask Mathon to send in some tea?"

"I can't tell you how much I appreciate having Major Wyndham here to advise me," Byron said after Wyndham left the office. "His own service in the command of Lord Wellington was exemplary, and now I have his sage military counsel at my disposal." He flashed a beguiling smile that, while illuminating his pale cheeks, also showed several of his discolored teeth. As if suddenly conscious of the blemish the smile revealed, Byron's countenance became serious again.

Xanthos started to retrieve from his briefcase the letters from Kolokotronis.

"Leave the letters with me," Byron said. "I'll read them later. Major Wyndham has told me enough about you so you don't require any further reference."

"Thank you, your Lordship."

Byron's pale cheeks flushed.

"You don't need to constantly refer to me by that title," he said. "It is a foolish appellation but one that impresses some of the local petitioners. You may simply call me Byron as my friends do."

The door opened, and a young page brought in a tray with tea in a fine china pot and two gold-rimmed cups that he placed on the table between the sofa and the chair. He was a comely boy but not as handsome as Lukas. The youth withdrew quietly.

"I understand you have served General Kolokotronis a long time," Byron said as he poured tea into their cups.

"I became his aide in Zante during the years he lived there in exile," Xanthos said. "When the revolt broke out in Greece, we traveled to the Mani to ally ourselves with Prince Petrobey. We were together at the terrible battle in Karitena and again at the siege and fall of Tripolitza. Since then, I have served the general at Navplion."

"The general is fortunate to have your support," Byron said. He sipped his tea slowly, his slim, white fingers gracefully holding the cup. "Major Wyndham also tells me that you are writing a history of the revolution?"

"That is my hope, sir," Xanthos said. "At this point they are mostly entries in a journal but when the war is over, I hope to coalesce the impressions and events into a completed work."

"A most worthy undertaking," Byron said. "I have read Herodotus and Thucydides several times and have been greatly enlightened. They have provided me eyes and a soul to understand Greece and the Greeks."

There was a knock at the door, and the face of the clerk appeared.

"Your Lordship," the clerk said nervously, "the delegation from the Acheloos Council is here for their appointment."

"Ask them to wait," Byron said.

Xanthos rose to leave, but Byron motioned him to sit again.

"Please stay a few minutes longer," he said. "I am sorry my schedule is so harried. If I'd known of your arrival earlier, I would have allotted us more time. But we will plan to meet again soon." His large eyes fixed earnestly on Xanthos. "Greece has always been for me, Xanthos, as it must be for all men of any sensibility or education, the promised land of valor, of the arts, and of liberty throughout all ages. It is a land where every stone tells its haunting story. On my journeys across Greece, I marvel that I have seen pines and eagles, vultures and owls similar to those once seen by Themistocles and Alexander!"

His voice had risen in pitch, trembling with an emotion he obviously felt deeply. "But that is the hallowed past. Now we must deal with the reality of the present. Tell me candidly, Xanthos, do the military leaders like General Kolokotronis and Prince Petrobey, do they understand my mission here and appreciate what I seek to accomplish?"

"I am sure they have no doubt about your devotion to our cause."

"Not only to our cause but to Greece itself, a land I deeply love," Byron said. "I first traveled here fourteen years ago. I thought then that the slavery of the Greeks was a desecration of that precious tradition we hold in classical drama, art, and philosophy." Byron sighed. "Along with the great beauty, I saw the horrors perpetrated by the Muslims on the Greeks. In Constantinople, I witnessed the execution of a Greek elder accused of trafficking with the Russians. His body lay where he had been executed, the poor man's severed head thrust between his legs as a sign of disgrace. I will never forget the sight of scavenging dogs lapping up the blood that oozed from his neck. It perverts any feeling of decency to think that human beings can be so brutal to one another."

His voice altered, grew pensive. "In Athens when I saw the Acropolis tragically mutilated, the dismembered pillars strewn upon the ground, I pledged then to return someday to Greece to aid in her liberation in any way we could." He paused. "Yet, I am being criticized by some as having come to Greece seeking only glory for myself. That is not true!"

"General Kolokotronis has no doubt of your desire to aid Greece."

Byron rose from his chair and limped toward his desk. "I am grateful for his understanding. I believe that true patriots understand my mission. Did you know the hero Markos Botsaris?"

"I only knew of him by his exploits and mourned as everyone did at the news of his death."

"He was a great loss to Greece and to the Greek cause," Byron said. He rummaged in the drawer of his desk. "When I was still in Cephalonia, I had this letter from Botsaris. . . . If you'd indulge me, I'd like to read you a few lines."

He opened the envelope and began to read in a clear, modulated voice.

Your Excellency is exactly the kind of person we need. Let nothing prevent you from coming to this part of Greece. . . . I shall do battle tonight against a corps of six or seven thou-

sand Albanians encamped close to this place. The day after
tomorrow I shall set out with a few chosen companions to
meet Your Excellency. I thank you for the good opinions you
have of my fellow citizens, which God grant you will not find
ill founded.

Byron put the letter aside, and Xanthos felt the intensity of his
gaze.

"Botsaris died in that battle," he said, and emotion caused his voice
to falter. "A terrible loss to me and to all of Greece."

Once again, there was a knock on the door.

"Just a moment!" Byron called, a strain of impatience in his voice.

Xanthos rose and started to the door, and Byron came limping to
bid him farewell. He gripped Xanthos's hand tightly.

"I want you to come back soon," he said earnestly. "I am anxious
for us to speak about many things with which I know you can help
me. If you'd be kind enough, perhaps you might also assist me in my
desire to master the Greek language so that I might use it to clarify,
with whatever eloquence I can, my motivation and my mission."

"I'll be pleased to assist you in any way I can, my Lord," Xanthos
said and reached for the handle of the door.

"Have you seen Lukas yet?" Although Byron tried to ask the question casually, his tone had altered. For the first time, his voice sounded
guarded.

"I saw him briefly last night after my arrival."

"He's a fine young man," Byron said. "Sensitive and honorable. As
with Major Wyndham, I am glad to have him with us in the service
of Greece."

In the month that followed, despite Byron's harried schedule, Xanthos
visited with the English poet several times a week. At Byron's urging, they studied Greek together, and the poet proved a quick and
proficient pupil, his ability to speak the language improving swiftly.
He was delighted and grateful to Xanthos, who was able on several
occasions to bring up the issue of funds for Kolokotronis.

"I assure you, Xanthos," Byron told him, "when Colonel Leicester
Stanhope, who is the other official envoy of the London Greek Com-

mittee, arrives with the first installment of the loan, the money will be equitably apportioned to those leaders who valiantly serve our cause. Among those leaders, General Kolokotronis holds a principal place."

Xanthos began to feel about Byron as Wyndham had before him, that the English poet manifested a nobility of spirit and resolute purpose. Byron also seemed willing to share his aspirations and dreams. At times, Xanthos was surprised at the candor with which Byron spoke in self-deprecating terms.

"Now, if I can claim to know myself," Byron said during one of their visits, "I should have to admit that I am sorely lacking in character. I am so changeable, beginning many things and staying with nothing very long."

This same candor applied when he spoke of his life in England. His father had died when Byron was three and a half, and at six, he was made heir to the family estates. At the age of ten, he was elevated to the aristocracy and took his seat in the House of Lords in 1809 when he was twenty-one.

"I was like a puppy hurled in among the wolves," Byron said. "The speeches were tedious, old men pontificating endlessly on one or another topic having nothing to do with beauty, truth or the fate of the common man."

Byron proved astute in his comprehension of the international context within which Greece struggled.

"There are the great powers, England, France, and Russia, each driven by its own national interest," Byron said. "If the interests of Greece happen to coincide at a given time, they may help the country in its revolt. If those interests come into conflict, poor Greece will be the loser."

He also spoke to Xanthos of his unhappy marriage to Annabella Millbanke in January of 1815 and how he fled from England less than a year later after the marriage collapsed. For the following seven years he had traveled, delaying returning to England, as if reluctant to confront the shambles of his past.

"I am afraid, dear Xanthos," Byron said pensively, "that I don't believe such a thing as a happy marriage exists. That is less the fault of the ladies than that we men are fools. We cry for a plaything, which when we have it, like children, cannot wait until we break it."

Only in regard to Lukas did Xanthos find Byron wary and nervous. Yet, Xanthos felt that of all the topics that passed in conversation between them, Lukas was what Byron wished to talk about most.

Several times, Xanthos accepted an invitation from Byron to ride with his entourage in the early morning and felt part of an imposing procession. The swashbuckling captain of the Suliot guard with a squadron of his soldiers preceded Byron, Xanthos riding beside him. Behind them rode Lukas on a splendid roan given to him by Byron and, beside him, Byron's chief aide, Pietro Gamba. Another length behind were Byron's physician, Dr. Bruno, and Eric Wyndham, followed by two of Byron's servants: Benjamin Lewis, his black groom, and the Venetian, Tita, both dressed elegantly like the courtiers who rode behind the carriages of monarchs. The stately procession was trailed by half a hundred rowdy Suliot guards, brandishing their weapons and, from time to time, firing them in the air to agitate any birds perched in the foliage of the trees.

Riding ahead of Lukas, Xanthos felt the youth's eyes piercing his back as if they were daggers. After their first visit, he had seen Lukas a number of times coming to or going from Byron's headquarters. They exchanged only the briefest greeting, Lukas treating him with obvious coldness and disdain.

Xanthos had written a long letter to Kolokotronis, apprizing him of the events taking place in Missolonghi, of his favorable impression of Byron, as well as of their conversations regarding the monies from the London committee. He added a postscript about how unhappy Lukas was and how much the youth wished to return to Navplion or to his family in Genoa.

> While I anxiously await to hear news of what took place in the battle between your forces and Khurshid Pasha, I fully understand and respect, General, your feeling that each of us must serve in whatever capacity most benefits our cause. But, in all candor, I feel we are imposing a most unnatural hardship on Lukas. It is obvious that Lord Byron is smitten with him, but Lukas has no feeling for him whatsoever. Indeed, if Lord Byron once senses the distaste and low esteem in which Lukas regards him, his anger may weigh heavily against any benefit we might gain from having Lukas here.

Meanwhile, Prince Alexander Mavrokordatos, who headed the provisional government based in Missolonghi, remained a regular and zealous visitor to Byron's headquarters. In several instances, Byron asked Xanthos to act as interpreter for the meetings. Xanthos knew that Mavrokordatos would have preferred to see Byron in private.

In late January of 1824, as president of the senate, Mavrokordatos gave Byron official sanction for an assault on the fortress of Lepanto, vesting him with full military and civil powers. He also promised the backing of Notas Botsaris, uncle of the fallen hero, Markos Botsaris. Mavrokordatos pressed Byron on the urgency of undertaking the assault as soon as possible.

"A successful attack now on Lepanto, your Lordship," Mavrokordatos said, "would give the Greeks control of the gulf and force the Turks to abandon Patras! Your leadership of that expedition will kindle the enthusiasm of our people across the land! I urge Your Excellency not to delay any longer!"

Xanthos translated the impassioned words of Mavrokordatos as faithfully as he could. Still, the little black-coated man with the owlish eyes remained distraught and suspicious.

"What are you telling him?" he asked Xanthos sharply. "Are you sure you're translating exactly what I said?"

"I am translating your precise words, Prince."

"I think we are agreed on this expedition against Lepanto," Byron spoke, and Xanthos translated the words. "My military advisors caution me, however, to wait until my firemaster William Parry arrives with his weapons, which will include Congreve rockets. He will also be bringing with him English mechanics skilled in artillery weaponry who will aid us in producing the rockets here. He is due very soon now, and we will then commence our campaign."

Byron stopped and let his expression indicate to Mavrokordatos that their interview was over. Mavrokordatos flushed slightly at the abruptness of the dismissal. He rose to leave and looked with hostility at Xanthos, as if resenting the interpreter being able to remain with Byron.

"Is his Lordship aware of your close association with Kolokotronis?" Mavrokordatos asked Xanthos.

"He knows it very well." Xanthos said.

Mavrokordatos stared at him in disapproval for another moment and then bowed brusquely to Byron and departed. Xanthos suspected, although he did not speak of his suspicions to Byron, a major part of the reason Mavrokordatos was urging action by Byron was to associate himself with a successful military adventure and help erase the shame of his defeat with the Philhellenes at Peta.

After Mavrokordatos had left the office, Byron leaned back in his chair, closed his eyes, and uttered a fervent sigh. "So many of these leaders who come to me seem obsessed with their own schemes," he said. "One can say of them that they are greedy. But in fairness, Xanthos, what they all want is power, and money is the means of power. From my own experience in England, I understand that greed for power is not usually reckoned as a sin." He laughed. "If it were, no English politician could ever hope to go to heaven."

In the meetings with various primates and captains when Xanthos served as interpreter, he came to understand the dichotomy of emotions that motivated Byron. Two different souls seemed to occupy the poet's body, one of which was generous, tender, and full of empathy for human suffering. But Byron also had a realistic ability to assess facts and examine their consequences with logic and accuracy. Several of the officials who sought to bully him found their blustering arguments soundly rejected. The most engaging element about Byron was his ability to find humor in his own vanities. He promised if he survived the Greek adventure, he would write two major poems about it.

"One will be an epic!" he laughed. "The other a burlesque in which none shall be spared and myself least of all!"

On another occasion, he walked to the corner where the majestic helmets were displayed that he had ordered made. He placed one on his head.

"How do I look, Xanthos?"

"Like a warrior out of the *Iliad*, Your Lordship."

"Like a buffoon is what you really mean, Xanthos," Byron said ruefully. "I don't know what I was thinking when I ordered them for my dear friend Trelawney and myself. Of course, he was too sensible to wear it."

He removed the helmet and turned to Xanthos with a smile. "Yet it is true that martial ornaments have their place in any conflict," he gestured toward the weaponry that adorned the walls. "What makes a regiment of soldiers a more noble object of view than the mass of a mob? It is the soldiers' arms, their uniforms, their banners, and the art and symmetry of their movements. In that respect, a Highlander's plaid, a Muslim's turban, and a Roman centurion's armor are more visually inspiring than the tattooed buttocks of a New Sandwich savage."

Byron was also haunted by morbid fears that he might lose his mind. His maternal grandfather and great-grandfather both had drowned, apparent suicides, and his mother had been markedly unstable, with violent swings of mood. A great-uncle was known as the Wicked Lord, and Byron's father was known as Mad Jack.

"None of these distinguished forebears suggests an inheritance of stability," the poet said. "The best I can hope for, friend Xanthos, is to hold my demons at bay."

Byron also repeated the story Xanthos first heard from Lukas, about the fortune-teller in his youth who had warned Byron of his thirty-sixth year. "If it proves true that I will not live to attain an old age, I pray to avoid the horror of a deathbed scene," he said wistfully. "As I've told others, I would far prefer to end up among the dead on a field of battle. But, as I have not been famous for my luck in life, most probably my death won't be much different. I fear I may draw my last sigh, not on a field of glory, but on a bed of disease."

The most aggravating of the pressures Byron faced that winter of 1824 in Missolonghi, were the incessant demands of the Suliot soldiers for more commissions. Byron paid out of his own pocket for a contingent of five hundred of them while the Mavrokordatos government paid for a hundred more. That did not satisfy the Suliots, and a day didn't pass when they did not pursue Byron like a pack of jackals demanding he enroll more of them on his payroll.

One morning in February, almost fifty of the soldiers pushed past the clerks and crowded into Byron's office. They raised a clamor until Byron impatiently demanded their silence.

"Tell them, Xanthos, that I simply cannot afford to employ any more of them! I have more men in my pay now than I need!"

Xanthos's efforts to explain Byron's refusal were met with cries of anger and derision.

"The Englishman needs us!" a swarthy, pockmarked captain of the Suliots cried harshly to Xanthos. "When the battles begin, who will he have to support him then? Farmers? Tradesmen? He needs us, and in order to be available for him, we must be paid!"

"He has no money," Xanthos sought to explain. "The money hasn't arrived yet."

"You are a liar!" a captain cried, his face contorted with blood and rage. He turned to Byron, flourished his musket, and cried out in a guttural Greek dialect, "Pay us! Pay us, or we'll go home and leave you at the mercy of the Turks!"

When they were finally out of the office, Byron slumped in his chair.

"They'll be the death of me before we ever see a battle," he lamented.

The closer the bond between Xanthos and Byron became, the more Byron confided in him of various relationships in his life before he had traveled to Greece. He spoke of women he had known and loved describing them vividly with a poet's ability to fashion metaphor and image. He spoke of Teresa Guiccioli, who had been his mistress for four years, longer than any other. He told Xanthos that he remained devoted to her despite finding her emotional demands exhausting. From time to time, Byron raised the name of Lukas and struggled for a way to convey to Xanthos something of his deep affection for the youth. Each time, his courage faltered, and he ended up offering a vague comment about how pleased he was to have a fine young man like Lukas in his service.

In the middle of February, Leicester Stanhope arrived bearing the first installment of the English loan. His ship's cargo also held several printing presses with which Stanhope planned to set up a newspaper. The money was placed on deposit in a bank on Cyprus to be drawn upon when Byron and Stanhope determined how it might best be used. The printing presses were set up in an abandoned warehouse.

Xanthos found Stanhope a haughty and unfriendly Englishman whose conceit and pedantry were in sharp contrast to Byron's friendliness and charm. Within a few days of his arrival, the two men began to quarrel. Stanhope accused Byron of adopting "the contrived and perverted ways of the Turks" and pressed on him the importance of quickly establishing a newspaper to confirm the London Greek Committee's belief in a free press.

"I also believe in a free press!" Byron said to Xanthos after Stanhope had left. "But I don't believe Greece is ready because most Greeks cannot yet read. Besides, I question why Stanhope with his smug English superiority should have a monopoly on running any newspaper! Does he really understand Greece and the Greeks?"

Despite Byron's reservations, within a couple of weeks, Stanhope had the presses running and published a paper called the *Greek Chronicle*. The slogan on its front page read, "The Greatest Good of the Greatest Number." Its circulation in Greece, Byron said scornfully, was forty copies. As if to defy and aggravate Byron still further, Stanhope started a second paper, the *Greek Telegraph*, whose slogan was, "The World our Country and Doing Good our Religion."

Yet, for all of his haughtiness and vanity, Stanhope proved capable of achieving some worthwhile goals. He set up a school and a dispensary, using Byron's and the committee's medical stores. Yet, when Stanhope finally left Missolonghi for Athens to introduce some of his projects for the Greeks there, Byron was heartfelt in his expressions of relief.

"Stanhope is the quintessential Englishman," he told Xanthos. "All his endeavors, wise and foolish, stem from his vainglorious feelings that he is superior to everyone else."

All through February, Byron waited impatiently for the arrival of firemaster William Parry. When word was brought to him that Parry's ship had been sighted and was anchoring in the Missolonghi harbor, Byron was jubilant.

"Now, Xanthos, by God, we'll see some action!" Byron cried. "Enough sitting around enduring endless petitions. The time has come for us to take the field and strike a blow at the Turks!"

Byron led a colorful contingent of fifty mounted Suliots down to the harbor to greet Parry. Xanthos, who was not present, imagined their first meeting to have been boisterous and effusive. A short while later, Byron brought the firemaster back to his headquarters and introduced him to the staff as well as Xanthos.

Parry was a big, strongly built man with a shock of unkempt red hair. His huge hand enfolded the Xanthos's hands in a powerful grip.

There was something impressive about the firemaster, and Xanthos understood the confidence Byron felt about his arrival.

Byron had arranged for the sailors on board Parry's ship and the Suliots to unload the ship's cargo of weaponry and then transport it to be stored in an abandoned Turkish seraglio, the largest building in Missolonghi.

The letters Byron had received about Parry praised him as a master of all the latest weaponry and, in particular, that he had been the right-hand man of General Congreve, the inventor of the Congreve rocket, which had been used against the French fleet before Trafalgar and then later at Waterloo. Byron expected Parry not only to have brought a supply of rockets with him but also to have the ability to manufacture additional ones at Missolonghi.

But, to Byron's bitter disappointment, Parry's ship did not carry any Congreve rockets. What was even more distressing was that neither Parry nor the mechanics he had brought with him had the faintest idea how to manufacture a Congreve rocket. Far from being an expert in weaponry, Parry's sole previous experience had come from his service as a firemaster in the British navy with knowledge only in basic firepower. Parry proved as painful a disappointment to Byron and Mavrokordatos as Missolonghi was for Parry.

"In all my travels around the globe," Parry grumbled to Xanthos and Wyndham, "I doubt I've ever come across a more godforsaken place! I vow I've seen pigsties brimming with slop more appetizing!"

With each day that passed, Xanthos perceived that Parry seemed to be all bluster offering little substance. Beneath his surface joviality, he was belligerent and quarrelsome. He argued with his own technicians, clashed with the Philhellene officers who had knowledge of weaponry and challenged him, and bickered bitterly with the Greeks.

For all the disillusionment Byron felt in Parry's lack of experience about weapons, he appeared to take a perverse liking to the loud, swaggering seaman. Byron enjoyed Parry's scurrilous and hilarious descriptions of the various Greek leaders. Xanthos believed that Byron also found Parry's crude, candid language a happy relief from the affectations of the foreign officers, the sneering superiority of Stanhope, and the tortuous subtlety of the Greek primates who could never say what they really meant. Byron also appreciated Parry's faith in brandy as a cure for every human infirmity. The two men shared a number of intemperate drinking episodes.

"He may be a rogue who does not understand what it means to act responsibly," Byron described Parry to Xanthos, "but the man is unafraid to boldly speak the truth as he sees it."

Meanwhile, despite the absence of the expected artillery, plans for the attack on Lepanto were finalized. By the end of February, everything seemed ready for the momentous undertaking. The first-wave assault was to begin with an advance guard of Suliots commanded by Byron and his chief aide, Pietro Gamba. Wyndham, accompanied by Mavrokordatos, would follow with a contingent of Philhellenes.

But on the day scheduled for the attack, the Suliots refused to move, once again demanding more pay. They also insisted that Byron should appoint two generals, two colonels, two captains, and about 150 junior officers from their force of five hundred men. Each of these appointments was to be allotted an officer's pay.

When Mavrokordatos brought word of these demands, Byron burst into a violent fit of temper and cried that he would have nothing more to do with the "scurrilous wretches!" Mavrokordatos, aided by Wyndham and Pietro Gamba, pleaded in vain with the unruly Suliots. They would not budge from their extravagant demands, which caused the Philhellenes to begin mocking the Suliots as cowards. That produced a battle in which the two sides actually fired on each other. A Swedish officer was killed, and the Suliots besieged the arsenal to appropriate the weapons and ammunition stored there.

In the midst of all the turmoil, Byron fell ill with what everyone feared was an epileptic fit. But despite the pleas of Dr. Bruno that Byron remain in his bed, when it appeared a full-scale war between Suliots and Philhellenes was about to erupt, Byron ordered the Suliot captains to his office. His servants helped him struggle into his full-dress uniform. While they waited in the office for the Suliots, Xanthos saw Byron trembling, his face flushed with fever. But when the Suliots came crowding into his office, blustering and threatening, the man they had heard was seriously ill confronted them with so fierce and martial a demeanor, they were shocked into silence.

"You are descended of heroic figures in world history!" Byron stormed at them. "Now, on the eve of a battle that may add your names to that glorious legacy, you quarrel and rebel! You make me regret the day I journeyed so far to be here with you in Missolonghi! You will receive the pay you have coming to this day, and then I want you gone!"

The Suliot captains and the soldiers in the office squirmed and muttered, overwhelmed by the anger of the regally dressed English lord. Finally, they filed sullenly from his office. After they were gone, Byron collapsed in his chair, his face ashen. He asked for his servants to help him undress and return to bed.

Later that evening, while at dinner with Wyndham, Xanthos spoke of Byron's plight.

"He was magnificent today in the way he confronted the Suliots," Xanthos said, "but for so proud a man, he could hardly have suffered a worse humiliation. He came to Missolonghi dreaming of leading his troops into battle and then failed to lead them from his compound. His enemies will savor his defeat."

"In these last weeks and with all I have learned of Greek politics, I cannot help but believe that Lord Byron's mission has been doomed to failure from the beginning," Wyndham said. "He came to Missolonghi as a foreigner to turn unruly brigands into a disciplined force and to merge them with European volunteers who mistrusted them. Meanwhile, men like Mavrokordatos are so blinded by their own self-interest that instead of warning him of what dilemmas lay ahead, they flattered him and watched him collapse into the chaos of this mutiny and failure."

It seemed to Xanthos that he also bore blame for Byron's plight. During the years he had spent with Kolokotronis, he had gained firsthand knowledge of the intrigues that engulfed Greek politics. He should have warned Byron of what, in retrospect, seemed inevitable. But he was also in Missolonghi as part of that intrigue, his mission to gain money for the general. His own loyalty to Kolokotronis had taken precedence, and a warning to the English poet might have been a betrayal of that trust.

After the failure of the planned assault on Lepanto, Byron's health and spirit seemed to fail. He spent a good part of each day in bed or sitting listlessly in his office. He became irritated over trifles and seemed in the grip of a growing depression. Dr. Bruno and Pietro

Gamba tried to persuade him to return to Cephalonia, a healthier
island in which to recuperate, but Byron refused.

"How can I retreat?" he lamented to Xanthos. "I cannot quit Greece
while there is still a chance of my being of any help! I must remain
loyal to my mission!"

He had lost much of his enthusiasm for learning Greek, and there
were days when Xanthos did not see him. Yet, from time to time
during the month of March, Byron sent word for him to visit.

On one such day when Benjamin Lewis brought word that Byron
wished him to visit, Xanthos found the ailing poet reclining on one
of the sofas in his office. Despite the heat of the afternoon, Byron was
covered with a blanket, his face moist with perspiration. His Newfoundland, Lyon, lay beside the couch, and, when Xanthos entered,
Byron was gently stroking the dog's ear.

"You know, Xanthos," Byron said pensively, "a dog will never lie
to you, nor will he deceive you."

He asked Xanthos to read to him, something from Herodotus's
history of the Greek wars against the Persians. For almost an hour,
Xanthos read passages from the ancient historian. He thought Byron
had fallen asleep, but when he paused in his reading, Byron opened
his eyes.

"The Greeks of that age were heroic figures facing adversity," Byron
said. "They overcame what seemed certain defeat and won their place
in history." His voice sounded weary and melancholy. "Another lesson
from Herodotus is how, when life grows burdensome, death becomes
for man a refuge."

In this time, Xanthos learned that Dr. Bruno was treating Byron by
bleeding him with leeches, which accounted for his pale complexion.
He seemed thin and on edge and feeling a nameless dread.

"I find myself recalling events from my childhood," Byron told
Xanthos. "The pain and shame I endured because I was lame. The
yearning I felt for the love and closeness of my mad mother. It was
as Homer wrote in the *Odyssey*, 'Thrice she spoke, and I longed to
embrace my dead mother's ghost. Thrice I tried to clasp her image,
and thrice it slipped through my hands, like a shadow, like a dream.'"
He sighed. "There are times I envy Shelley's swift death."

"Your presence in Greece has been an inspiration to so many all across this country, Your Lordship," Xanthos said in an effort to relieve the poet's melancholy.

Suddenly, inexplicably, Byron improved. When Xanthos arrived at his headquarters one morning, he found Byron dressed and ready for a ride, his mood more buoyant than it had been in weeks.

"Xanthos, in the grip of my illness, I had a revelation!" Byron cried. "Freedom from despair can only be attained by a brave heart resolved to ride forward and not flinch from the enemy's onslaught!" He laughed vigorously. "Now to launch this new regimen, Pietro Gamba and I are going to take a ride today! I have been confined to these dismal rooms for too long. I need air, even the malodorous air of Missolonghi!"

Dr. Bruno, alerted of Byron's intention to ride out, came anxiously to dissuade him.

"There are dark clouds gathering and a threat of rain, Your Lordship," the physician warmed. "In your weakened condition, it might not be wise to venture out."

"Nonsense!" Byron said and flashed his beguiling smile. "Soldiers in the field fight in all kinds of storms. I should be able to endure mere rain!"

But Dr. Bruno's fears proved true. At the end of the day, Byron and Pietro Gamba returned, soaked and cold. They had been caught in a severe thunderstorm and been drenched. Byron was put back to bed.

To treat his assorted disorders, another medical specialist, Dr. Julius Millingen, educated in England and a graduate of the Edinburgh Royal College of Physicians, traveled to Missolonghi. From the beginning, the diminutive, anxious Dr. Bruno and the towering, gloomy Dr. Millingen disliked one another and had trouble agreeing on their diagnosis and the course of Byron's treatment. The only thing on which they could agree was that Byron required more bleeding. Xanthos heard Byron's adamant refusal.

"Is bleeding the only word each of you has in your vocabulary?" Byron cried, weakness making his voice shrill. "You have bled me empty! I vow neither of you will be satisfied until you have every last drop of blood out of my veins and leave my carcass dry as bone!"

But as Byron's condition worsened, and his protests became weaker, the doctors prevailed in their treatment and continued to attach the leeches to his flesh. A catastrophe was narrowly averted when the leeches came too close to Byron's temporal artery. He recovered, but more of his strength had been drained from his body. It seemed obvious to everyone in the household that Byron was dying.

In those days of his illness, Byron's headquarters teemed with activity, a swarm of captains and primates anxious to have their demands satisfied before the English poet died. Mavrokordatos was no longer among the petitioners, because as rumors began to circulate of another civil war breaking out among the Greek factions, he left Missolonghi for Athens to meet and ally himself with Odysseus Androutsos. Xanthos later learned that Mavrokordatos and Androutsos planned a council of chieftains at Salona.

To protect Byron from the crush of petitioners, Pietro Gamba set up a contingent of Philhellene officers as guards around Byron's house and placed others at the door of his bedroom. They were given strict instructions to admit only the physicians and those individuals Byron asked specifically to see. Byron began complaining of violent headaches and of severe pain in parts of his body. Once, in the presence of Xanthos, Gamba, and the two physicians, Byron cried out.

"I am in terrible pain! If I must die, then let me die, but I cannot bear this pain!"

He began to run a high fever, and while in the throes of it, he reaffirmed the prediction made by the soothsayer his mother had consulted, that he should beware his thirty-sixth year.

Xanthos was among those few individuals Byron requested to visit him. He sat beside the bed that held the pale-faced poet in the sickroom with the oppressive smell of impending death. Byron's cheeks had receded into the hollows, and his large luminous eyes had become even more prominent. His hair had the dry, brittle look of straw. An odor of rank sweat and decay rose from his body.

"You know I have grown very fond of you, Xanthos," Byron said wistfully during one of the visits. "You remind me of the close relationship I once had with Shelley. We spent hours talking of poetry and literature, of life and of death."

"And you know how fond I have grown of you, Your Lordship," Xanthos said earnestly. "I also feel a great admiration for all you have done and are doing for Greece. God grant you the strength to survive, and you will aid us still more."

He wasn't deceiving Byron. Xanthos had ceased thinking about his mission for Kolokotronis to obtain the London committee's money. He had grown genuinely fond of the volatile, capricious poet and regarded his illness with the empathy and concern of a friend.

"When you write in your history of my life and death in Greece," Byron said, "I know I can trust the things you record about me will be honest and faithful to my feelings." A faint, wan tremor of a smile creased his cheeks. "Perhaps you will become my faithful Thucydides."

"I will try to be worthy of you and of Thucydides, Your Lordship," Xanthos said.

"I have asked you before to cease using that ridiculous appellation," Byron said wearily. "I am no longer lord or any other foolishly titled mortal but a poor wretch expiring in a foreign land."

In what became their last visit together in mid-April, while the churches of Missolonghi and the town's inhabitants celebrated the Christian rituals of Easter, the poet spoke of Lukas.

"You are a perceptive man, Xanthos," he said. "You know I love the boy."

"I do understand," Xanthos said quietly.

"I have had other infatuations," Byron said, "but this one seems to me more profound than any I have ever experienced before. Perhaps . . . perhaps it is because I sense it may be my last."

"Has he been here to visit you?"

"He comes when I send for him," Byron said, "but he says little. He sits beside my bed watching me, and I fear he does not wish me to recover. I ask nothing from him now but to be able to gaze upon his beauty and, perhaps, have him offer me a few words of affection such as one might show a sick dog." He made an effort to shrug. "But both of us understand that love must be freely given."

His eyes, sad and reflective, gazed earnestly at Xanthos.

"I know that you and Wyndham came here at the behest of General Kolokotronis to gain money from me for his cause," Byron said. "That is your purpose, isn't it?"

Xanthos nodded.

"And Lukas?" Byron asked, his voice so low Xanthos could barely hear. "Knowing my weakness, the general also sent Lukas here to ensnare me and win my favor in your cause?"

"That is true, Your Lordship." Xanthos had never uttered words about which he felt more ashamed.

Byron sensed his distress. "Don't disturb yourself with remorse, my friend," he said, a weak smile fluttering his lips. "The youth could be commanded to come to Missolonghi but no king or general can command a person to love. Still, I'm thankful that for all these weeks I've had your heartwarming friendship and grateful that I've also had the beauty of Lukas to look upon and to love. It is a vision I will carry with me on my pilgrimage into eternity . . . "

Expressing the truth of his emotions about Lukas had exhausted him, and Byron slept for a while. Xanthos waited silently beside his bed fearing that any movement he made might disrupt his rest. After a while, Byron opened his eyes.

"Still here?" he asked in a low voice.

"I'll remain with you as long as you wish," Xanthos said.

"Thank you, friend Xanthos. Now let me share with you what others will someday read. You will understand."

Byron fumbled for some papers beside his pillow and found what he was seeking. Holding the paper in his trembling hands, he began to read.

> 'Tis time the heart should be unmoved,
>   Since others it hath ceased to move,
> Yet though I cannot be beloved,
> Still let me love!
>
> My days are in the yellow leaf:
>   The flowers and fruits of love are gone
> The worm, the canker, and the grief,
>   Are mine alone!

The page slipped from Byron's hand, and Xanthos moved to retrieve it. Byron waved him away and continued reciting the poem by heart.

Tread those reviving passions down.
    Unworthy manhood! Unto thee
Indifferent should the smile or frown
    Of Beauty be.

Seek out, less often sought than found,
    A soldier's grave, for thee the best;
Then look around and choose thy ground
    And take thy rest.

Xanthos left Byron sleeping that afternoon and returned to his
own lodgings. He was there when he received word from Wyndham
that Byron had died. It was Easter Monday, the nineteenth of April,
in the year 1824.

In the days that followed, as government authorities and the primates ordained a national period of mourning and planned a great,
lavish funeral, Xanthos began another letter to Kolokotronis.

All of Missolonghi is in mourning for Byron's death. I am
sure, General, that when the news circulates farther, that all
of Europe will be moved by his death. The feeling will be that
this extraordinary poet who so loved Greece came to die on
her behalf in a cause worth fighting and dying for. It is true
that he failed at Missolonghi, failed to reconcile the Greek
factions, failed to maintain discipline and amity among the
various forces here, and, finally, in his single military undertaking failed to capture the fortress at Lepanto. But all these
failures will be overshadowed by the enormity of his sacrifice.
His spirit will be as the phoenix resurrected from the ashes.
With all my heart, I believe his death will become a "dying
into life" and will do more to win Greece its freedom than
anything he might have accomplished had he lived.

CHAPTER
FIVE

During the centuries of slavery under the sultan's rule, the inhabitants of the mainland of Greece endured the greatest hardship and suffering. Meanwhile, the Greek islanders to the east of the mainland, also subjects of the sultan, paid their taxes and were left unhindered to conduct their commercial trading along the ports of the Black Sea. A few islands prospered in spite of their bondage, and among them, the island of Psara had been especially blessed with good fortune. Its bustling trade not only filled its own ships with cargo but also that of ships from other islands it leased for transport.

A few of Psara's shipowners, not satisfied with this prosperity, sought illicit bounty by engaging in privateering, their ships preying on towns along the coast of Asia Minor. But this was true of only a minority. Most of the Psariot merchants and captains were respected as principled commercial agents from Marseilles to Odessa and from Moscow to Alexandria.

When the revolution in Greece broke out in 1821, Psara joined the islands of Hydra and Spetsia and a few smaller islets in converting its merchant brigs into ships for battle. Although their vessels had carried cannon for protection against Barbary pirates, additional guns were installed on the upper and lower decks, the masts of the brigs reinforced, the spars and rigging bolstered. The ships' captains turned their concerns from trade to war.

For Leonidas Kontos, captain of the brig *Odysseus*, the war had made the sea his home. Since the outbreak of the revolution, he rarely spent more than a few days at a time in his port of Psara. His seasons were passed at sea, scanning the horizon for enemy sails, and then tracking and harassing the larger Turkish frigates. These skirmishes sometimes resulted in battles and, at other times, if conditions did not favor the Greek ships, prudent retreats to keep their vessels out of range of the heavier firepower of the Turkish frigates.

Seas and oceans were among the mightiest of earth's powers, as devastating in their fury as earthquakes, volcanic eruptions, and deadly hurricanes. Although there were days when the *Odyssey* lay becalmed without a single sail flapping, at other times the ship was rocked and battered in fierce gales. The worst of these brutal storms left their ship with damaged sails and splintered masts, requiring the *Odyssey* to falter into port to make repairs. They used these intervals to refill their casks of water and reprovision their larder with fruits, vegetables, hardtack, and dried mutton.

To compensate the crew for their weeks at sea, Leonidas granted his sailors a few nights of leave when they made port. He knew the seamen would stagger back to the ship in the morning, besotted with drink and smelling of harbor whores. But men sequestered from spirits and women too long became quarrelsome. After a long spell at sea, at least a half dozen of his crew would be confined to sickbay because of knife wounds incurred in shipboard quarrels.

From the age of ten when Leonidas made his first voyage with his father, who captained the fine brig *Miltiades,* he had loved the days and nights spent at sea. He savored the moment when the sheets went aloft, and the masts billowed with white sail. He'd sit near the helmsman, whose strong, sure hands controlled the great ship, and anticipated the day when he'd hold the giant wheel in his own hands. He'd spend hours on the quarterdeck, watching the forecastle men, the strongest and most valorous of the crew charged with the headsails and studding sails of the topmast, working aloft with confidence and skill. He recalled those journeys with his father as a series of mostly tranquil days broken only by the surging waves and sounds of the sea and by the cries of gulls soaring above the peaks of the masts.

During these early journeys, Leonidas became a favorite among the crew, who spoiled him and regaled him with stories of sea monsters and ghost ships that had sailed the seas since the time of the legendary Greek kings.

"Aye, sonny," an old grizzled seaman named Demetrios told him, "a ship is a living thing, breathing like we breath, bearing a spirit of its own. Treat her fairly, keep her shipshape, and be a fair captain to your crew.

Then, by my word, a time will come when, at night, listening to the creaking of the spars and rigging, you'll hear the ship speaking to you."

Leonidas believed these tales. At night in his berth, he heard the spars and rigging creaking and moaning above him. He asked Demetrios what message the ship was trying to convey.

"Don't be impatient, sonny," Demetrios reassured him. "You got to sail for years before you understand what a ship has to tell you. Believe me, someday you'll know what I mean."

In his nineteenth year, Leonidas continued his studies on the nearby island of Chios. He remained there for three years, returning to Psara during the summers, until the year his father was lost in a storm at sea. Leonidas grieved for his passing and for the sailors who perished with him, yet he felt no bitterness against the sea.

He gave up his studies to follow his father's path by taking to the sea. To replace his father's ship *Miltiades* that had been sunk in the storm, he designed and supervised the building of a brig he named *Themistocles,* which was his father's name.

In the years that followed, Leonidas captained the *Themistocles,* sailing the trade routes his father and he had followed to the ports of the Black Sea. During the hours he spent on the bridge, from time to time relieving the helmsman at the wheel, he considered himself among the most fortunate of men. Captain of a splendid vessel on a sea as free as God's sky, the sails snapping and whipping in the wind, the sleek ship's hull skimming and dipping into the waves.

Those journeys Leonidas made in the years before the war lasted only a few weeks, and then he'd eagerly return home to his wife, Aspasia, and their three daughters, Asmene, Caliope, and Nikki. When his ship anchored in the harbor of Psara, he'd be among the first to leap into the longboat to be rowed ashore. He'd hurry through the noisy port teeming with peddlers hawking their wares, pausing only to buy a bouquet of fresh-cut flowers. As he entered the great iron-hinged front door of his dwelling, his beloved daughters ran to greet him, clutching his legs, crying their greetings. Beyond their golden-haired heads, he'd see his wife, Aspasia, still as strikingly beautiful after bearing three children as she had been when they first married.

Aspasia's shimmering blonde tresses, pale-green eyes, and flawless complexion contrasted starkly with even the most beautiful of the island women, who were dark-haired and dark-eyed with olive-tinted

skin. She had inherited her golden hair and complexion from an an-
cestor who was a Venetian princess at a time when the Venetians
occupied regions of Greece.

With the open windows carrying the languid scents of hibiscus and
bougainvillea into their bedroom, their desire nurtured by the weeks
of separation, Leonidas and Aspasia made fervent love. With the faint
light of the lanterns glistening over his wife's slender legs and thighs
and across her breasts and delicate nipples, Leonidas fantasized once
again that his wife's flawless beauty might have been fashioned by a
classical sculptor like Phidias. Then, a benevolent deity who could not
bear such beauty to remain cold and inanimate stone transformed
her into life.

All those joyful reunions belonged to a time of peace. Now, absent
from Psara for months at a time, sailing endlessly from one horizon
toward another, he had only his memories of home and those nights
of love to console his loneliness.

When the *Odyssey* was anchored in a foreign port for repairs or to
take on provisions, Leonidas did not join his crew on shore but chose
to remain on board, secluded in his cabin, drinking despondently
from a decanter of brandy. He envisioned his wife and daughters in
Psara, sitting before the large fireplace in their home, the girls playing
while Aspasia sewed or read.

In those times, his imagination fortified by the intoxicating brandy,
his longing to see his family became so compelling, he felt if he closed
his eyes and stretched out his hand, he could touch them.

During their time at sea, the *Odyssey* crew practiced daily gunnery
drills under the stern tutelage of the ship's first mate and gunnery
specialist, Skylos Yarkas. The Psariot seaman, who had been sailing
with Leonidas since the voyages he'd made with his father, towered
six inches above six feet, with a body as lean and robust as a mast.
His other distinctive features were the tattoos on his right and left
forearms, one embossed with an angel, the other with a devil.

"I had them engraved onto my carcass by an artist in Algiers," the
first mate told Leonidas. "They're there to remind Skylos he needs to
balance his intemperate appetites." His broad grin revealed a stockade
of strong, white teeth. "While I could never abide living as an angel,
I must also beware the bloody devil enslaving my soul."

Signaling the start of gunnery practice, Skylos's strident whistle sent the crew scurrying to their stations. The seamen swiftly tugged off the cannons lashings, pulled the guns inboard, removed the wadding from the muzzles, and sponged the barrels.

"Run them out!" cried Skylos.

The wheels of the gun carriages rumbled along the deck as the crew strained against the tackle to thrust the cannons' heavy muzzles back through the gunports. To conserve ammunition, the men usually practiced without firing cannonballs. But, one day every few weeks, in more realistic rehearsals, the cannons were loaded and fired.

"Faster, you worthless sons of luckless fathers!" Skylos shouted at the crew during these practices. "Do you think the bloody Turks will wait while you fumble at the breech? Load those barrels faster, or you'll find a Mussulman cannonball blown up your ass!"

The gun crews increased the pace of their efforts, swiftly inserting powder, cartridges, and ball into the cannons, jamming rope yarn solidly between the powder and wads.

"Quicker, Vasili, quicker!" Skylos bellowed at one of the seamen lagging behind the others. "Stop worrying about your wife cuckolding you with some landlubber, and move your lazy shanks!"

Standing to windward, the seamen primed the touchholes with powder, heaved on the tackle, and pushed the gun carriages forward beyond the ports. The gun chiefs ignited the powder on the base rings. The balls thundered from the cannons, the force of the detonation hurling the gun carriages backwards against the bulky breeching ropes. Explosions and geysers of water marked the entry of the balls into the water about two hundred yards distant from the hull of the ship.

"Under a minute, captain, and landing dead on target!" Skylos said gleefully to Leonidas. "I vow our boys are still the best gunners in the fleet!"

It was true that the crew of the *Odyssey* was composed of good and loyal seamen, their bonds forged by the months they lived and fought together at sea. The commander of the fleet from Psara, Admiral Konstantine Kanaris, who captained the *Pericles,* praised the *Odyssey* as a model for other ships because of the discipline, skill, and fidelity of its crew.

Unfortunately, those virtues weren't always evident on the ships that sailed under the flags of the islands of Hydra and Spetsia, whose fleets Psara joined in battle. Their ships sometimes held selfish and unruly seamen who scorned discipline and who, at times, even refused to sail to battle unless they had received their full pay. On more than one occasion, all of Greece had been shamed by the spectacle of seamen disobeying the injunction to join their fellow Greeks in battle and, instead, forcing their captains to sail back to their home islands.

In this time of war, the Greek seamen sorely needed discipline as well as valor and skill if they were to successfully battle the Turks. The Turks had more-imposing battle fleets with heavier warships that carried twelve- and eighteen-pound cannons. The largest of the Muslim frigates, awesome juggernauts of the sea, had crews of as many as six hundred men and huge, twenty-four-pound cannon that when firing and striking a brig broadside could blast and tear the smaller vessel into fragments.

The principal resource the Greeks had to rely on to combat the more powerful Turkish ships was the superior seamanship of their crews. During the years of slavery, Greek islanders had been conscripted as sailors into the Turkish navy and merchant marine, service that Turks thought too menial for a devout Muslim. When the war broke out, those seasoned seamen formed the backbone of the Greek battle fleet. They were aided by the daring of their comrades acting as bruloteers, the incendiaries who manned the fire ships.

The fire ship, a brig or brigantine primed and loaded with explosives, had to be sailed under cover of fog or darkness to ram the hull of a Turkish warship. The powder train was then ignited, and the fire ship was swiftly abandoned by its seamen before the hold packed with powder and combustibles exploded. The maneuver required precise coordination between the lighting of the fuses and the seamen fleeing the ship. The bottom of the sea held the bleached bones of Greek bruloteers who had not escaped in time and perished on the decks of their flaming ships.

In the years since the war began, the Greek fleets had achieved some stunning successes in the use of fire ships. Leonidas's *Themistocles* was successfully used as a fire ship in the burning of the Turkish frigate at Eressos in May of 1821. Leonidas with Papanikolis, his fellow Psariot, had manned the ship for its final journey in a feat that became renowned in all of Greece. Another fire ship captained by the great Hydriote Admiral Andreas Miaoulis later destroyed the Turkish flagship in the Dardanelles in December of 1821. Other fire ships sank Turkish frigates in the battle of the straits of Spetsia in early September of 1822.

The fear Leonidas lived with during his months at sea was for the safety of his family and the security of his island. His fear had become terror after the destruction of the island of Chios by the Turks in March of 1822. Chios, a much larger island, was like Psara also located perilously close to the mainland of Turkey. The invasion and destruction of Chios by the Turkish Admiral Kara Ali had been brutal and devastating. Along with the sailors under the Turkish admiral, mobs came in boats from the mainland of Turkey to join in the ravaging of the island. As a warning to those islanders who dared to resist, the merciless Ali hung a hundred Chiot elders and senior officials from the trees leading along the road to the harbor. After the massacre, the pathway became known across all of Greece as the Road of the Martyrs.

The Turks butchered the men of Chios with shot and sword while thousands of Chiot women and children, many of them raped, were shipped to the slave markets of Constantinople, Egypt, and Barbary. The beauty of these women and children attracted Muslim purchasers from across Asia Minor.

Following the massacre at Chios were rumors that the islands of Kasos and Psara, both also enticing targets, might be the sultan's next goals.

The population of Psara had numbered about seven thousand, but in 1824, so many refugees from Chios, Kydonies, and Smyrna had fled to the island that the population exceeded twelve thousand. Hoping to escape the fate of Chios, the Psariots fortified their small island with two hundred artillery pieces mounted on the ramparts above the harbor. In addition, two thousand Rumeliot soldiers, the mercenaries called *armatoli*, were hired to aid their island's defense. The islanders, women as well as men, daily practiced shooting their pistols and muskets. Fishing sloops stationed on alert in the sea between the island and the coast of Turkey watched for warships leaving Anatolian ports and bearing a course toward the island.

Leonidas knew that despite these precautions, Psara could not withstand a major Turkish assault. Foreign officers from German and French armies with military knowledge had pointed out the defects of the island's batteries. They also warned that the mercenaries hired to protect the island couldn't be trusted not to bargain with the Turks to save their own lives. During battles in the past, other bands of *armatoli* would accept the assignment and the pay and, when confronted by the enemy, would abandon their posts.

But the Psariots, ignoring the counsel of leaders like Admiral Kanaris who had fought the Turks and understood how tenacious and ruthless they could be, arrogantly disregarded the warnings. Psariot leaders spoke contemptuously of the Turks as "cowards" and of Sultan Mahmud as a "tyrant and fool" who would not find Psara as easy a target as Chios.

In a council meeting, Leonidas heard one of the island elders, Mamounis, a vain and stupid man proclaim, "Any Turk that dares set foot on our island will gain nothing but his grave!"

Leonidas did not share that foolish bravado and had expressed his fears to the island's leaders on more than one occasion. Faced with their obstinate refusal to pay attention to the many warnings, he urged Aspasia to flee with their daughters to safety.

"You must understand, my darling," Leonidas pleaded. "Fears for your safety bedevil my days and nights at sea. The thought that you or the girls might come to harm torments me."

"Where in Greece today, in the midst of war, can anyone be truly safe?" Aspasia asked quietly. "Then there is our family honor and pride. Many of the seamen who serve with you also have wives, sons, and daughters on the island, and they are without the means to flee their homes for sanctuary elsewhere. It would shame us all if the wife and children of their captain fled."

He acknowledged the truth in her reasons for not leaving, but after the destruction of Chios, he finally convinced Aspasia to send their daughters to relatives living on one of the islands closer to mainland Greece. Separated from their home, the girls pined for their mother and father. When several months passed, assailed by repeated pleas from Aspasia and his daughters, Leonidas reluctantly allowed the girls to return home. Now he lived each day and night with the fear that the war might entrap his family and his island.

By the spring of 1824, the *Odyssey* had been at sea for more than three months and during that time had fought several battles with Turkish warships. In the middle of May, it sailed to a rendezvous planned with other Psariot ships off the northern coast of the island of Euboea.

After the *Odyssey* anchored alongside a score of Psariot ships in the harbor, Leonidas received a message relayed from the flagship of the fleet, the brig *Pericles* captained by Admiral Kanaris, calling the captains to counsel.

In the sea battles since the beginning of the war, Admiral Kanaris had not only proved himself a valorous captain but also an astute and resourceful patriot in the tumultuous politics of the revolution. He was a voice of reason among the various warring factions, recognized by all as a man of character, and, unlike some other Greek leaders, willing to sacrifice personal ambition for the cause of his nation's freedom.

The only other captain in the island fleets whose ability and renown matched that of Kanaris was Admiral Miaoulis, who had also confirmed his brilliant mastery of war at sea by winning several major battles against the Turks including his great victory at Bodrum (the ancient Halicarnassus). So laudatory were his achievements that the admiral had been honored in a popular song sung across Greece.

> Were there but two like Miaoulis
> They had burned the Turkish fleet entire
> Were there another ship like his
> They had finished off the Armada!

Leonidas wasn't concerned which admiral might be the greater hero. He was thankful that Greece had two such valorous leaders in its struggle for freedom.

Leonidas ascended the rope ladder from his longboat onto the *Pericles* and joined a score of captains assembled about Kanaris on the quarterdeck. They greeted Leonidas and then returned to crudely taunting one another.

"Nikolaos, you're the only sea captain I know who grows fatter at sea!" Captain Anagnos said, pointing derisively at another ship's commander. "You must have provisioned your larder from the table of some affluent pasha!"

"Man, if you can no longer distinguish between fat and muscle," Captain Nikolaos retorted tartly, "the sea air must be causing your eyesight to falter!"

"Dimitri," Captain Cosmas said, "what happened to your ship in that gale last month off Kasos? We lost sight of the *Apollo* for almost ten days."

"The storm tore down part of our foremast, and we had to put into port for repairs," Captain Dimitri responded."

"I've been told you fancied a Circassian woman in that port and lingered an extra few days to savor her favors before putting back to sea."

"That's a damnable lie spread by that scurrilous Hydriote Kalimeris!" the captain said indignantly. "Within an hour after our mast was mended, we put to sea!"

"My friends," Kanaris soothed the tumult, "let us save our taunts and barbs for the Muslims. Dimitri, calm your ruffled temper with another tumbler of this fine Cypriot brandy."

After the men had quieted, Kanaris spoke. "The reason for this meeting is to share with you distressing news I have from Trilakis, who is in touch with our agents in Asia Minor. The captains waited in silence for Kanaris to continue. "In this last year, the war in the Peloponnesus has not gone well for the Sultan. The armies of Anagnostaras and Kolokotronis have defeated the Turks in several battles. The klephts hold the mountain strongholds. Our ships have prevented the Turkish fleet from reinforcing their besieged fortresses along the coast. The sultan, who is frustrated and enraged, has called upon his ally Mohammed Ali of Egypt for help. Ali is sending his son, Ibrahim Pasha, with a powerful army to subdue the revolt. If Ibrahim Pasha manages a landing on Crete and uses that island as a base to move north across the Cretan Sea to invade the Peloponnesus, it will pose the gravest danger to our survival the revolution has yet faced."

"We will defeat him as we have defeated all the other vassals of the sultan!" Captain Yannaros blustered. "When night falls over the Turkish frigates, their captains and crews tremble in fear of our fire ships!"

"We have been fortunate in gaining victories in our battles," Kanaris said, "but Ibrahim Pasha poses a new and dangerous threat to us at sea and on land."

"On a voyage I once made into Cairo before the war, I saw this Ibrahim Pasha," Captain Skandelis said. "The Muslims were celebrating some religious holiday, and this Egyptian monarch was perched like an imperious Roman emperor on a throne reviewing the parade. He is a short, grossly fat man whose face is deeply marked with the scars of some pox. He makes a ridiculous and unimposing figure."

"Whatever his appearance, it would be a mistake to underestimate this man," Kanaris said. "He has had years of military experience. He helped his father suppress the uprising of the Mameluks, who ruled Syria and Egypt, and he led the Egyptian forces to victory against the Wahhabis in Arabia. He has in his service veteran officers of Napoleon's armies, who have taught his soldiers how to campaign in the European manner. He also shares the hardships of his soldiers in the manner of Alexander. The man has also demonstrated that he can be as merciless as the Roman general Tacitus—willing to destroy a city, kill its inhabitants, and call it peace. His goal is to annihilate the Greek population of the Peloponnesus and repeople the land with settlers from Egypt and Africa."

The captains broke into an angry muttering, and some referred to Ibrahim Pasha as a "monster" and a "barbarian."

"Are the Greek generals in the Peloponnesus aware of this threat from Ibrahim Pasha?" Captain Yannaros asked.

"At the same time Trilakis sent me news of Ibrahim Pasha, he dispatched couriers into the Peloponnesus to alert the generals and primates," Kanaris replied. "Those couriers brought word that Kolokotronis and Petrobey are assembling an army south of Corinth to confront Ibrahim Pasha. Makriyannis is also joining them with a force from the western mainland. They will confront Ibrahim Pasha if he lands his army in the Peloponnesus, but our ships must prevent those landings. We must also prevent his fleet from supplying food and ammunition to the Turkish fortresses we are besieging."

"How large an army does this Egyptian butcher have at his disposal?" Captain Nikolaos asked.

"Trilakis estimates Ibrahim will have around fifty thousand well-trained soldiers," Kanaris said. "He will also carry numerous cannon. His fleet will number three hundred ships, at least fifty of them heavily armed frigates."

As the captains grasped the magnitude of the enemy's force they would confront, they fell into a gloomy silence.

"God help us," Captain Makris said. "Even with the ships of Hydra and Spetsia, we cannot muster more than a hundred vessels, none matching the firepower of their frigates."

"We will continue the tactics we have used in the past," Kanaris said quietly. "We will hound and bedevil them while staying out of range of their cannons. When we locate their ships in port or at anchor, we'll attack with our fire ships."

The captains broke into a tumult of voices, offering advice about the methods to be used in fighting the Turks. Kanaris gestured brusquely for silence.

"I must also tell you that we have another danger besides Ibrahim Pasha to consider," Kanaris said. "You know that Khosref Pasha has had his fleet of warships anchored for some months in the Dardanelles. Now, perhaps believing that our fleets will be occupied with the movements of Ibrahim Pasha, there is word from our ships watching his movements that he has sailed with his fleet to make port at Mytilene. With that island as his base, he might be planning an attack on Kasos." Kanaris paused again, his countenance as grave as his voice. "Or on Psara . . ."

An uneasy silence settled over the assembled captains. Leonidas felt fear clutch his heart.

"If an imminent threat to Psara exists, we must sail at once to reinforce our island defenses!" Captain Yannaros cried.

"We cannot yet be positive that Khosref Pasha plans to invade Psara," Kanaris said. "Until we know for sure, we are honor bound not to abandon Miaoulis and the Greek fleet for the sake of our own island. If Ibrahim Pasha lands his army in the Peloponnesus, he may crush the revolution. If all of Greece falls before his force, it would be only a matter of time before he attacked Psara as well."

"You're telling us to ignore the threat to our homes and families, Konstantine!" Captain Cosmas spoke in outrage. "Let the mainland Greeks look after their own homes! My first loyalty is to my family and our island!"

"My family faces the same danger as yours on Psara," Kanaris said sternly. "That is true for every man here. Believe me, my first reaction is to sail at once to Psara. But that would be a betrayal of an even greater cause, the struggle for Greek freedom."

The captains fell to sullen muttering, their voices angry.

"Admiral," Leonidas said quietly, "my fear for my family is equal to that of any other man here. But I accept the good sense of what you are saying. Tell us what you wish us to do."

Kanaris nodded approvingly at Leonidas. "We will send the major part of our fleet to join Admiral Miaoulis in preventing Ibrahim Pasha from landing in Crete. We'll also send three of our swiftest brigs to track the movements of Khosref Pasha. If his intentions are to invade Psara, word can be sent to us via the Malta pigeons. We'll then sail as swiftly as we can to join our island's defenses."

"Which of our ships will return to Psara?" Captain Apostolis asked.

"The fastest ones will be sent," Kanaris said. He gestured toward Papanikolis. "Your ship, the *Epaminondas*, is one. Then the *Jason* of the Velisarios brothers and, finally, the *Odyssey* of Leonidas Kontos."

There was some grumbling about the selections but no one could quarrel with the fact that Kanaris had chosen the swiftest brigs.

At the conclusion of the meeting, Kanaris asked Leonidas, Niko-laos, and the Velisarios brothers to remain. He motioned them close around him on the quarterdeck.

"I did not wish to speak of it before the other captains," Kanaris told them, "but Trilakis is certain that Khosref Pasha has chosen Psara as his target. It would provide him the wealthiest prize, and, afterwards, Kasos and even Skorpelos would be easy prey."

"For sure then, it is Psara," Nikolaos said, a tremor in his voice. "God help our island."

"Prayers alone won't help anymore than they helped those poor souls on Chios," Gorgios Velisarios said grimly.

"Even if an attack seems certain and despite our concern for our families, we cannot ignore the greater threat of Ibrahim Pasha," Kana-ris warned. "If every time one of our towns or villages was threatened, portions of the armies rushed to their aid, the revolution would be in chaos. So now, my comrades, let us do what we can to meet the threat. Set sail at once for Psara. Admiral Miaoulis has promised to dispatch two fire ships from his fleet to help us. You will rendezvous with those ships off the coast of Prasonissi, and if the Turks attack our blessed island, then do all you can to repulse them until we are able to join you."

"Konstantine," Demetrios Velisarios said, his voice revealing his frustration, "you have assigned us an impossible task! What can three brigs and two fire ships do against a fleet the size of Khosref Pasha's? How in God's name can we hope to stop them?"

For several moments, Kanaris did not answer. Finally, he said, "My friend, I have no answer for you. I have feared such an assault ever since Chios was destroyed. I don't know what we would be able to accomplish even if our entire Psariot fleet confronts Khosref Pasha. Short of evacuating the entire island population, forsaking our homeland, I don't know what else we can do but battle as valorously as we can."

The captains stood silent, recognizing the harsh truth Kanaris spoke.

"All right, my compatriots," Nikolaos said finally. "Enough talk about what might or might not happen. Let's return to our ships and set sail."

The captains dispersed from the quarterdeck and Kanaris motioned for Leonidas to remain. As the longboats ferrying the captains to their vessels pulled away from the *Pericles,* Kanaris spoke quietly.

"There is a favor I wish to ask," Kanaris said. "You may have heard forecastle rumors about a seaman named Petros Baltas, who sailed as second mate with Captain Kalafatis on the *New Carthage.* That ship was seriously damaged in a battle off Santorini and may never be seaworthy again. Baltas has asked to be reassigned to another ship, and I would like him to sail with you." Kanaris paused. "I must warn you there are seamen who swear the man carries misfortune with him. Before serving on the *New Carthage,* he was chief mate on the *Semiramis* when she was struck broadside by a Turkish warship. Most of her crew was lost, Baltas, once again, among the few who survived." Kanaris sighed. "It isn't only seamen who believe the man to be cursed. There are even captains who would not abide the man crossing their gunwales. So I will fully understand, Leonidas, if you refuse."

"I have heard stories of cursed seamen and doomed ships since my childhood voyages," Leonidas said. "I'd be a poor captain if I allowed them to guide me. Battles are won and lost by the abilities of the seamen and the sturdiness of their ships."

"I knew I could count on your good sense, Leonidas," Kanaris said. "Baltas may also prove helpful. The man is gifted in the surgeon's trade, able to skillfully amputate a mangled arm or leg. He also has a preacher's gifts and has spoken the last rites over those unfortunate seamen whose bodies we sew in shrouds and commit to the sea."

"Any ship at war can always use a good surgeon," Leonidas said. "And we may well have need for this man's preaching abilities, as well."

Back on the *Odyssey*, Leonidas called Skylos to his quarterdeck.

"We'll set full sail at once for Psara," Leonidas said. "As soon as the boat brings one more seaman to join us, send the topsail men aloft."

As Skylos moved to alert the crew, a longboat approached to starboard of the *Odyssey*. A seaman ascended the rope ladder to the deck where Leonidas waited to meet him.

Baltas was a barrel-chested man with craggy features and a face so weather-beaten by wind, rain, and sun that his flesh resembled the grain of an aging tree. He had rust-colored and unruly hair and long sideburns mottled with gray. A metal-beaded necklace bearing an ivory amulet dangled around his throat. He saluted Leonidas with a seaman's big, calloused hand.

"Welcome aboard the *Odyssey*, Baltas."

"You show trust in letting me join your crew, captain, and I thank you," Baltas said, his voice as rough as his face. "There's many a commander would set off a nine-pounder to keep me away."

"Your reputation doesn't concern me," Leonidas said quietly. "Your service on my ship begins today."

At that moment, Skylos joined them. He stared at Baltas and then gazed uneasily at the necklace and amulet around the seaman's throat.

"This is my first mate, Skylos," Leonidas said. "He'll see you are quartered properly." He spoke to Skylos. "This is Petros Baltas, who will sail with us. When he has become familiar with our ship, we'll assign him the duties of a second mate."

Skylos hesitated, and then, a certain foreboding evident in his face, he brusquely thrust out his hand. Baltas grasped it.

"I can tell by your eyes you've heard of me, mate," Baltas grinned.

"Aye, I've heard of you," Skylos said somberly. He turned to Leonidas. "Are we ready to sail, captain?"

Leonidas nodded. Skylos moved to the stairway.

"Stand by the capstan!" he cried, his voice resonating across the ship. "Hands aloft to loose the topsails!"

The *Odyssey*'s seamen scrambled aloft to unfurl the headsails and studding sails of the topmast. In a few moments, the ship's masts and rigging billowed with white sail.

To starboard of the *Odyssey*, the brigs of Papanikolis and the Velisarios brothers were also unfurling sails. Fluttering from the topmasts of each ship was the flag of their island of Psara—anchor and cross against a white background with a red border. On each flag was inscribed "Freedom or Death."

Leonidas felt a surge of pride in his island and confidence in its fighters. They were confronting a vastly superior force, but no alien army could match their zeal to liberate their long-suffering and anguished land. The souls of all those who had perished throughout the centuries of bondage would reinforce their spirits and strengthen their arms.

Within minutes, the *Odyssey* was racing through the open sea, her bowsprit digging into the heavy swells, casting up torrents of water. As twilight fell, they were still favored with a strong breeze. They sailed on under the glow of a full moon, the night sky dotted with stars shining in all their brilliance. On the port and starboard of their racing vessel, waves scudded up as if they were leaping dolphins.

Skylos stood on the quarterdeck beside Leonidas, who held the wheel. The first mate's face was streaked with spray from the waves, and his tall, strong frame braced against the whip of the wind.

"A ship under full sail skimming the sea in a stout breeze!" Skylos cried, his voice almost lost within the clamorous flapping of the sails. "Nothing to match it anywhere on God's earth!"

As Leonidas prepared to retire to his cabin, he asked what provision Skylos had made to quarter Baltas.

"I'll be honest, captain," Skylos said grimly. "The men aren't eager to have him on board let alone anywhere near them in the crew's quarters." He shrugged. "I've strung a second hammock for him in my tight little cabin."

"You know his reputation for spawning disaster?"

"God's truth, captain, after what's befallen the ships he's served on, I hope that voodoo necklace the grizzled old salt wears doesn't prove a noose for us, as well. As for bunking with me," Skylos shrugged, "I've bedded with two-legged species meaner than snakes. Who knows? This ill-omened preacher may even attend to my spiritual needs."

"Your spiritual needs require at least an archbishop!" Leonidas laughed as he waved Skylos good night.

Leonidas descended the stairwell to his cabin. His quarters were small and cramped, his cot suspended from the deck beams. The cabin held a chair, a small bookcase, and a mirror on the bulkhead above a canvas basin. His desk was clamped on the opposite bulkhead, with his sea chest stored beneath it. A wooden hook hanging from the deck beams held his clothing.

Before lying down to sleep, Leonidas wrote the day's entry in his ship's log.

> May 20, 1824: Met with Admiral Kanaris and other Psariot cap-
> tains off the coast of Euboea. Kanaris informed us of the threats
> of Khosref Pasha and Ibrahim Pasha. In response to his order, at
> mid-afternoon we set out with the *Jason* and the *Epaminondas*
> under full sail for Psara. We are sailing in fair weather and hope
> to make Psara in timely fashion.
>
> Petros Baltas, a second mate who is also surgeon and preacher,
> has joined our ship. Our crew has not received his presence
> kindly. I trust he will not prove a troublesome addition.

In a separate, personal log he kept for his Aspasia to read, he made an additional entry.

> May 20, 1824: My dearest: We are sailing for Psara under a strong
> wind so before long I hope to hold you in my arms. Know that I
> think of you and the girls many times during the day and in each
> waking moment of my night. God keep you and our islanders

under his watchful eye. I will sleep for a while now wishing I might be blessed by seeing your beloved face in my dreams.

Leonidas did not know how long he slept when he was shaken awake by the quick, sharp rocking of the hull beneath his cot. He rose quickly and, bracing himself against the desk and walls, slipped into his shoes and ascended the stairwell. The moment he emerged onto the deck, he was buffeted by a strong wind that fought him every step of the way as he lurched and stumbled to join Skylos on the quarterdeck. The first mate was hunched over the helm, using all his strength to hold the wheel steady under the pounding sea. At that moment, the wheel broke free, its spokes whirling. Leonidas joined him, and the two men managed to get the wheel under control once more.

Across the bow of the *Odyssey*, a strip of crimson light was visible along the horizon, a frail harbinger of daylight marooned within black, swirling clouds.

"A devil's storm it is, captain," Skylos cried, his voice almost lost in the wail of wind. "Struck just like that! The topmen took in the studding sails and royals but trying to furl the top-gallant yards, part of the mainsail tore!"

The wind grew stronger, the *Odyssey* rocking and tossing more violently in the sea. Baltas joined them on the quarterdeck, his burly body braced against the power of the gale. He replaced Skylos at the wheel, and the first mate went below to see whether the ship was taking in water. Leonidas and Baltas joined their strength to restrain the wheel from tearing loose.

Across the horizon, once again ragged patches of crimson and purple struggled to start the day. As quickly as slivers of light appeared, the dark clouds plundered them.

Over the port and starboard of their ship, Leonidas witnessed a sea in greater fury than he ever remembered seeing before, the waves cresting as high as the peaks of their masts, water cascading across the decks, drenching the men where they stood. The wind lashed the masts and battered the hull.

Skylos returned, stumbling along the deck, clutching the grab rails until he reached the quarterdeck. Shouting and using hand gestures, he let Leonidas know that the ship had sprung several leaks and, despite the pumps working at full capacity, was taking in water.

For the balance of the day, under a sky dark as night, the howling gale continued. Waves struck the bow, exploding huge pillars of spray. Other waves beat the ship's stern with a sound of thunder.

Leonidas knew his ship could not endure such sustained pounding, and, that afternoon, as he feared, a part of the foremast splintered with a sound like the detonation of an earthquake. If the crippled mast collapsed and shattered the hull, the *Odyssey* would sink with every man on board hurled into the sea.

With the wind and water lashing his face, Leonidas prayed to the ancient and powerful God of his fathers for the salvation of his crew and the salvaging of his ship. In the flashes of lightning that illuminated the quarterdeck, he saw the water-streaked faces of Skylos and Baltas, both men spitting words into the wind. He couldn't be sure whether they were joining him in prayer or cursing the merciless storm.

In his years at sea, Leonidas had experienced storms before, violent gales that had battered and lashed his ship. But the one that struck the *Odyssey* only hours after they'd departed the sanctuary of the harbor at Euboea was the most savage he could ever remember.

More than half his crew, including men who had spent most of their lives at sea, was heaving with seasickness. Leonidas felt his own stomach churning. Meanwhile, each time it seemed the wind might weaken, a fresh squall spawned a cloudburst of rain.

Not until evening did the full fury of the gale lessen slightly, although the wind remained strong. As night descended, the last streamers of frail daylight dissolved into blackness once more. Leonidas felt a pervasive despair added to his overpowering weariness. In addition to the danger the storm posed, they might be snagged on a sandbar or driven upon rocks that could tear holes in their hull and send them to the bottom of the sea.

In this time of tribulation, he was grateful for the strength of Baltas, who performed valiantly holding the wheel resolutely against the force of the wind.

Skylos had been directing the seamen at work in the hold where the water level continued to rise. He reported to Leonidas that casks of water, bales of canvas, and piles of timber and cordage had broken free from their moorings and were floating loose in the hold. Most of the crew not working on the pumps was huddled below, fearful, and exhausted. After a day and a night of being soaked and cold, men developed hoarse coughs, their bodies shaking and fever bringing a flush and sweat to their faces. The forecastle reeked of vomit and excrement. With the gale diminishing, Leonidas had the windsails raised to divert the breeze below decks and provide ventilation to the most stifling part of the ship.

As night advanced slowly into morning, the wind abated and the pounding sea receded. For the first time in almost twenty-four hours, daylight appeared on the horizon. The raven-black sky lightened to gray and, finally, to streamers of orange. The corona of the sun appeared at the horizon. As the sky altered from orange to crimson, it tinted the battered masts and torn sails of the ship with a deep scarlet hue.

Chilled and shivering seamen emerged warily from their refuge below deck. Many of them feared the monster squall was only momentarily passive. Standing along the gunwales staring in awe at the eerie blood-red sky, men knelt and prayed in gratefulness for their survival.

After another trip below deck, Skylos rejoined Leonidas and Baltas on the quarterdeck. The first mate's strong face was slack with exhaustion.

"I never thought to see the blessed sun rise again," Skylos said grimly.

"What is the condition of the crew?" Leonidas asked.

"Two score of men bear one bruise or another," Skylos said, "but none appear mortal injuries."

"I'll take a look at any injured men," Baltas said.

"The men have their own forecastle herbs and poultices," Skylos said in a wary voice. "Best leave them look after their own."

He turned again to Leonidas. "We counted heads and found one man lost, captain, probably washed overboard in the storm. Whatever cry he was able to make for help was smothered in the blow."

"Who was he?" Leonidas asked

"Gorgios Laras from Antipsara."

"Does he have a wife?"

"No, captain," Skylos said. "Only a swarm of harlots in assorted ports who won't ever know or care the poor devil is dead."

Leonidas recalled the dead seaman, a slightly built man with an engaging laugh and a gift of mimicry with which he entertained the crew.

"God rest his soul," Leonidas said. "When we reach port, we'll light a candle for him. Since there's nothing we can do for the dead, Skylos, look after the living. Have the men change to dry clothing, and let them rest as they can. Add a double ration of brandy to warm their bellies, as well. When the day lightens, we'll muster whatever canvas we have left and pray we can hobble into some port for repairs."

"Aye, Captain," Skylos said. "They can use both the brandy and the rest. I'll check the pumps again, too. If we can't drain the water still flooding the hold, we may all get more rest than we're looking for."

After Skylos left the quarterdeck, Leonidas gestured at Baltas. "Let me take over now."

"I'm fine, Captain!" Baltas said crisply. "My father was a bull, and I've inherited his strength. Why don't you dry off yourself. The wheel won't be a problem in a calmer sea."

Leonidas marveled how Baltas seemed the one man on board least affected by the fury and power of the storm.

"Then, I'll be thankful for the rest," Leonidas said. "Skylos or I will spell you at the beginning of the watch. By that time, we should also be able to assess how badly we have been damaged."

Leonidas left the quarterdeck and went wearily to his cabin. He changed into dry clothing and collapsed across his cot. In spite of his exhaustion, he could not sleep. He was filled with despair at the ill fortune that had befallen them and swept with foreboding because he did not know how his battered ship would make it to Psara.

After a while, weary and sleepless, he rose from his cot and returned to the quarterdeck. Baltas was still at the wheel, his body swaying with the roll of the ship.

"Give me the wheel now, and get below." Leonidas said. "You've earned several rations of brandy and more."

"I'm fine, Captain," Baltas said, his voice hoarse, "but, God's truth, the brandy will be welcome." He relinquished the wheel to Leonidas and left the quarterdeck.

Standing at the helm, Leonidas surveyed the shambles of his ship, a broken vessel adrift in an open sea. Until he calculated their navigational position, he could not be sure how many leagues they had been blown off course. He wondered again at what had happened to the ships of Papanikolis and the Velisarios brothers. Their ships could not have fared any better in the storm.

Skylos ascended to the quarterdeck with a final assessment of the damage. He stared at Leonidas in silence.

"A Turkish frigate delivering a broadside couldn't have inflicted any greater destruction on us," Skylos said, his voice burdened with futility. "The hold is still flooded in spite of the pumps, our topsails in shreds, our foremast splintered. The lower rigging is torn, and half dozen of the lower-gun-deck cannon have broken loose from their moorings and overturned. We'll need chains and a crane to move them back into place." He shook his head wearily. "As far as whether we can sail, we're still afloat, Captain, but not much more than that. I've sent the best topsail men aloft to cut away the shreds of flapping canvas and unfurl whatever sail we have left."

Skylos hesitated. "One more thing, captain," he said, his voice low and troubled. "The men are bitter and angry. They're saying the new seaman, Baltas, carried his curse onto our ship. They blame him for the storm that nearly did us in."

"The storm is nature's doing!" Leonidas said impatiently "Blaming any single man is ignorance! Baltas proved himself a first-class seaman at the helm. He did as much as any other man on board to keep this ship afloat!"

"Aye, captain," Skylos said. "I told them something like that. But they're worn out and fearful of what might still be ahead."

"We'll meet whatever fate decrees for us as proud, courageous seamen!" Leonidas said, his voice rising angrily so crewmen on the deck below could hear. "I won't allow my crew to be unbalanced by superstitious omens and curses! If any man makes a move to harm Baltas, I'll clamp him in irons!"

"Aye, captain," Skylos said, his voice resigned. "That's what I'll tell them."

After the first mate had left the quarterdeck, Leonidas stood help-lessly amidst the ruins of his crippled ship. Despite his stern, reproach-ful words to Skylos, he could not suppress the same frustration and dread that agitated his crew. The worst storm he had ever experienced at sea had assailed them only hours after the seaman had come aboard. That might have been a merciless coincidence but then how to explain the calamities that had befallen the previous ships on which Baltas served. Was that all coincidence as well?

"For shame, man," he berated himself scornfully. "The vaunted good sense Admiral Kanaris praised you for has been scattered like a leaf in the gale!"

All the remainder of that day, the crippled *Odyssey* drifted in the open sea. The exhausted and disheartened crew labored to reinforce the splintered mast and keep it from toppling. A score of men were repairing and patching the torn sails. The navigational charts Leonidas studied showed their ship had been blown far south of Psara and left them disabled somewhere in the western Aegean.

Not until the second day following the storm were they able to patch and tie together enough canvas to take advantage of the wind. For two days, they sailed feebly through an open sea, vainly seeking sight of land or another ship. The only hope Leonidas could muster was that the *Jason* and the *Epaminondas* might have suffered lesser damage than the *Odyssey* and made it to Psara in time to track the fleet of Khosref Pasha. When he considered whether those two ships were as battered and adrift as his own vessel, terror stormed his heart.

Meanwhile, as the *Odyssey*'s patched canvas limited their ability to take advantage of the wind, the mood of the seamen grew bitter and wrathful. Their anger was compounded because some of the casks of fresh water stored in the hold had sprung leaks during the storm and been contaminated with seawater. Water had to be rationed, and men began complaining of thirst.

In all his years as a captain, Leonidas had never before felt the malice and hostility in the glances his seamen cast at him from the lower deck. At different times during the day, they converged in small groups whispering with urgency and fervor until he approached when the men fell silent. For the first time when their vessel was not facing battle, Leonidas strapped on a pistol under his waistcoat. Despite his authority as captain of the vessel, he understood that it was probably only the crew's fear of and respect for Skylos that restrained them from attacking Baltas.

Baltas appeared unafraid of the loathing and hate cast at him wherever he moved on the ship. During the day, Leonidas took the precaution of keeping Baltas beside him at the helm. At night, Skylos kept the door of his cabin bolted. But the longer the ship drifted without glimpsing another vessel or the sight of land, the more ominous the mood of the men became.

On the afternoon of the fifth day following the storm, still without sight of land or another vessel, a tall, craggy-faced Psariot named Panos, with half a dozen seamen following him, came to the base of the quarterdeck stairs. A powder explosion during a battle a year earlier had blinded the seaman in his left eye, now covered by a black patch. The other eye glared at Leonidas as malevolently as the eye of a vengeful Cyclops.

"Captain," Panos called up harshly, "the men and me would like a word with you!"

While Baltas held the helm, Leonidas moved to the top of the stairs to confront the men. For a moment, Panos stared at him in resentful silence.

"Speak up, Panos," Leonidas said brusquely. "If you've got something to say, don't stand there like a bristling dog! Speak up!"

"By God, Captain, we've had enough!" Panos cried, his face twisted with wrath. "That hell-borne storm has driven us from our own sea, set us adrift in some devil's channel without a trace of land or the presence of another ship. If we don't do something, why the men and me feel we're doomed to sail on forever, a ghost ship manned by a crew of the dying and the damned!"

The men grouped behind him muttered in surly and agitated agreement. Leonidas waved them sternly to silence.

"Where on the navigational charts is this devil's channel you're babbling about, man?" Leonidas asked. "Don't be a fool! We're still afloat in the Aegean, waters our ancestors have sailed on for centuries! Somewhere to the north and east of us is our island, Psara, as well as all the other Greek islands where we've made port in the past!"

"That's what I'm trying to tell you, Captain." The one-eyed seaman's voice shook with rage. "These are not our waters or our sea!" He pointed toward Baltas. "It's his fault! As soon as that spawn of Satan stepped foot on our ship, we were damned! Either we toss the bastard overboard, or else . . . " The seaman's voice faltered.

"Or else what, Panos?" Leonidas asked brusquely.

"Or else, by God, we'll take over the ship and deal with him ourselves!"

Before Leonidas could respond to the threat, Skylos pushed through the cluster of men and took a stand at the base of the stairs. The first mate's imposing height towered over the angry seaman.

"Mutiny now, is it, Panos?" Skylos said, his voice quiet and firm. He stared with feigned pity at the other men. "And you, Vasili and Aris, Gorgios and Michali, are all of you also driveling on about curses and omens?" Skylos shook his head in disbelief. "I can't believe you're the same men who fought the Turks so valiantly at Eressos. Panos himself led the gun crew that brought down the frigate's mast. Now you stand here quaking like children, mumbling about our ship having sprouted wings and flown to another body of water. You shame our ship and shame yourselves."

"Stand aside now, Skylos!" Panos blustered. "Our quarrel isn't with you!"

"When you challenge my captain on my ship, you challenge me!" Skylos said, his voice no longer conciliatory but angry and his eyes glowing. "And you'll deal with me!"

Other members of the crew who had been standing nearby suddenly surged forward to form a menacing circle around Skylos. Several of the men carried belaying pins they made no effort to conceal. Their presence emboldened Panos.

"We want that devil's spawn off the ship!" Panos cried. "That's all we want! If you and the captain don't try and stop us, you won't be harmed! But, by God, we mean to have our way!"

"Panos is right, Skylos!" one man cried. "There's Satan's work afoot here, and we've got to put it right!"

"Twenty years at sea and I've never before seen a blow like the one that struck us!" a second man shouted.

"God knows what's still ahead if we don't rid our ship of this scourge!"

Leonidas stepped forward and gripped the railing of the stairway.

"Listen to me, men," he said in a final effort to reason with the crew.
"During the storm, no man on this ship did his duty as valorously
as Baltas. He held the helm in that fierce gale as ably as any seaman
I've ever sailed with. He had our survival in his hands and did not
fail us. It is absurd to think of him as cursed."

The men angrily rejected his entreaty, and Panos started to mount
the stairway to the quarterdeck. Skylos grabbed him roughly by the
arm. The other seaman pressed in around them. When violence seemed
inevitable, a robust cry rang down from the lookout in the loft at the
peak of the mast.

"Land ho! Off the starboard side!"

Every man on deck, including Skylos and Leonidas, raced to the
starboard side. Barely visible in the distance was the murky outline
of what was undeniably land. The men let loose a thunderous cheer.
With his own heart pounding, Leonidas heard his voice raised in a
jubilant cry as well.

When they anchored in the harbor, Leonidas recognized the port
as the island of Tinos and never had land looked so appealing. The
sight of the island turned the concerns of the crew from mutiny and
an assault against Baltas into an eagerness to get ashore. They drew
lots to see which crewmembers would be in the first longboat rowing
into port. Skylos took charge of the landing party.

"See what their facilities are for repair, Skylos," Leonidas said, "and
hire whatever workmen you can find. Return with the boat, and I
think it prudent to take Baltas with you on your next trip. The men
seem reassured for now, but we'll get him off the ship for a few days
as a precaution."

As the longboat filled with jubilant seamen pulled away from the
ship, on the quarterdeck Baltas gazed at Leonidas in silence.

"Thanks to you and Skylos for defending me, Captain," Baltas said
quietly. "I did not mean to bring trouble to your ship."

"We were fortunate, Baltas, that the lookout spotted land," Leonidas said. "My crew are usually sensible, stalwart seamen. The gale
unbalanced them and sparked old superstitions. I think a stint on
land may help them regain their reason."

"There's no need to concern yourself about me any longer, Captain. When I go ashore, I won't return to the *Odyssey*."

"I'm not asking you to forsake the ship, Baltas," Leonidas said. "The men were frightened by the ferocity of the storm. A spell of leave on land will bring them to their senses."

"It's not the men I'm concerned about, Captain. I've begun to fear myself. Perhaps they're right, and I carry a curse."

"That is foolishness, Baltas."

"Can we be sure, Captain? What if from time to time Lucifer selects a human, some witless wretch on whom he endows his capacity for evil? The hard truth is that all three ships I've sailed on now have suffered disasters."

"That is simply a malignant coincidence of fate," Leonidas said. "Whatever befalls us, Baltas, we must not abandon reason."

"Forgive me for standing against you, Captain," Baltas spoke with finality. "I mean no disrespect toward your command, but I've made up my mind. I'll help with the repairs to the *Odyssey* as best I can. When your ship is ready to set sail again, I'll bid you farewell and a safe journey."

For an instant, Leonidas hesitated in pressing Baltas to remain on board. Despite his stern response to the fears of his crew and his words of reassurance to the seaman, it might be better not to have Baltas as a source of contention on his ship. As if he'd understood what Leonidas had been thinking, Baltas did not speak, and he turned away.

When Skylos returned in the longboat to the *Odyssey* for a second load, the crewmembers waiting impatiently to go ashore scrambled halfway down the rope ladder to meet him. As soon as the bow of the longboat bumped the hull of the *Odyssey*, men leaped into it from their perch on the ladder.

"Careful, you benighted wretches!" Skylos cried at the men who sprawled in the longboat around him. "You'll break your bloody legs and spend months in some pestilential island infirmary!"

"Did you see any whores in the port, Skylos?" a seaman asked.

"Only your sister," Skylos snapped. "She has your same crooked-eared head!"

"My first stop will be to an island priest for confession and communion," another seaman said fervently.

"That poor pastor better have a fortnight to spare," Skylos said.

"I'm not looking for either a whore or a priest," a third man said, "but ground that's steady under my feet."

"That will last only as long as you stay sober," Skylos said.

With his seabag slung over his shoulder, Baltas sought out Leonidas to tell him good-by.

"Thank you again, Captain," Baltas said. "Your crew is lucky to have you in command. If things were different, I'd be proud to serve under you again."

"You were as fine a seaman as any I've ever had on my ship, Baltas," Leonidas said. "I regret you're leaving."

Baltas was the last man into the longboat before it pushed off from the hull of the *Odyssey*. The other crewmembers avoided him so he sat alone in the stern of the boat.

The longboat made its way to the port, the seaman's solitary figure growing smaller. Leonidas could not suppress a feeling of remorse because he had not pressed harder for Baltas to remain on his ship.

By the afternoon of the following day, eager to begin the repair and refitting of his ship, Leonidas sent Skylos and a squad of his strongest, most reliable seamen to scour the taverns of the port for the carousing sailors of his crew.

"They've had enough time to celebrate," Leonidas said. "We must now complete our repairs and sail for Psara as swiftly as we can."

"I'll round them up, Captain," Skylos said. "And once they're on board, I vow I'll make sure they're fit to work."

Throughout the afternoon, Skylos and his crew carried several boat-loads of seamen suffering hangovers back to the ship for harsh sobriety treatments with black Asian tea and a foul-tasting elixir brewed of acidulous roots and herbs. When the seamen recovered, they began repairing and refitting the *Odyssey*. The men labored through the day-light hours and continued working at night by lantern light. Almost two score island women worked at sewing new sails and mending the canvas of the torn ones. All three masts of the *Odyssey* had been damaged by the storm: two could be mended and strengthened, but the third needed to be replaced. To set the new mast, they used a vessel in the harbor of Tinos rigged to erect masts onto a brig. New topsails and gallant sails were hoisted, and the cracks in the hull were patched. By the use of winch and pulleys, they remounted the cannons torn loose from their moorings. Finally, cartons of fresh vegetables, fruit, and casks of spring water were taken on board and stored in the hold.

While the *Odyssey* was anchored in the port, Baltas labored along with the seamen and islanders at making the repairs. He directed the crew of men when they replaced the broken mast, working with the same diligence he had shown during the storm.

That period spent in port waiting for the repairs to be completed was agonizing for Leonidas. The hours of daylight passed quickly as he worked with the crew on the ship, but at night, despite being exhausted by the day's labor, he was unable to sleep. His thoughts raced like a vessel in a strong wind. The entries he made in his log reflected his impatience and his fear.

> June 5, 1824: Our eighth day in Tinos repairing and refitting the ship. We are doing all we can but the time slips by, each day and night like a boulder on my back. I cannot escape the fear we may be too late. God help our island and my family.

His entries in the log written for his wife were feverish affirmations of his love and his concern for her safety and the safety of his daughters.

Finally, the morning of the tenth day after they first entered the harbor at Tinos, the *Odyssey*, its hull gleaming under a new coat of paint, its masts looming like three sturdy pillars against the sky, appeared as gleaming and seaworthy as a newly launched vessel. When the time came to set sail, a half dozen of his crew, mostly single men without families on Psara and fearing for their lives in another gale, deserted, going into hiding on the island to avoid reboarding the ship.

"Shall I track the cowardly wretches down, Captain?" Skylos asked.

"If we bring them back by force," Leonidas said, "they'll make poor and sullen seamen. See if you can recruit a few islanders with sailing experience willing to take their place."

As Skylos prepared for this last longboat trip, Leonidas pulled him aside.

"We have hard days of sailing and battle ahead of us, Skylos," he said, "and I'm unwilling to spare as able a seaman as Baltas. I want you to find him! Tell him that I want him back on our ship!"

"By God, Captain," Skylos grinned in approval. "I was hoping that would be your decision! I'll be proud to tell Baltas we want him as a shipmate! And if I hear a solitary grumble or a groan out of any of the crew, the halfwit will feel a belaying pin across his mold-riddled head!"

When the longboat returned with the islanders, Leonidas waited impatiently at the gunwales. As the boat neared the rope ladder to the deck, he was gratified to see the stocky figure of Baltas standing beside Skylos in the stern. Leonidas greeted each of the islanders as he climbed onto the deck, welcoming him on board and thanking him for joining his crew. When Baltas appeared before him, seabag slung over his shoulder, for a moment, the two men faced one another in silence.

"I'm pleased you responded to my request, Baltas," Leonidas said.

"If I'd raised any objections, Captain," Baltas chuckled, "Skylos threatened to bring me back by force. I still have concerns but I also concede that all manner of humanity is packed within a ship's forecastle. Among the thieves and scoundrels, heroes and saints, maybe there's also a place for an ill-omened seaman."

The *Odyssey* sailed through fair weather for the following two days, its sails billowing in the wind, its hull skipping along the surface of the sea. Any fear and hostility the men felt toward Baltas were subdued in their eagerness to reach Psara.

The morning of the third day after leaving Tinos, the lookout shouted, "Land ho! Off the starboard bow!"

Leonidas peered through his spyglass into the distance and recognized his beloved island.

"Psara!" he cried jubilantly to Skylos and Baltas standing nearby. "We are home! Home!"

The crew swarmed along the gunwales of the *Odyssey* and shouted with excitement.

As they sailed closer, his spyglass revealed a scene of carnage and devastation. The elation Leonidas felt at first sight of his island became dread and despair. The ships the Psariots had placed in the harbor as stationary batteries to repel the Turkish attack were wrecks, with fragments of masts and sails floating on the water. Lingering black smoke rising from the roofs of houses beyond the harbor provided further proof that Khosref Pasha had already struck their island. In the midst of these wrecked ships was a three-masted brig with undamaged masts and the flag of Psara fluttering from her main mast.

"God willing it be the *Jason* or the *Epaminondas*," Leonidas said to Skylos.

The excitement of the crew had become a shocked and somber silence, but when Leonidas shouted, "It's the *Jason*!" the deck below echoed with the jubilant cries of the seamen.

After they anchored in the harbor, a longboat was quickly lowered to carry Leonidas to the *Jason*. They crossed the narrow stretch of water separating the ships, and his anguished thoughts were whether, by some miracle, his wife and daughters had survived.

When he ascended the rope ladder to the deck of the *Jason*, he found the ship had been converted into an infirmary crowded with wounded survivors. Men were on pallets, some moaning and pleading for help. One man with a bloodstained bandage covering the stump of his arm still bled from his wound onto the deck. Another man coughed up blood. Sailors moved among the wounded, providing water to those who could drink.

Stricken men held out their hands to Leonidas as he passed, their weakened voices calling the names of loved ones and asking if he knew their fate. Suffering and despair enveloped the ship like a shroud. Papanikolis came from the quarterdeck to clasp Leonidas's hands tightly in his own, murmuring, "Thank God . . . thank God!"

On the way to the captain's cabin, Leonidas gave him a summary of what had happened to the *Odyssey*.

"A miracle that you and your crew were saved," Papanikolis said. "Now, let us pray to God that the Velisarios brothers survived that dreadful storm as well and have put into some port for repairs."

"My ship was blown off course as yours was by the storm and damaged, too," Papanikolis said as he poured a brandy in his cabin. "We made repairs at Hydra and sailed for Psara as soon as we were seaworthy. But we were too late . . . too late . . . " His voice faltered.

"We arrived here a week after Khosref Pasha's assault. When you go ashore, you will find wreckage and disaster everywhere. What the vandals could not carry off, they burned. The island has also been stripped of its population. Only the dead and a few souls who managed to survive are left."

Leonidas dreaded asking the question foremost in his mind.

"Have you found any of the women and children?" he felt his voice trembling.

Panikolis only stared at him. "So far only a few old women and dead children," he said, his voice hoarse and low. There may be others we haven't yet found, but from what the survivors have told us, the women and children who weren't murdered were shackled and carried onto Turkish ships."

Leonidas knew the suffering his wife and daughters would endure on those ships bound for the slave bazaars of Smyrna and Constantinople and what their lives would be like after they were sold. He was overwhelmed with rage and despair.

"I tried many times to get Aspasia to leave," he cried bitterly to Papanikolis. "She would not go! I'll damn myself forever for not insisting and making her go!"

"My wife ignored my pleas the same way," Papanikolis said. "She told me a captain's family does not flee."

"So did Aspasia," Leonidas said. "Now we may still find survivors. God help us, some of the women with children might have managed to hide."

"It is true we haven't yet searched the entire island," Papanikolis said. "Your men can now join the search for those who may have hidden." He made a gesture of futility. "But it is best, Leonidas, if we do not raise our . . . " He left the sentence unfinished.

In the silence, the laments and moans of the wounded on the deck above them carried into the cabin.

"From the accounts told us by survivors," Papanikolis said, "when the ships of Khosref Pasha entered the harbor, they opened a heavy cannonade on the ships we had equipped as batteries. They were swiftly destroyed by the heavier firepower of the Turkish frigates." He shook his head in disgust. "The fools had been told those stationary ships would be useless but they would not listen. Afterwards, the Turks turned their cannonades on the batteries of the town and quickly disabled them as well. Meanwhile, other ships landed Janissaries and Asiatic troops at stretches of beach along the coast. They overran a fort manned by the Rumeliot *armatoli*, and then they scaled the mountain above the town, displayed the Turkish flag, and proclaimed themselves victors."

Papanikolis shook his head in resignation.

"While those troops were slaughtering our people, boats filled with rabble from the mainland of Turkey landed and joined the soldiers in pillaging and looting. They killed the men, but when the women resisted, they slaughtered them, too. . . . The dreadful stories I have heard from these survivors, Leonidas, atrocities against mothers while their children watched, the severing of ears and tongues as punishment against those who resisted . . . even the senseless killing of animals . . . " The captain's voice trembled with outrage. "In the main town square, we found the greatest atrocity of all, the severed heads of more than a thousand men piled into one of those bloody pyramids the cursed Muslims construct to celebrate their triumphs! It took us days to dismantle the bloody relic and bury the heads in a grave!"

From the deck, a ship's bell rang, its resonance muffling for a few moments the moans from the deck.

"The gravest danger we face now, Leonidas, is disease from the unburied bodies rotting in the sun. We are burning the corpses as quickly as we can, but those bodies still unburied are being eaten by packs of wild dogs, maddened by hunger and the smell of blood. Those animals are also spreading disease. When we find the living with symptoms of the disease, we quarantine them in the monastery of the Assumption. My men are too terrified to do any more than carry in those afflicted and then flee."

"Who is looking after them?"

"The poor devils are being cared for by a pair of sisters, angels from the monastery who survived the Turkish raids by hiding under the altar in the chapel of Saint Nectarios."

The chronicle of misery and savagery seemed to have exhausted him, and Papanikolis fell silent and stared helplessly at Leonidas.

The immensity of the catastrophe overwhelmed Leonidas, as well, and he couldn't hold back his tears. Papanikolis reached out to him, and, in an awkward and futile effort to console one another, the captains embraced and wept together.

The longboat carried Leonidas, Skylos, and members of his crew ashore, and the seamen dispersed quickly to go to their houses.

"Will you go to your home, Skylos?" Leonidas asked.

"Captain, it shames me to confess that I've women and a few bastard children in several ports but no one any longer on Psara. As for a home here, I have only one if you can call a roach-riddled room in a scurvy port boardinghouse, home. But I'll be glad to go with you and offer whatever help you need."

"Thank you, Skylos," Leonidas said. "God knows I expect to find nothing, so it might be better if I went alone. When the men return, we'll begin our search of the island."

Leonidas walked through abandoned streets of wrecked and burned-out shops and dwellings and remembered the port as it had been before the attack. Its streets had bustled with shops and stalls, teeming crowds, the clamor of street vendors hawking their wares, sidewalk cafes filled with festive patrons.

He recalled, as well, his anticipation at arriving in Psara after a voyage. From the terrace of his house, which overlooked the sea and the harbor of Psara, his wife and daughters would have seen the *Odyssey* anchor and would be preparing to welcome him.

Their home, built by his father half a century earlier, was one of the most elegant dwellings on the island. One entered the spacious twin-story structure of stone and marble, with gleaming, whitewashed walls and red-tiled roof, through an ornate, wrought-iron gate. The gate opened into a courtyard garden that bloomed throughout the year with hibiscus and bougainvillea. Inside the house, the floors were inlaid with terra cotta, and the bathrooms appointed with Greek marble. Each room had huge mahogany-framed windows that had been transported by ship from artisans in Italy, windows so expansive they suffused the house with sunlight. When the panes were open, every room in the house was cooled by the breezes from the sea.

Within the house, as well, were all the artifacts and mementoes Leonidas had acquired during his years of voyaging. There were linens and silks from Damascus, thickly fleeced floccati rugs from Trikkala, brocaded silk tapestries from Marseilles. There were works of art that included a gold samovar from Odessa, icons of the Virgin Mary and the Saints from Jerusalem, oil paintings of the Assumption from Alexandria. All of these treasures would have gone to their daughters and their chosen husbands after Aspasia and he were gone.

As he neared his house, his despair growing at what he feared he would find, none of these material possessions mattered. They were simply artifacts that encircled the presence of his beloved family.

He found his house wrecked and burned. The garden was in shambles, the flowers trampled as if by a herd of animals. The great front door was broken, the windows shattered, the walls a heap of blackened ruins. Fire had brought down the great central beam of the ceiling, which collapsed the roof, leaving cracked pieces of red tile scattered amidst the ashes. What had not been carried away had been broken and burned. The house's scorched and crumbled walls enclosed only debris. He was overwhelmed at the totality of the devastation.

Scavenging like a beggar among the ashes and rubble, he retrieved a few meager remnants of his family's life. Several charred pieces of silver had escaped the looters, as had a pearl comb belonging to Aspasia and a small, copper bracelet he'd given one of his daughters.

As he stood amidst the ruins, his heart savaged with grief, something strange and haunting assailed him. When the breeze that blew from the sea subsided, an eerie and alien silence lay in its wake. He understood then what were absent were the songs of birds, melodies so prevalent about his house for as long as he could remember. Now, even those small, winged, and feathered creatures had fled the afflicted terrain where his family once lived.

Leonidas returned to the port to rejoin his crew. Each man had found the same wreckage and desolation as Leonidas, and they grieved with others at lost family and burned-out homes. Some wept bitterly, others shouted with rage. All vowed vengeance on the barbarians who had taken their families and devastated their homeland.

"We can remain here in mourning for what we have lost," Leonidas said, "or we can begin to search for survivors. If we don't find any of our own families, we may save loved ones belonging to others."

With hope they might find a few survivors, the crew began a search of the island. Skylos led one force to scout the outlying settlements while Leonidas led another group to search the farms located below the slopes of the mountain. The farther they traveled inland from the harbor, they discovered there wasn't any part of the island untouched by devastation. Villages were in shambles, houses looted and burned, barns and sheds stripped of their implements. Even the livestock—donkeys, sheep, and chickens—had been carted away.

And everywhere they searched, in the ruins of houses and farms, in barns and in fields, there were the bodies. Bodies dumped on the ground like scraps of waste, bodies riddled with bullets or slashed by swords. Bodies sprawled face down on the ground, arms flung out and fingers burrowed in the dirt as if they were seeking to escape into the earth itself. Sometimes the wounds exposed the viscera of the organs, kidneys and bladders, hearts and lungs. All of these littered within the sculptured framework of bones that glistened like porcelain, the crooked bones of the old and the strong bones of the young.

Above the corpses lingered air poisoned with the smells of blood, urine, and feces forced from victims in their final moments of terror. Sometimes, the bodies disclosed the atrocities inflicted upon them before death. In a small farmhouse where a couple had been slaughtered, the man's corpse had empty sockets—from which his eyes had been gouged. The woman's corpse lying near him was naked from the waist down, her pale thighs streaked with blood. She had been struck with a weapon that shattered her skull. In her broken cranium, Leonidas saw the brain itself, pulpy and ridged like furrows made by a plough in the earth.

In one horrifying tableau, the searchers found the head of a small child severed from its body. In a savage parody of maternal fidelity, the head had been placed between the breasts of a dead woman who might have been the child's mother.

After a while, the rage Leonidas and his men endured at the gruesome spectacles of slaughter passed into a numbness and silence. Their eyes and hearts could no longer absorb the horror.

There was little they could do with the corpses except to consign them to funeral pyres that blazed into the sky and filled the air with the stench of burning flesh.

As twilight fell and they were about to cease their search for the day and make camp, they discovered in the fruit cellar of a burned-out farmhouse an old man and old woman who might have been husband

and wife, beaten bloody and left for dead. The men handled the old pair gently, eager to save the first living souls they had found all day. They attempted to move them from the charred debris, but both died within minutes of one another.

Because they had found the couple alive, they did not burn their bodies but buried them together under the shadow of the mountain. On their graves, they placed a small, wooden cross that bore no name but merely the words, "A man and woman are buried here."

That night, wrapped in his blanket in the midst of his restless men, Leonidas lay sleepless as well. He could not forget the sights and smells of the day, the remnants of slaughter and brutality they had witnessed. Now, in the stillness of the night, under the stars that shone down on the living and the dead, he wondered whether God himself wept at the atrocities committed by the humans he had created.

Leonidas's final, grieving thoughts were of his wife, Aspasia, and his daughters, severed fragments of his body and his heart, suffering under those same stars.

When they resumed their search the following day, they located a few other survivors, a score of men and a few women and children who had managed to evade capture by fleeing farther inland and hiding in the forest. Some were injured, a few seriously, while all suffered from hunger and thirst. The crew gave them food and water and, moving them on litters or astride their backs, carried them to the infirmary and surgery compound Baltas had set up in the square of the port. The large tent would shield the wounded and ill from sun and wind.

One of the injured men, a handsome youth in his early twenties with auburn hair and dark eyes that girls must have found bewitching had his arm shattered by a musket, and his wound was festering. Baltas told him he'd have to amputate the limb to save him dying from gangrene. The young man wept and pleaded with Baltas.

"What will I do?" he cried. "How will I live? What woman will have a one-armed man?"

"Your spirit and courage do not rest in a single arm," Baltas said to him quietly. "You're young and strong and will be able to do more with one arm than older men do with both. And you will still bear strong children who will help you do those things that need to be done."

Because they had not yet found any of the island's priests alive, Baltas also conducted final rites for the dying and spoke a few simple prayers for the dead.

"Lord, accept this soul into your keeping. As he came forth of his mother's womb, naked shall he return as he came. Grant him peace for his suffering, leniency for his sins. And forgive us who remain for not having been better shepherds of his mortal body. Earth to earth, ashes to ashes, dust to dust. Amen."

From the survivors, Leonidas and the seamen heard more stories about what transpired after the invasion. When the cannonade from the Turkish ships overwhelmed the port defenses and destroyed the town batteries, the Turkish troops had landed. The islanders fled in panic, seeking refuge wherever they could. The principal hiding places were in cellars or in the fields. Some hid their children inside the ovens of the houses. They also hid in barns, in cemeteries by burrowing into graves beneath the tombstones, and in bell towers of churches. One father hid his small children in the hollow trunk of an olive tree and saved their lives. Another mother attempted to save her child by lowering her into a bucket down a well. Later, when she pulled her up, the girl had drowned. A male attendant in a small island hospital told of patients pulled from their beds and slaughtered. A woman hidden in a hayloft told of her neighbor who fought the Turks like a tigress to protect her children until one came up behind her and ran his sword through her back. A shepherd told of seeing a father fling himself across his children, shielding them with his own body before all were killed.

A young mother they found still alive clutching a dead baby in her arms was paralyzed with grief. Others who survived told her story. While she hid with villagers in a cave while Turks searched nearby, her child had begun to cry. In fear that the infant's crying would endanger all their lives, they had smothered the child.

There were stories of mystical transfigurations. A sexton hiding in the bell tower of a small village church had witnessed Turkish soldiers desecrate the church altar by stealing the gold chalice and were then struck blind.

"I swear to God I saw them blinded!" the sexton said fervently. "They staggered around squeezing their eyes and howling like madmen!"

In another story, Turks who had murdered several families of Psariots they had discovered in a settlement were themselves destroyed. A survivor hidden farther up the mountain swore he had seen their bodies caught in a whirlwind that hurled them into the air along with fragments of trees and houses.

Some of the recitals had victims overcoming their captors. A Turkish soldier was leading a group of captive Greek women toward one of the ships when they stopped to rest near the edge of a cliff. The Turk stood near the precipice smoking his pipe when one of the women, managing to get loose from her shackles, rushed him from behind and pushed him over the cliff. They heard his screams as he tumbled to his death.

One old man who had been hiding in a plane tree saw a pair of Turkish soldiers capture a farmer who, in return for having them spare his life, vowed to show them where island girls were hidden. After he had exposed the girls' hiding place, the Turks killed him.

An account of extraordinary courage and sacrifice involved a group of *armatoli* militia who fought and held off a horde of Turks long enough to allow a score of women and children to escape. The women, some mothers with infants cradled in their arms, fled up the slope toward the summit of Mount Candara, taking refuge in a cave used by Psariots to store casks of gunpowder. After the Turks had slain the *armatoli*, they stormed the cave. The women inside set fire to the cache of gunpowder, and the great explosion killed both attackers and defenders.

Leonidas recalled having heard, as a young man, a similar tale about the women of Suli, a mountainous region in the north of Greece. Fleeing before the attack of soldiers of the notorious Ali Pasha, the tyrant who ruled the region, the women had retreated with their children up the mountain of Zalongos. As the Turks closed in on them, the Suliot women began to dance in defiance, and, one by one, holding their infants and children in their arms, they leaped to their death.

As the story of the women of Suli would remain eternal, Leonidas knew the stories of the women of Psara would also live on long beyond their deaths.

As Papanikolis had foreseen, the gravest threat facing the seamen and the island's survivors was the spread of disease. The sisters in the

monastery who were caring for the ill and dying victims appealed for
help to bring in food and water and to remove the bodies of those
who had died. Several islanders who had been helping perform those
tasks had grown fearful and refused to continue. Baltas assembled
medical supplies, food, and water and accompanied by Leonidas and
a group of seamen carried them to the monastery.

Before entering, Baltas spoke to the men.

"I am going into the monastery to bring those victims who are suffering and the blessed sisters looking after them food and water and
medications," he said. "We must also remove the bodies of the dead."
He stared gravely at the circle of men. "Now, who will join me?"

The men stared nervously and silently at one another. Concealing his own anxiety about entering the monastery, Leonidas stepped
forward.

"I am joining Baltas," he said. "I will not order any man to enter
with us. But I also ask for volunteers."

Skylos raised a hand in protest.

"Hold on a minute now, captain." His voice held a plea. "Your survival is more important than that of any of the rest of us. The *Odyssey*
and the war for our liberation need you. Let me go in your place."

"Thank you, Skylos," Leonidas said, "but allowing you to go in my
place would so dishonor me, I'd be unfit to command ship or crew.
But I'll be pleased to have you join us."

"You're my captain, on land as well as at sea, so I'll join you," Skylos
said. "I always anticipated I'd die in a gale or a battle at sea. If God
decrees I perish on land, at least it will be a dry death!" He looked
sternly at the circle of seamen. "All right, my hardy shipmates, who
are the brave ones among you who will join the captain, Baltas, and
me carrying in food for the living and hauling out the dead?"

Only Panos stepped forward.

"Good for you, Panos!" Skylos cried. "I knew you were a brave
man!"

"Meaning no disrespect to the captain," Panos shrugged. "All my
volunteering proves is that there are at least four foolhardy souls on
the *Odyssey*. Our captain, his first mate, a shipmate we were ready to
cast overboard, and a one-eyed seaman."

The four men, their faces masked with cloth and wearing gloves
to protect their hands, carried the food and casks of water into the

monastery. The only light in the cavernous and shadowed church that had been converted into an infirmary fell in narrow ovals from small windows high in the dome and from candles flickering on tables and ledges. As the men moved deeper into the church, they were assailed by a stench of decay and pollution rising from the ill and dying lying in heaps on blankets along the floor.

"God save us," Skylos muttered. "Month-old ship's garbage smells like a flower beside this stink."

The sisters, a pair of cloaked and ghostly figures with only the barest portion of their faces visible in their cowled heads pointed out the bodies of the dead.

While Baltas treated the patients with palliatives and ointments, Leonidas walked among them, seeking a familiar countenance. He was shocked at faces so bloated and disfigured that any identification was impossible. For the ones most critically afflicted and dying, a thin, bloody mucus trickled from their mouths, and the skin on their cheeks and throat appeared infested by tick-like insects feeding on the flesh. Leonidas could not help drawing back in revulsion.

For the following few hours, Leonidas joined Skylos and Panos in carrying out a half-dozen dead bodies. He was surprised at how strangely weightless the corpses seemed, as if the disease had eaten away their bones as well as their flesh. They placed the corpses onto a pile of branches and brush the other seamen had built in a nearby field. When they set the pile afire, plumes of black, stench-riddled smoke spiraled into the sky.

The following day, the three men reentered the monastery with additional food and water and to carry away the bodies of several men who had died during the night. After Baltas instructed the nuns on the further care of those ill and left them ointments and powders, he returned to the port infirmary to care for the wounded survivors there.

On the third morning, as Leonidas, Skylos, and Panos prepared to go to the monastery again, Skylos once more asked for volunteers from the crew.

"Enough standing around watching us perform our Christian duty," he said brusquely. "We've confronted Turkish frigates with twenty-four pound cannon that could blow a man to pieces. Inside this enclave, there are only poor devils whose affliction is not of their own doing. You've seen us entering and leaving for several days now without harm. Will we allow our fellow Psariots to die of starvation and thirst? Be stout lads, and give us a hand."

He added a measure of sardonic humor to his entreaty. "Consider how much more I'm risking than any of you. There's more of my long-boned body to become afflicted. Besides, if this bloody scourge lays me low, think of the satisfaction you'll have tossing my carcass onto the funeral pyre."

By his coercing and cajoling, half a dozen additional men volunteered.

At the end of the week, the *Apollonian*, a brig commanded by Captain Vergis and carrying a shipload of volunteers from the island of Samos, arrived to aid the victims on Psara. The valorous Samiots took over the duties assisting the nuns at the monastery and joined the search for survivors. They also set about rebuilding some of the wrecked and burned-out dwellings.

The Samiot captain also provided Papanikolis and Leonidas news on the progress of the war. From the last dispatches, he'd learned that Kolokotronis and Petrobey Mavromichalis were marching for battle against Khurshid Pasha, who had invaded the Peloponnesus from the north with his armies. At sea, the Greek fleet, through the use of fire ships, thwarted the Turkish fleet of Ibrahim Pasha in its efforts to attack Samos and saved that island from suffering the fate of Psara.

"It was a great victory for Kanaris and the fleet!" Captain Vergis told them enthusiastically. "Their fire ships blew up a Turkish frigate and two Turkish brigs. Thanks to the courage of our seamen, the Muslims decided the cost of attacking Samos was too great and sailed off to find easier prey!"

"Where are Kanaris and the fleet now?" Papanikolis asked.

"The last I heard they were sailing from Samos toward Crete to prevent Ibrahim Pasha landing his armies. If he gains a foothold on that island, he'll make his next move against the Peloponnesus."

Additional good news from Captain Vergis was that the *Epaminondas* of the Velisarios brothers had survived the storm. The ship, refitted and repaired, was ready to sail once again.

"All this news is welcome!" Papanikolis said. "We have lost blessed Psara, but the war continues, and we must do our share. Kanaris will need us, and it is time for us to return to sea."

The two captains agreed that as soon as they could provision their ships, they would sail.

During one of the final searches Leonidas and his men undertook before departing Psara, they found a solitary survivor in a cave on the mountain above the village of Lagonissi. When men first entered the cave and heard a shrill moaning, they thought it might have come from an animal that had taken refuge. The searchers moved deeper into the cave and discovered a man hiding behind a mound of rocks. When he saw the flame of their torches, he broke into cries of terror that echoed piercingly through the cave. They spoke to him loudly in Greek, trying to reassure him. He continued to shriek and hurl stones.

Leonidas moved closer and spoke to him quietly and reassuringly, "We're Psariots and friends. We're here to help you."

Whether the man finally understood they meant him no harm or had simply become exhausted, he quieted down and allowed them to approach. In the light of the torches, they saw a gray-bearded and haggard old man. Leonidas had never before looked on a human face that so starkly conveyed terror and anguish.

The man struggled feebly against the men seeking to lead him from the cave. Leonidas clasped him gently by the shoulders and felt his bones under the emaciated layer of skin.

"Come now from this cold, damp cave," he said quietly, "let us take you where you can be looked after."

The old man stared mutely at Leonidas. Finally, he ceased struggling and let them lead him from the cave. Once outside, he raised his hands quickly to shield his eyes from the bright sunlight. He was barefoot, his feet bloody from the rocks in the cave, and his clothing was filthy and tattered. The flesh of his cheeks appeared dry as parchment, and his neck was as scrawny and wrinkled as the neck of a rooster. One of his ears was missing, the orifice crusted with dried blood, a fragment of cartilage visible within the tangle of his hair.

The old man fumbled at his dry, caked lips. "Water," the word came in a croaking whisper. "Water . . . "

They brought him a flask of water, and he drank thirstily, the liquid dribbling down his chin.

As they washed and tended his wounds, in a low, hoarse voice, the old man moaned a lament. "Hear now, foolish people, who are without understanding, who have eyes and see not, who have ears and hear not. We are sheep who have gone astray. O earth, earth, earth, hear the word of the Lord!"

The sun descended, the cypresses and plane trees along the slope of the mountain slipping deeper into shadows. In the encroaching darkness, light from the campfires glittered across the rocks and trees. The old man, sitting near the fire, asked again for water. When they offered him food, he waved it away. Leonidas tried to feed him soup, slowly and patiently, the way one would feed a child, but the old man resisted opening his mouth. When he did accept nourishment, he had trouble swallowing. A morsel stuck in his throat, and a harsh bout of coughing wracked his frail body. Through the evening, he sat staring at the fire, his arms clasped about his raised knees, rocking silently back and forth. From time to time, he broke again into a lament, an eerie elegy that whirled into the night.

"As he came forth from his mother's womb, naked shall he return and shall take nothing of his labor which he may carry away in his hand."

He fumbled in his ragged trousers and brought up a small gold crucifix that he held aloft.

"Hear my cries, O Lord! For my voice is the voice of one crying in the wilderness! By thy great mercy, defend us from all perils and dangers of the night! Earth to earth, ashes to ashes, dust to dust!"

All their efforts to calm him were futile. He continued his wailing, his voice growing weaker, his breathing hoarser. When he stared up at the seamen who listened nervously to his raving, his eyes glowed like specks of flame in the pale circles of his face.

"Whatever the poor devil has seen and endured has driven him mad," Skylos said somberly.

After a while, as the fires burned down, the last embers glowing in the dark, the old man's body and voice succumbed to exhaustion, and he fell silent. Skylos brought a blanket to drape across the old man's shoulders. One of the men boiled water for tea, and in the coolness of the evening air, sweet fumes of vapor rose from the pot.

Leonidas brought tea to the old man and sat beside him. The old man held the cup and sipped slowly, and when he was done, his hands trembled as he placed the cup on the ground and lowered his body wearily to the pallet. Leonidas covered him with the blanket.

"Sleep now, friend," he said quietly. "You're safe, and we'll look after you."

Shielded from the firelight, the old man's eyes had become small and dry like the pits of olives, his lids heavy, as if they longed to close.

In the recesses of the night, Leonidas was wakened by an urgent tugging at his shoulder. He looked up into the grim face of Skylos.

"The old man tried to slice his wrist with a piece of jagged rock," Skylos said. "Venetis heard him and stopped him before he could finish himself. We wrapped the wound, and the men are watching him. I'm sorry to wake you, Captain, but you're the only one who's been able to calm him. It might help if you talked to him."

Leonidas went to the old man slumped on the ground under a tree. His body appeared limp and exhausted, and stains of fresh blood seeped through the cloth wrapped around his forearm and wrist. Several men stood sentry around him. One added wood to the nearby fire, and the flames flared more brightly. The old man raised his head and stared at Leonidas with despairing eyes.

"Why won't you let me die?" he said wearily. "I want to die."

"No man should seek to die before his time," Leonidas said quietly. "Your wounds will heal, and you'll grow stronger. What about your family?"

The old man looked back at the fire.

"I'm cold . . . so cold," he said, and a tremor swept his body. Skylos brought him another blanket. In the firelight, the old man's face looked skeletal, barren of flesh. When he raised one hand to fumble at the bandage covering his forearm, his fingers seemed shriveled appendages, as well.

"I am Father Christos, the priest in Lagonissi," he said in a low trembling voice, "I had a family. . . . Now, all are dead."

As men whispered to one another that the man they had rescued was a priest, others formed a silent, attentive circle around him, waiting for him to speak again. He did not look at the men but stared into the fire.

"My family and I took refuge in my church," he said. "We were kneeling . . . praying . . . when they broke in." He lowered his head, drew in a breath.

"Before God's holy altar, they ravished my wife . . . my daughter." The words came torn from his lips. "Because they fought, both were killed. Then they seized my grandchildren."

The priest's frail body trembled in small spasms, his fingers groping restlessly across the blanket.

"They were innocent!" he said, "Infants who had never harmed anyone! I pleaded, begged, cried on God to save them. . . . Let the children live, let them live!" His voice rose and became an anguished cry. "They slit their throats!"

His words echoed in the night, and the naked force of his grief swept across them in waves. Leonidas felt his heart shattered at the brutality of what had taken place. Near where the priest sat, a tiny lizard darted across the ground. The priest watched its passage and then stared back at the fire.

"They tore off my robe, held me down while one man sliced off my ear." He paused. His tongue moistened his dry, caked lips. "I cried out, waiting for them to sever my other ear, slice off my nose, cut out my tongue . . . but they left me there, beside the bodies of my family." He shook his head. "They had found other villagers who were hidden, because I heard women screaming. I did not want to leave my family, wanted them to kill me, as well. But I was terrified at what they would do to me. I ran from the church into the woods. When it became dark, I came up the mountain . . . to the cave."

The priest ended his story with his shoulders slumped, his voice fallen to a whisper. For the first time, he turned his gaze away from the fire and stared with anguish at the circle of silent men.

"Why should I live and my dear ones be dead?" His tormented question accused them. "What use are my days now? I can never forget the way they died before my eyes." His voice faltered and became a mournful plea. "I pray to God, let me die, too."

Leonidas looked beyond the priest at Skylos and understood both his first mate and he were trying to remember whether they had found the priest's family. There had been so many bodies, many of them victims who had sought refuge in churches only to be slaughtered there.

Father Christos lay down on his side, his pale cheeks reflecting the glow of the fire, and began his mournful chant again.

"They that wait upon the Lord shall run and not be weary; they shall walk and not be faint. For the Lord is my strength. He will swallow up death in victory and will wipe away tears from all our faces."

In a somber silence, the men returned to their blankets to sleep.

"Make sure he's not left alone," Leonidas whispered to Skylos.

Leonidas tried to sleep himself, but the priest's anguished story would not let him rest. Even as he grieved for the tormented old priest and the family he had lost, his thoughts were of his own wife and daughters. For a terrible instant, he wished that they had died on the island, as well.

In the morning, they secured Father Christos onto a litter to transport him back to the port. On the journey, he resumed his litany of despair.

"I am the voice of him that crieth in the wilderness! Prepare ye the way of the Lord, make straight in the desert a highway for our God! Then shall the dust return to the earth as it was, and the spirit shall return unto God who gave it!"

Walking alongside the litter, Leonidas envisioned what the priest's life might have been like before the calamity that had befallen his family. He imagined him holding services in the small village church on Sunday mornings, his family and his flock gathered with him. How serenely he must have conducted the comforting ritual he had performed so many times.

In his quieter, more lucid moments, Father Christos stared sorrowfully at the men who were carrying him on the litter and at Leonidas walking beside him.

"Why should I live and my dearest ones be dead?" he asked. "Why, O my God, why?"

By the time they reached the port's infirmary, the journey had exhausted the priest. He had grown feverish, his face flushed and his skin hot to the touch. Inside the enclosure, the air swollen with the stench of blood and festering wounds, Baltas gently cleaned the priest's wounds and replaced the bloody bandage on his arm with a poultice. He coaxed the priest into swallowing some medicinal liquid.

"You'll be better soon, Father Christos," Baltas said. "With rest, you'll get stronger. Other survivors will have need of your prayers and counsel."

The priest stared at Baltas in silence. "You don't understand," he said, his voice low and despairing. "My soul and heart have fled. Nothing in me still wants to live." He looked entreatingly from Baltas to Leonidas. "Pray to God to let me die."

Baltas rose from beside the priest and looked helplessly at Leonidas.

"When God granted Adam the right to bring death into the world," Baltas said quietly, "it may not have been for punishment but as an act of mercy."

Leonidas slept fitfully once again that night in the barracks set up near the infirmary. His thoughts teemed with images of his own family. Each succeeding day increased the enormity of their loss. He rose at dawn and spent the first few hours of the day making final arrangements with Skylos for the departure of the *Odyssey* the following morning. He packed his clothing and a few other possessions in his sea bag and returned to the infirmary. Among the rows of the ill and wounded, the pallet of the priest was empty.

He found Baltas attending a patient and asked him about the priest.

Baltas faced him, his eyes moist and red, the lids heavy as if he also had spent a sleepless night.

"Father Christos died during the night," Baltas said. "I had given him some broth and sat with him a little while. He died peacefully in his sleep."

They stared at one another in silence. The question Leonidas might have asked remained unspoken.

"In the morning, Captain Papanikolis and I sail to join our other ships in the waters north of Crete," he said. "You are welcome to sail with us."

"There is so much more that I can do here, Captain," Baltas said. "The infirmary is full of survivors, and then there are the poor souls

in the monastery. I can be of greater help here on Psara than I could
be on the *Odyssey*." He paused. "But I'll keep you and the crew in
my thoughts, Captain, praying for your safe voyage and victory in
battle."

"Thank you, Baltas."

"And will you pray for me, too, Captain?" Baltas asked quietly.
"Pray for God to understand and forgive those poor mortals who
sometimes dare to play God."

"I will pray for you, Baltas," Leonidas said.

The following morning, the *Odyssey* and the *Jason,* their anchors
hoisted and secured, sailed from the harbor of Psara. They would
voyage south from the island, down the fourth degree of longitude,
keeping the wind on their port quarter.

Soon after clearing the harbor, the seamen surged up the shrouds,
and along the swaying yards, their bodies small and dark against
the sky. As canvas thundered loosely from the masts, the ship gave
a long-drawn shudder. In a few moments, every sail on the *Odyssey*
was billowing, the ship skimming along the waves.

Standing on the quarterdeck, feeling the spray of water across his
face for the first time in weeks, Leonidas experienced the freshness
and deliverance of the winds that blew across the sea. He gazed back
at Psara, the island receding in the morning mist. On the deck below,
seamen lingered along the gunwales, gazing back at the island, too.
They were leaving a scorched and devastated island that would never
be the same for them. Nor would they ever be able to look forward
with joy to homecoming after a voyage. Nothing was left of the lives
they once shared but the memories of wives, children, parents, friends
who had died or been enslaved.

Consumed as he was with bitterness and a desire for vengeance,
Leonidas understood that such slaughter against the innocent wasn't
restricted to the Turks. No race bore a sole claim on cruelty. He knew
his own countrymen had massacred Turkish women and children.
That humans could commit such violence and savagery upon other
human beings questioned their origins as God's creation.

But those were enigmas to be pondered by wiser men. He was a sea
captain, his only home now his ship, his mission to battle and liberate

his country so that the children of those who did survive would grow up free and unchained as human beings had a right to live.

He turned away from the fading vision of his island and spoke to his first mate, standing at the wheel.

"The wind's holding steady, Skylos," Leonidas said. "Set our course south by southwest for the Cretan Sea."

"Aye, Captain," Skylos said.

CHAPTER
SIX

The winter of 1825 was the harshest the villagers of Krava-saras had experienced in many years. At night, a cold wind, wailing like a stricken animal, blew with such force that the roofs of houses shook and the windows rattled. Goats and chickens had to be quartered inside to keep them from freezing. In the morning, as the wind subsided, a chilling mist descended from the mountain, a thick, palpable fog that obscured the houses and streets so it became hazardous to venture outside.

For several weeks in February, the sun remained obscured, and the light that managed to emerge from under the dark swirling clouds of night seemed dimmer than normal. Villagers nervously made their cross and whispered that the sun hiding for so long a period was an evil omen.

When Father Markos slipped out the door at dawn to relieve himself in the crude lean-to behind the house, within minutes his extremities felt frozen. He made a labored effort to bend his stiff limbs quickly up and down, groaning at the sharp pain these movements caused in his knees and back. He also flapped his arms to move the blood to warm him. He imagined what an absurd figure he would have appeared to anyone who saw him, an aged priest, thrashing about as if he were possessed by the devil.

Along with other regions of Greece where the harvest had been destroyed by war, Kravasaras suffered a scarcity of food. The shortage had begun near the start of the rebellion four years earlier, and each successive year of conflict saw conditions worsening. That winter, the villagers subsisted on a carefully rationed supply of corn, parsnips, beans, peppers, and dried tomatoes they had stored from the previous summer. A limited supply of precious garlic was used not only to spice foods but also for medicinal purposes. Their diet was supplemented by an occasional rabbit or quail caught in the nets and traps the villagers set in the fields. These catches were rare because of the intense cold that kept the creatures secluded in their lairs. The supply of milk for the children was also diminished because the village goats had to be nourished on thistles and shriveled husks of corn in place of the customary diet of flowering cereals and grasses, barley and oats. Even the hens, in spite of being sheltered in the houses, felt the effects of the cold and produced fewer eggs.

Yet, despite the severity of the weather and awareness that the war now being fought in the country beyond the village could engulf them at any time, the winter was one of the most content and fulfilling Father Markos had spent in years. He understood that his euphoria came because of the young mother, Maria, and the infant, Lefteris, living in his house. He delighted in seeing them during the day and listening to them at night. If the child sometimes fretted and cried in the dark, his mother sang to it softly with a voice so sweet and haunting it returned the priest to the lullabies his own mother had once sung to him.

Their confinement in the small house that included a few chickens and the priest's goat, Minerva, was cramped. Privacy was achieved by means of a curtain that hung between their sleeping quarters at night. During the day, the curtain was removed, and they shared meals that Maria prepared in the fireplace.

Since her bruises had healed and her fears eased by the sanctuary she had found in the priest's house, the girl's beauty flourished. Father Markos observed with awe that she was not only lovely but also seemed imbued with a spiritual essence. This sensitivity was reflected in her eyes that were as luminous and dark as those of the Shulamite maiden in the Old Testament. When she knelt at the fireplace to cook, her long, thick, black hair tumbled across her shoulders. When she smiled affectionately at the priest, his heart felt embraced by gratitude and warmth.

Despite the shortage of food, her child, Lefteris, grew with amazing swiftness. His infant's face filled out, the shade of his cheeks beginning to reflect his mother's flawless complexion. His body grew sturdier, his arms and legs stronger. At first, he tottered on unsteady legs, then walked, and, finally, began to run. When the priest entered the house, the child ran to embrace him, calling him grandfather, "Papou! Papou!" In those endearing moments, the priest felt blessed by God.

Father Markos made certain that however scarce food became, the child was the first one fed with eggs from their chickens and milk from their goat. When he wasn't visiting ailing parishioners or holding services in his church, he played for hours with the child. Their games often included the chickens and Minerva in the bin of straw in a corner. When Lefteris found a newly laid egg from one of the hens, he brought it to the priest with delight—"Look, Papou! Look how white this one is!"

The child and the goat seemed to have formed a special bond. As Father Markos milked Minerva, the child stood at the goat's head, animal and child gazing steadily into one another's eyes.

At the times Minerva needed to be milked, the priest would teach the child about goats. "You see how Minerva watches you, Lefteris? She is pleased she can provide you milk to help you grow tall and strong."

As the boy drank the still-warm milk, the priest provided him a stream of information about goats.

"The milk of a goat, Lefteris, is sweet, nourishing, and medicinal," the priest said. "And, believe me, much less likely to curdle in your stomach than the milk from a cow."

When the boy finished the milk in the cup, a trace of chalky film lingered around his mouth.

"When goats are content and in good health, my child," the priest continued, "they are full of energy and playfulness, curious and mischievous."

"Why does Minerva sometimes cry, Papou?"

"That isn't really crying, my child, it is bleating. There are many reasons for a goat to bleat. A goat will bleat to tell you when it is hungry, when it is thirsty or feeling ill." He omitted adding the goat might also bleat noisily during the breeding season, saving that information for when the child grew older.

"You can always tell a healthy goat by the way it stands, feet planted squarely and well balanced, its tail held high, or busily chewing its cud when lying down to rest. The coat of a healthy goat should also be shiny. And the eyes are most important. Look into Minerva's eyes, my child, and you'll notice they are bright and alert." He smiled. "As your blessed eyes are bright and alert."

Resentments remained among the villagers about the girl and her son born of a Turkish rape. Father Markos noticed the hostile and malevolent glances directed at the mother and child in church and even malicious whispering that ceased quickly in his presence. But the villagers also recognized that Father Markos had become guardian to Maria and Lefteris, and, with a few exceptions, they embraced the mother and infant. Even more significant in preventing anyone from maligning or abusing the mother and child was that the klepht leader Manolis Kitsos was godparent to the infant. No one dared to offend the stalwart young warrior or make him an enemy.

During the coldest days of that winter, the villagers remained secluded in their houses for most of the day except for those necessary chores that required them to go outside, the setting of traps and gathering wood for the fires.

When men and women fell ill from the damp and cold, their houses were visited by the canny old women who specialized in cupping. They dripped oil into a cup, and after setting a quick flame to the oil, placed the cup on the afflicted person's bare back. They muttered incantations while the flesh inside the glass puffed up and reddened. When the cups were removed, they left red swollen circles on the back.

The villagers also assembled for morning prayers and evening vespers and on Sunday mornings for the liturgy. Father Markos, breaching the rituals of the church on holding a lengthy service, shortened his Sunday sermon in the cold church to lighten the discomfort of the weather on his parishioners. In his sermons he expressed fervent gratitude to God because the village, protected by the colossus of the mountain, had been spared the ravages and despoilment so many other villages had suffered. Yet everyone understood that if the war continued and grew in scope, that safety of sanctuary might not continue.

After the liturgy on Sunday, the villagers lingered in church to eat their communal meal. The children were also able to play with their friends and the grandparents to exchange village gossip as they used to do in the more benign period before the war.

In the years since the refugee band had brought Maria and Lefteris into the village, some of the refugee men returned to pick up the women and children they had left behind. A few women and children without husbands chose to remain in the houses with the families that had given them shelter.

There were four deaths in the village that winter. Father Markos carefully transcribed them in the old ledger where he had been recording the births and deaths, marriages and baptisms that transpired in Kravasaras for more than fifty years. Three of the deaths involved aged villagers who had lived well beyond the span of an average lifetime. They were properly mourned and then interred in the village cemetery beside the church. The fourth death was the unhappy demise of a village youth—Sifis, the son of Artemis and Soto Dokakis—who had been fighting in the north and, even though wounded, had made it back to his village. Shortly afterwards, his wounds worsened, and he died in the arms of his bereaved parents. In addition to mourning the loss was the problem for any funeral during those frigid months of digging the grave in the frozen, stony earth.

In the middle of that winter, like creatures emerging from another world, a band of gypsies came to Kravasaras from the south. The villagers, weaned by age-old superstition that gypsies were portents of ill fortune and prone to stealing and deceiving, met them warily. Because gypsies were also suspected of kidnapping children, their appearance mandated that all the children be kept secured inside their houses.

The gypsies carried for sale an assortment of trinkets and charms as well as pots and skillets they had fashioned on their anvils. They also brought with them fortune-tellers, who offered any villager willing to pay a pittance a medley of predictions, enigmatic enough to be interpreted in numerous ways.

"Tell your fortune, your holiness," an old gypsy crone, her face rampant with guile, leered at Father Markos. "Find out about that gold lurking in your future."

"I do not seek gold," Father Markos replied sharply, "but to bring God's word to my flock."

"Suit yourself," the crone snapped, "but when calamity strikes, remember that old Karkenitza offered you a chance to escape the devil's embrace."

For an uneasy moment, Father Markos wondered if he shouldn't have given the crone a copper to appease any malevolent spell she might be inclined to cast on him. He quickly rejected the craven impulse. "When you start believing in the omens of gypsies," he scolded himself, "then it is time to doff your vestments and don the garb of a fool."

Another visitor that winter was a traveling peddler who entered Kravasaras leading a caravan of three mules bearing a cargo of hides from animals trapped in the fertile woods in the south. The villagers eagerly purchased his wares, cutting up the hides and sewing the pieces together to make boots and shoes, replacing those that had worn out. They also wove blankets from the hides and fashioned thick rope mats that would be used in the oil presses during the olive harvest.

The peddler's name was Zigoris, and he had been visiting the village for years. He was a small, wiry man with a face so cratered with creases and wrinkles that it was impossible to estimate his age. He traveled swathed in layers of clothing and a long, wool cape that dragged on the ground behind him. In addition to his hides, he brought news. The villagers gathered in the church to hear his hodgepodge of chatter and gossip gleaned from a dozen other villages.

"In the village of Arnitsa, a wife whose husband is fighting in the north bedded her brother-in-law," he said, excitedly shaking his head. "Both sinners were driven out of the village."

Barely pausing for breath, Zigoris rushed on.

"In Likekatsro, in the church of Saint Andreas, they have an icon of the Panagia that, from time to time, weeps living tears. I confess I did not see the icon weeping myself, but villagers swore to me that her tears appear regularly."

"What do you hear about the war, Zigoris?" Botsakis, one of the elders, asked.

Moving from village gossip to the more serious news of the war caused the peddler's tone to become somber.

"I hear rumors of our valiant forces winning some major battles." Zigoris spoke slowly, punctuating each word with a knowing nod of his head. "But there are also rumors they are losing some major battles. Meanwhile, our bold, resourceful leaders are conscripting armies from all parts of the land to prepare for other major battles in which they hope to crush the Muslims."

"But, Zigoris," Leontis, another elder, asked, "if we are both losing and winning battles, how can we tell which side is truly winning?"

"That is a most meaningful question!" Zigoris praised the elder. "However, in order for me to answer, you must understand that before victory there has to be a defeat. Any victory that follows will then be succeeded by another defeat, which in turn will lead to another victory. However . . . " The wiry peddler paused to emphasize the acuity of his observations. "We must be cautious in any final assessment because there are right and wrong kinds of victory. And . . . " His voice became quieter, and the villagers strained forward to hear. "We must not forget that there are also times when a battle produces neither victory nor defeat!"

The most comprehensive information the villagers received on the war was from Manolis Kitsos. He returned to Kravasaras on two occasions during the coldest months of that winter, and Father Markos marveled at how the young man had managed to traverse the snowbound passes and icy ravines of the mountains to make his descent to Kravasaras.

On his first visit, when he emerged from beneath the layers of clothing that sheltered him through the mountain's snowy wastes, Father Markos saw that following his near-fatal wound, the young klepht had regained his good health. His tall frame appeared strong and fully restored, his handsome face cured by the sun and wind to a deep brown. Visible just beneath the collar of his shirt, the skin of his neck gleamed white.

Although everyone in the village understood Manolis came to visit his godson and the child's mother, his arrival was always reason for all the villagers to celebrate. In his saddlebags, he brought almonds, figs, wild berries, and artichokes that he shared with the villagers. He carried as well a substantial quantity of *paximadia*, those dark-brown snacks of twice-baked bread, which for centuries had been the staple fare of shepherds. The villagers regarded them as savory morsels, especially when eaten with slivers of cheese, sprigs of garlic, and a glass of homemade red wine.

Before a gathering of elders with Father Markos in the church, Manolis also related the grim tidings regarding the rebellion.

"The disheartening news I bring you is that even as our forces seek to resist the attack of Ibrahim Pasha's armies who are attempting to land in the Peloponnesus," he said somberly, "we have reports there are Greek armies in the west fighting one another in a civil war."

The villagers expressed their consternation by fervent sighs and exclamations of dismay.

"This will be the second time since the start of the rebellion that Greeks are fighting other Greeks," Manolis continued, his voice reflecting his bitterness, "but this conflict seems even more violent."

"Why are Greeks fighting one another, Manolis?" Leontis asked.

"There are groups in both the western and eastern parts of our country who claim they are the legitimate government of the new Greece," Manolis replied. "On one side are the prosperous Greeks who owned land under Turkish rule, and they are allied with islanders from Hydra and Spetsia. Against them are the military leaders, led by Prince Petrobey of the Mani and General Kolokotronis. Our captain, Vorogrivas, and men of our band joined their force in battle this last year. But when Greek took up arms against Greek, Vorogrivas became disheartened and returned with our men to the mountain camp. Now, the landowners and islanders seem to be in control. The most unhappy news is that this group has arrested General Kolokotronis and put him in prison on the island of Hydra."

"Unbelievable!"

"Shocking!"

"How could such a thing happen?"

The villagers crossed themselves fervently, their fingers darting nervously from their foreheads to their waists and then from their right shoulders to the left.

As he listened to the bleak news from Manolis, Father Markos felt his hopes for the victory of their rebellion faltering. That Kolokotronis, one of the legendary, victorious heroes in the early battles of the war, could be imprisoned by other Greeks seemed a betrayal of the revolution itself.

But not unexpected, the priest thought sadly. From the time of the Peloponnesian War, which pitted the city-states of Athens and Sparta against one another in a brutal and exhausting conflict, fratricide was the great tragedy of Greece. Beset by jealousies and arrogance, by malice and mistrust, as their earth was saturated with the blood of tyrants who sought to invade and conquer them, so was it also soaked with blood spilled in warfare between brothers.

During his brief visits to the village, Manolis spent most of his time with Maria and Lefteris. The child called him *Nouno*, for godfather, and accorded him the same jubilant affection he offered his mother, Papou, and Minerva.

With Lefteris well bundled in clothing, Manolis took him for walks along the perimeter of the village, the child usually riding on his shoulders. When they returned to the house, the child's nose was beet-red from the cold but his eyes gleamed with joy at the adventure he had shared.

These visits by Manolis were for no longer than a day before he began the arduous journey back up the mountain.

"There are battles to be fought, Father," Manolis said. "Our band is always outnumbered so every fighter is crucial. I would never forgive myself if a comrade was mortally wounded because I was not there to protect his back."

The priest played with Lefteris in one of the farthest corners to allow Manolis and Maria time alone. Pretending to be intent only on the child, from time to time Father Markos stole a furtive peek at the two of them. He noticed the warmth of the glances they exchanged, the whispered words and soft laughter between them that had the tangible contact of touch.

The priest pondered the sequence of events that had brought the young people together. If Manolis hadn't been concerned about the refugee band harming the villagers, he wouldn't have traveled to Kravasaras. Nor would he have met Maria and become godfather to Lefteris. Now, the two young people were forming a closer attachment, one that might bind them together in marriage.

"Lord, O Lord," the priest whispered as he gently stroked the child's soft hair, "Thy ways are a mystery beyond human understanding."

The following morning, Manolis prepared for his departure. He cradled Lefteris in his arms and gently kissed the child's forehead.

"How soon will you return?" Maria asked plaintively.

"As soon as I can," Manolis said. He put the child down and then, shyly, kissed her on the cheek.

Father Markos, clothed in cape, scarf, and cap, walked with Manolis to the nearby shed that sheltered his horse. After Manolis had saddled and led his mount from the shed, he bent and kissed the priest's hand. Father Markos embraced the young klepht with the affection he would have shown the son he had been denied.

"Forgive me, Manolis, for speaking to you as if I were your blood father," the priest said. "Have you and Maria made any decision about what you wish to do?"

"I love her, Father," Manolis said quietly. "And I feel she loves me. But if you're asking whether I spoke to her of marriage, I did not dare. I have no heart to make her a bride one week and a widow the next. More important than anything we wish to do, this war must first be fought and won."

Manolis gently stroked his horse's withers and swung up into the saddle. Above their heads, a flock of gray rooks passed, their cawing reverberating loudly and harshly and then receded as the flock disappeared into the snow-crested peaks of the mountain.

Manolis stared pensively down at the priest. "Look after them, Father."

"With my life, my son," the priest spoke the words as if they were an oath.

After the young klepht had ridden off, the priest could still inhale the scent of mountain thyme from his clothing that lingered in the cold air.

With the departure of Manolis, their house seemed somber and silent, and a melancholy descended over Maria. She sat in a corner, her hands folded in her lap, staring at the small square of the window. The only brightness in the house came from the buoyant laughter of Lefteris playing with Minerva.

Several weeks later, at the end of March, winter still veiling the village and the berry trees still barren of any budding, half a dozen horsemen appeared on the road from the south leading into Kravasaras. They were first seen by Ares Scarpas, whose house was built on one of the higher levels of the village with a longer view of the road at the foot of the mountain. He alerted the villagers, who carried word to Father Markos during his visit to an ailing parishioner.

Although it was unlikely that Turks would be traveling into the village from the south, the riders could be a band of Muslims that

had eluded Greek forces. They might also be renegade Greeks intent
on thievery. While the villagers set about concealing their meager
food stores, Father Markos hurried home to Maria and Lefteris. He
cautioned them to remain within the house, and then he waited
nervously on his porch.

Many of the villagers had locked themselves inside their houses,
leaving the streets deserted except for the prowling of a lean cat or
mangy dog. Father Markos imagined the inhabitants peering nervously from slits in their shutters, watching as the strangers rode
by. And then, with his heart pounding, Father Markos watched the
horsemen, swathed in hoods and cloaks, riding at a slow gait up the
street toward his house.

When they reined their horses before his porch, the lead horseman
tugged down his hood. Father Markos was shocked to see the bale-
ful countenance of the monk, Papalikos, the fiery renegade cleric he
hadn't seen since the spring of 1821 when the revolt broke out.

Papalikos leaped down from his horse to stand towering over the
priest. He greeted Father Markos with a harsh, derisive laugh.

"God be praised, my esteemed Brother in Christ!" the monk cried
in the same abrasive voice the priest remembered. "Your face welcomes
me as though I were a carrier of plague! I expected you'd be delighted
to greet an old friend!"

The monk looked many years older than the four years that had
passed since the priest last saw him. His huge head still appeared
sculpted from granite. His raven-black and densely planted hair grew
low on his forehead above his dark, deep-socketed eyes, which seemed
to reflect the vindictive thoughts seething behind them.

"I am always pleased to see my Brother in Christ," the priest tried
to make his words sound sincere.

He looked uneasily beyond the monk at the other horsemen, a
rough and sullen band. The men had swarthy faces the color of earth
with eyes like black holes under their hoods. All of them bristled
with firearms, cartridge belts slung across their chests and shoulders,
pistols and daggers stuffed into their belts. They stared at the priest
with unsmiling faces that lacked any vestige of friendliness or human warmth.

"You and your companions are welcome to whatever hospitality our village can offer," the priest said. "Alas, there isn't much. The war has made us all paupers."

"Don't worry about us," Papalikos said brusquely. "We'll find whatever we need. What we're looking for now is a place to shelter and rest. We have been through some devil-damned battles. Would you believe," he gestured toward the ragged crew, "this is all that remains of what had been a band of fifty brave fighters?!"

Bunching his body, he spit violently at the ground.

"But we are consoled, little Father!" he cried. "With the Lord blessing our arms, we dispatched to the eternal fires of hell many times the number of men we lost! But the filthy heathen kept coming at us in howling hordes, and, in the end, those of us who had not fallen were fortunate to escape with our lives!" He paused. We were in search of a safe haven to rest, and I remembered your isolated little hamlet here, and," mockery was evident in his voice, "I recalled your kindness during my last visit."

The priest remembered that earlier visit by the monk as one filled with tense hours waiting for Papalikos to take his leave. Seeing the priest and the visitors conversing, villagers in the nearby houses felt emboldened to come and join them. They welcomed the visitors warmly, greetings that the riders accepted in surly silence.

"God be blessed that you and your men have come through your battles safely, Brother," Father Markos said. "My neighbors and I will be pleased to provide whatever assistance you need."

He addressed one of the elders. "Cleon, please take these men to the church. Have our people arrange houses where our visitors might stay."

"Rest assured, Father," Cleon said, "we'll do everything we can to make them welcome."

The monk gestured to one of the riders, a weather-beaten, stocky-bodied man whose slanted eyes and bronzed skin drawn tight across his high cheekbones made him resemble a Mongol or a Hun.

"Tzangas, go with him, and get our men settled," the monk said. "I'll lodge here with my Brother-in Christ as I did during my last visit."

The priest felt a lance of foreboding. "I'm afraid that won't be possible, Brother," he said hesitantly. "There are others now living in the house with me."

The monk looked at the priest in surprise, an expression that became a smirk. "Don't tell me, Father, that in your well-ripened years, you have taken a second wife?"

"No, no!" the priest said quickly. "But there are a pair of refugees, victims of the war, staying with me."

"Bless your kind and benevolent Christian heart," the monk said, a parody of civility lacing his voice. "At least, grant me your hospitality long enough to offer me a glass of water. My throat is as dry as a riverbed in summer drought."

Beset by anxiety at having the monk see the girl and her child, the priest struggled for reasons to prevent him entering his house.

"Alas, Brother, one of the refugees is an infant who I believe may be sleeping," he uttered the lie with what sincerity he could muster.

"Your Reverence," Cleon respectfully addressed the monk, "we'll gladly find you comfortable accommodations in another house."

Papalikos ignored the elder.

"I'll be quiet as a dormouse, Father," the monk said. Without any further delay, he brushed past the priest and strode into the house, his towering height requiring him to bend by half a foot to pass through the doorway. The priest followed nervously behind him and entered the house in time to see the monk's glance fall on the figures of Maria and Lefteris sitting in the corner. Papalikos let loose a hoarse, suggestive laugh.

"Are these your refugees, Father?"

"This poor mother and her child were victims of the war and in need of food and shelter," the priest spoke quickly. "They were among a number of refugees we have sheltered in other houses."

"Now that you've explained how they came to be here, Father," the monk said, "why don't you let me meet this young woman and her seedling?"

"The mother's name is Maria, and her son is Lefteris," the priest made a gesture of deference toward the monk. "Maria, this is Brother Papalikos, who, since the beginning of our rebellion, has fought valiantly in the cause of our country's freedom."

The monk walked closer to Maria and Lefteris. He gave the child a cursory glance, and then his gaze turned to the mother. He stared at her, boldly and intently, and Father Markos was shaken by the rampant lust visible in the monk's face.

"I'm pleased to see that age hasn't dulled your craftiness, Father," the monk smirked. "You've obviously culled the choicest of the refugees to share your snug little dwelling." He continued to stare brazenly at Maria. "It has been a long time since I have looked on so beautiful a young woman. Most of the village girls one sees now are scruffy shrews resembling their hag mothers. I envy the lucky man who sired her child."

As if she sensed the menace in the monk's presence, Maria did not speak but clasped her son tightly.

"Come sit by the fire and warm yourself, Brother," Father Markos said. "I'll pour you a glass of water or wine and offer you a *paximadi*, as well."

"The last time I was here, Father," Papalikos said while continuing to stare at the girl, "you were Christian enough to allow me to rest my weary bones for the night before your fire. I hope you might extend me your hospitality again."

The priest shifted restlessly. "Last time I was alone and pleased to offer you hospitality in my humble dwelling," Father Markos said. "As you can see, there are now three of us, plus the goat and those few chickens in this space, which you must find cramped. I'm sure our elders will find more comfortable lodgings for you in another house."

"Will another house provide me such beauty as this madonna and her child?" Papalikos asked. "If you cannot promise my poor eyes such bounty in another dwelling, Father, the only Christian thing to do is to allow me to rest my battle-weary bones here, by your heart-warming fire."

Despite the priest's efforts, the monk would not be denied. A moment later, when his lieutenant Tzangas called to him from the porch, the monk left the house to talk to him. During the brief interval Papalikos was outside, the priest quickly hung the sheet across the corner of the room that provided Maria and Lefteris privacy from the remainder of the house.

"I cannot prevent him staying the night," the priest told her hastily. "But, Maria, please, remain behind the curtain. If he asks why you aren't joining us, I'll tell him you are ailing." He looked at the girl's frightened face and tried to reassure her. "I'm sure he doesn't mean you or the child any harm, but these are men whose blood has been inflamed by war, and we best be cautious."

The monk returned, tugging off some of his outer garments. The black shirt he wore buttoned to his throat was tattered, his trousers were frayed, and his boots patched and worn.

"You see what a warrior for the revolution is reduced to wearing, Father?" the monk's voice was bitter. "The cursed politicians gorge themselves on the fat of the land while fighting men scrounge for food and clothing just to keep warm and stay alive!"

"Have your men been accommodated all right?" the priest asked.

"Don't worry about my men, Father," the monk snapped. "They are resourceful as wolves in taking whatever they need."

His weapons clattered noisily as he pulled them off. He set them on the floor close beside him. Then he settled himself before the hearth while the priest heated beans and broth at the fire. He offered them to the monk with a chunk of wheaten bread.

"Won't the sweet mother and her child secluded behind that inhospitable curtain be joining us for a bite of supper, Father?" Papalikos asked, speaking loudly enough so that Maria would hear. "Here I am, weary from battle defending our land and homes from the Muslim heathen and longing only to share a crust of bread with a Christian family."

"I'm sorry to say that Maria is ailing, Brother," the priest said. "I'll take her and the child a little food now, and then I think it best to allow her to rest."

Father Markos carried a bowl of broth and milk to the mother and her child. He motioned again for Maria to remain behind the curtain.

A moment later, there was a knock on the door. The priest answered to find Leontis, the village mayor. Father Markos stepped outside to speak to him, pulling the door partially closed.

"They're all bedded down for the night, Father," Leontis said. "We put three of them in the blacksmith's barn with Gorgios, and the other two with Tsoumas in the bakery." He lowered his voice. "I'm sorry to say, Father, they are an unruly, bad-tempered lot."

The priest peered into the house to assure that the monk remained seated before the fire. He turned back to Leontis.

"First thing in the morning, I think it wise for me to send Maria and Lefteris to your house," he whispered.

"I'll look after them, Father," Leontis said gravely, and he slipped away into the darkness.

As the monk ate the meager supper, Father Markos took a decanter from the cupboard and poured a cup of wine.

After a sip, the monk grimaced and shoved it away. "Your village brew tastes more like cat piss than wine," he said in disgust. He fumbled in his saddlebag and brought out a flask. "Try a drop of this juice of the gods." The monk extended the flask. "It is *tsikoudia* from Crete. The Cretans distill it from dragons' bones and the kidneys of eagles."

"Thank you, no, Brother," Father Markos said. "My aging stomach would not be able to digest that strong a potion."

The monk put the flask to his lips and drank thirstily. Afterwards, wiping his mouth with the sleeve of his shirt, he exhaled a deep sigh of pleasure. "You're missing a treat, Father! This concoction has magical qualities. They say that drinking substantial amounts of *tsikoudia* is the reason Cretans believe that one day a new savior will return, born of a male." The monk's raucous laughter resonated through the house. "That's why Cretan males wear baggy breeches so they won't risk bruising the infant's head when it appears! Can you believe such stupidity?"

The monk brought his chibouk from his saddlebag and lit it with a taper from the fire. Soon the house filled with the rank smell of pungent tobacco. Several times, Papalikos stared fretfully toward the curtain.

"Maybe I should just slip behind that shroud for a moment, Father, and bid the young mother and her child goodnight."

"I'm sure they're both asleep," the priest said quickly. He walked to the edge of the curtain and pretended to peer behind it.

"Both are sleeping soundly," he lowered his voice. "I pray the poor girl feels better in the morning."

The monk picked up several walnuts the priest had given him and cracked them between his huge fingers. For a chilling moment, Father Markos imagined how easily those powerful fingers and hands could throttle a man.

"Why is this young woman living in the village alone with her offspring?" the monk asked. "Where's the child's father?"

"He is fighting with our forces in the north," the priest said, lamenting at how easily the lies were slipping from his lips.

"All the better for you, Father," the monk leered at the priest. "I expect, from time to time, with the girl living under your wing, you manage a fleeting glimpse of the enticing naked flesh she conceals under her frock?"

"I assure you, Brother," the priest couldn't suppress his indignation. "I regard her as I would my own daughter!"

"Calm your ruffled feathers, little father," the monk snickered. "I doubt she has anything to fear from you. But whether your feelings are paternal or not, living this close to any woman rattles a man's senses. Women can't help themselves because they give off different scents. Females who fight alongside men in battle give off the same stink as men. Then there are the pungent, overripe smells from a wanton woman." The monk's black eyes glowed in the firelight. "In this house, I can smell that young mother's scent, an aroma of virginal purity and maternal devotion."

"You're most welcome to take my bed for the night, Brother," the priest sought to deflect the monk's reverie. "I will be fine sleeping on the floor."

"My body hasn't felt anything but rocky, rutted earth in months," the monk grunted. "Keep your old shanks where they belong."

The monk picked up a large log from the stack beside the hearth and tossed it into the fire, causing a flaring of sparks. He spread his blanket before the fireplace and, with a long, noisy swallow, finished the *tsikoudia* in the flask. The reek of the wild liqueur mingled with the smell of tobacco and filled the house with a dense, oppressive odor. Fearing the mordant odors might sicken the child, the priest considered opening the window for fresh air. Not wishing to offend the monk, he repressed the urge.

The monk tugged off his boots and tossed them against the wall. He sprawled on his side, facing the fire.

Father Markos removed only his shoes and cassock before lying down across his bed. For a little while, the only sound in the house was the crackling of the burning logs.

"Living in your village, secluded and safe, little father," Papalikos said, his voice slurred by drink, "you cannot imagine the butchery rampant across the land. A fog of blood shields the earth from the stars." The monk twisted noisily onto his back, the firelight glowing across his strong, chiseled features. "In Laconia, in a small, drab village the Turks had attacked a few days before we rode in, we found twenty naked Greeks, hanging like rotted carrion from the plane trees. They'd had their genitals hacked off, their mutilated bodies hurled into eternity with bloodied holes like a woman! Other villagers had been slaughtered in their houses, children violated, babes like the one you shelter here, skewered on the blades of scimitars!"

The priest lay tensely in his bed, listening to the monk's bitter voice echoing from the corners of the room.

"But that cursed Muslim barbarism only fans our zeal for vengeance!" the monk said, his breathing harsher and more labored. "We answer fire with fire, blood with blood! A week after we found those poor wretches dangling, we ambushed a caravan of Turks near Sigala and, by good fortune, snared a wealthy Vizier, a bloated, overfed swine with diamonds glittering on his fleshy fingers and jeweled earrings in both his jackass ears. I severed the diamonds still attached to his fingers and collected his earrings along with his ears. After that satisfying antipasto, I began slowly, believe me, little father, very slowly, slicing away at his bloated carcass, trimming layers of his fat as one would carve a pig, careful not to cut too deep and have him bleed to death before I'd finished. The cowardly scum screamed so loud the bastard sultan must have heard him all the way to Constantinople!"

The priest, shaken by the grisly recital, lamented that Maria had to be hearing the terrible tale.

Papalikos abruptly lurched from the floor to his knees, and, with a surge of fear, the priest remembered his pledge to Manolis to protect the girl with his life. He fumbled for the stout shepherd's crook he kept near his bed, his fingers trembling and clammy around the rough, carved wood of the handle.

The monk remained kneeling before the fireplace, his body swaying slightly before the fire. After a moment, Father Markos heard the sound of his voiding, the flames hissing and the sparks flaring as the stream struck the burning logs.

Afterwards, the monk sprawled down on his blanket. For a while, he was silent, and the priest thought he had fallen asleep.

"You think because I journey with a band of men that I am not lonely, little father." A strange pensiveness had entered the monk's voice. "But there are moments when I endure a solitude you cannot imagine, when I feel alone as newly created Adam, driven from God's garden into the merciless world for the first time." His voice became quieter and strangely gentle. "In those periods of loneliness, I look forward to a time after we have won our freedom, a time when I might take a wife, Father, someone lovely and pure as that girl in the corner, a maiden to nourish my aching spirit and comfort my loneliness. We would share bread warm from the oven in the morning and share supper together before the fire in the evening. In the summer, after working together in the fields, we'd rest and savor golden, ambrosial honey . . ."

The monk's voice, succumbing to weariness, faded. A few moments later, he began to snore. In the farthest corner, Minerva responded to the noisy snores with a low, skittish braying.

Throughout that night, Father Markos could not sleep. He watched the logs burn down to glowing embers, the final sparks fluttering to the ceiling. In the stillness of the night from some mountain crag sounded the desolate howling of a wolf. Several times Papalikos thrashed in his sleep, barking an oath or a command. The goat responded with a low braying.

Once, during the night, Lefteris began to cry, his voice carrying in a low, fretful wail through the house. Father Markos heard Maria's soft voice soothing him, and, after a few moments, the child became quiet again.

As the first traces of dawn became visible through the window, Father Markos rose and walked quietly on stockinged feet behind the curtain to the bed where Maria slept. The child was asleep, but the girl's eyes were open, revealing she, too, had spent a sleepless night.

"Everything will be all right, Maria," Father Markos whispered, offering her a false reassurance. "But, I think it best you take the child and go to the house of Leontis. Carry only a few things you and the child may need, and then, I beg you, don't leave their house for any reason until I send you word that the Brother and his band have gone. Tell Leontis no one in the village is to know that you are secluded there."

The girl rose quickly to gather her clothing. The priest returned to his bed, warily watching the figure of the monk still sleeping heavily. After a while, he heard Maria and Lefteris leave the house, the door closing quietly behind them. For the first time, then, he closed his eyes and slipped into an exhausted sleep.

Sometime later, brighter daylight illuminating the interior of the house, the priest was awakened from sleep by the noisy clatter of the monk rising, coughing loudly and hoarsely to clear his throat.

"Good morning to you, Brother," the priest called from his bed.

The monk grunted in response and bent to pull on his boots. He walked with a heavy tread to the door, and the priest heard him in the lean-to behind the house. Papalikos returned, stamping his booted feet and clapping his hands briskly to warm them. He gestured toward the curtain.

"Why isn't she up?" he asked sharply. "What good is a strong young female in the house if she can't kindle a morning fire and brew a cup of coffee for a guest?"

The priest struggled from his bed, and bent to tug on his shoes.

"Maria woke me early, Brother," the priest said. "She still wasn't feeling well, and, in order not to disturb us and to have some help looking after the child, she took herself to the house of a neighbor."

The monk glared at the priest for a moment and then turned and walked to the curtain. He roughly tore it down, revealing the empty bed. He turned balefully back on the priest.

"Was she really ailing, or did the ungracious minx decide she didn't want to remain in the house with me!?" he snarled. "I must tell you, Father, this discourtesy offends me! It offends me greatly!"

"I'm truly sorry, Brother," the priest said. "I'm sure Maria meant no offense. You must remember that, as a refugee, she suffered injury and ill health from which she hasn't yet recovered."

"Whose house in the village has she gone to?"

"I'm not sure," the priest said. "She has a number of friends she might be staying with." Under his breath, he asked the Lord to forgive the unwavering sequence of his lies.

"Perhaps your memory will improve later in the morning," the monk said brusquely. "Now, Father, be a decent Christian host, and kindle a fire so I can get a bloody cup of coffee."

After the fire had been lit and the coffee brewed, the monk's lieutenant, Tzangas, arrived at the house.

"My man and I need to talk of private matters, Father," the monk said brusquely. "You'd oblige me if you stepped outside."

"That's all right, Brother," Father Markos said. "I am already late to church for my morning liturgy."

The priest left the two men and walked through the brisk early-morning air to his church. The village square was occupied by the men of Papalikos. They had drawn water from the well, which they drank and splashed on their faces.

"On your way to save some souls, Father?" one asked mockingly.

"Grant me a few hours this afternoon, Your Eminence," another man called. "I vow my confession will sear your ears."

"Will you hear my horse's confession as well, Your Holiness!" a third cried. "He'll confide what he does when he smells a mare!"

Greeks who fight for freedom can also be louts, the priest thought sadly as he walked on.

When he passed the house of Leontis and Dafni, where Maria and Lefteris were hiding, he carefully averted his eyes. He wondered with a tinge of remorse if he was doing the monk an injustice in suspecting that he was brute enough to actually harm the young mother. Yet, nothing in the ferocity of the monk's demeanor or his grisly recitals of his conduct in war provided any assurance the girl would be safe in his presence.

Father Markos also feared how Papalikos might react if, by unhappy chance, he learned Maria had no husband and that her child had been born after a rape by a Turk. When the priest considered all these possible dangers, it confirmed the good sense of sending Maria and the child away.

His apprehension about Papalikos and his band was reinforced when he arrived at the church and found a group of embittered villagers. They besieged him with complaints about the monk's men trespassing into their houses the night before in search of food and wine.

"When I told one of the scoundrels who burst in that we had no food or wine to spare, he threatened to give our young grandson a beating," Spirakes said indignantly. "We were frightened and gave him whatever we had. Now we're left with nothing."

"They are truly brutes, Father!" Daminaos said indignantly. "One of those men who accepted my hospitality demanded I sleep on the floor, and he took my bed!"

"The pair of rogues who came into our house searched our cupboards and cabinets and broke some of my wife's pottery!" Vasili joined the grievances. "They might be Greeks, but, I swear, Father, they are no better than common thieves!"

"However rough and rude these men are," the priest appealed for patience, "we mustn't forget they are fighters for the revolution. There is little in our village for them to steal, and, therefore, no reason for them to stay with us for long. Let's bear with them as well as we can."

After Father Markos finished his morning liturgy, the villagers dispersed, except for Leontis.

"Maria and Lefteris are fine, Father," Leontis whispered. "This morning, Dafni fed them a warm breakfast. We'll be watching carefully, and, if any of that scurvy band come near our house, we'll have them hide in our fruit cellar. You know that underground room is well concealed, Father, and they'll be safe there."

"Thank you, Leontis," the priest said. "It relieves me to know you're caring for them. Make sure the child gets milk." He sighed. "As for that unholy crew, God willing, I hope they don't harm any of our people before they leave."

Later that morning, as the priest was cutting crusts of dried bread into small pieces for the evening's communion, the door was tugged open, and someone entered the church. When the figure came in a quick, lurching gait up the aisle to the altar, Father Markos recognized Kandoula Minoti. She was a straggly-haired, hump-backed old woman who had lost all her teeth to disease years earlier so she ate with gums grown tough as bone. Her husband, Ezekial, had been a caretaker of fields and orchards. After a fall from a tree he had been pruning, he suffered from a limp and a useless arm.

The old woman hastily made her cross before the altar and bent to clutch and kiss the priest's hand. When she straightened up, he saw her distraught and tear-streaked face. She did not speak but stood there, whimpering through her toothless gums.

"What's wrong, Kandoula?"

The old woman continued staring at the priest in suffering silence for a moment more and then erupted in a torrent of words.

"They break in house, Father!" she cried. "Search for wine, for money!" she labored for breath. "We tell we poor people, we have nothing." Her frantic voice echoed from the shadowed alcoves of the church. "One strike my Ezekial . . . like this!" She flailed at the air with one clenched and bony fist. "God help, Father, I think our end! They find nothing, then ask where Maria who lives with you hides. We say we know nothing! They kick Ezekial, knock him to floor! God help, Father, kick his stomach so hard, he cry in pain! I beg leave us be . . . we know nothing!"

"Did you tell them anything, Kandoula?" He felt his heartbeat quicken.

"They mean kill old man . . . maybe kill Kandoula, too!" the old woman cried. "God help forgive me, Father, I tell!"

"Told them what, Kandoula?" His voice trembled because he knew the answer.

"I fear they kill old man and me!" Her lips quivered. "Kandoula tell how baby is born, how mother come our village!"

The priest was shattered with terror.

"God help, Father," the old woman cried, "show mercy and forgive!"

He struggled to pull his hand away from the woman's frantic grasp.

"All right, Kandoula, it's all right. I forgive you, and our Lord forgives you. Where are the men now?"

"They leave, and I hurry here," she said. "Forgive old woman, Father!"

"I forgive you, Kandoula. I forgive you, and God forgives you. Now go home and look after Ezekial. Go."

"God bless you, Father!" Kandoula said, her voice choked with gratefulness. "I pray God mother and child keep safe!"

She turned then and with her lopsided gait hurried from the church.

After the door closed behind the old woman, the priest's first panicked impulse was to take flight, believing the monk might resort to torture to make him tell where Maria was hiding. He recalled the zeal with which Papalikos described his carving up the Vizier! But where would he hide? Whichever house he chose for concealment would endanger the inhabitants who gave him refuge. He had no choice but to remain in God's sanctuary and await whatever was going to happen. His fingers shaking so badly he feared he might cut himself, he resumed slowly and carefully cutting up the dried crusts of bread.

Father Markos did not have to wait long before he heard a horse gallop up outside the church. The door was hurled open. The monk's body blocked out the light. He came with his long, swift stride up the aisle toward the sanctuary. When he reached the altar, his dark and angry figure towered over the priest.

"You senile, despicable old fool!" the monk cried. "You lied to me and deceived me! Did you think I wouldn't find out the truth? Poor refugee and her child, indeed! Her brave husband fighting with our forces in the north! One shameful, abominable falsehood out of your craven mouth after another!"

He raised one of his huge hands bunched into a fist that he brandished threateningly before the priest's face.

"All those wretched deceptions to conceal the truth that you took into your house a bitch-whore with her devil-spawned bastard! You provided safe haven to minions of Satan! You miserable simpleton, you two-faced, old imbecile!"

"The girl was attacked, Brother," the priest felt his words like frail leaves caught in a fearful storm. "What happened wasn't her fault! She loved the child she bore, as any mother might love!"

"She should never have allowed that cursed devil-seeded viper to ripen in her womb and uncoil between her legs!" Papalikos shouted. "The bitch should have slit her own swollen belly and cut out the poisoned fetus! If I had found her in time, I would joyfully have done it for her!" His raging words lashed the priest like the blows of a rod. "God forgive the weakness of my flesh, I absorbed her Satanic wiles the moment I entered your house! When I first set eyes on the bitch, some evil core of me was lured and hypnotized. Thank God, I kept my senses long enough to discover she'd been put here by Satan himself to tempt me! If I'd laid a hand on that soiled harlot, my soul would have been damned forever!"

Papalikos paused for breath, his face teeming with rage. He grasped the handle of the dagger sheathed in his belt. Father Markos felt himself a flutter away from death.

"She had suffered, and I wanted to protect her," the priest said. "We baptized the child in our village. His godfather is the klepht captain Manolis Kitsos! The child is under his protection!"

"I don't care if St. John himself baptized that cursed spawn!" the monk thundered. "The whore-mother and her bastard need to be dispatched back where they came from, to the eternal fires of hell!"

"No!" the priest's voice rose. "You must not harm them! I will not allow that to happen!"

"Not allow it to happen?" For a moment, the monk stared at Father Markos in disbelief. "You lying betrayer of your habit and disgracer of your church! Be thankful I maintain a shred of regard for your withered age and that soiled cassock you wear, or here, before God's holy altar, I'd gut your lying throat!" His voice rose to a roar. "I want to know in what house you have hidden them! Tell me where they are!"

"I don't know," the priest's voice trembled. "I sent them to find shelter. I don't know into whose house they have gone!"

The church door opened once again. Tzangas came up the aisle to the altar.

""We are searching the houses," he said to Papalikos, "but I don't think the bumpkins know anything. We've knocked a few of them around, and all they do is whimper and whine for mercy." He loosed a raucous laugh. "Some shit on themselves in fear, but they don't tell us anything."

"Keep searching!" Papalikos cried. "They have to be hiding somewhere in the village! We'll find them if I have to tear apart every last hovel and slit the throats of every damned liar!"

He looked balefully back at the priest. "If we don't find them, you fork-tongued old wretch," he said, "I vow we'll be back! My patience will have expired, and I'll no longer regard you as a priest but a creature as worthless as a Turk! I won't soil my hands on you but turn your lumpish carcass over to Tzangas. Believe me, Father, he is known to be able to make even a mute sing like a dove!"

After the monk and Tzangas had left the church, the priest was shaken by a seizure so severe he feared he would fall. He grasped the railing of the altar, holding on with both hands to steady himself. In the span of his lifetime, he had never before looked upon a countenance so full of unfettered rage. The priest marveled that he had been left alive. He gazed up at the paintings of the saints, the small oil wicks burning before their austere and desiccated faces. They had been martyrs for their faith, their lives more consequential than his own wretched life, their deaths more meaningful than anything his own death might achieve. Yet, what happened to him did not matter. If the monk found the mother and child, he'd murder them both. If the monk let him live, Father Markos would have to tell Manolis that he'd failed to protect the blessed pair as he'd vowed.

Releasing his hold on the railing, he turned and knelt before the sanctuary. He spoke to the saints in their icons, to the image of the crucified Christ above the altar, to the loving visage of the Panagia Mother.

"O Lord, my Lord," he said, and his voice sounded frailer, more despairing than in any prayer he had ever spoken. "All across our anguished land, thousands suffer and die, the old and the young, every poor soul with a prayer to you on their lips." He shook his head in resignation. "I know you cannot answer the prayers of such a multitude, that many who pray must die. I understand that truth, O Lord, and still in that chorus of voices raised to you in prayer, I beg you listen to my poor, woeful voice. I pray not for myself but for that girl and her helpless child. She has suffered so much, Lord, and in your bountiful mercy, I beg you spare her further suffering. Take my worthless life, but spare their lives. If I cannot keep the pledge I made to Manolis, then I should not live."

His prayer continued, the words tumbling from his lips, and still he babbled on, pleading and praying, trying to make his prayer longer and more fervent than all the legion of prayers rising in that moment to God. After a while, his prayer changed, his pleas transformed into verses from all the holy texts he had ever read—from Samuel and Joshua, from Jeremiah and Job.

"The souls of the righteous are in the hand of God, and there shall no torment touch them. For though they be punished in the sight of men, yet is their hope full of immortality. Who can number the sand of the sea? And the drops of rain and the days of eternity?"

His prayers evoked a stark vision of frail human beings weaving their own bits of the web of sorrow and suffering. The young and the old, the healthy and the infirm driven by the cruelties of men and the brutalities of war from sunshine to the sunless land.

"Man born of a woman is of few days and full of trouble. He cometh forth like a flower and is cut down. He fleeth also as a shadow."

From outside the church he heard the noisy barking of dogs, the jangling of a goat bell, and the shouts of a shepherd driving his flock.

"Naked came I out of my mother's womb and naked shall I return, the Lord hath given, and the Lord hath taken away. Blessed be the name of the Lord."

Finally, his body aching, his voice grown hoarse and weak, his throat so dry his prayer became a croak, he was overcome by exhaustion. He no longer had the strength to kneel, and he prostrated himself before the altar. When his voice failed, he continued praying in his aching and despairing heart.

He did not know how long he lay at the base of the sanctuary, drained of strength and barren of tongue, when he heard what at first seemed the thunder of an approaching storm. That was followed by the crisp firing of muskets, a few random gunshots that became noisy volleys. For an instant, he feared that Papalikos and his men were murdering the villagers. He struggled to his knees, and the firing receded and then ceased.

As if from a great distance, he heard the church door burst open, and then the jubilant voice of Leontis rang through the church.

"Father, we are saved!" Leontis cried. "Manolis Kitsos rode in with a band of his men! The bloody brutes have fled! They're gone! Father, they're gone! Come, and see for yourself!"

The door closed, and the priest was alone once more. Still on his knees, he stared at the sanctuary, at the flickering candles, at the austere faces of the saints.

"O my God," he prayed. And the tears ran like rivers down his cheeks. "O my God! Blessed and merciful God! O my God!"

Later, the priest and the villagers were provided a plausible explanation for the timely appearance of Manolis and his band of klephts. They had raided a Turkish arms convoy near Kratoria, about twenty kilometers from Kravasaras. After killing some and then driving off the remaining Turkish soldiers, they discovered that in addition to muskets and gunpowder, the convoy was a cornucopia of provisions. There were baskets of Arcadian figs and grapes, round loaves of sesame-seeded bread, tubs of Kalamata olives and Messenian cheeses as well as kegs of fine Anatolian wine.

Wishing to share their bounty with the villagers, Manolis had altered the route of the band's return journey to stop in Kravasaras. A shepherd on the road beyond the village had informed the klephts of the renegade monk who occupied Kravasaras and was abusing the villagers. Manolis and his band galloped into the village and attacked Papalikos and his men, who, after exchanging a few volleys of gunfire with the klephts, fled.

The villagers marveled at the benevolent fortune that brought Manolis into Kravasaras to save them and to rescue, as well, Maria and his godson, Lefteris, who had emerged from the fruit cellar of Leontis to join the celebration.

But, in his heart and without speaking of it to others, the priest knew that Manolis and his men were only instruments of the Lord. He understood that in the declining years of his life, near the culmination of his priesthood, after decades of feeble chants and ineffectual sermons, he had been witness to a miracle as profound as those the Son of God had performed in His brief span of life on earth. The priest's anguished prayer, rising into the firmament alongside the prayers of countless other poor souls—his prayer had somehow caught God's compassionate ear. And in His mercy and by His power, He had altered the path of the journey Manolis and his men had made.

Later in the day, Father Markos held a special liturgy of prayer and thanksgiving attended by villagers and klephts. Still weak from his desperate prayers, his voice and chants sounded hoarse and weary, but his heart was gladdened to see the elated faces of the villagers grateful for their deliverance. After the service, Manolis and Maria lingered to speak to Father Markos. In the foyer of the church, Dafni waited with the child Lefteris.

When Maria and Manolis attempted to kiss the priest's hand, he pulled it gently away and, instead, embraced them warmly.

"Bless you again, Father, for Lefteris and me," Maria said, her eyes moist. "Sending us away when you did saved our lives."

"Our thanks belong to Manolis and his men who saved all our lives."

"We must also be grateful to the Turks for the opulence of their cargo," Manolis smiled. "The harvest of food we liberated was so bountiful I felt I had to share it with the village." He paused, his tone quieter and his expression more serious. "Father, my men and I cannot remain here more than another day or two before we have to start back. I understand now I cannot leave Maria and Lefteris unprotected in the village. If they aren't in danger from a rogue band such as the one we drove off, some other vengeful Greek may do them harm."

He drew Maria closer. "After my last visit here, Father, a group of refugees straggled into our mountain camp, mostly poor and exhausted women and children who had been in flight for weeks. Vorogrivas allowed them to set up a camp not far from our own. The mountains are a harsh terrain, but they felt safe and were reluctant to leave. Our men built shelters for them and set up ovens for the women to bake bread. Their camp has become a small community. We have even given it a name—Akropolis—because the settlement sits so near the peak of the mountain." He paused. "When you last asked me, Father, I told you I had no heart to make Maria my wife one week and my widow a week later. But now, Father, I take back my words." Elation warmed his face. "I've asked Maria to be my wife. She hasn't accepted my proposal for reasons I don't think are important. So I come to you, Father, asking that you plead my proposal to her as well."

"What is it that troubles you, Maria?" Father Markos asked gently.

"Before God, Father," Maria said, her voice low and tremulous, "I am grateful and proud that Manolis wishes me to be his wife. I thought no man would ever want me again." She gestured in resignation. "What Manolis doesn't understand is that in our village, from the time I was born, my mother began preparing my dowry. She put aside tablecloths, bedcovers, linen, pots, and embroideries of the Holy Family and the holy saints. My father pledged when I married, he would provide my husband and me a house."

The young woman's face revealed her grief.

"When the Turks raided and burned our village, all that was lost. I no longer have parents alive to share my joy. I would bring nothing to this marriage but the clothes Lefteris and I wear and even those have been provided by the kindness of the villagers." She stared plaintively at the priest. "Father, I'm ashamed . . . ashamed to bring so little to someone as good and worthy as Manolis. Any number of women with houses and orchards would be proud to have him as a husband."

"I don't want a wealthy woman!" Manolis said, his voice echoing from the corners of the church. "I care only about Maria and Lefteris! Let us marry, and I'll take them to live near me in the settlement. God willing, we survive the war, and we'll make this village our home." His voice turned somber. "Father, even if the worst happens, and I am lost in battle, then Maria would be the widow of Manolis Kitsos. My comrades would make sure she and Lefteris were cared for and safe."

Father Markos struggled for a way to judge their pleas.

"In a time of peace, the proper marriage customs would have been observed," he said slowly. "There would be a dowry and preparations made weeks ahead for an exchange of vows. But we are now a land at war and nothing is the same."

He spoke gently to Maria. "My child, all of us are in danger but you and the child most of all. If you consent now to marry Manolis, I will gladly marry you. The village is poor, and the wedding celebration will be sparse, but more important than anything, else, Maria, is the question, Do you love Manolis and wish to have him as your husband?"

The girl stared at the priest and then looked at Manolis. She lowered her head shyly.

"I love him, Father."

Her words heartened Manolis.

"I love you, too, Maria!" he said fervently. "Since we love one another, tell Father Markos you will marry me. I want to hear you say it!"

"I will marry you, Manolis," Maria said quietly. "I'll be a scarecrow bride who will bring you nothing but a child in her arms and the love in her heart."

"That's all I want!" Manolis said jubilantly.

"The matter is settled then," Father Markos said. "I will speak at once to Leontis and have him prepare the wedding papers. With God's blessing, we will bypass the other formalities." He smiled. "My dear Maria and Manolis, it will provide me great joy to marry you tomorrow."

In all the years Father Markos had been a priest in Kravasaras, never had a marriage been put together so quickly. As soon as Manolis and Maria left, the priest sent his sexton to notify Leontis. He also called in Christos Lambridis, the most talented artisan in the village, asking him to fashion a pair of *stefana,* the wedding crowns, as well as a set of rings for the marriage service.

"It's a shame, Father," Ephemia Karras, the pastry maker in the village told the priest when she heard the news, "that we don't have time or the means to prepare the grand pastries such a noble wedding deserves. But I've been saving some flour and honey, and, I promise you, we'll prepare some pastries including *baklava* for the wedding feast."

Under the supervision of Ephemia, the village women began baking that afternoon and worked through the night by candlelight and oil lamp. Another group of women prepared the *koufeta,* the sugar-coated almonds, wrapped in tiny packets of tulle that would be placed on the wedding tray. In past years, following the marriage ceremony, the *koufeta* were handed out to the unmarried women, who placed them under their pillows as amulets to aid in finding husbands. But that custom was not needed this year since there was not one young single woman of marriage age still living in the village.

From among her belongings, Dafni Makris retrieved her own turquoise wedding skirt, a flowing garment stitched with gold thread. Despina Daros provided a white, silk blouse, and Fotini Lambridis lent a richly sheened velvet jacket. The best seamstress in the village, Katerina Tsokas, adjusted the garments to fit Maria.

Several village men contributed wedding attire for Manolis, including a blue, silk broad-sleeved shirt and a finely tailored, silver-flecked jacket. Petros Scarpas offered an elegant velvet sash and a small, jeweled scimitar.

"These belonged to my son Ares, who was killed in the first year of the war fighting in Rumeli with Delayannis," Scarpas said gravely. "He would be very proud, I know, if you wore them."

"I will be honored," Manolis replied.

Leontis and Dafni Makris made plans to stay with a cousin and offered the bride and groom their house for the wedding night. A half-dozen women made up the marriage bed using Dafni's white embroidered linens that had been part of her dowry decades earlier.

The morning of the wedding, a stream of visitors entered the Makris house and were offered a glass of wine with *paximadi*. Afterwards, they entered the bedroom to place a few gifts for the bride and groom on the bed. In more prosperous, peaceful days, the gifts for so prestigious a wedding would have been fine linens and even gold coins. But the poverty of the village meant the gifts were few and meager in value. Yet, they were still presented with heartfelt good wishes and fervent prayers for the happiness of the bride and groom. Finally, the youngest village children were allowed to recline briefly on the bed, a ritual to invoke fertility for the bride and groom.

In the late afternoon, with a cloudless blue sky as a harbinger of spring, the bell in the church tower began pealing its joyous message across the countryside. Inside the nave, the candles and oil wicks were glowing. In preparation for the ceremony, Father Markos had carefully trimmed his beard and brushed his disheveled head of hair. He had scrupulously wiped the most evident stains off his faded vestments.

He was in the altar room back of the sanctuary when he heard the laughing, boisterous klephts entering the church. He peered through a small slit in the doorway to see the young men escorting a well-scrubbed and regally dressed Manolis to a position at the altar. His *koumbaros*, Zarkas, was with them, as well. He had also acquired several articles of colorful clothing. Unaware they were being overheard, the klepht engaged in a rough and acerbic banter.

"Hard for me to understand why Maria would choose Manolis when she has me around," a handsome young klepht boasted.

"You might ask her," Manolis said. "But hours would be needed to list all the reasons she'd prefer me."

"If you need any help in the marriage bed tonight, Manolis," another klepht smirked, "I'll be available."

"Thanks, Sotiris," Manolis laughed. "If I need someone to empty the chamber pot, I'll be sure to call you."

"I've never seen a more ragged and uglier *koumbaros*," another klepht taunted Zarkas. "If I were the groom, I'd make you wear a sack over your shaggy head."

"Don't worry about the kind of *koumbaros* I am," Zarkas snapped back. "Save your concern about how you'll ever find a woman willing to marry a lout who doesn't bathe but once a month!"

"If you ever have a daughter, Zarkas, will you promise to let her become my bride?"

"I'd rather she married a one-eyed, one-legged farmer than a licentious, worthless wretch like you!" Zarkas scowled.

Their taunting was curbed when the villagers began to enter the church. The klephts joined them, leaving Manolis and Zarkas at the altar. A short time later, a sound of music carried from the street outside, and a trio of musicians playing a fiddle, a *bouzouki*, and a *santouri* led a group of laughing, singing women escorting the bride into the church. As Maria entered the nave, the crowd in the church called their blessings and opened a path for the procession. The women led Maria to the altar to stand beside Manolis before the altar table, which held the crowns and rings.

Father Markos emerged from the sanctuary and took his place on the opposite side of the table. Whispers of excitement roiled the church, and then the crowd quieted.

The sexton lit and handed a pair of long white candles adorned with white silk ribbons to Father Markos, who passed them to Maria and Manolis. The candles were symbols of their willingness to accept Christ in their lives.

With the candlelight glowing across the faces of Maria and Manolis, Father Markos observed with awe that they were, without a doubt, the loveliest bride and handsomest groom he had ever married. Maria's luminous dark eyes and raven-black hair made her appear a reincarnation of matchless beauty from a classical myth. Manolis, tall and strong beside her, might have been a noble young prince in the lineage of the Mycenaean kings. He quickly recanted the imprudent thoughts for fear they might invoke some minion of ill fortune.

Standing beside the groom as stalwart witness and zealous guardian of the couple's joy, the stocky *koumbaros*, Zarkas, beamed, his teeth flashing like pearls in the dark, bearded forest of his face. Beside Zarkas, Dafni held Lefteris by the hand, the child mesmerized by the candles and the solemnity of the ritual. The faces of the villagers appeared equally enthralled by the first marriage held in the village in the four years since the war began.

"Blessed are all they that fear the Lord," Father Markos began the service of betrothal and the blessing of the rings. Beside the glittering candelabra at the farthest side of the altar, old and lean Spirakes the cantor, his mellifluent voice that age had not weakened or dulled chanted the response. "Glory to Thee, O our God, glory to Thee."

"And walk in his ways," the priest said.

"Glory to thee, O our God, glory to Thee."

"Blessed be the kingdom of the Father and of the Son and of the Holy Ghost, now and forever and from all ages to all ages."

"Amen," the cantor sang.

Father Markos raised his hands above the heads of Maria and Manolis.

"O God, most holy and maker of all creation, who through thy love to man didst change the rib of our forefather Adam into woman and didst bless both and say increase and multiply and have dominion over the earth—"

From the rear of the church, a small child raised a piercing cry that spiraled toward the dome of the nave as her mother pulled her quickly into the foyer. As the child's cry faded, in the sky above the bell tower, like an augury of good fortune, a flock of birds flew by, their throaty clamor carrying clear and resonant for a moment and then receding slowly as they passed.

"Remember them, O Lord our God, as thou didst remember thy forty Holy Martyrs, sending down upon them crowns from heaven. Remember them, O God, who are come together in this joy."

A few old women, perhaps reminded of their own long-past nuptials, began to weep tears that mingled joy and nostalgia.

"Grant them of the fruit of their bodies, O Lord, exalt them like the cedars of Lebanon, like a luxuriant vine. Give them seed in number like unto the full ears of grain. Let them behold their children's children like a newly planted olive orchard round about their table, that they may shine like the stars of heaven in Thee, our God."

The couple exchanged the marriage rings three times. The ceremony of the sacrament of marriage began as Father Markos picked up the first flowered crown from the altar table and placed it upon Manolis's head.

"The servant of God Manolis is crowned . . . "

He placed the second crown on Maria's head, the flowers gleaming vividly above the white sheen of her veil.

" . . . for the servant of God, Maria."

Zarkas stepped forward, grinning broadly and, as Father Markos had diligently instructed him before the ceremony began, reached up and grasped the crowns. In an awkward tangling of his hands, he exchanged the crowns three times on the heads of the bride and groom.

Father Markos led bride, groom, and *koumbaros* three times in a slow circling around the altar table in the Dance of Isaiah, symbolizing the journey of husband and wife through life. As they circled, Zarkas, struggling to hold the crowns in place on the heads of the bride and tall groom, stumbled. A billow of laughter rose from his comrades in the church. Zarkas swept the assemblage with a fierce glare that threatened bodily harm to anyone he perceived laughing at him.

When they had finished circling, the bride and groom returned to their places before the altar table. Father Markos raised the crowns from their heads and replaced them on the table. He made a final sign of the cross.

"In the name of the Father, and of the Son, and of the Holy Ghost, beloved Maria and Manolis are now man and wife." His voice trembled with the emotion he felt then. "And we beseech God grant them a long and happy life."

Manolis turned to Maria. Bride and groom faced one another as if they were the only two mortals who existed in the world. The priest poignantly recalled the words of Hesoid, "From their eyelids as they glanced at one another, dripped love."

Manolis gently and chastely kissed his bride. A chorus of joyous, approving laughter swept the church.

Klephts and villagers formed a ragged line to congratulate Maria and Manolis. The klephts, with bold eyes and suggestive looks, swaggered by. The elders filed by slowly, gravely offering their blessings and best wishes. Gero Sotiris, one of the oldest men in the village with six sons and two daughters all fighting the Turks in the north, clasped Manolis's hands and with his voice trembling expressed his fervent prayer that the groom live to see one of his own children married. The old women shuffled by, their cheeks still moist with tears, and fervently kissed the hands of the bride and groom and wished them good fortune.

"May you have ten children," Katerina Tsokas said.

"May they be nine boys and a girl!" her husband added.

The wedding celebration was held in the village taverna. The large room had been swept, scrubbed, and decorated for the occasion with tinsel and bunting. Nikos Psomas played the *bouzouki*, and Mitsos Collis the fiddle. After the wedding feast, which came from the provisions impounded from the Turkish caravan, people formed lines to dance. For the first dance, bride and groom led the line, circling in a graceful *syrtos*. The people watching clapped and cheered.

When the young klephts began to dance, feeling their movements restricted by the walls of the taverna, they ignored the night chill and with the musicians moved outside to dance under the bright moonlit sky. Within a ring of torches, the strong men with lithe, battle-hardened bodies, taking quick steps forward and quick steps back, vaulted and leaped vigorously to the beat of the music.

For an interval, Manolis led the line of klephts, holding one end of a handkerchief with the other end held by Zarkas. As the circle of dancers shouted and cheered him on, Manolis performed a series of nimble leaps. As he whirled in mid-air, he swiftly slapped his booted heel, then landed lightly back on his feet. At once, he bent into a crouch, his hand fleetingly grazing the ground before he sprang back erect.

Pausing only long enough to drink liberally from the casks of wine, the klephts took turns leading the dances that grew wilder. The dancers leaped and whirled, their bodies spinning and gyrating, the boisterous shouts and raucous cries inciting the leaders to faster and brawnier feats. As one riotous dance followed another, they became athletic contests marked by dazzling jumps and daring leaps, each man seeking to overwhelm and outdance the rest. With the flame of the torches sweeping shadows across the surrounding trees, the ground reverberated under the pounding of booted feet.

From under a nearby tree, Father Markos watching the klephts compete, thought this was how the warriors of Achilles and Odysseus might have danced celebrating under Homer's glittering moon. After a while, the night cold chilling his bones, Father Markos retreated into the taverna to take a chair with a group of elders. A stream of people came to speak to him, toasting the welfare and happiness of the bride and groom. Everyone offered blessings as well for their young sons and daughters, brothers and sisters fighting in the north against the Turks, looking to the day they'd return to weddings of their own.

Leontis kept refilling the priest's glass, and, after a while, the room beginning to sway, Father Markos knew he had drunk too much. In the midst of the tumult and celebration, the bride and groom had slipped away, and he decided it might be prudent for him to stop guzzling and get himself home, as well. Holding carefully to his chair, he rose to leave.

"Will you need an arm to lean on, Father?" Cleon Pitsas asked, his own words slurred by wine.

"I'll be fine, Cleon!" Father Markos spoke with more vigor than his condition warranted. "I'll be fine!"

Despite his assurances to the elder, Father Markos walked from the taverna feeling the ground strangely unsettled under his feet. He left the klephts still engaged in their wild dancing. The priest knew they would continue to dance through the night until the last man collapsed from drink or exhaustion.

Walking slowly and praying under his breath that he make it safely home, Father Markos was doing well until he turned a corner, when a vagrant cat, perhaps agitated by the wedding clamor, darted directly in front of him. The priest stumbled, his arms flailing, but awkwardly regained his balance. After uttering an unchristian oath against the miscreant creature, he quickly made his cross in penance and, for the balance of his journey, walked with even greater caution. He was relieved when he arrived at his door. He entered the dark, silent house, and lit the oil wick in a lamp.

"I am home, Minerva," he greeted the goat reclining placidly in the bin in the corner. "Believe me, it was a truly splendid wedding!"

He kindled a fire to warm the chilled house and then fed Minerva. Afterwards, finding it difficult to muster the will to tug off his shoes and remove his cassock and clothing, he sat for a while before the fire. The wind rose and lightly rattled the sash of his window and shook the rafters. In those moments when the wind subsided, he could still hear the sound of the music carrying across the crisp, clear night. He envisioned the young klephts still frenzied in the dance.

In the flicker and glow of the fire, he pensively recalled the life of the village as it had been before the outbreak of the revolt. Despite being a subjugated people, they had lived in a generally benign amity with their Turkish neighbors and, on a few occasions, even celebrated together. He remembered the pleasant interludes when he visited his dear friend Ahmed Bajaki. That honorable Muslim, along with many of the other Muslims of Kravasaras, respected their Christian traditions and their faith.

In that time in the life of the village, young people still courted and married. In addition to the weddings were the baptisms for the newborn, the solemn feast days of the church, the birth of Christ at Christmas, the death and resurrection of their Savior at Easter. Of course, there were the funerals, which were also an inevitable part of life.

Those nostalgic memories faded, and Father Markos considered his future. He had been resigned to living a solitary existence for so many years, and then the beloved mother and child entered his life. He rejoiced in their warm and endearing presence, the sharing of suppers, seeing the girl's lovely countenance when he woke in the morning, the delight he felt when he played with Lefteris.

He suddenly understood that all the fulfillment and pleasure he had savored for the past few years would be lost to him now. That sense of loss swept him with a bleakness of spirit more painful than any he had experienced since the death of his wife. He could not help himself, and, putting his head in his hands, he released a forlorn wail of lament. At once, he was shaken with a remorse.

"Shame on me, Minerva!" he cried loudly and with agitation to the goat. "Will you believe this old, wine-soaked fool of a priest sits here mourning his own fate instead of rejoicing for the happiness of those young people? That only proves that old men are children for a second time. When Maria and Lefteris are in the mountains with Manolis, they will be loved and protected, safe from harm. The child will have a chance to grow into young manhood in a land that may someday, God willing, be free!"

After purging his remorse to Minerva, he rose from his chair before the fire and wearily prepared for bed, tugging off his shoes and removing his cassock and outer clothing. He bent his head and spoke his prayers and then entered his bed, pulling the quilt to his throat. On his side, he watched the fire dying slowly, the glowing embers emitting their last sparks.

He drew some solace in knowing that the winter was nearly over, that spring was imminent, the earth stirring and blooming with new life. The warmer air would kindle the scents of new buds blooming on the trees and in the gardens.

Perhaps the spring and the passage of another year would see their revolt victorious, the last Muslims driven from their land. Manolis, Maria, and Lefteris as well as the other young people fighting valorously for the cause would return to the village. Living as a free people would bring them a contentment they had never before known. Yet, even if freedom came soon to their anguished land, the benefits to Father Markos would be useless because he was in the twilight of his life.

At times, the thought of dying frightened him. His faith granted him the bounty of believing that he would join the great legion of the deceased in the Elysian fields beyond the perimeters of the Earth. In that eternal garden, there would no longer be winters to contend with, cold and inclement storms to endure. He would be relieved of the frailties of his aging body and the fears and anxieties that burdened his daily life. God willing, he'd find his beloved wife waiting for him. He wondered suddenly whether she would have aged as well or whether he'd find her young and vibrant as he remembered her before her death.

As he listened to the faint strains of the buoyant music carrying across the night, he felt himself slipping seamlessly into a flow of darkness, a repose that embraced him with such totality that, for a frightened and yet anticipatory instant, he felt as if he were entering the domain of death itself.

CHAPTER
SEVEN

Xanthos spent the winter of 1825 secluded in a small village twenty kilometers west of Navplion and working on his journal of the war. While he understood his limitations as a historian, he hoped his personal observations of the politics and warfare might supplement the more scholarly histories of the revolution that would be written later.

In many ways, the conflict between the political factions presently in Greece was reminiscent of the internal struggles recorded by Thucydides, who many centuries earlier had written his history of the Peloponnesian War. That fratricidal conflict between Athens and Sparta left both Greek states exhausted and impoverished. The virulent seed of self-destruction remained part of the Greek psyche.

The tragedy of Greek politics, as Xanthos noted in his journal, was that the various factions were only united when an external foe confronted them. When that threat temporarily abated, the absence of a common enemy provided a breeding ground for bitter quarrels between military and political factions. As the revolution progressed into its second and third years, there were times when it appeared this rancorous discord would doom the struggle for freedom. By the fourth year of the revolution, the quarrels, jealousies, and heated disputes erupted into civil war for the second time.

From the beginning of the revolution, various groups had vied for control of the newly proclaimed Greek government. At the time Xanthos was recording his chronicle, the party claiming to be the legitimate government was the New Executive led by Gorgios Koundouriotes, a primate from the island of Hydra. His party, which had taken control in January of 1824, included leaders from Hydra as well as the island of Spetsia. Among these leaders was an unscrupulous politician named Yannis Kolettis, who had taken over the War Ministry. Kolettis had been versed in intrigue as a physician at the court of Ali Pasha, the Butcher of Ioannina. He was the man in the New Executive most resolved to break the power of the military chieftains of the Peloponnesus.

The leader among the military chieftains was Theodoros Kolokotronis with his sons Panos and Gennaios and his nephew, the warrior Nikitas. These chieftains defied the government and questioned its legitimacy. They refused to allow the government's tax collectors into their provinces and appropriated the local revenues for themselves. While Koundouriotes attempted to fashion a compromise with the chieftains, Kolettis, acting on his own initiative, broke off negotiations and dispatched several regiments of Rumeliot troops as well as Bulgarian mercenaries into the Peloponnesus. After several bloody battles, the outnumbered military chieftains were defeated.

Xanthos recorded in his chronicle that the victory of the New Executive hadn't been achieved by any strategic or moral superiority but because they had the substantial monies from the English loan committee. These funds allowed them to purchase the services of the Rumeliot and Bulgarian troops.

After defeating the chieftains, the Rumeliot soldiery and the Bulgarian mercenaries, forsaking any allegiance to the government that had hired them, plundered the villages of the Peloponnesus. They stole stores of food from the villagers, carried off their sheep, goats, and donkeys.

In that lawless time, treachery and murder were also weapons of choice. Odysseus Androutsos, one of the great fighters of the revolution, had been accused of treason against the New Executive and imprisoned in the Frankish Tower at the western end of the Acropolis. For weeks, he was chained in his cell and tortured, it was said, to reveal the whereabouts of the treasure he was reported to have gathered. One morning, the rising sun disclosed the lifeless body of Androutsos at the foot of the tower. Gouras, the tower's commander, claimed that Androutsos had been trying to escape and that the rope with which he was lowering himself had broken. But it was generally accepted that the valiant soldier had been strangled and his body thrown from the wall to make it appear he had died while attempting to escape.

Another loss that occurred in the savage fighting between the government and the military chiefs was one that struck directly at the heart of Kolokotronis—the death of Panos, his eldest son.

Xanthos witnessed the general's terrible grief when they brought him the body of his son. Kolokotronis secluded himself with Panos for the span of a night. When he left the next morning to make arrangements for the funeral, it seemed to Xanthos the general had aged by years. His eyes were bloodshot, and his cheeks were swollen with his tears.

"The death of a young son destroys a father's dream," Kolokotronis told Xanthos sadly, "the dream that after his death, men might say of his son, 'He was far greater than his father.'"

But the leaders of the New Executive were not content with defeating Kolokotronis on the battlefield. They feared his influence with the people and accused him and one of his associates, Kanellos Delayannis, of treason. They were ordered to stand trial in a proceeding motivated by vengefulness and deceit.

Xanthos, who was present at the trial, recognized that Kolokotronis was not without flaws. He was a proud and stubborn, at times, even an arrogant man who was reluctant to share power. But he was also an exemplary patriot and brilliant military leader who had devoted his life to the cause of his country's freedom.

Yet, none of his victories or accomplishments seemed to matter when a procession of witnesses, motivated by the government's resolve to find him guilty, testified against him. In the process, words and meanings were distorted. The general's victories in battle were labeled a strategy to gain power. His courage was held to be recklessness. His loyalty and generosity were scorned as weakness. In the end, the verdict of guilty foreordained, Kolokotronis and Delayannis were sentenced to exile and imprisonment on the island of Hydra.

Meanwhile, the threat from the Egyptian armies of Ibrahim Pasha became increasingly dangerous. During the previous summer and fall of 1824, Admiral Miaoulis, who commanded the Greek fleet, had managed to thwart the invasion of the Peloponnesus by Ibrahim Pasha and his troops.

Because no naval force had ever attempted to cross the Cretan sea during the stormy winter season, Admiral Miaoulis sailed his fleet home at the beginning of winter in 1825 to rest his seamen, to repair his ships, and to plan strategy for the battles that would resume in the spring.

But the tenacious Ibrahim Pasha ignored the winter, assembled his fleet once more, and, with the sea between before him barren of Greek ships, sailed on the twenty-fourth of February 1825 from his base at Souda Bay on the north coast of Crete. Two days later, he had reached the coast of the Peloponnesus. His ships returned to Crete and brought back additional troops and horses. Within the span of ten days, Ibrahim had disembarked at the fortress of Modon what Greek scouts estimated as at least ten thousand Egyptian soldiers, a thousand horses, and several hundred pieces of artillery that included howitzers and six-pound cannons.

The landing of the Egyptian army had shocked the Greeks, who began desperately assembling forces to resist it, but the bitter civil war had bred resentment and hostility that made concerted action among the leaders impossible. Even under the best of conditions, the Greek forces might not have been able to prevent Ibrahim Pasha from invading the Peloponnesus, but with their forces weakened by rivalries, the Greek chieftains seemed helpless.

Living as he was in the isolated village, it took weeks before Xanthos learned that Ibrahim Pasha had landed in the Peloponnesus. He anticipated that the Greek government would be assembling an army to confront him. He also knew that in the battles to come, the military abilities of the imprisoned Kolokotronis would be sorely missed.

At the beginning of spring, Xanthos received permission to visit Kolokotronis on Hydra. He had written half a dozen letters pleading with government officials in the New Executive, assuring them that his visit had no military significance but was only motivated by his long friendship with the general. Finally, permission was granted with the strict proviso that his visit should last no longer than a day.

Xanthos packed a few belongings and traveled from the village to the port in Navplion. While seeking to hire a boatman with a caique to carry him to Hydra, for the first time Xanthos heard that Ibrahim Pasha and his forces had taken the island of Sphakteria and were attacking the fortresses of Old and New Navarino.

On the crossing from the mainland, the sea was turbulent, the surging waves crowned by whitecaps rocking the caique.

"See how the waves gallop along the water like horses?" the grizzled boatman said. "For that reason, we Hydriotes believe that Poseidon, the god of the sea, is also the creator of horses."

As they approached, the island emerged from the sea, a great mound of barren rock, silent, watchful. Within a cloudless, blue sky, the sun radiated a blazing panorama of light across the stone. After he'd disembarked in the port, Xanthos was confronted by a squad of surly Rumeliot soldiers, who scrutinized the papers authorizing his visit.

"Why do you want to visit that scurvy old rebel?" a soldier sneered.

"That old rebel has given our revolution some of its greatest victories," Xanthos said brusquely.

The man grunted and motioned him to move on.

Xanthos arranged for a donkey and guide to take him up the mountain to the monastery where Kolokotronis was imprisoned. As they began their ascent, the sun rose higher in the sky, its rays igniting the rocks, which reflected a heat like fire.

"If the sun burns so fiercely in the spring, what is the summer like?" Xanthos asked.

The guide, a wizened and wiry old islander, grinned. "The island becomes the anvil of hell."

Seeking a momentary respite from the heat, they sheltered under a thickly foliaged plane tree. A nearby spring was dry.

"Most of our springs dry up because our island is volcanic," the guide said. "Underground eruptions destroy the freshwater springs. If it were not for occasional rain and the barrels of water we transport from the mainland, we would all perish from thirst in the space of a few weeks."

When they reached the monastery, in the courtyard outside the cloisters Xanthos was again accosted by soldiers. These were Bulgarian mercenaries, hairy, bellicose men with the eyes of assassins. They were commanded by a ferret-faced Greek sergeant, who brushed aside the papers Xanthos presented.

"My orders are that no one is permitted to see the prisoner!" the sergeant snapped.

"These papers authorize my visit," Xanthos said, for an anxious moment fearing he had made the trip in vain. "You can see they have been signed by the government of the New Executive."

The sergeant continued to bluster and deny him entry. The Bulgarian soldiers clustered around them, snarling and threatening Xanthos with their muskets. Xanthos finally understood the sergeant was denying the papers because he could not read them.

Xanthos spoke in a loud voice, demonstrating a confidence he did not feel. "These orders come from President Koundouriotes himself!" he said sternly. "If I leave without seeing the general and inform the president his orders weren't obeyed, he will have the flesh hot from your back!"

His show of force intimidated the sergeant, and his face dark with frustration, he gestured for the soldiers to stand back. Xanthos entered the monastery and encountered a lean-figured monk, his face gleaming like a pale melon in the shroud of his hood.

"I am here to see the general," Xanthos said.

The monk raised his arm, his wrist and bony hand emerging like an arid stalk from the sleeve of his habit. He pointed along a corridor leading into a courtyard.

"The path leads up the mountain," he said. "You will find the general there."

When Xanthos left the cooler confines of the monastery, and walked into the sunlight, he felt once again the oppressive heat. As he ascended the stony path toward the peak, around him the island flowers shone in luminous bloom. There were violet delphiniums, golden thistle, and the pink blossoms of oleander. Their fragrances scented the burning air.

On a ridge beneath the peak of the mountain, Kolokotronis was seated on the ground, his back braced against the trunk of a battered, wind-swept pine tree. The general was motionless, staring at the sea.

Pausing for a moment to regain his breath, Xanthos stared across the horizons that Kolokotronis gazed upon. From that angle of vision, he felt as if he were standing at the pinnacle of the Earth itself. Beyond the great moon-shaped bay of Hydra where his caique had moored, the vistas on all sides were endless. There were the misted outlines of mountains marking the other Saronic islands. To the north, he could see the contours of Poros. To the south, the open sea extended all the way to the great island of Crete. Beyond Crete, hidden by distance and the mist, lay the alien regions of Africa.

Some intimation of his presence must have alerted Kolokotronis. He twisted around and, when he saw Xanthos, he uttered a low, hoarse cry and rose quickly to his feet.

"Xanthos, my friend!" the great voice rumbled from his throat. A moment later, Xanthos felt himself engulfed in the powerful arms of Kolokotronis. As he struggled to catch his breath, the general released him.

"I cannot recall ever looking upon so welcome a human face!" Kolokotronis said, his voice choked with emotion. "How did you manage to obtain permission for a visit? They haven't allowed a soul beside the monks near me for months now."

"I wrote half a dozen letters pleading my case as a friend," Xanthos said. "I think it helped that I was not a military man. In the end, I believe it was Prince Mavrokordatos who championed my request."

"Bless the man for that favor," Kolokotronis said.

"Is Delayannis with you here?" Xanthos asked.

"They have jailed him elsewhere on the island," Kolokotronis shrugged. "They fear that by placing the two of us together, we'll hatch another rebellion."

Afterwards, when he'd returned to the Peloponnesus, Xanthos would try to recall the conversation that took place that first afternoon he sat with Kolokotronis beneath the gaunt pine tree.

What he remembered most clearly were the grievous changes in the demeanor and figure of the general. His long, thick hair was whiter and unkempt, his swirling mustache coarse and untrimmed. His strong frame seemed thinner, and the contours of his hawk-like profile sharper. His cheeks were pale, lacking the ruddiness of vigorous health he'd reflected in the past.

But it was the general's eyes that Xanthos found most changed. They held a sadness and a weariness that seemed to emanate from his soul. When he spoke of the war and the bickering among the factions, his voice reflected his despair.

242   THE SHEPHERDS OF SHADOWS

"Victory for this war rests in the hands of the soldiers," the general said, "but they are betrayed by the sorry words of scheming men, those so-called leaders, Xanthos, who conceal one emotion in their hearts and with their mouths utter something else."

Xanthos told Kolokotronis the news about the invasion of Ibrahim Pasha and the attack on the forts at Navarino.

"That invasion has been expected ever since we learned the Egyptians were entering the war," the general said. 'All the battles we have fought so far will be minor skirmishes compared to what lies ahead. Ibrahim Pasha will prove more dangerous to our cause than any of the Turkish leaders we have fought in the past.

In a more pensive moment, Kolokotronis spoke of his son.

"Now that there is nothing for me to do but sit idly and wait. I don't spend my time thinking of those men who betrayed me but of my son. It is hard for me to believe that Panos is dead. I find myself remembering him as a boy, the way he laughed, how proudly he sat on the horse I bought him for his twelfth birthday." He fell silent, staring sadly across the sea. "During those years we lived in exile on Zante, I would take my sons to the ridges of the mountain and point to the peaks of the Peloponnesus across the sea. I told them our destiny was to liberate our homeland. 'I will help you, Papa!' Panos said. 'When I grow up, I will help you bring freedom to our land!'"

Kolokotronis shook his head. "Panos gave his life for our cause, but we are nowhere near liberated. If we do not find the wisdom to heal our quarrels, I fear we are now as close to defeat as we have been since the fighting began."

"Do you know where Gennaios is now?" Xanthos asked.

"Fearing they will imprison him, as well," Kolokotronis said, "I suspect he has gone into hiding, perhaps joining one of the klepht bands."

When Kolokotronis spoke of the leaders of the New Executive who had imprisoned him, anger wracked his voice.

"They called us rebels," Kolokotronis said bitterly, "but we earned our right to speak in the councils by the blood we shed. Where were they in the early battles of the revolt? Where were they when we fought so fiercely and defeated the Turks at Valtetzi at a cost of two hundred of our own brave dead strewn on the earth? Where were they when Petrobey and I led the Maniots against the Turkish cavalry at Karitena and saw our men cut down like sheaves of corn before the Muslim yataghans!"

The melon-faced monk brought them a pitcher of cold water and some *paximadia*. They lingered, the afternoon passing slowly. Little swirls of parched wind trembled the branches of the pine tree above their heads. From the harbor below drifted up the sounds of the surf. Later, across the sparkling, azure sky, the first clouds of twilight appeared like ships adrift in an open sea.

"Are you in danger here, General?" Xanthos asked. "Is there a chance the government won't be content to keep you imprisoned but might try to harm you? They wouldn't dare do it openly but remember what they did to Odysseus, making his death appear an accident."

"There is always that possibility, Xanthos," Kolokotronis said. "I don't believe I'm in immediate danger because they know the people regard me as a champion of the revolution. Of course, as with Androutsos, they could claim I had an accident, that I fell from a crag or drowned in the sea. If that is what they decide to do, there is little I can do to prevent it." He smiled. "Let us hope the more noble souls among that pitiful lot prevail."

Several moments passed in silence before Kolokotronis spoke again.

"I am less concerned with my own fate, Xanthos, than with what will become of our sorrowing country," he said sadly. "This poor land, so often assaulted and violated. The question I ask myself over and over is whether we will succeed in gaining our freedom, or if after all the blood that has been shed, we tumble back into the abyss of slavery once again."

In the late afternoon, they walked down the mountain to the monastery, and, seated at a small rough-hewn wood table on the stone terrace, they ate a sparse meal of hard bread and greens sprinkled with a few drops of olive oil to dilute the bitterness.

"I am sorry there isn't any wine," Kolokotronis sighed. "When my supply ran out, I asked the soldiers who guard me for a few flasks, but those louts said they required orders to bring in wine. I have asked them several times to obtain that permission, but the days pass, and there is no wine." He smiled ruefully. "I must be grateful they allow me water. When summer comes, without water, one would shrivel up and die."

Despite the order that his visit to Kolokotronis not be any longer than a day, no soldier intruded on them to enforce the edict, and Xanthos remained with the general for several days. They passed the hours discussing strategies for the war. Kolokotronis spoke grimly of the consequences of Ibrahim Pasha ravaging in the Peloponnesus.

"Now that he has captured the island of Sphakteria, he'll have an easy time attacking and overrunning the Navarino forts," Kolokotronis said. "They won't be able to hold out against a sustained assault. After the forts fall, he'll move his army into the heartland of the Peloponnesus, against Argos, Corinth, and Tripolitza. God help us then."

He shook his head somberly. "Why should we believe that after the centuries of suffering we've endured, we'd gain our liberation without anguish, struggle, and many defeats? From the hordes that streamed down from the north, the invasion of Persians, Venetians, Franks, and Turks, Greeks have come to understand that freedom can never be taken for granted. It is elusive and impossible to maintain without constant struggle. We are like the shepherd who must, night after night, vigilantly defend his flock against marauding and hungry wolves."

On the morning of the fourth day of the visit, Kolokotronis told Xanthos to prepare for his departure from the island.

"I will be pleased to remain with you as long as they don't force me to leave, General," Xanthos said.

"Glad though I am for your company, Xanthos, there isn't reason for you to stay," Kolokotronis said. "You are not the one sentenced to prison, so why should you remain in jail? More important, you accomplish nothing by remaining with me here. You best rejoin the struggle, helping wherever you can be of most use."

He stared from the monastery window across the sea.

"I have considered those Greek chieftains now engaged in the struggle," the general said gravely. "It grieves me to say not all of them can be trusted. The man for whom I hold the highest regard is a soldier, not a politician. He is Captain Yannis Makriyannis from Lidoriki. We were both impressed with him when he visited our headquarters at Navplion last year."

"But he has been allied with the government of the New Executive," Xanthos said. "He led a force of government soldiers against you."

"I haven't forgotten that confrontation," Kolokotronis said, "but during my trial, I learned Makriyannis had become disillusioned with the government. He sent word with one of my jailers that he wished me well, and he vowed never again to raise his weapon against another Greek. But what is more important is that he is a valorous and able soldier. Until I am released, Xanthos, and you can join me again, it is my wish that you find Makriyannis. I will provide you a letter that you will deliver to him. I will tell him how highly I regard your abilities and ask him to avail himself of your good services."

"Will he trust me?"

"He will trust you. He will look into your eyes and see the reflection of his own honest heart. And he will have urgent need of your counsel in dealing with the intrigues of the politicians."

The following morning, Xanthos prepared to leave, and Kolokotronis and he embraced a final time.

"It isn't fair, General," Xanthos said, and he could not conceal his despair. "At a time when our nation needs you most, it is an injustice that they keep you imprisoned."

"Let us be patient and not lose faith, Xanthos," Kolokotronis said quietly. "I tell you now that by the time the fruit of the orange and the tangerine turn golden, I will be released to join the struggle." He smiled wryly. "However much they denounce my politics and fear my influence, I have proved many times I am an able soldier. When the Egyptian hordes of Ibrahim Pasha threaten to overwhelm them, they will open my prison gates and entreat me to join the struggle once more."

Xanthos made the crossing from the island to the mainland and traveled back to the village. He packed his manuscript carefully with the remainder of his belongings and left them in the care of a friend. After purchasing a sturdy horse and saddle, he began his journey to locate Makriyannis.

He rode from the village west toward Tripolitza. In midday, the fields he passed gleamed in the spring sun that also reflected across the tiled roofs of houses in small villages nestled along the slopes of the mountains. Here and there, a cluster of women labored in the fields, their dark-clad figures bent against the earth. That was the way they had labored before the revolution and the way they would labor even if Greece gained its freedom.

In the early afternoon, a bearded old priest riding a donkey passed him on the road. The cleric's cassock was stained, and crumbs of bread littered his shaggy beard. He raised one hand and nervously proffered Xanthos the sign of the cross.

"They burned our village and slaughtered most of the inhabitants. I hid under the altar and escaped." His voice was low and weary. "Do you know of any village that might need the services of a priest?"

"I'm sorry, Father," Xanthos replied.

The old priest nodded in resignation and rode on.

To escape the oppressive heat, Xanthos paused in a glen shaded by several wild fruit trees. He ate a lunch of olives, cheese, and bread. Afterwards, he napped for a while and woke to the songs of birds hidden in the foliage of the trees.

By late afternoon, his body weary from the hours of riding, he reached the outskirts of Tripolitza. He encountered a cordon of sentries who, he was told, were under the command of the military leader Donatos, who had fought valiantly with Kolokotronis at Valtetzi.

Seeking Donatos, Xanthos rode deeper into the camp and saw more soldiers sitting around fires over which they cooked shards of meat. The men looked defeated, their shoulders slumped with weariness, their clothing soiled and ragged, their faces reflecting resignation. A short distance beyond the main encampment, Xanthos passed a cluster of wounded men sprawled or reclining in a small grove. Some wore ragged bandages round their head and arms. Few of them bothered to look up and note his passage.

Xanthos asked a young soldier cleaning his musket where he could find their captain. The soldier pointed toward a tent a short distance away. Outside the tent, Xanthos found Donatos standing before a small fire. A soldier crouched beside him, slowly turned a spit on which a trio of pigeons was skewered. As Xanthos approached, the chieftain peered at him sharply and then, when he recognized him, raised his hand in greeting.

"You appear out of the landscape like a ghost, Xanthos," Donatos said. He was a tall, unruly-haired fighter with a face the wind and the sun had burned to a deep copper. He gestured toward the pigeons on the spit. "You are welcome to share what we have."

"Thank you," Xanthos said.

"Have you any word about your general?" Donatos asked. He spit contemptuously into the dirt. "I couldn't believe the news the scoundrels jailed him. That foul nest of vipers needs to be cleaned out! By God, I wish I had the force of men to do it."

"I visited the general a few days ago on Hydra," Xanthos said. "He is well and anxious to rejoin the fray."

"God knows we'll need him," Donatos said. "You see around you in this camp the remnants of a beaten army, in retreat from the debacle at Navarino we suffered at the hands of the Egyptians." He shook his head somberly. "We'll have little time to rest our veterans, tend to our wounded, and muster new conscripts before we have to fight again. Even now, that Egyptian devil and his horde are marching north, hot on our heels."

In the hour that followed, as they ate the grilled pigeons and drank red wine, Donatos told Xanthos about the battles that had taken place at the fortresses of Old and New Navarino.

"It was a catastrophe," Donatos said scornfully, "made worse because our leaders were worthless. You should have witnessed the sorry spectacle of our valorous president, Koundouriotes, setting out to confront Ibrahim Pasha. He was mounted on a richly caparisoned horse over which he hung like a sack of hay, supported on either side by two grooms. He was followed by a retinue composed of secretaries, guards, and pipe-bearers." Donatos paused and again spit violently at the ground. "You would think he was marching to a festival and not riding to do battle with a formidable enemy. Anyway, his ride came to nothing. After a while, he rode back the same sad spectacle he made as he rode out."

He scratched his beard. "When my men and I joined the fighting at Old Navarino, Ibrahim Pasha had already captured the island of Sphakteria. With that island lost, we could no longer receive supplies of bread and water. Using Sphakteria as his base, Ibrahim began bombarding Old Navarino both from his frigates in the bay and from the landward side of the island. Without ammunition for our artillery and our force badly outnumbered, we gave ground and retreated. More

than half my men were wounded or killed." Donatos shook his head
gloomily. "The final outpost to fall was New Navarino, which was being defended by the garrison of about a thousand men. Makriyannis
was there with a force of several hundred men. His band and the forces
of the garrison were attempting to hold off thousands of Egyptians."

"How long were they able to resist?"

"Less than a fortnight," Donatos said. "Gunpowder was short,
and water was also a problem. Once Ibrahim Pasha had cut off the
Venetian aqueduct supplying the fort, there was only a dwindling
supply of water in the cisterns. When the men began to riot over the
water, I was told Makriyannis himself took over the distribution of
the water, threatening to shoot any man who did not obey. In the end,
some of the defenders negotiated a surrender with Ibrahim. Others
like Makriyannis managed to flee."

"Where is the captain now?"

"The last I heard his battered force had lodged at Argos," Donatos
said. "He will be tending to his wounded and resting his men, as
we are doing. He will also be conscripting new recruits to face the
Egyptians. We know that devil Ibrahim Pasha will be coming. We
have scouts following him from the time he left Navarino. He would
have attacked us already but his army is moving slowly, stripping the
fields and villages of food, scorching the land." He shook his head
gloomily. "In all my years as a soldier, I have never before felt such
despair. God help us all."

Xanthos spent the night in the Donatos camp and, in early morning,
set off for Argos to find Makriyannis. The day was overcast, a hot wind
blowing from the south. He stopped at a small spring where water
flowed out of a rock into a hollowed log on which birds perched to
wet their beaks. When he approached, the birds scattered, uttering
shrill cries. After he had drunk the water and moved away, the birds
returned to their perch.

On the road a few kilometers outside Tripolitza, Xanthos encountered two raggedly dressed girls between ten and twelve years of age.
Both were beautiful children, barefooted, and their bare brown legs
laced with the scars of thorns. Their faces seemed strangely comatose,
as if they were unaware of what they were seeing.

"What are you doing alone on the road?" Xanthos asked. "Where are your parents?"

The girls did not look at him, nor did they speak. Still holding tightly to one another's hands, they walked on aimlessly. Xanthos wondered what horror they might have experienced to render them so unresponsive. He felt apprehensive what further misfortune might still befall them in the cauldron of war.

For a moment, he considered taking the children under his protection until he could find them a safe haven. But he kept riding on and, when he finally looked back, the two girls had receded into the distance.

The sun was beginning its descent, making long shadows sweep across the rocks and trees when Xanthos arrived in Argos. On its outskirts, he found the camp of Makriyannis. As with the force of Donatos, the soldiers he encountered had the demeanor of defeated men.

"Where is your captain?" Xanthos asked one of the soldiers.

The man stared at him without answering.

"He's with the wounded farther back in the camp," another soldier finally told him.

In a barn set up as an infirmary, Xanthos found Makriyannis walking among rows of wounded men, bending to press the arm of one in reassurance, crouching to speak a few consoling words to another. Along with the smells of blood and decay, the barn held a strong aroma of lemon. Xanthos remembered that the smell of a freshly cut lemon was reputed to cure fever. Here and there, a soldier held one of the golden pomanders to his nose.

Xanthos approached Makriyannis kneeling beside a young soldier whose pale face was contorted with pain. The captain looked up, but for a moment, he did not appear to recognize Xanthos.

"I am, Xanthos, captain, scribe, and adjutant to Kolokotronis. We met in Navplion when you visited last year."

"I remember now," Makriyannis said. "I will be with you shortly, my friend. Let me now finish my rounds and offer what comfort I can to my palikaria."

Later, Makriyannis invited Xanthos to join him at his fire. He seemed melancholy from his rounds of the wounded.

They ate their meal in silence.

"To see strong young men cut down by sword or shot in the full flower of their strength is a burden," the captain finally said. He looked across the fire at Xanthos. "What brings you here, scribe?"

Xanthos told of visiting Kolokotronis on Hydra and of the general's wish that he offer the captain his services.

"I am sorry to have taken up arms against the general," Makriyannis said sincerely. "I feared that if the new government was not respected, there would be chaos. I did not understand that the government itself was not only in chaos but corrupt, as well."

When Xanthos sought to present him the letter of reference Kolokotronis had written, Makriyannis waved it aside.

"There isn't any reason to offer me a letter, scribe," he said quietly. "There were no teachers in my village, so I never learned to write or read."

"Shall I read it to you?"

"You've told me the general offers me your services," Makriyannis said. "There is no need for me to hear the letter. I will be grateful for your help."

Makriyannis fell silent again, staring moodily into the fire. Somewhere in the darkness beyond their campfire, a soldier played a reed flute, the sound carrying plaintively across the darkness. From the sky above them, the raucous cry of a crow pierced the night.

Seeing the captain's face gleaming in the firelight, Xanthos marked the differences in his appearances from that of Kolokotronis. The general was of average height and built as brawny as a bull. His features were sharp and strong, his head looking as if it had been carved from stone. In his presence, one felt an aura of raw, restless power.

Makriyannis was a taller and much handsomer man, his body reflecting strength but his build more slender. He had fine features, fair skin, and large, expressive, dark eyes as striking as the eyes of a beautiful woman. He had a small, curled mustache in contrast to the great swirling mustachio favored by Kolokotronis. His beard was also well trimmed and burnished slightly by the sun.

Makriyannis lit his chibouk, the tip glowing in the shadows.

"You heard what happened to us at Navarino, scribe?"

"Before I reached Argos, I visited with Donatos at Tripolitza," Xanthos said. "He told me about the battle and the rout."

"Donatos and his men fought valiantly," Makriyannis said. "But valor wasn't enough to carry the day." He sighed. "I haven't fled from many battles, but at New Navarino, it was either flee or surrender. Victory wasn't possible."

He shook his head.

"The fort we sought to defend was rotten and falling to bits," he said. "Gunpowder was short. And when Ibrahim cut off the Venetian aqueduct supplying us with water, we had to rely on the water in several cisterns. Thirsty men were stealing it, so I distributed the water myself, at first half a pint a day and later only half that. We knew when the water ran out that the battle was lost. The wisest course of action was to flee and survive to fight again."

A soldier came to tell the captain that one of the seriously wounded men was asking for him.

"I'm not sure if I'll return tonight, scribe," Makriyannis said as he rose to leave. "My men will find you a place to sleep. We can speak again tomorrow."

Xanthos slept that night in a small barn at the edge of the camp. His companions were several soldiers who had not washed for weeks, and Xanthos endeavored to remain as close to the solitary window as he could.

With daylight, the soldiers rose, and, in a small, stone enclosure outside the barn, they lit a fire and brewed a pot of strong coffee. As they drank the pungent brew, they also spoke to Xanthos about the battles at Navarino.

"The Egyptians are not like Turks," a swarthy soldier they called Panaki said. "They are smaller and don't appear as strong. But, believe me, the little bastards advance steadily, take fire without cowering, and they don't give ground." He grinned, showing a brace of discolored teeth. "But just like Turks, they can still be killed." He fumbled in a pouch at his waist and brought up four small, pale ears. "Souvenirs," he said gleefully. "When I return home to my village, I'll present them to the girl I take as my bride."

A short while later, a soldier brought Xanthos word that Makriyannis wished to see him. Xanthos joined the captain at his tent and asked about the condition of the soldier he had visited the night before.

"He was dying when he sent for me," Makriyannis sighed. "He wanted to be sure his mother back in his village learned of his death. He was twenty years old, a handsome lad who, if he lived, would have bred fine, strong children."

Several soldiers nearby raised their voices in strident argument. Makriyannis called to them sternly, and they hushed.

"Once we measured our days by the weather and the seasons, by the needs of animals and by the growing of crops," the captain said pensively. "Now our days are measured by battles and by the death of good men."

They turned their conversation to the leaders of the government, Makriyannis of the opinion that many of them were driven by ambition and greed.

"In the beginning, I respected them because they were our leaders," he said, "but as I came to know some of them, I became disillusioned. Koundouriotes is a pompous figurehead, Kolettis a deceitful schemer."

He stared out thoughtfully across the landscape of the camp.

"I moved against Kolokotronis because I supported the government." He shook his head wearily. "But I became sickened at shedding the blood of other Greeks and disheartened at the way any victory we won in the field was betrayed in the council of politicians. I told them I would no longer take part in any civil war."

Later that morning, a soldier brought Makriyannis a half-dozen farmers as prospective recruits. The men, who were raggedly dressed, appeared nervous and suspicious.

"Our people are joined in a great struggle for freedom," Makriyannis said earnestly. "If you join our band, you will at once gain several hundred brothers, men who will fight beside you in our sacred cause."

"What pay are you offering?" a peasant with a pockmarked face asked.

"When we obtain any monies, we share it among all," Makriyannis said. "But the greater pay must come from the knowledge that you are helping free your country from slavery and tyranny."

Several of the men chose to enlist. One man pleaded he could not leave his mother, who was ill. Another said he had a pregnant wife. Makriyannis allowed both men to leave.

"Some of the captains conscript men against their will," he said, "but they make poor and resentful soldiers. If a man does not fight with his heart, he is worthless."

"The history of our land bears out that truth," Xanthos said. "When our ancestors fought the Persians, the Persian officers drove their men into battle by lashing their backs with whips. In contrast, the Greeks, who were free men, ran joyously into battle."

That validation of his decision to accept only men willing to fight pleased Makriyannis.

"You see, scribe?" he smiled. "Even an unlettered man like myself can make a wise choice!"

As they were eating a morsel of lunch, Makriyannis spoke again of the battle at Navarino. "I tell you what impressed me during those dark days, Xanthos—the men who came from other countries across the world to join our struggle. There was an Italian Philhellene named Santa Rosa who fought valiantly and who gave his life defending Sphakteria. There were two men from far off America. One was George Jarvis, a valorous captain, who led a group of Greek irregulars. I heard Ibrahim offered him a command in his army, but the American scorned his proposal.

"The other American aiding us was a remarkable man, a surgeon. I remember thinking it odd because he bore three names, Samuel Gridley Howe. But he tended our battle casualties with devotion, removing bullets, treating wounds. I saw him amputating mangled legs, and he did it skillfully and with compassion for the suffering the men were undergoing. Xanthos, that is one of the most hopeful signs in our struggle. How many generous souls from around the world are coming to assist us. That means our battle is known in other countries, and our effort is being supported by many diverse peoples."

During one of the evenings Xanthos spent with the captain, Makriyannis, in a nostalgic mood, spoke of his birth in a village in the district of Lidorikion in the western Peloponnesus.

"My parents were very poor, and their poverty was caused by the rapacity of the Turks and the cruelty inflicted on them by the Albanians of Ali Pasha," he said. "We also had a large family, and the story I was told later on was that when I was still in my mother's womb, she went one day to gather firewood in the forest. With the wood on her back, burdened and alone in the wilderness, the pains came upon her, and she gave birth to me. After the birth, she tidied herself, took up the burden of firewood, put some green leaves on top, laid me on the leaves, and went back to the village."

Xanthos's admiration for the man grew the more time he spent with Makriyannis. What impressed him was that the captain had a genuine feeling for their Hellenic heritage.

One morning, several soldiers were brought to Makriyannis. They had found some antiquities and had been arrested while trying to sell them to foreigners in Argos. Makriyannis examined the small stone figures, one of which was a woman, by her attire most likely a princess or a queen. The other was of a young man who might have been a prince. The statues were in remarkable condition, so exquisitely made that one felt at any moment the figures might move and speak.

"You must never give away or attempt to sell such antiquities, not for any amount of gold," he reproached the soldiers. "They must not be taken from our country. They are precious artifacts of our past, and it is for the greatness of that past that we do battle now."

But Makriyannis could also be merciless when his orders were disobeyed. He had issued a stern edict against any pillaging or looting by his forces, and when he learned that several of his men had abused some farmers and threatened their wives in a nearby village, he had the culprits brought before him. He denounced the frightened men with a vengeful fury.

"You knew my orders!" Makriyannis thundered. "I will not tolerate a dishonorable or thievish man in my troop, a scoundrel who preys on his own people! You have been warned of the punishment such conduct would bring more than once! Now you will taste that punishment from my own hand!"

Makriyannis had the four men thrown on the ground, and with a long leather belt, he fiercely thrashed them until their clothing became stained with blood from their buttocks and backs. When he had finished beating them, his breathing came in short, hard gasps, and his own hands were bleeding. He ordered the men's wounds tended, and then he discharged them from his band.

"If I hear of any of you harming or mistreating another Greek," he said grimly, "I vow I will hunt you down and put a bullet in your heads!"

Makriyannis became more at ease with Xanthos and asked him to write messages to some of the government leaders.

"I will be grateful for your help, because the sad reality of my life is that I am an illiterate," he confessed to Xanthos. "But I am still fortunate because God has granted me the gift of speech, a gift that no one has the right to take away from me. Therefore, I must not abuse this gift by using it to speak falsely, to demean others, or to elevate myself in undeserving ways."

Xanthos noted that the captain, despite his illiteracy, spoke with confidence and with color, often fashioning phrases to give his words an added power.

Once, upon hearing the news of an untimely retreat by a band of Greeks, he dictated to Xanthos an angry, scathing letter directed at the leaders of the government.

"You put a captain in the fortress of Corinth, and his name was Achilles! And hearing the name of Achilles, you imagined this was the great Achilles of the Trojan War, and you let the name fight the Turks. But fighting is not done by a name—what does the fighting is boldness, patriotism, courage!"

Makriyannis grew more impassioned as he paced heatedly back and forth, his words erupting faster than Xanthos could transcribe them.

"And your Achilles had in the fortress everything necessary for fighting, and he also had an army. He saw in the distance the Turks of Dramali, and, at the very sight, Achilles fled from the fort without striking a blow. Now, if Nikitas had been there, would he have done that? Would Hadjichristo have done that? Both men proved their iron when they fought Dramali and routed him in the plain and not from a well-stocked fort like that of Corinth."

While Xanthos was in the camp of Makriyannis, word arrived from Donatos that his scouts reported the forces of Ibrahim Pasha were less that fifty kilometers south of Megalopolis and that another attempt to thwart Ibrahim had been made by the veteran chieftain Karatassos, who suffered a decisive defeat with many of his men wounded or killed. The battle also reconfirmed the harsh reality that the Arab soldiers, trained and disciplined by European officers, made formidable antagonists.

Fearful of any further effort to confront Ibrahim in force, Donatos and some of the other Greek captains adopted the tactic of harassing the Egyptian army along its route, making quick forays at night and driving off their horses or blowing up their ammunition wagons. None of these efforts did any more than momentarily delay the Egyptians.

Donatos had called an urgent meeting of Greek captains to be held in Nemea, a small town less than a two-hour ride west of Argos, to decide a unified strategy against Ibrahim. Makriyannis asked Xanthos to accompany him as he led a band of half dozen men to attend the gathering.

Nemea was crowded with captains and their troops, a total of almost two thousand men bivouacked there, many of them newly conscripted farmers and villagers. After the first meeting, which had deteriorated into a shouting match, Makriyannis was dismayed by the bitter disagreements among the captains. The discord encompassed not only differences in strategy but also conflict between personalities who disliked one another. In their arguing and ranting, the captains displayed jealously and resentment against other captains who might overshadow their own chances for victory and glory.

"They don't seem to understand that we are in mortal danger," Makriyannis complained to Xanthos. "If we cannot agree on a unified course of action, this Egyptian invader will eat us, bones and all!"

Meanwhile, the efforts at Nemea to instruct and train the motley assembly of troops and meld them into a cohesive fighting force also seemed destined to failure. There were problems getting peasants to relinquish their carefree behavior and observe rules of simple discipline. Fights broke out between men from different villages and regions. A Spartan accused a Corinthian of cowardice, and a dozen men were injured in the general melee that followed. A band of about twenty men abandoned their captain and rode out on their own to join the klephts harassing Ibrahim. About a hundred men, weary of having to conform to discipline, decided to return to their villages.

Foragers were sent into the countryside to gather food, but it was carelessly prepared, and men fell ill with loose bowels and cramps. The latrines were crude pits dug in the earth, and, when they were full, they were covered over, and new pits dug. Worms flourished in the earth, and great black flies swarmed overhead. Devout captains demanded their men refrain from using profanities and drinking, and other captains drank intemperately with their men until all collapsed into a drunken stupor. Men shot off muskets at random, ignoring the orders not to waste powder. Other men assigned guard duty wearied of standing watch at night and left their posts to sleep.

"Why should I stand there, all alone in the night, being laughed at by rabbits and owls?" one man protested.

"It is frustrating," Makriyannis told Xanthos bitterly. "We have this citizen's army tugging in every direction while Ibrahim marches his highly disciplined force to meet us."

Numerous strategies were presented to counter Ibrahim. Some captains felt the soundest tactic was to continue to harass the Egyptian army without directly confronting their superior force. Others felt such methods were useless and that Ibrahim had to be met in force and defeated.

Amidst the disorder and contention, there was some heartening news. The Koundouriotes government, frightened at the threat posed by Ibrahim Pasha, granted amnesty to all political prisoners. As part of the amnesty, Kolokotronis had been released from his prison on Hydra.

"The old warrior is already in the field!" Makriyannis told Xanthos jubilantly. "I heard that wherever he marches, the peasants flock to his banner. He is not wasting time in councils and meetings but is moving quickly to assemble an army and once again confront Ibrahim!"

At the end of the second fruitless day of meetings, the sole survivor of another battle against Ibrahim Pasha was brought into camp by soldiers who had found him wandering a few kilometers from Nemea. He was a young farmer in wretched condition. His body bore several wounds, his flesh was scaly and swollen from infection, and he was exhausted and nearly starving. His wounds tended, he was given warm food and then allowed to sleep for the span of a day. After he'd awakened, a group of the captains that included Makriyannis with Xanthos gathered to hear his story.

The survivor, whose name was Volakis, had a sunburned face and unruly flaxen hair and was from the region of Agrinio. He had been part of a force totaling about fifteen hundred men under the command of half a dozen captains.

"We were marching east for Sparta when we were attacked by a party of Ibrahim Pasha's cavalry," Volakis said. "We drove them off, but they returned and pursued us with a much stronger force. We set up bulwarks to defend ourselves at the village of Maniaki near Gargaliani."

Someone handed the soldier a flask of water that he put to his scabbed lips and sipped slowly.

"I am ashamed to tell you that at the sight of the Egyptians who appeared to have a great army stretching as far into the distance as the eye could see, some of our men and even a few of the captains panicked and fled," Volakis said. "But among the captains who stood their ground was a leader who rallied our men to stand and fight. He was a giant of a monk, tall as a pine tree and with a countenance fierce as a lion. He led men in charge after charge against the Egyptian ranks, each time killing enough Egyptians to prove they were mortal. I saw him pull an Egyptian cavalryman off his horse and then holding him in his long arms, break the man's neck as one would snap the neck of a chicken."

The man stopped to catch his breath, his voice grown weary and hoarse.

"I was wounded in the fighting and fell among a mound of dead bodies. From there I saw that fierce monk's final struggle. The Egyptians had surrounded him, moving closer, tightening the circle. He towered over his attackers, a yataghan in each of his hands, cutting Egyptians down like sheaves of wheat. He was slashed and cut, shot and struck, and still, by some miracle, he remained on his feet and kept killing Egyptians. When he finally collapsed and went down under the assault of fifty men, I swear I felt the earth beneath my body tremble."

His voice was shaking from his effort to continue, and again he raised the flask of water to his lips.

"I lay there for I don't know how many hours, terrified to move, soiling myself, terrified to breathe, praying to God for my survival.

When darkness fell, I heard the vultures and wild dogs roaming the battlefield, heard the sounds they made feeding on the carcasses of the dead. I burrowed deeper under the corpses around me. It was the longest night I have ever known, but, finally, daylight came, a strange crimson mist floating over the bloody earth. That morning I saw the pasha, Ibrahim himself, inspecting the battlefield on horseback with his troop of guards. Where they found a Greek still wounded and alive, they butchered him. I whispered my prayers then and prepared to die."

The captains remained silent, hanging on the survivor's words.

"Because I had buried myself beneath the corpses, I was spared. From my human grave, I saw them bring the pasha the severed head of the monk. I knew it was his because I had never seen so massive a human head. And yes," the man's voice fell to a husky whisper, "I saw the pasha kiss the monk's lips in homage to his bravery." He shuddered. "It is a sight I will carry with me to my grave."

At their camp, Makriyannis said to Xanthos, "I have met that monk the man spoke about. He was called Papalikos, and I knew him as a vengeful and murderous man, driven by lust for wealth and power. But look now, even such a man can achieve a noble death."

The acrimonious disagreement about coordinating a strategy continued among the captains. Finally, at the end of the fifth day, Makriyannis despaired of any consensus and left with Xanthos to return to Argos.

"Whichever towns and forts in the Peloponnesus Ibrahim Pasha attacks as his forces move north, his goal must be to capture Navplion," Makriyannis said. "That will provide him access to the sea from which his army can be provisioned and reinforced. We must prevent him taking Navplion."

Makriyannis resolved to make his stand at the Mills of Lerna on the bay opposite Navplion. The location was renowned as the place in legend where Hercules killed the multiheaded monster Hydra. The Mills held the main stores of grain and ammunition for Navplion, and the stream that turned the mill wheel supplied the town with water.

Agreeing with Makriyannis that the military objective of Ibrahim Pasha would be Navplion, two other captains joined him. One of them was Konstantinos Mavromichalis, a stalwart son of Petrobey, prince of the Mani. He brought with him a hundred seasoned Maniot warriors, hard-bodied men with resolute faces, fierce, black eyes, and great swirling mustaches.

"Just one of these men is worth twenty farmers," Makriyannis told Xanthos. "I am grateful to have them fighting beside us."

The other noted leader who joined them at the Mills was Demetrios Ipsilantis, the Phanariot prince who had been one of the first fighters of the revolution. He brought with him a contingent of several hundred men.

Makriyannis spent the week preparing the Mill's buildings for defense, extending the walls to the west and east, and redirecting the millstream to flow underground into the enclosure. They also reinforced the battlements, adding boulders and the trunks of trees. In the watchtowers that adjoined the Mills, he established sniper's nest at those loopholed windows that allowed a clear view of the battlefield.

To prevent any of his men attempting to flee when Ibrahim Pasha attacked, Makriyannis with the help of an American Philhellene named Jonathan Miller transported the horses from the camp into Navplion. The captain also ordered the caiques in the bay to be sailed away during the night while the soldiers were sleeping.

"If any coward decides he doesn't have the mettle to fight," the captain told Xanthos grimly, "he will have to take his chances fleeing on foot, not escaping by horse or on water. That may make him think twice about deserting his comrades in battle."

While they waited for the Egyptian attack, a courier brought them news from Donatos that the troops under Kolokotronis had been defeated by Ibrahim Pasha. What was left of the general's force had been compelled to take sanctuary in the mountains.

"That is unhappy news indeed," Makriyannis said somberly. "But the general has only lost a single battle. Kolokotronis will regroup and prepare to fight again. Meanwhile, his defeat makes it all the more urgent that we hold back the Egyptians at the Mills."

The morning their lookouts brought them word that Ibrahim Pasha's army had moved into Argos, Makriyannis suggested that Xanthos leave for a safe haven beyond the battle.

"Your general has entrusted you into my care," Makriyannis said. "After all, you are not a soldier. And it is also important that you survive to record the history that ignorant men such as myself are unable to write."

"My life is no more important than the life of any other soldier," Xanthos said quietly. "I have been in battles before, Captain, at Karitena and at Tripolitza. I have a set of good pistols given to me by the general. While I do not think of myself as a warrior, I will fight as well as I can."

"As you wish," Makriyannis said. A wry smile creased his lips. "Having come to know you through these last weeks, my friend, I would have been surprised if you had chosen otherwise."

Ibrahim Pasha's attack came on the evening of June 25 in late afternoon after the midday heat had passed. Earlier that day, a solitary eagle had been observed soaring above the battlements, a sighting some men took to be a felicitous augury. As if sensing the impending conflict, all that day the birds in the surrounding trees had been restless and noisy. Close by, among the rocks, the cicadas kept up a dry, shrill drone. Even the dogs and cats seemed to have absorbed the aura of tension and danger and had gone into hiding, leaving the pathways around the Mills deserted of animals. From a nearby pen, a shepherd led out a last small flock of sheep, herding them toward the safety of the mountain.

On the eve of the battle, his anxiety growing with each hour, Xanthos thought of his history still unwritten and wondered if he would survive to complete it. He also recalled with a surge of nostalgia his beloved Chryseis and their nights of love. He consoled himself that at least he would not die without having tasted the sweetness of union with a woman. At the same time, he lamented he had no child, no son or daughter, to deliver him from the finality of what might be his death.

That day, as if seeing it for the first time, he was also conscious of the beauty of the earth around the encampment. The full bloom of summer enriched the fragrance of budding trees and blossoming flowers. A little later, he heard in the distance the bells of far-off churches, perhaps tolling to warn of the approach of the Egyptians.

The hot afternoon sun streamed down across the battlements, swirls of dust rising from the dry earth under the men's booted feet. As the hours passed, the enclosure and the surrounding areas faded into the shadows of the waning sun. Beneath a plane tree where a small fountain splashed and gurgled, a steady column of thirsty, nervous men lined up to drink and splash water on their flushed faces. Earlier that day, the men had been laughing and boisterous, speaking confidently to one another, boasting of the defeat they would wreak upon the Egyptians. But, as the afternoon wore on, they grew tense and silent.

Xanthos took his place behind one of the battlements, beside Elias Karnezis, who had become his closest friend. He was a tall, handsome farmer with mischievous, hazel eyes, an unruly shock of russet-colored hair, and a thick, sandy mustache. The back of his neck had been burned dark by the sun in contrast to his complexion that was unusually fair for a Greek. Elias was from a village in Boeotia, north of the Gulf of Corinth and on the slopes of Mount Parnassus. He had been with Makriyannis since the beginning of the fighting. As a farmer, he knew the crops and the seasons in which they grew best. He was also genial, quick-witted, and gifted as a storyteller.

Securing the flank to the left of Xanthos, Elias, and the other men under Makriyannis was the band led by the trimly uniformed and slightly built figure of Ipsilantis. Although the Phanariot prince did not have the stature of a warrior, Xanthos knew he had more than once proved his courage.

At their right flank were PetrobeyMavromichalis and his Maniot warriors. Befitting their notoriety as fierce and legendary fighters, the Maniots were the most ornately dressed of the defenders. Along with their long-barreled Albanian muskets, they had silver-embossed pistols and ivory-handled daggers secured in the bright sashes around their waists.

"I wish this battle was being fought under the snow-peaked crags of Taygetus," one of the Maniots grumbled to Xanthos and Elias. "Those mountains of our homeland hold the bones of our ancestors who fought valiantly in old battles." He shook his head somberly. "These cursed lowlands are no place for a man to fight or die."

Near the final hour of the afternoon, they saw the vanguard of the Egyptian forces. They appeared, at first, as a red mist wavering in the distance. At the same time, there resonated across the fields the thumping of kettledrums and the jangling of tambourines, the instruments the pashas favored to herald their attacks.

The mist took form and became columns of red-jacketed troopers, marching steadily forward, the sun glinting on their high-crowned helmets and on the bayonets attached to their muskets. They moved in steady, orderly fashion, without urgency, as if marching to parade instead of to fight.

"Those soldiers are well disciplined," Makriyannis said. "That is evident in the way they advance."

The captain reassured his men with banter and jest.

"Fight without fear, Panos," he told one soldier, a small, wiry man with a lean, crafty face. "You are too cunning a scoundrel to be injured or killed in any battle. The devil is saving you for other villainy."

He spoke next to a sturdy young Greek whose blazing red hair made him appear a stranger from some alien land among the dark-haired Greeks.

"Tassos, I expect that you will fight with honor and bring further distinction on your valorous father, a hero at the battle of Dhervenakia."

"If I did any less, captain," Tassos said, "he wouldn't allow me back into our house."

Makriyannis spoke to a third soldier, a stocky, powerfully built farmer with a pocked complexion and teeth stained yellow by the tobacco beans he constantly chewed.

"In any hand-to-hand combat, Stavros," he said gravely, "I expect you to overpower at least six Egyptians. Anything less would disappoint me."

"I promise I will, captain!" Stavros spoke with fervor. "Six at the least!"

When Makriyannis encountered several young men who were pale-faced and obviously frightened at the prospect of battle, he sought to bolster their spirits.

"Remember these Egyptians are only mortal," he said quietly, "and they will die like mortals. Hold your fire until they are within range, and you hear my signal. Don't aim for their heads, which make too small a target. Use their red jackets as a bull's-eye to guide you to their hearts."

When he returned to Xanthos and Elias, his demeanor became more reflective.

"Which men will be the bravest in battle?" he asked quietly and then answered himself. "Those who have the clearest vision of what lies before them, glory and danger alike, and yet go forward to meet it."

At that moment from a ridge somewhere behind the columns of advancing troopers, the Egyptian cannons exploded, the howitzers and six-pounders supporting the infantry attack. The puffs of smoke momentarily obscured the columns, while the cannon shots, gun after gun firing in rapid succession, whistled above the heads of the defenders.

"Those Egyptian gunners would be dangerous if they closed their eyes before firing," Elias grinned.

After a while, the howitzers and six-pounders ceased firing. As the smoke cleared, and the medley of kettledrums and tambourines was heard again, the troopers reappeared, this time much closer, advancing in wide columns stretching as far back across the fields as the eyes could encompass. There had to be thousands of soldiers, and Xanthos was swept with a sweat of fear. He understood suddenly the compulsion of men to flee in panic from a battle.

As the columns of red-jacketed soldiers moved still closer, the kettledrums and tambourines abruptly stopped, leaving an eerie, suspenseful silence, as if the earth itself were holding its breath. The silence brought tremors of anxiety to the defenders, who, with a clatter of muskets, laid their guns upon the battlements and took aim. The red-haired Tassos wet his finger and raised it to check for any trace of wind.

"Steady, hold your fire!" Makriyannis called loudly. "They are still out of range. Steady . . . "

The columns of troopers marched closer, for the first time the faces of the men becoming visible, small, pale, half-moons under their stiff, high hats.

As Xanthos and Elias leveled their muskets along the parapet, beside them Panos, Tassos and Stavros also took aim.

"Keep coming, you bloody heathens," Stavros, the burly farmer, muttered. "Keep coming, and see what we're planning for you."

The voice of Makriyannis shattered the silence.

"Now!" he cried.

An instant later, hundreds of muskets rang out a deafening volley. Swirls and coils of smoke obscured the fields, and when it cleared, the columns of troopers seemed to have been blown apart, gaps visible where seconds before men had stood. As quickly as the gaps appeared, they were filled by other troopers, and the columns moved inexorably forward.

The Greeks reloaded hastily, aimed their muskets, fired again. More troopers fell, but the soldiers behind them instantly took their place. From the towers at the side of the Greek battlements, puffs of smoke burst at the loopholes as the snipers aimed for the officers leading the columns.

The soldiers advanced, and for the first time Xanthos saw the feared bayonets of the Egyptians clearly, shafts of glistening steel so long they made the guns to which they were attached appear to be lances.

As the columns of troopers neared the battlements, they increased their pace to double-quick time, muskets lowered to their waists, bayonets looming before them.

One of the Maniots did not wait for their charge. Loosing a ferocious roar, the man rose upright and scrambled across the battlement, pistol in one hand, yataghan in the other. He raced toward the Egyptian line, brandishing gun and sword, and bellowed a valorous, reckless challenge. For an instant, the columns of troopers faltered, as if fearing the man charging them might not be human but some supernatural demon. Then, a score of Egyptians quickly took aim at him and fired. The Maniot was struck by a fusillade of bullets, the impact causing his body to bound weirdly off the ground. He made a final mighty effort to continue his charge before pistol and yataghan dropped from his hands. He raised his arm in a final flourish of defiance, and then he sprawled on the earth.

The man's daredevil charge inspired the other Maniots, and they, too, did not wait for the Egyptians but leaped across the battlement to race toward the enemy line. Maniots and Egyptians struck one another like herds of cattle colliding. Muskets and pistols were fired at close range, swords clashed against bayonets, and the screams of wounded and dying men added to the bedlam.

Those troopers advancing against the positions of Makriyannis and Ipsilantis, who had survived the musket fire of the Greeks, came running toward the battlements. The defenders met them with a withering volley of fire. Many troopers fell before they could scale the barrier, while others scrambled across, bayonets brandished before them. The Greeks rose to meet them, and attackers and defenders engaged in a fierce hand-to-hand struggle.

As troopers crossed the battlements, Xanthos confronted them, pistol in one hand, saber clutched in the other. In the instant before becoming engulfed in the action, he was startled to notice the Egyptians were small men the size of adolescents, their skin a peculiar shade of brown.

The battle became a brawl of men catapulted against one another, firing pistols, thrusting bayonets, slashing sabers. When a trooper loomed before him, Xanthos fired his pistol squarely at the man's red jacket. The trooper halted as if he'd struck a wall. His musket flew from his hands, and he tumbled to the ground. Another trooper who'd scrambled across the battlement was felled by a shot from Elias. Not far from him, Xanthos saw the crimson thatch of Tassos struggling with a trooper, and then he broke free with a triumphant cry, the trooper sprawling on the ground. Meanwhile, Stavros had grasped two of the diminutive troopers in both his great hands, lifted them squirming and kicking from the ground, and smashed them violently together. As if they were a pair of broken dolls, he tossed them aside.

Men died instantly, their bodies sprawled in graceless forms upon the earth. Others lay wounded, thrashing on the ground, screaming in pain. Xanthos saw a Greek run through the chest by an Egyptian bayonet, the tip of the blade driven through his back. Another defender shot the trooper, his body falling on top of the slain Greek, the two men strangely embraced in death.

A Greek staggered around bellowing, his belly slashed open, his smoking intestines dangling from the hole. Near him, an Egyptian trooper was cut by a sword across the face, and a gaping cavity ran across his forehead. His anguished eyes seemed to burst from his head.

THE SHEPHERDS OF SHADOWS

Adding to the frenzy and fury of the action was a thunderous clamor of screams and curses that assailed the ears and paralyzed the senses.

Then, as quickly as it had begun, the attack was over. The Egyptians had been driven back across the battlement. Many of those scrambling to flee were cut down by the Maniots who roamed the battlefield like wolves, slaughtering with a vengeful fury.

As the Egyptians retreated, a wild elation swept the defenders. Men laughed hysterically, waving their bloodied sabers and yataghans in the air, cheering and shouting with the merriment of jubilant children. Tassos and Panos hugged one another, and stocky Stavros beat his chest in a primordial gesture of triumph.

Xanthos was grateful to see the sweaty, powder-stained face of Elias, his teeth gleaming white in an exulting smile.

"We beat them off, Xanthos!" Elias cried. "By God, we showed them what Greek fighters are like!"

Makriyannis came to review the condition of his men. His clothing was disheveled, one of his cheeks bore an ugly bruise, and bloodstains covered his jacket and sleeve. His left hand was swathed in a bandage.

"You've been hurt, Captain," Elias said with concern.

"It's nothing," Makriyannis said. "A wound that will heal quickly." He gestured excitedly at the men. "Bravo, lads!" he cried, his voice exultant. "We have drawn first blood! But do not celebrate victory too soon! They have been stung, but they have strong reserves, and they will regroup and attack us again!" He gestured grimly toward the bodies of the wounded and dead sprawled along the ground. "Now, let's take care of our wounded comrades, and then look after the bodies of those who have given their lives in our cause."

He moved closer and spoke in a voice so low that only Xanthos heard.

"Kolokotronis would be proud of you," he said quietly.

Xanthos turned away quickly to conceal his pleasure at the praise.

Men ceased their celebrating and bent to look after the wounded. The more seriously hurt were carried to an infirmary set up back of the lines. Makriyannis offered words of reassurance to the wounded men before they were carried away.

"Don't despair, Vasili," he told one. "I suspect your wound is not lethal, and you will see your family again."

To another, he said, "I have seen men more severely hurt than you, Kyriaki, and they are on their feet in a few days."

Xanthos and Elias joined others in wrapping the bodies of the dead in shrouds to carry them away.

"God grant them peace in heaven," Elias said somberly and made his cross.

A man near them, bending to lift one of the dead soldiers, let loose an anguished cry. Crouched beside the corpse, he began to wail, rocking his body back and forth in grief.

"The dead man is his brother," Makriyannis told the men quietly.

On their right flank, the Maniots had carried in their dead comrade who had made the first reckless and defiant charge. They wrapped his disfigured, bullet-torn body gently in a shroud, vowing to give him a hero's funeral.

"A foolhardy but noble death," Makriyannis said to Xanthos. "If that man had died fighting behind the battlement, he would have been one fallen soldier among many. Now men will speak his name with reverence, and his exploit will be told and retold to future generations."

As Makriyannis spoke of the fallen Maniot, Xanthos thought of the lines from the *Iliad*, "I, too, shall lie in the dust when I am dead, but now let me win noble renown."

"What do we do with the bodies of the Egyptian troopers?" Panos asked Makriyannis.

"We treat their bodies with the respect soldiers show other soldiers and bury them, as well," Makriyannis said. "And if their comrades enter the battlefield to gather their dead, I do not wish them harmed."

As Makriyannis walked away, one of the Maniots who had overheard him spit scornfully.

"To hell with respecting the enemy dead!" the Maniot snarled. "These vermin poison the earth on which they fall! Killing them is holy work! For every heathen we kill, God will abolish one of our sins!

Xanthos had been busy carrying away the bodies of the dead but now, for the first time, an awareness that he'd survived the battle swept over him like a bracing wind. Concealed from the others, he felt his arms and legs to make sure he had not incurred any wound. When he considered the injuries other men had suffered and what might have been his fate, his legs trembled so violently he feared he'd fall.

Elias, who also appeared exhausted but unwounded, sprawled on the ground nearby. When Panos, Tassos, and Stavros joined them, the men reviewed the battle.

"The captain was right," Tassos said. He bore a small cut on his temple where his blood had dried into the color of his hair. "They are mortal, and they died like mortals."

Stavros shook his head somberly. "I'm sorry to say I did not kill six as I pledged. To my shame, I didn't manage to dispatch any more than three or four."

"I tell you what I think," Panos said. "I've killed a number of them, and as yet they haven't managed to kill me. Perhaps it's time for me to go home."

The men laughed boisterously, a laughter reflecting their own relief at having been spared. As he shared the camaraderie and laughter, Xanthos marveled how attached he had become to them. He understood that when men live, eat, sleep, and fight together, they form a deep and abiding attachment.

"What did you learn in this battle today, Xanthos, that you will put into your history?" Elias asked.

Xanthos thought for a moment.

"I learned that in a battle a man thinks of nothing but killing or being killed," he said quietly. "All thoughts of country, family, home vanish, and only the instinct for survival remains."

Although they knew the morning would bring a renewal of the Egyptian attack, Xanthos noted a different mood among the men than the one that prevailed before the battle. Despite the wounding and death of comrades, the survivors displayed a fresh and bracing confidence and swagger. The veterans had reaffirmed their steadfastness and courage, while the recruits who had experienced battle for the first time felt a newfound power because they had fought well, and they had survived.

Nightfall came, shadows lengthening across the battlements, the darkness seeping in around them. The trees altered color and loomed charcoal-black against the sky.

Xanthos and Elias found a resting place for the night under a plane tree, its branches and leaves making a soft, rustling sound. Elias lowered himself to the ground with a sigh.

"I make a confession to you now, Xanthos," Elias said wearily. "In my dreams, I don't think about victory and freedom for our land but simply of being victorious so I am able to return home and embrace my son and sleep in bed beside my wife."

He stretched out on his side beneath the tree and covered himself with his goat-hair cape. Cradling his head in the crook of his arm, in a moment he was asleep.

But his own body still inflamed from the day's fierce fighting, sleep eluded Xanthos. In the darkness around him, he heard the faint, dry scratch of lizards crawling across the stones, and he imagined such tiny creatures crawling across the ruins of columns in ancient Greece where men then fought. In the great vault of the sky above him glittered the stars that had shone down on the conflicts of men since time began.

He wondered where Kolokotronis had sought sanctuary and begun recruiting men for another confrontation with Ibrahim Pasha. If Xanthos survived the battle at the Mills, he would travel to join him.

He also thought anxiously of the next day's battle and whether he would again find the will and courage to fight well. He had never conceived of himself as a warrior, and he wore that appellation uneasily.

That certainly wasn't true of the Maniot warriors. He felt strangely reassured at having them as allies. Perhaps their bloodthirsty ferocity came because they were bred on a stony, harsh land that could not provide sustenance for all its people, so it spawned warfare among them simply to survive. Generation after generation of fratricidal warfare continued until it had bred a race of warriors resembling the ancient Spartans.

Weary as he was and yearning for rest, the noises of the night prevented Xanthos sleeping. From the infirmary in the rear of the camp, the moans of wounded men carried in a mournful chorus across the night. Meanwhile, from the darkness of the battlefield, he heard the shrill shrieking of a sorely wounded, horse that had been overlooked by the soldiers assigned to kill the injured animals.

Listening to the anguished cries of men and the solitary shriek of the dying horse, Xanthos considered the barrier that separated living creatures from one another. Nothing more clearly illustrated that division than suffering, which, along with its consort death, was always an individual experience and could never be shared.

When the passing hours brought colder air, Xanthos rose and quietly tugged the goat-hair cape that covered Elias higher over his comrade's shoulders. He stared at the handsome, sleeping face of the man who had become his dear friend. If one of them had to die in battle, he thought pensively, it would be just that his own life be the one lost. He had no family who would mourn him, while Elias had a wife and young son waiting for his return.

He wrapped himself in his cape and felt weariness envelop him like a second blanket. The last sound he heard before he fell into exhausted sleep was the cry of a loon.

With the first traces of dawn shredding the sky, the camp awakened, the soldiers tense and quiet in anticipation of the coming battle. A line of men with trousers crumpled around their boots squatted at the holes of the malodorous latrines. Afterwards, a column of men waited in line to have a quick wash at the spring. Others lit fires and brewed strong, black coffee they would drink with hard-crusted bread.

Elias brought back tin cups of coffee and several ears of corn from one of the campfires. He offered an ear to Xanthos, who had no stomach for food, but he drank the rank, black coffee. Elias husked an ear of the corn and chewed the kernels.

"My wife and son will be rising now, too," Elias said. "She'd be kneading the goat's udders for milk, gathering eggs from our hens, a little warm bread she baked in our oven." He closed his eyes. "Xanthos, I can see them clearly."

Afterwards, with Panos, Tassos, and Stavros, they joined the columns of men moving to take their places at the battlements.

"I pray I kill my six Egyptians today," Stavros said and made his cross.

"No heroics for me," Panos said. "My only prayer for today is to stay alive."

Muskets and pistols were primed, ammunition boxes filled, sabers and yataghans placed nearby.

"I wonder if there are other battles as crucial as this one being fought anywhere in our land today?" Tassos asked.

"I'm sure there must be more important battles," Elias said.

"Any battle in which a man lives or dies is a crucial battle," Panos said.

The captains moved again along the line, rallying their men. Makriyannis joined their group. He appeared unrested, a gray, weary pallor on his face. His hand was still wrapped, with stains of blood seeping through the bandage. Xanthos suspected his wound was more serious than the captain had revealed.

"If we can hold the line today, they may become faint of heart about attacking us again," Makriyannis told them. "And a courier brought us word that Kolokotronis is on the move again and approaching Argos. Ibrahim must be worried about being attacked from the rear."

"We'll do our part, Captain," Elias said.

"I know you will," Makriyannis smiled.

As the tension of waiting for the attack mounted, Xanthos felt his throat parched. He drank from his water flask several times, but it did not appease the dryness.

When a morning wind rose, it carried toward the battlement a foul, putrescent odor from the field where the dead troopers and horses lay, their rigid forms appearing strange shrubs sprouted from the earth. Black flies swarmed over the corpses, and an occasional butterfly fluttered a tiny circle of color in the air.

Xanthos and his comrades waited in silence. That wasn't true of the Maniots, who laughed and chattered excitedly. They were the only fighters impatient for the battle to begin.

The shadow of the earth's eastern rim descended like a curtain and the first glow of the rising sun appeared on the horizon. The landscape, crested by a thin-spun mist, hung strangely motionless, as if the earth itself were holding its breath.

That stillness was shattered by the explosion of the Egyptian howitzers and the six-pounders. Small puffs of smoke erupted and then floated in small clouds above the horizon. Once again, the shells whistled uselessly above their heads.

"Those same gunners are still taking aim," Elias laughed nervously.

Makriyannis walked along the line, steadying the men. He paused a moment beside Xanthos and clasped his arm in a gesture of support. He bent closer so Xanthos heard him above the cannonade.

"Another chapter for your history today," the captain said.

The cannon fire continued, the shells flying overhead. One of the shells exploded much closer, a thunderous blast landing not far behind their line. For a moment, the detonation deafened Xanthos, and then he heard the shouts and shrieks of men. Word passed among the men that the infirmary with the wounded had been struck by one of the rounds.

"The poor devils survived the battle yesterday only to get struck today by the only shot that landed anywhere near us," Elias said.

The cannon fire ceased. Afterwards, there was a sound they had not heard before, a rumbling like distant thunder and, with it, a trembling of the earth beneath their feet.

"Cavalry," Makriyannis said, and the word flew fervently from man to man. "Steady now . . . Aim for the horses that make bigger targets. Reload quickly, and use your sabers and yataghans on the riders who survive. Remember, their infantry will attack close behind the horsemen."

The men laid their muskets along the battlements. Xanthos could feel the rapid heartbeats around him joined to his own quickened pulse.

The Egyptian cavalry sprang suddenly out of the mist, crossing the ground much more swiftly than the infantry had the day before. They rode in four compact squares, cantering toward the battlements, the morning light glinting on their lances and sabers. As they advanced, the canter changed into a trot and then became a gallop. The closer the horses came, the more violently the earth vibrated beneath the feet of the waiting men. Xanthos also heard the metallic jangling of spurs.

Nearer to the battlements, the columns of cavalry opened like a fan to extend to the length of the defender's line. When the riders were so close that Xanthos saw the sweat glistening on the horses' heaving flanks, the Greek captains shouted the order to fire.

The defenders fired, reloaded as quickly as they could, and fired again. Those horses struck by bullets reared up with piercing shrieks of pain and tossed their riders. The battlefield was suddenly strewn with tumbled horses and fallen men. Several riderless horses raced blindly

toward the battlements. Beyond the horsemen, Xanthos saw the vanguard of red-jacketed Egyptian infantry advancing across the field.

As the horses and riders that escaped the first volleys galloped up
to the Greek line, the defenders repelled them with another salvo of
musket fire. The hard, dull thuds of bullets piercing fleshy parts of
the animals sounded like stones thrown into a swamp. When a bullet
struck the bone of a horse's leg, there was a loud, snapping sound,
and the animal tumbled to the ground.

Some riders who had been thrown lay motionless on the ground
while others scrambled to their feet and clutching their weapons raced
toward the battlements. These were not the small-bodied Egyptian
troopers who formed the infantry but bigger, brawnier men that Xanthos knew were the Bulgarian mercenaries, men who would be harder
to vanquish in hand-to-hand combat.

Directly across the rampart from Xanthos, a horseman came galloping out of the smoke, with his saber raised. Xanthos fired at the
rider, who lurched and fell from his horse. The horse, relieved of its
rider, came to a bewildered halt, tossed back its head, and whinnied.
It wheeled around, seeking a direction to flee, and then was struck by
several bullets. The mount shuddered, its great eyes wild with terror,
its mane tossed as if shaking off flies. Then it dropped to its knees,
hung trembling for an instant before collapsing, blood streaming
from its neck.

Somewhere along the left flank where the men of Ipsilantis defended the line, horsemen had broken across the battlement. Now,
the riders wheeled about and attacked the defenders from the rear,
swinging sabers right and left. Xanthos saw a Greek's head fly off as
if it were a melon. Another man jumped about screaming, waving a
bloody stump that had held his arm. A third man, blinded by a saber
slash across his face, fell to his knees, shrieking and flailing his arms.
Another horseman trampled him into the ground.

Makriyannis, his saber raised, led a charge to support the line
that had been breached, followed by Xanthos, Elias, and other men
from the center. In a wild tangle of bodies, they slashed with their
sabers and yataghans at humans and horses alike. The stricken horses
stumbled and collided against other horses, reared back on their heels,
forelegs flailing the air. Their hoofs struck the earth, trampling men
beneath them.

Bending low to avoid a horseman thrusting with his lance, Xanthos thrust his saber into the rider's thigh. As the rider screamed, Tassos pulled him from his horse and killed him with a saber thrust through the chest.

At that moment, segments of the Egyptian infantry, advancing at a run, reached the battlements and scrambled across to join the battle. A trooper lunged at Xanthos with his bayonet, the blade so close he felt his clothing ripped. He struck out desperately with his saber, a blow delivered with all his strength that cleaved through the trooper's jacket, plunging into his chest. The handle tore loose from Xanthos's hand and hung quivering in the man's body. The trooper sprawled on the ground, and Xanthos pulled the saber free.

Elias was wrestling with a cavalryman thrown from his horse, a giant Bulgarian, who towered over him. The two struggled. The trooper battered Elias with a savage blow to the head that dropped him to his knees. The Bulgarian slashed down with his saber at Elias, who twisted his body in a futile effort at escape. The saber shattered his left thigh, the blade cutting deeply through the muscle to the bone. Elias, his face frozen in shock, dropped his saber and sprawled on the ground.

With a cry of rage, Xanthos attacked the Bulgarian, using both hands to swing his saber across the man's body, the blade slashing through the man's tunic and piercing into his flesh. The man shuddered, bellowed in fury, and lunged to attack Xanthos. Stavros assaulted him from the side, slashing the Bulgarian a second time. Still, the giant remained erect, still brandishing his saber. It took the desperate efforts of both Xanthos and Stavros, hacking and chopping at the man's body, before he was driven to the ground. Even after he had tumbled onto his hands and knees, Xanthos continued hacking fiercely at the man's body. His final saber blow split the back of the Bulgarian's neck, the trooper's great hairy head flopping forward as if it were about to fall off. His torso floundered in a final, violent effort to sustain life, and then he struck the ground like the trunk of a massive tree, his head attached to his body only by a thin strand of tendon and muscle. The blood cascaded from his severed neck and drenched the ground.

The hand-to-hand battle turned in the Greeks' favor when the Maniots, who had taken control of the battlefield came racing in force to attack the Egyptians who had broken the line. They scrambled across the battlements, roaring their wild battle cries and swinging their yataghans and sabers, slashing and cutting across the Egyptians and Bulgarians, severing heads and arms. The horsemen who were still mounted fled back across the fields. Those Egyptian troopers seeking to escape on foot were pursued by the Maniots, who slaughtered them mercilessly. One wounded trooper fallen to his knees crawled helplessly along the ground, dragging a shattered leg. A Maniot leaped on his back, roughly jerked back the trooper's head, and with a swift stroke of his dagger slashed his throat.

Another enraged Maniot stamped on the head of a rider he had pulled from his horse, his booted foot kicking and smashing the man's skull half a dozen times, until the trooper's head was a mass of pulp.

The remnants of enemy infantry and cavalry that managed to escape left behind a battlefield littered with the bodies of dead and dying horses and men. Here and there, a riderless horse, empty stirrups jangling, raced in blind circles, trampling the wounded as well as the dead. Several crippled horses thrashing on the ground joined their frantic bellows to the shrieks of wounded men. A stench of carnage rose like a poisonous mist from the field.

Angered that some of the Egyptians had managed to escape, the Maniots foraged across the battlefield, shooting the dying horses and finishing off the wounded troopers and fallen riders with pistol and yataghan.

Xanthos knelt beside the stricken Elias. The Bulgarian's saber had slashed across his thigh and left a gaping wound from which bright-red blood flowed. Xanthos removed his sash and fashioned a tourniquet that he tied around his comrade's thigh to stem the bleeding. Elias watched him numbly, his face teeming with pain. A great shudder wracked his body, and he closed his eyes. Xanthos feared he had died, but suddenly Elias's eyelids fluttered, and he stared mutely at Xanthos. He made an effort to speak, but no words passed his lips.

Stavros and Xanthos carried Elias to the infirmary. His face had become gray and pinched, his nostrils constricted, a dry scab formed across his lips. The infirmary soldiers removed his boot and sock and cut away the clothing covering his leg. The injury was a grievous one, the flesh of his thigh slashed to the bone, blood leaked through the tourniquet. Working quickly and carefully, they washed the wound. While Xanthos and Stavros held Elias tightly, a soldier skilled with needle and thread made an effort to suture the broad gash and bandaged and bound the thigh with a clean cloth.

While Xanthos remained beside Elias, Stavros joined others who were carrying wounded soldiers to the infirmary. Other men gathered the bodies of the dead.

Driving back the Egyptians the day before had produced jubilation, but this retreat and victory provoked no joy. The cost had been frightful, the ground on both sides of the battlement littered with the bodies of gravely wounded and dead Greeks as well as the bodies of Egyptians and Bulgarians.

Elias, from time to time, opened his eyes. His lips quivered in an effort to speak, and, leaning closer, Xanthos heard him whisper the names of his wife and son.

All around them wounded and dying men moaned and prayed. Xanthos aided several of them with water from their flasks. Some pleaded with him to relieve their pain. He felt helpless; the smell of blood and the sight of suffering made his head reel. He was grateful when Stavros and Panos came to join them.

"How is the poor soul doing?" Stavros asked.

"He keeps calling for his wife and son," Xanthos said.

"We will stay with him now," Stavros said. "You better get some rest."

Xanthos tried to find a place under a tree to lie down, but the moans and pleas of the wounded wouldn't allow him to rest. He returned to Elias and told Stavros and Panos they could go.

He spent the balance of that night keeping vigil beside his friend. He put a wet cloth to his friend's lips and washed away the sweat from his forehead and cheeks. He assisted other wounded men who begged him for help. At some point, Elias began to burn with fever, and Xanthos feared his friend would die in the night.

In the midst of pain and death and distraught about Elias, Xanthos recalled the Bulgarian he had savagely butchered. His attack after the man had fallen helpless went beyond avenging the assault against Elias. Xanthos had been so consumed with rage he not only wanted to kill but also to dismember the man as mercilessly as the

Maniots dealt with their foes. He wondered if that ferocity for killing had always existed deep in the self he thought he had known during his years on earth. Perhaps from the time of Cain and Abel, that compulsion not only to kill but also to mutilate and destroy resided within the heart of every human being.

The night dragged on. Xanthos heard men draw their last breath quietly, while others died uttering anguished cries. One severely wounded man lying not far from them kept up a litany of curses.

"Whoremongers! Sons of bastard fathers and harlot mothers! Spawns of wolves and snakes!" On and on, all his pain and rage funneled into obscenities.

Another young man lying nearby who had asked several times for water, which Xanthos had given him, wept and called for his mother.

With the first traces of dawn lightening the horizon and finally fallen asleep beside Elias, through some disordered dream Xanthos heard his name spoken. He woke to see Elias with his eyes open, staring at him, struggling in an effort to offer Xanthos some reassurance. His fever appeared to have broken, and his cheeks were cooler to the touch.

"Xanthos," the name faltered weakly from his lips. "Friend . . . " The effort to speak exhausted Elias, and he closed his eyes once more, his body motionless except for the toes of his torn leg, each toe twitching as if it had a life of its own and was struggling to escape.

As a gray and dismal daylight crept slowly across the earth, Makriyannis came to visit the wounded. He paused beside Xanthos, staring down at Elias in silence.

"Look after your comrade, Xanthos," he said quietly, "but recognize that in any battle, you grieve, and then you accept the reality of what might happen."

Despite the fear of everyone in the camp that Ibrahim Pasha would return to attack for a third day, no further assault was launched against them. The mounted scouts sent out to track the Egyptian army brought word that Ibrahim Pasha had broken camp and was moving his forces west, away from Navplion, back into the heartland of the Peloponnesus.

The initial reaction of the men was exultation at what they felt was their heroic victory. Their enthusiasm was tempered when Makriyannis spoke to them later in the morning.

"The Egyptian has retreated," he said gravely. "He has decided the price we are making him pay to take Navplion is too great. Yet, do not make the mistake of thinking he has been defeated. Wherever his army marches, he controls the land. All our forces can do is harass, him but we cannot prevent him resuming what he had been doing before the attack on Navplion—burning and destroying villages, stealing the animals, leaving our people homeless and starving."

Throughout that day, Xanthos, joined by Panos, Tassos, and Stavros, tended Elias. They could do little more than provide him water that he sipped through his parched lips. He had lost a grave amount of blood, and his breathing was labored and hoarse with pain and exhaustion.

In the field alongside the infirmary, soldiers mourned beside the bodies of dead comrades, a number of men that Xanthos had known. One of them was Vasilios from Megalopolis, the finest fiddle player in the camp. His friends dug him a solitary grave and placed his precious fiddle in the earth beside him. Another soldier killed was Seraphim from Kalamata. He had a pet gamecock that slept beside him and crowed raucously every morning. The day following Seraphim's death, the gamecock sat listless and mute. There was also a young soldier named Alexios from Metzovon, who, in the frenzy and disorder of battle, had shot and killed his best friend. He sat alone, secluded within a small shelter of rocks, shaken by fits of crying, tormented and inconsolable.

In early afternoon, several soldiers came to examine Elias's leg. One of them was a tall, white-haired old veteran in charge of the operations. He took Xanthos aside and told him that Elias's leg would have to be amputated above the knee.

"It's the only way to save his life," the old soldier said. "His discolored feet reveal that infection has set in. If we don't amputate his leg, it will become gangrenous, and I doubt whether he'll live another night."

As the man moved away to get his instruments, Panos spoke quietly to Xanthos.

"He is called Macheris, and I have seen him at work before," Panos said. "He is truly a marvel with a knife. Believe me, he'll do what is best for Elias."

Someone brought a flask of brandy, and the men managed to get a few swallows of the fiery liquid between Elias's clenched teeth. The young farmer seemed to understand what was about to happen. As the men lifted him from the ground to a makeshift table, Elias grasped Xanthos by the arm, tension and terror seething within his cheeks.

"Help me, Xanthos!" he pleaded weakly. "Don't let them take my leg! How will I live and look after my family? In God's name, help me!"

"There's nothing else to be done, my friend." Xanthos was barely able to restrain his tears. "If they don't cut off the leg, you will die."

Xanthos wanted to be spared the grisly sight of the amputation, but he felt his presence might reassure Elias. He remained close as Macheris bent over Elias and whispered a few words to him that no one else could hear. Then the veteran grasped Elias's shoulder in reassurance, a clasp conveying such compassion that it was almost a caress.

Xanthos felt compassion wasn't something a man carried with him from the fluids of his birth. He understood this old man had acquired it by witnessing and then treating the terrible wounds that human flesh suffered in battle.

From a sheath at his side, Macheris drew out a foot-long knife, its gilded handle decorated with mother-of-pearl, its serrated blade made of fine steel. Bending over a small fire burning nearby, he passed the knife several times through the flame to sterilize the blade. To further disinfect the blade, he poured brandy over its cutting edge. He turned to Elias, who was being tightly held by Stavros and Tassos. Holding the knife as carefully as a musician would hold the bow of his fiddle, Macheris lightly placed the edge of the blade against Elias's thigh. He pressed the knife down, cutting into the skin a few inches above the wound.

The old soldier peeled back tiny flaps of flesh, exposing the bone, which gleamed brightly in the sunlight. Xanthos thought of the skeletons of the countless dead, lingering long after the transitory flesh had been rotted away. The durability of bones turned white, bleached by sun, wind, and rain, covered by layers of earth, yet remaining indestructible for centuries.

Macheris cut through the fibrous layer encasing the muscles and moved slowly and surely through the thigh, finally cutting away what remained of the mangled leg.

As the severed limb fell away from his body, Elias uttered a cry of pain and despair that burst from the recesses of his being, a cry so primal in its agony that anyone hearing felt the torturous suffering it conveyed. The cry rose to a shrill scream and then abruptly ceased as Elias lost consciousness.

Macheris soaked up the blood with a sponge, wrung it out, and dipped the sponge into clean water. He gently washed the stump. Using a long needle looped with thread, he began stitching the flaps of skin over the stump, crisscrossing the thread deftly back and forth, each time drawing the flaps more tightly together. When he finished, he wrapped the stump carefully in a sleeve of sheepskin.

"Thank God, that's done," Stavros said, his strong cheeks wet with tears.

"For this young man only," Macheris said. "There are a dozen more amputations I have yet to do today."

Elias's comrades, including Xanthos, took turns tending to him. Other men labored in the camp to bury the bodies of their comrades, all placed in long, deep trenches. They also dug trenches into which they consigned the bodies of their enemies. Other men built pyres out on the battlefield where they dragged the dead horses to cremate them. The stench of scorched flesh tainting the air about the camp made it difficult to breathe.

Elias improved slowly, eating a little more each day. By the fifth day, he was able to sit up and with a man holding his arm hobbled to wash his face at the fountain. Xanthos and the others tended him diligently, making sure he ate a little and that his bandages were kept clean. Macheris came daily to check the stump and expressed satisfaction that it was healing well.

"When your leg has healed," he told Elias, "have a good craftsman in wood build you a peg leg. I have seen men who get used to those second limbs dance as well as, if not even more vigorously than, men still bearing their own legs."

On the morning of the seventh day after the battle, with Xanthos beside him, Elias spoke of his desire to return to his village.

"I am no longer of any use as a soldier," he said. "And here in camp, I'm a burden, wasting the energies of men who must look after me." His voice became a shaken plea. "I know you are eager to join Kolokotronis, Xanthos, but I cannot make it home alone. That emboldens me to ask you, now that I have grown a little stronger, will you help me go home?"

Xanthos spoke of the request to Makriyannis.

"Kolokotronis has set up his headquarters, I know," Xanthos said. "No matter how much I wish to help Elias, am I neglecting my duty to be with the general?"

"It is true that in a time of war duty comes first, Xanthos," Makriyannis said. "But a week or two more before you go to Kolokotronis will not make much difference. He will be doing what we are doing here, tending his wounded, getting his veterans rested, recruiting and training new men, preparing to fight again. You can help Elias to his home and then rejoin your general."

When Xanthos brought the news to Elias, the stalwart young farmer could not hold back his tears.

"Poor soldier, that I am, Xanthos," he offered an apology. "But my gratefulness and relief that you'll help me return to my family is greater than any shame I might feel about crying like a woman."

CHAPTER
EIGHT

The morning of their departure, Makriyannis came to bid them farewell. He embraced Elias and aided him in mounting his horse. Elias sat stiffly in the saddle, his face already drawn with pain that Xanthos knew would only grow worse.

"God protect your journey, Elias," Makriyannis said. "He has chosen to let you live, and I pray he also grant you the bounty of returning home safely."

Makriyannis handed Elias a stout wooden staff with a handle carved in a fine, ornate replica of an eagle's head. "This staff belonged to my Great-Uncle Kyriakos. During his life as a klepht in the mountains, he killed many Turks and lived to age ninety-one. After his body became scarred and weakened with many wounds, he used this staff for support until his death. I want you to have it now."

"Thank you, Captain," Elias said. "I'll be honored to use it." He slipped the staff beneath the straps of his saddle.

"I am grateful to have had you with us even for this short time, Xanthos," Makriyannis said as he embraced Xanthos. "Thank you for your help with my letters." His voice turned pensive. "If we'd had more time at peace, you might have taught me to read and write." He smiled. "Thank you, as well, for the valor you showed as a soldier. You came to my camp a scribe, and you leave it, still a scribe but also a warrior."

After Makriyannis had left, Panos, Tassos, and Stavros came to bid them good-by. As parting gifts, they brought a flask of raki, a few ripe plums, and a small sack of almonds.

"In a few more days, you lucky devil," Tassos spoke to Elias, "you'll be warm and snug in bed beside your wife."

"There will be little time for sleeping," Elias said. "I must find ways for a cripple to take care of his family."

The men roughly embraced Xanthos. He was suddenly aware of the deep affection he felt for these men who had been his comrades in battle. There was also sadness in the farewell, because Xanthos understood that he would probably never see any of his three friends again.

"When you finish that history of the war, Xanthos," Panos said, "be sure you write how many of the enemy Panos Zeros of the village of Chrysovitzo killed."

"You pipsqueak!" Stavros growled. "If he includes anything about what you've done, he'll be obliged to write ten times as much about me!"

"You're a burly brute, dependent on strength alone," Panos scoffed. "My victories were achieved because I'm a craftsman with pistol and saber."

"I'll make sure you're all included in my history," Xanthos smiled. "I'll write that no man in battle ever had more brave and loyal comrades."

Xanthos and Elias rode slowly through the camp, accompanied by their three comrades who held on to the bridles and the straps around the horses' flanks. Elias swayed awkwardly in the saddle, leaning slightly to one side to favor the tender stump of his left leg, which was wrapped in sheepskin as a cushion against the impact of the ride. They went past men washing at the spring who waved them farewell. Other men brewing coffee and heating beans over small fires also called good-bys.

Xanthos saw the men he was leaving as a formidable army. The fierce days of warfare had tempered their bodies and spirits and made them resolute warriors under their tattered pennants. Joining Makri-yannis in the beginning as farmers and villagers, they had become lean and battle hardened, even the youngest recruit baptized in the fire of war. Elias and he were also leaving behind in the camp the graves of men who had been breathing, laughing soldiers only a few days earlier and who were now buried under the shadows of the Mills of Lerna.

Long after the deaths of all of those who had fought there, Egyptian, Bulgarian, and Greek alike, perhaps the battleground would live on in history as a place where the invincible power of Ibrahim Pasha had been thwarted and forced to retreat.

At the edge of the camp, the group stopped. They had spoken their farewells, and now, without needing to say anything more, they parted in silence. At a bend in the road, Xanthos looked back and saw their three comrades still standing there. He waved one last time, and the men raised their hands in a final farewell.

As they rode north in the direction of the Gulf, the sun rose, and the rocky, rutted landscape around them gleamed as though on fire. They rested at noon in a small glen over which wild fruit trees dropped black pools of shade.

The morning ride had exhausted Elias, lines of pain etched deeper in his cheeks. Xanthos helped him dismount and aided him to a resting place under one of the trees. Elias could barely muster the strength to eat some of the bread and cheese they carried in their saddlebags.

"Perhaps we shouldn't try to ride any farther today," Xanthos said. "Let's rest here where it's cool the remainder of the day. We can start again first thing in the morning."

"If we only ride three, four hours a day, it will take an eternity to reach my village," Elias said impatiently. "I can bear the pain. Help me back into the saddle, Xanthos, and let's be on our way."

A short while after they resumed their ride, at a crossroads, they came upon the sprawled body of a dead Greek soldier. He had been stripped of his weapons, his knife sheath emptied, and the bandolier around his chest cleared of bullets. He had been a handsome young man, his sunburned face strangely placid and untroubled in death. They could not know who he was or how he came to die at those crossroads, but his corpse recalled for Xanthos the line from the *Iliad* "by the road lies a dead man, unwept, unburied."

Using the short spade he carried on his saddle, Xanthos dug a shallow grave and dragged the dead soldier into it. He shoveled the dirt back and piled a mound of stones above the grave to secure the body from foraging animals. High above the grave, a hawk, black wings extended, glided with a graceful slowness through the sky.

They rode into the afternoon, entering the region of Corinth. The trail ran beneath a rampart of mountains and gorges, the slopes dark with forests of fir sweeping upward to the highest ridge.

By the time the shadows of late afternoon darkened portions of the landscape, Elias was riding with his head down, his shoulders slumped, his body swaying loosely to the gait of the horse. Xanthos rode close beside him, fearing he might tumble from the saddle. By the time they paused for the night beside a small spring, Elias was delirious with pain.

"I'll be all right," he mumbled as Xanthos helped him to a blanket. His cheeks were pale, his eyes reflecting his suffering. He made an effort to smile.

"What amazes me, Xanthos," he said weakly, "is how much pain I feel in the leg that isn't there."

Xanthos carefully unwrapped the sheepskin sheathing and exposed the stump, which was swollen and irritated, trickles of blood leaking through the bandage. He gently washed the stump and applied a compound of oil and herbs Macheris had given them back in camp. Afterwards, Xanthos wrapped the stump carefully in the sheepskin once again.

During the night, the fire burning down slowly to glowing embers, both men slept restlessly. Elias thrashed under his cape, his labored breathing indicating he was in pain. From time to time, he mumbled sentences that Xanthos couldn't understand.

In the morning, despite his restless night, Elias felt better, buoyed by his eagerness to continue their journey. Holding the staff Makriyannis had given him, he hobbled around a few steps. Xanthos walked beside him to protect him from falling.

"I must practice with this staff every day!" Elias said earnestly. "It must take the place of that missing part of my body!"

After they'd eaten breakfast and mounted their horses, Elias spoke apprehensively of his wife's reaction when she saw him.

"I don't know what I expect her to feel, but I fear for the worst." Elias's voice was somber and resigned. "She sent away a husband with all his limbs, and he returns to her a one-legged cripple."

"I'm sure she'll be grateful that you're alive," Xanthos said. "Even with a missing leg, she still has a husband, and your son has a father."

"You are right, Xanthos! I am alive! I still have a pair of strong arms and one good leg. By God, I vow I'll find a way to care for my family."

As they rode on, in the distance they saw black plumed smoke of fires spiraling into the sky. They also heard the faint sound of gunfire.

"A battle is being fought there," Xanthos said, "perhaps a Turkish or Egyptian patrol encountering a band of Greeks."

Later that afternoon, they reached Kiato on the Gulf of Corinth. They rode the ferry across the water with a boatload of exhausted and lamenting refugees from a village farther south that had been attacked by a detachment of Ibrahim Pasha's army.

"We had placed sentries in the mountains to alert us of their approach, so when their patrols attacked, we were hidden in the woods, and our lives were spared," a villager told them during the crossing. "After they had gone, and we returned to our village, we found only ruins. They took our sheep and chickens and burned our houses to the ground." He somberly made his cross. "God knows what will happen to us now."

An old woman told of the Egyptians killing her husband. "They left him lying there with the blood soaking the ground beneath his body," she said, all emotion drained from her voice. "They left me alive so I could suffer and mourn. I buried him myself, and then I piled stones above him so people would not walk on his grave." She shook her head sadly. "Only the wind will keep my old Thanos company now."

When they reached the northern shore of the gulf, Xanthos and Elias rode off the ferry and continued their journey. That night they rested under the shadow of fabled Delphi. In the hours of darkness, the wind swirling from the hidden gorges became a wail. Xanthos imagined such a wind carrying the voices of the oracles who had centuries earlier counseled princes and kings.

In the morning, they resumed their journey under a dark, threatening sky. By noon, swirling thunderclouds gathered low in the west, black and sulphurous, charged with lightning. The wind rose, lashing their faces and tossing the manes of their horses. A heavy rain began to fall, and they took shelter under a ledge of rock. When the rain ceased, and the sky cleared, a stunning rainbow glistened across the horizon.

"A good omen, Xanthos," Elias said gratefully. "It means we will make our journey safely to my home."

At dusk, they saw before them the lights of a village built along the slope of the mountain of Parnassus, the tiled roofs of the houses glinting under the light of a crescent moon.

"I know this village," Elias said excitedly. "It is called Kravasaras, and it is only a single day's ride from my village. Sometimes on those mornings when the air was clear and crisp, we'd hear the bell tolling in their church tower. I tell you, Xanthos, it rang a sound more beautiful than any bell you've ever heard."

They entered the outskirts of the village, the dogs raising a clamor as they rode by. They could sense villagers watching them from behind the shuttered windows of their houses. When several bolder villagers ventured out and learned the strangers were Greeks and that Elias was from the adjoining village of Pentemes, they shouted excitedly to their neighbors. Soon, a cluster of men and women swarmed around them.

Someone sent for the village priest, who came to greet them. He was a gentle-faced, white-haired, and white-bearded old cleric whose name was Father Markos of the parish of Saint Athanasios in Kravasaras. He invited them into his house and sent word to the village women, who, in a short while, brought them a savory repast of beans, lentils, cooked snails, and herbs. One woman brought them a roasted rabbit.

"I had been feeding and fattening this rabbit for months now," saving it for the return of my own son," she said fervently, "but this is a special day so I cooked it for you! Your safe arrival might mean my son will come home safe, too!"

"Melpo, you are a kind Christian lady," the priest offered her a blessing.

As she came closer to the table, the woman caught sight of the stump of Elias's leg. Her face paled, and she quickly made her cross. Mumbling something about an urgent chore, she fled from the house.

After dinner, when Father Markos and Xanthos left the house to bring in firewood, the priest spoke remorsefully about the woman's panicked flight.

"I hope Elias wasn't grieved by her hasty departure," the priest said. "Our people are superstitious, and some consider a severed limb a curse decreed by the devil." He shook his head. "I'm afraid Elias may find that same fear and aversion about his amputation in his own village."

"He worries most about his wife," Xanthos said.

"If she is a good and loving Christian woman," Father Markos said firmly, "she will understand and accept it as a price he paid fighting for his country's freedom."

Xanthos and Elias slept that night before the priest's fire, the first time under a roof in weeks. Early in the morning, they accompanied Father Markos to church for the liturgy. Standing in the shadowed nave, the candles gleaming before the visages of the saints in the icons, the tolling of the bell confirmed what Elias had told him of the beauty and richness of its tone.

Afterwards, Father Markos took them back to his house for a breakfast of milk warm from his goat and eggs from his chickens.

"We are grateful for your hospitality, Father," Elias said. "We haven't eaten this well in months."

"Bless the Lord for giving us the animals to provide such meals," the priest said.

Father Markos held the horse's bridle as Xanthos helped Elias up into his saddle.

"Give Father Basil in your village my warm regards," Father Markos smiled at Elias. "After you are settled and feel stronger, bring your wife and son to Kravasaras for church on Sunday. We will hold a special service of thanksgiving for your safe return. Your family, of course, is welcome to stay with me then, as well."

"Thank you, Father," Elias said. "I promise we will return as soon as we can."

The priest offered Xanthos and Elias the sign of the cross to bless their journey. They waved him a final farewell, and as they headed for the trail to Pentemes, the church bell tolled once again. Even after they had traveled some distance from the village, the bell's melodic resonance carried across the mountain with such purity of tone that it seemed to Xanthos even the birds who heard it were humbled and fell silent.

They rode all day across the foothills of the mountain, Elias stubbornly resisting any suggestion they pause to rest. The nearer they came to his village, the greater his impatience. From time to time, as he urged his horse into a rapid trot, Xanthos had to dissuade him from spurring into a gallop. He marveled at the force that drove Elias despite his weariness and pain.

"I'm not asking that we slow down for your sake alone," Xanthos lamented, after they'd been riding without rest for hours, "but have mercy on me. I'm exhausted and ache in every part of my battered carcass."

"We are so close now, Xanthos!" Elias said, his voice trembling with anticipation. "I beg you let us keep going! When we reach my village, we'll have days and nights to rest!"

Late in the afternoon, as the sun began its descent, the mass of the mountain above them altered shadow and texture. The higher crags were transformed into dark silhouettes against the sky, and the mountain's peak reflected the scarlet hues of the waning sun.

As the trilling of cicadas hidden among the rocks grew to a louder chorus, they saw on the slope of the mountain in the distance the clustered houses of a village.

"Home, Xanthos! I'm home!" Elias cried jubilantly. His shout echoed and reechoed from the canyons.

He spurred his horse into a gallop, the stump of his leg flapping against the saddle with what Xanthos knew must have been an agonizing measure of pain. As he urged his own horse into a gallop, Xanthos called a plea for his companion to slow down. Elias laughed, and for a few moments, they galloped side by side.

"I've brought you this far to reunite you with your family," Xanthos cried. "If you fall on your ass now, your wife will blame me!"

"I won't fall, Xanthos," Elias laughed buoyantly. "I feel wings rising from my shoulders. I'd be able to fly the rest of the way home!"

Elias only slowed down at the outskirts of Pentemes. Along the cobbled street, an old man was leading a donkey with a basket of olives lashed to its flank. At the approach of their horses, the old man tugged at the halter of his donkey to pull the animal out of their way. He stared up at them in fear.

"Barba Vasili!" Elias cried, as he reined in his horse. "Don't you recognize me? It is Elias . . . Elias Karnezis!"

"Elias!" the old man cried in disbelief. He quickly made his cross and came to the stirrup of the horse to peer up. He fumbled to touch Elias's hand on the pommel, as if to confirm that he wasn't an apparition.

"Is it really you, Elias?" he cried hoarsely.

"It's me, Barba," Elias laughed. "I'm not a ghost!"

The old man turned toward the houses and let out a vigorous shout that belied his age. He released another even-louder bellow that brought a number of villagers from their houses.

"Elias Karnezis is back from the war!" he cried. "Our warrior is home!"

Xanthos and Elias rode deeper into the village. More villagers hurried toward them, gesturing excitedly and calling effusive greetings.

"Welcome home, Elias! God be praised!"

"I prayed for you every night you were gone!"

"Elias, did you see my husband, Panfelio? I haven't heard from him in two years!"

The old man leading the donkey briskly slapped the animal's flank, prodding it along ahead of him, and continued to shout, "Elias Karnezis! Our Elias is home!"

After a while, the size of the crowd impeded their passage, and Elias pleaded for them to move aside and let them through. As men and women converged around them, those who noticed the stump of Elias's leg fell into shocked silence. Several old women exchanged low, stricken whispers. Others crossed themselves and turned away in fear.

"It's all right!" Elias sought to reassure them. "I lost one leg in the war, but, believe me, what remains of me is in fine shape!"

Elias and Xanthos slowly pressed their way through the crowd. Aroused by the excitement of their elders, a group of children formed a rag-tail vanguard, stamping and shouting, leading the parade. There were infants on wobbly legs, whose hands were held by older children with cropped hair and great round eyes.

As they neared Elias's house, a woman emerged from the courtyard to watch the mass of children followed by Elias and Xanthos with the villagers milling around them.

The excited children clustered around her, shouting and gesturing. Xanthos and Elias reined in their horses, and the woman in the midst of the tumultuous children stared up at them in bewilderment.

In the tawny light of the late-afternoon sun, Xanthos saw Anna Karnezis was an attractive, full-bodied woman with auburn hair, ruddy cheeks, and strikingly pale blue eyes. She wore a red kerchief around her brow and a red print apron about her waist.

The children fell silent.

"My beloved," Elias said, his voice choked. "My dearest Anna."

The children made way as Anna walked toward Elias and with trembling hands reached up to touch him, a touch that became a frantic caress.

"In God's name, Elias," her voice trembled. "Is it really you?"

"Yes, my dearest, it is me," Elias said. "A part of me is missing"—he motioned to reveal the stump of his leg dangling from the side of the saddle—"but I pray to God you'll be grateful for what is left."

Anna stared at the stump in shock and caught her breath. Then she reached out and with her body and both her arms gently embraced the stump.

"I don't care what you've lost!" she cried. "I'm grateful to see your blessed face!"

The children resumed their shouting and holding hands encircled Xanthos, Elias, and Anna. From the same courtyard, another woman about Anna's age came leading a small child by the hand.

"See, Matina!" Anna cried over the shouts of the children. "Elias has come home to us!"

When the woman and child reached them, Anna raised the child in her arms and lifted him up to Elias.

"Here is your son!" she said. "Here is your Kimon! How often have I feared this child would never see his father again!"

Elias took the tousle-haired, handsome child of about three in his arms. He held him gently, peering into his fair-cheeked face and light-blue eyes. The child stared at his father without any sign of recognition, but neither did he show any fear.

"He doesn't know me," Elias said.

"He will come to know you and love you," Anna said.

Elias bent from his saddle and handed their child to her. He dismounted and took the staff from the saddle.

When those villagers who hadn't noticed before now glimpsed the stump, a distress and anxiety swept the crowd. Several made their cross and turned away, muttering supplications against malevolent spirits. Anna glared a warning against anyone daring to utter a word of reproach.

Elias braced himself upon the staff and gestured toward Xanthos.

"This is my comrade Xanthos," Elias said. "We fought side by side in battle, and then, with a brother's love and devotion, he brought me home."

"God bless you, Xanthos, and welcome to our house," Anna said. She embraced Xanthos fervently, kissing him on both cheeks.

"Welcome home from me, as well, Elias," the other woman spoke for the first time, her voice low and gentle. She stepped forward and warmly embraced Elias.

"This is my sister-in-law, Matina Vrouvas," Anna said to Xanthos.

"You have my gratitude, friend Xanthos, for your devotion to Elias," Matina said. "I offer you my thanks, as well."

In a first glimpse, Xanthos saw Matina was a lovely woman about Anna's age, in her middle thirties. She was taller than Anna and more slender. She had skin so pale it appeared silky. Her eyes were oval-shaped and dark, with delicate burnished brows making them appear even larger. She wore her thick black hair plaited in austere braids fastened tightly about her head revealing her small shapely ears. The frock she wore was black and plain, without a trace of color or adornment. As she stared earnestly at him, Xanthos felt the glowing force of her eyes.

Anna spoke to the villagers. "Tomorrow you can all hear Elias tell what has happened to him these last three years. But I beg you now, let him rest and spend time with his son."

The crowd dispersed slowly, whispering to one another their wonder at the miracle of Elias's return. A few old women in black lingered, gesturing at the stump.

"Let us go into the house now," Anna brusquely dismissed them. "Those crones can go prattle in their own houses."

Anna, carrying Kimon, led the way. Elias hobbled along on his staff with Xanthos and Matina following. Inside the shadowed house, the women hurried to light the wicks of the lamps.

"To save on oil, we usually go to bed at twilight," Anna said, "but tonight is special. God has brought my Elias back to me! I want to be able to see him clearly!"

The room glowed in the light of the lamps. In that brightness, Xanthos watched Matina moving with a gracefulness unusual among the more stolid village women. When she stretched on her toes to bring down a kettle that hung on the wall, he noticed she wore black cotton stockings tied into a knot just below her knees. As she bent to light the wick of one of the lamps, her black frock gaped at her throat, and he glimpsed a trace of lighter flesh just below the neck of her dress. He had an unsettling image of how soft and pale her breasts must be beneath the dark cloth. The erotic fantasy made his cheeks burn, and he feared his face might reveal his licentious thoughts.

He was also conscious suddenly of his body crusted with smudge and sweat. In the ride from the camp, Elias and he had been drenched in rain and enveloped in dust that had dried into a second skin on their bodies. He also smelled of horse's sweat and the hot, sun-baked leather of the saddle on which he'd ridden for days. With a feeling of despair, he feared that Matina would be repelled by him. As if she sensed his concern, a reassuring smile curled the corners of Matina's mouth.

"Come and wash your hands in the basin now, Xanthos," she said. "Then sit and rest while Anna and I prepare as good a meal for you and Elias as our poor village can offer."

After a quick wash, Xanthos and Elias sat before the fire, Elias holding Kimon in his arms. While the father looked lovingly at his son, the child's eyes raptly watched the flames. Anna and Matina worked quickly and, within a short time, set on the table bowls of bean soup, a platter of macaroni, wheaten bread, and tumblers of dark-red wine.

"We make our own wine here in the village, Xanthos." Elias lowered Kimon gently from his lap to the floor and hobbled on the staff toward the table. "Strangers who taste it agree it is the best in the region."

"If we'd known of your arrival, I would have tried to buy a rabbit or chicken," Anna apologized as everyone sat down. "This poor supper is all we have in our home."

"This is wonderful, my darling," Elias said. "I know Xanthos agrees. For months now, our diet has been scraps of cheese and hard bread and, a few times, those small animals our comrades were lucky enough to catch in their snares. Believe me, this is a feast!"

Elias bent his head and whispered a prayer that Anna echoed softly. Afterwards, husband and wife stared silently at one another across the table. Xanthos saw the tender, endearing glance that passed between them.

As Elias began to eat, he gestured at Xanthos.

"Now, Anna, you and Matina should know that Xanthos, my devoted friend who brought me safely home, isn't just another village bumpkin barely able to read and write! He is an educated man, who serves as an aide to our great General Kolokotronis! He is also a scholar of history who is writing the story of our struggle for freedom." He smiled proudly. "He has promised he will put me into his book!"

"That is truly a marvel!" Anna said.

Matina looked at Xanthos with an admiration that brought a rush of warmth to his cheeks. "Perhaps you might share some of your experiences with us, Xanthos," she said.

Before he could respond, Elias broke in with another salvo of praise, "Xanthos is also a splendid storyteller. He had the men in camp hanging on his tales!"

"In God's name enough, Elias!" Xanthos pleaded. "Your family will think you brought home one of the classical historians instead of a simple scribe who aspires to write something meaningful about our struggle."

The conversation turned to plans Elias had for his future.

"First thing in the morning I'll talk to the village carpenter, Panagos, about cutting and carving a peg leg for me," Elias said. "I'll also speak with our elders about some work I might do. Anna and Matina know that even with one missing leg, I am very strong!" His voice was firm with resolve. "I'll look after Kimon and you, my darling! Don't worry about that!"

"I'm not worried," Anna said quietly. "We will work together, and we will be fine."

After they'd eaten, Anna brewed a small pot of thick, sweet coffee the men sipped slowly. The women carried the utensils to wash in the basin.

The long day of riding and the excitement of being home had exhausted Elias, his face now pale, his eyes revealing his pain. Elias noticed Xanthos watching him.

"Don't worry about me, friend," Elias said quietly. "In spite of my body's pain, my heart is full, and I am grateful to be home. Thanks to God and to your friendship for bringing me back to my wife and son."

Anna overheard him. "We are also grateful to have you back," she smiled, "but you also bring back a body that smells like a stable that hasn't been cleaned in weeks."

"You are right, my darling," Elias laughed. "Before I enter our bed tonight, Anna, I must wash as well as I can. I am sure Xanthos feels the same way."

"Tomorrow we'll bring in water to heat for the tub, so you can both have a proper bath," Anna said. "Tonight I'll help you wash in the basin."

After the utensils had been washed, Matina rose to leave. "It is time for me to go now," She bent and embraced Elias once again and then clasped Xanthos's hand to bid him farewell. He found the fleeting touch of her fingers strangely pleasing.

"Do you have far to go?" he asked.

"Matina lives just two houses away," Elias said.

Xanthos resisted as too brazen a suggestion that he walk Matina home. After she left, it seemed to him that the room lost light and warmth.

Elias hugged and kissed Kimon goodnight, and Anna took the child into an adjoining room to put him to bed.

"Where is Matina's husband?" Xanthos asked.

"He was killed in the fighting the first year of the war."

The first reaction Xanthos felt at the news was sympathy for Matina at being widowed so young, but he could not suppress a selfish surge of gratefulness, as well.

"Stelios, who was Anna's brother, was a truly fine man." Elias spoke in a low voice. "Matina and he had been together less than a year when he left to join the revolution. He was killed in one of the first battles of the war fighting with the army of Odysseus against the invasion of Dramali."

Xanthos understood why Matina was dressed in black. In the villages, when a family member died, the women were destined to wear black for the remainder of their lives. Their bleak destiny was a life of constant toil, in the house or in the fields, at the olive press or at hand mills. If water had to be carried from springs outside the village, they trudged the distance with kegs on their backs. If they had small children, they worked with them cradled in cloth slings from their shoulders.

When Anna returned, she warmed a large kettle of water at the fireplace that she poured into the basin.

"All right," she said brusquely. "Now both of you strip to your underclothing. I will scrub your skin as well as I can."

"Be warned, my darling," Elias laughed. "In addition to being a scholar, Xanthos is a modest man who's not used to being washed by a woman."

"Modest or not, he will need to wash before entering a clean bed," Anna nodded reassuringly at Xanthos. "I grew up with brothers and know what men look like in their underclothing. First, I'll wash Elias, and then we'll get to you."

Elias removed his shirt and trousers, and Anna helped him to the basin. Using a bar of pungent soap and a washcloth, she bathed her husband, rubbing the cloth vigorously along his arms and shoulders and then down his back. She washed his sturdy leg.

"Your hand is the only pleasure my body has felt in many months," Elias sighed.

"The grime on your body needs a hard brush, not just a cloth!" Anna shook her head in dismay. "It will take weeks of hard scrubbing just to remove the crust."

"War doesn't allow time for a leisurely bath," Elias shrugged. "With several thousand men waiting their turn for a little water, a splash or two is all one gets."

Afterwards, as Elias sat by the fire, Anna knelt beside him and slowly removed the soiled sheepskin that bound the stump of his leg. Xanthos noticed her shudder when she first saw the ragged, still-swollen flesh that marked the amputation. She turned away quickly to conceal her tears.

"The stump looks worse than it really is," Elias said in an effort to console her. "With time, Anna, the flaps of skin will toughen so the peg leg can be attached. It will be all right, my dearest."

Anna washed the area around the stump gently and bound it again with a clean cloth.

"Tomorrow, we'll find some clean sheepskin and rebandage it properly," she said.

She brought Elias a clean nightshirt that he slipped on. When he was settled beside the fire, Anna gestured at Xanthos, who had stripped to the waist.

"All right, Xanthos," she said crisply. "Now it is your turn."

"Perhaps it will be enough, Anna, if tonight I just wash the upper part of my body," Xanthos said nervously. "My legs didn't really get dirty."

"That will not be enough," Anna said firmly. "Come now, and remove your trousers, and let me help you wash properly."

Xanthos yielded like a child being forced to obey his mother. With Elias obviously enjoying his discomfort, Xanthos slipped out of his trousers. Aware that his underclothing was tattered and soiled, he stood submissively and resigned while Anna briskly washed his back and arms. She bent, finally, and washed his legs. After his first feeling of embarrassment, Xanthos allowed himself the pleasure of having a strong young woman scouring the grime from his flesh.

"This is the first time anyone has washed me since I was a child," he said.

"The child remains part of the man for as long as he lives," Anna said. "When you have a wife of your own, you will learn that to be true."

She put his soiled clothing aside to wash and brought one of Elias's clean nightshirts for Xanthos to wear to bed.

"Tomorrow I'll wash whatever pieces of your clothing can be salvaged," Anna said, "and then we'll see if we can't find you a few clean garments. I'll speak to Matina. You are taller than Stelios was, but you might fit into some of his clothing."

She bent and gave Elias a quick kiss. "Our bed is ready," she said. "And I'll bring a blanket and pillow for the cot in the corner where Xanthos will sleep."

Before leaving the room, Anna poured a little milk and honey into a saucer that she placed on a small table near the door.

"To thank the fates for bringing my Elias home," she said quietly and quickly made her cross.

"I must tell you, Xanthos," Elias said with a smirk after his wife left the room. "I didn't wish to embarrass you in front of Anna, but I have seen better legs than yours on some of our village donkeys."

"For that disrespectful remark, my friend," Xanthos said, "your heroic exploits have lost their place in my history. I will write that Elias Karnezis was a craven coward who surpassed all others in fleeing from the battle."

Later, settled in his bed on the cot, with the oil lamps extinguished and the fire in the hearth burned down to glowing embers, despite his weariness from the days of riding, Xanthos could not sleep. After months of bedding down on hard earth under the stars, the house seemed a sanctuary isolated from the world, providing him a tranquility he hadn't experienced since before the war.

He recalled the sequence of events that had brought him to this moment. If Kolokotronis hadn't been imprisoned, Xanthos wouldn't have joined Makriyannis on the eve of his battle with Ibrahim Pasha. Elias wouldn't have become his comrade and friend. Then, if Elias hadn't been wounded, Xanthos wouldn't have accompanied him to the village and met Anna and Matina. Nor would he have experienced this serenity in the warmth of his friend's house.

For an instant, he couldn't resist a pang of envy when he considered Elias nestled against the warmth of his wife's body. He also thought of Matina, her beauty shadowed by her mourning, sleeping alone in her widow's bed. He was surprised, as well, by the erotic feelings she had evoked in him, the most intense such emotions he had felt since those nights on Zante when he had lain beside his beloved Chryseis. He had difficulty recalling the shimmering loveliness of the young girl he believed he would love forever. When he sought to bring her likeness to mind, an image of the young widow intervened. He recalled the lamplight shining upon Matina's lovely face, the gentle sound of her voice, the gracefulness with which she moved. She had roused feelings in him that had long been dormant.

Yet, he couldn't believe she saw him as any more than the ordinary man he was. If he wasn't a homely man, he, with a pale, irresolute scholar's face, was certainly not as handsome as Odysseus or Makriyannis, a man of unimposing presence. However, his confidence was bolstered by the war he had experienced. He had fought beside comrades against the fierce Egyptian assault without faltering. That tempering in battle provided him an esteem in himself he had never felt before.

His fantasies of Matina grew more tangible, and he could almost sense her presence, although she slept in a different house. He considered she might be awake in the darkness of her house as he was awake, grateful that Elias had come home, even though his return had to remind her of her own forlorn widowhood. Xanthos allowed himself the audacity of believing that Matina might also be thinking of him, finding something felicitous about him besides the loyalty he had shown to Elias.

His final thoughts before he slipped into exhausted sleep were lines of poetry that returned poignantly to him: "Girl of the fertile soil, by Pallas reared, daughter of Zeus, adorned with the honey of bees and the scents of flowers."

With the stump of his leg mending and his spirit nurtured under the devoted care of his wife, Elias quickly grew stronger. In the first few days following their return, the village carpenter, Panagos, carved a peg leg for him, adding several sturdy leather straps to attach it to the stump. In the beginning, Elias could only tolerate wearing the peg leg for brief periods because of the pain it caused his tender stump. But he steadfastly endured the pain as well as several falls and bruises he suffered trying to maintain his balance. The first time he walked unaided on his artificial limb, his face glowed with triumph.

"When you return to visit us someday, Xanthos," he cried, "I swear you will see Elias Karnezis leading a line of dancers in a *syrtos!*"

Elias found work as an apprentice for Kalogeres, the village knifemaker. During the first week, he invited Xanthos to visit the shop with the charcoal forge in which the knifemaker fashioned and tempered his knives.

Kalogeres was a grizzled old man with stained and blemished teeth. As Xanthos watched him work, the old craftsman began by heating the forge until it blazed and cast off waves of sizzling flame. Clasping the as-yet-untempered blade with a pair of iron tongs, the knifemaker suspended it in the fire until the metal glowed blood-orange. He drew out the blade and beat it vigorously with a hammer, slowly and laboriously shaping the molten metal. He repeated the process of heating and beating and then waiting for the metal to cool. Afterwards came the grinding and then buffing the metal on a whetstone. The procedure continued until the raw blade was tempered into a fine, sharp knife. The final step was to fashion a design for the handle.

"The blade of a knife can be used as defense against animal or human," the knifemaker grinned, showing his yellowed teeth, "or to cut bark or chisel wood, to dismember a rabbit, or to slice a layer of grilled lamb. To accomplish any of these tasks with the greatest ease, the blade must not only be sharp but the handle must also be crafted to securely fit the human hand."

Around the base of the knife, the old man slowly fashioned a casing made of leather, sheep hide, and bleached bone. He added a decorative flourish by embedding in the handle—tiny gemstones and slivers of silver.

Kalogeres calmly accepted the praise that Xanthos offered him on his handiwork.

"My father was a knifemaker, who taught me his trade," Kalogeres said proudly," and he learned it from his father. God willing, if they show any aptitude, my sons will follow this same craft." He gestured at Elias. "This man will also make a fine artisan. He not only has a strong arm for beating and shaping the knife but also a natural talent for the craft."

As they walked home together, Elias could not conceal his jubilation. "This is labor I can do despite my missing leg, Xanthos," he said excitedly. "You see, my friend, regardless what some in the village may think about me, Elias Karnezis isn't finished!"

During that time he spent in the village, Xanthos found a secluded nook under a plane tree, a sanctuary protected from the wind by large boulders. He spent hours there writing entries in his journal, recording the intrigues of the leaders of the competing factions and of the civil wars that followed. He wrote of the shameful imprisonment of Kolokotronis and, finally, details of the battle at the Mills of Lerna where the forces of Makriyannis fought off the army of Ibrahim Pasha. He tried to remember and accurately transcribe all the events.

Anna and Elias insisted he continue to live in their house and each evening join them for supper. While it was true that their country was shadowed by war that could engulf the village and disrupt their lives at any time, those evenings Xanthos spent at their table were marked by a quiet and reposeful joy. For the first time in years, he felt returned to a normal existence. He occupied a house glowing with a warm fire and where eating and drinking could be enjoyed without haste or fear.

He knew his pleasure was enhanced because the evenings often included Matina. The more time he spent with the young widow, the more attractive she became to him. When they were together, he sneaked furtive glances at her. When she caught him staring, he looked quickly away.

Despite his timid demeanor with her, his thoughts were brazen and unconstrained. He imagined how flawless her naked body must be beneath her dark, somber garments. He also indulged in a fantasy where he loosened her tightly braided black hair and allowed it to tumble free about her naked shoulders.

As much as he tried to conceal his feelings, both Anna and Elias noticed his interest in Matina.

"Matina would make you a fine wife, Xanthos," Elias said one afternoon when Xanthos sat with him at the forge.

Xanthos stared at him in shock.

"The war has unbalanced you!" Xanthos cried. "She's a widow still mourning her dead husband! She probably sees me as an ungainly, temporary visitor in your village! However grateful she may be for my help in bringing you home, she'll probably be relieved to see me on my way!"

Elias accepted his tirade calmly. "You may know something of history and of the writings of famous men, my friend," he said quietly, "but you know little of women. I have noticed the way you look at Matina, and I also see what you obviously do not see . . . the way she looks at you."

"You are crazy," Xanthos muttered and turned away, but he could not deny the words quickened his pulse.

The seed planted by Elias would not let Xanthos rest. Yet, every time he thought of a relationship developing with the young widow, obstacles flourished. Their country was at war, and, within a few days, he would have to leave to rejoin Kolokotronis. He had no right to expect any woman to love him, let alone wait for him.

Yet the audacious fantasy persisted. While they were often in the company of Anna and Elias, there were times when husband and wife were away with their son, and Xanthos and Matina were alone. He treasured those intimate moments, but he still couldn't muster the courage to confess his feelings.

One afternoon, returning from the grove where he wrote his journal entries, he passed the bank of a small stream that ran down to the village from a mountain spring. A cluster of village women were washing and wringing out their clothing and spreading it on the rocks to dry in the sun.

Xanthos saw Matina ascending the slope carrying a basket of dry wash, and he hurried to take the basket from her hands.

"I am used to carrying it myself," Matina said quietly, and he found her gaze unsettling. "You will spoil me."

"Then let me spoil you a little," Xanthos said.

For a short distance, they walked in silence. As they exchanged brief greetings with a few villagers they passed, Xanthos observed their reproachful faces.

"They disapprove of our walking together," Xanthos said.

"It doesn't bother me. Because I am from another village, they disapproved of me even before Stelios and I married. I have gotten used to their glares and whispers."

They passed a dog foraging nearby, its gaunt frame revealing the rack of bones beneath its skin.

"That poor creature doesn't care where we are from or that we are walking together," Matina said pensively. "All it wants from humans is not to be beaten and, from time to time, given a few scraps of food."

They continued for a while walking in silence.

"Anna told me you'd be leaving soon." Matina said.

"I need to report to General Kolokotronis," Xanthos said. "He will be recruiting men for an army once more."

"That means you'll be going into battle again."

Xanthos was grateful for the concern in her voice. "I won't be going into battle such as the one we fought at the Mills of Lerna," he said. "When I join the general, my task will be the writing of dry letters and boring dispatches to the other leaders. Braver men will be doing the fighting."

"How many of them will die or return to their villages wounded and crippled before this war ends?" Matina spoke sadly. "In the end, will we gain our freedom, or will all the suffering and the dying be for nothing?"

"I hope we achieve freedom for the sake of all the men and women fighting and dying for it," Xanthos said. "We must keep faith that we will win in the end."

They turned onto the street that held her house.

"When I was a little girl growing up in my father and mother's," Matina said, "I didn't think about our country being enslaved. I feared the Muslims because they were often cruel to the people in our village. But there were also some contented, carefree days, the holidays of Easter and Christmas, and the pleasure we experienced treading the grapes in autumn and harvesting the olives in winter."

"Someday we may share those pleasures again as a free people," Xanthos said.

Walking beside Matina, stealing glimpses at her lovely face, he felt unsettled once again at the turmoil of emotions that being in her presence kindled. They paused outside her house, and, when she moved to take the basket, he felt a reluctance to leave her.

"Let me carry the basket in for you."

"Thank you."

Xanthos followed her from sunlight into a small, shaded courtyard, where the air was cooler and fragrant with the scent of a lemon tree and flowers. Matina opened the door, and, still carrying the basket of wash, he followed her inside. Her house comprised a large main room with great wooden beams supporting the ceiling. A pair of long, narrow windows stretching from ceiling to floor had frames of bright sea-blue. The panes of glass were open, and a breeze rustled the diaphanous curtains and carried the scents of lemon blossoms from the garden. A large, stone fireplace occupied one wall. Along another wall was a couch covered with a crimson spread and several small, fringed pillows. A circular wooden table was covered by a bright maroon cloth and, around the table were four finely carved wicker chairs. A thick, white fleece rug covered a portion of the floor.

In an alcove adjoining the main room, he glimpsed the footboard of a large wooden-postered bed. On the wall above the bed was a shelf bearing a candle in a small glass container, its tiny flame flickering across miniature icons of the Virgin and the saints.

When Xanthos moved closer to the fireplace, he noticed beside the hearth what he had missed seeing when he first entered, a pair of knee-high men's boots, the leather lustrous and gleaming with polish. The boots appeared strangely out of place in the neat and sparsely furnished room.

Matina noticed him staring at the boots.

"They belonged to Stelios," she said quietly. "He had this male obsession about keeping his boots so well polished he could see his face reflected in the leather as though it were a mirror. He wore them proudly on holidays and for weddings and baptisms." She made a helpless gesture. "I feel I need to keep them polished as he had always done."

Suddenly, in the silent, tranquil house, Xanthos felt the brooding specter of the dead husband.

Matina spoke in a low, tense voice. "What did Elias tell you about Stelios?"

"Only that he was killed early in the war."

"That was the end of our life together," Matina said quietly. "But there was also a beginning. I told you I came from a different village, one twenty-five kilometers from here called Zapherion. Stelios and I met at a festival, and you know the marriage of strangers from different villages is discouraged, but we didn't care. We were betrothed, and then we married."

The first haze of late afternoon deepened the shadows in the corners. Xanthos saw Matina's pale face in the waning light.

"Stelios had been a resin gatherer," Matina said. "He would climb high in a tree and hang by one arm from a branch and with the other hand scrape at the trunk with a short hoe. He was very strong, and he knew when the sap runs best and how to make gashes in the trunk just deep enough to keep the resin flowing into the tin, yet not cut so deep as to kill the tree."

A sudden rise of wind rustled the curtains.

"We had been married less than a year when word of the revolution reached our village," she said. "Like all the other young men, Stelios was full of pride and swagger, wanting to prove he was as brave and ready to fight as anyone else. When some of the men made plans to leave and join the war, Stelios was wild to go with them. I was pregnant then and pleaded for him to wait just a few more months until our baby was born." She paused. "But he couldn't bear being left behind."

She fell silent, and from somewhere in the distance, a rumble of thunder sounded, its echo carrying into the house.

"I did not learn he had been killed for almost six months after our baby was stillborn."

She spoke quietly of the death of her baby, but Xanthos understood her anguish.

"What helped me survive those months after my baby's death was my prayer that Stelios would return," Matina said. "I only learned of his death when one of his comrades who had grown homesick and returned to the village brought me the news." She shook her head in resignation. "I loved Stelios very much and, even after all this time, I wonder why I shouldn't have felt some hint during those months, some premonition to tell me he was dead."

As the words emerged softly and sadly from her lips, she raised one hand, her fingers fumbling restlessly at the bodice of her dress. She suddenly appeared nervous at how much of her life she was confiding to Xanthos.

"Thank you, Xanthos, for carrying my basket home," she said.

As he rose to leave, he couldn't resist asking whether she'd be coming to dinner that evening.

"Yes," Matina smiled. "Anna is a good and loving sister-in-law who regrets my eating alone, so, yes, I will be there. And I will bring a small tray of baklava I'll bake with honey and nuts I have been hoarding. I hope you like baklava."

"Baklava is my favorite," Xanthos said. "I haven't had it for a long time." He couldn't find any excuse to stay longer. "Then I'll see you this evening."

When he reached the door, she called him back, "Xanthos, I will always be grateful to you for bringing Elias home to Anna and Kimon."

"Elias is my comrade and my friend."

"He will be sorry that you are leaving. . . . I will be sorry, too. . . ."

His pulse quickened and, f or an instant, he felt an urge to reveal something of his feelings to Matina. Yet, the sight of the gleaming, polished boots constrained him to silence. All he found the courage to utter were the lame words, "I will be sorry to leave, as well."

Even as Xanthos berated himself for neglecting his duty to rejoin Kolokotronis, he fashioned excuses for additional delay. Whatever reasons he offered Elias and Anna, the postponements were because he did not wish to be separated from Matina.

One afternoon that week at the knifemaker's forge, Xanthos confided his growing affection for Matina to Elias.

"I've told you we noticed," Elias laughed. "When you look at Matina, your face bears the anguish of a lovesick youth."

"I have never shown any ability at concealing my emotions," Xanthos sighed. "Yet I swear, Elias, much as I wish to stay, I feel guilty about the delay. If every soldier shirked his duty the way I am doing, the revolt would collapse."

"If you feel you must leave, Xanthos, why don't you at least first speak to Matina?" Elias said. "Confess your love. That makes more sense than remaining silent and then leaving without knowing what her own feelings about you might be."

"I haven't any right to speak to her," Xanthos said. "It would be disrespectful to her as a widow."

"Holding your tongue this long shows adequate respect!" Elias said brusquely. "You told us last night you had finally resolved to leave this coming weekend. That allows you only a few more days to muster the courage to speak up."

"God help me, Elias, I know."

That evening Elias must have conspired with Anna, because during dinner she suggested that before Xanthos's departure, Matina show him the ruins of a chapel on the slope of the mountain.

"The chapel has a dramatic history that should interest you," Anna said. "In the last century, a group of villagers fleeing from a band of Turks joined with the monks and barricaded themselves in the chapel of the monastery. They held out for three days. Finally, when the walls had been breached, and their capture was inevitable, the men killed their women and children so they wouldn't fall into Turkish hands.

Then they died fighting rather than surrender." She paused. "Before the war, every year hundreds of villagers from many kilometers away made a pilgrimage to the chapel to lay flowers on the stones. Priests came from the different villages to join in a sacred liturgy."

"If Xanthos wishes to see it, I will be pleased to guide him," Matina said.

"I would like very much to see the chapel," Xanthos looked gratefully at Anna.

The following morning, Matina packed a lunch of cheese and freshly baked bread. Anna gave them a small flask of wine. They left the village and followed a path leading up the mountain. Matina ran ahead, fleeter of foot than Xanthos, who plodded along behind. He was astonished at the ease with which she ascended. She sensed his chagrin as he lagged in her wake.

"Don't be concerned because you can't keep up, Xanthos," she smiled. "I have made the climb up this mountain with Stelios and then by myself many times."

They climbed in silence, conserving their breath, but at one point, Matina cried, "Look, Xanthos! Look!" She pointed to a higher ridge of the mountain and the sight of a wild ibex scaling a sheer face of rock as fleetly as if dancing on air.

At noon, they rested and ate lunch beside a small mountain stream. They drank small tumblers of the wine, which brought a flush to Matina's cheeks. She suddenly slipped off her shoes. Turning away from Xanthos, she bent and fumbled at the skirt of her dress and then tugged off her black cotton stockings. Xanthos removed his shoes and pulled off his socks. They sat on the bank and dangled their feet in the water as Xanthos hadn't done since his boyhood in Zante. He savored the sight of Matina's bare legs and slender feet, her toes shimmering like tiny shells beneath the surface of the water.

For the first time since they met, he felt the aura of mournfulness lifted from Matina. As she fluttered her toes in the water, her eyes glistened with a child's carefree pleasure. With the suddenness of a revelation, Xanthos understood how much he loved Matina. In that moment, he yearned for the eloquence of a poet like Lord Byron to convey that love into words.

While he struggled for a way to begin, Matina drew her feet from the water and rose.

"We better go on," she said. "If we delay too long, we'll have to make our way down the mountain in the twilight."

Using leaves to dry their feet, they put on their shoes and stockings and resumed their climb. The final span of ground they ascended to reach the chapel became a cobblestone path, the stones worn shiny and smooth by the passing years and the tread of pilgrims. The chapel itself stood beneath a row of lofty cypresses. The decades of wind had bent the peaks of the trees so they appeared to bear the posture of mourners above the chapel ruins.

As they entered the enclosure, the wind sweeping through the crumpled walls and broken windows whistled eerily about their heads. The base of the walls was overgrown with patches of moss and latticed by the webs of spiders. Small splashes of color were made by the geraniums and daffodils that sprouted among the ruins. Above them like tiny, winged sentries keeping vigil over the sacred ground, came the cawing of a flock of small gray rooks.

"Holy men lived here once," Matina said softly. "They spent their days in meditation and prayer never anticipating that young men, women, and children would die with them. Months after the massacre, villagers came secretly at night with lanterns to gather the bones of those who had died here so they might bury them. Their martyrdom has never been forgotten."

A late-afternoon wind rose carrying cooler air. Xanthos built a fire within the enclosure, and they huddled close beside the flames to keep warm. The peak of the mountain reflected the rays of the descending sun and the first trace of a pale, crescent moon appeared in the western sky. A scent of thyme permeated the fading light.

Xanthos knew it was time to start down. With a flare of panic, he also understood it might be his last chance to reveal his feelings to Matina.

"Matina," he said, nervousness causing his voice to tremble. "I mean no disrespect . . . but I didn't want to leave the village before speaking to you . . . " He managed that much and then fell awkwardly silent.

As if to embolden him, the fire suddenly leaped and hissed, scattering sparks. He drew a deep breath and began again.

"I didn't want to leave before confessing . . . I mean expressing my feelings for you." Through the firelight, he imagined he saw dismay in her face. "Forgive me if I offend you."

For what seemed an endless span of time, she didn't answer. He was conscious of the shadows lengthening, the sun descending, a stillness in the air.

"I know your feelings for me, Xanthos," Matina said finally. "I could tell by the way you look at me, by the words you keep trying to speak." She fell silent, and he felt her struggling. "I found it hard to tell you I also have such feelings," her voice faltered, "I have not spoken because I wonder whether my feelings betray Stelios. In God's eyes, I may still belong to him."

Even as Xanthos felt a surge of jubilation at her revelation of feelings for him, he was swept by a foreboding. He understood the dead husband could be an overwhelming obstacle.

"We better start back down," she sprang to her feet. "It will be dark by the time we reach the village."

As they began their descent, fireflies speckled the first shadows of twilight and night-flying moths fluttered about their heads. When the path down the mountain became darker, and he could no longer see the ground clearly, Matina took his hand to guide him. He felt the softness of her fingers as if they were a caress. She held his hand tightly until they reached the outskirts of the village.

By that hour, full darkness had fallen, the crescent of moon shining across the tiled roofs of the village. Within a few dwellings, oil lamps flickered tiny beams of light across the windows.

When they reached Matina's house, they entered the courtyard and stood for a moment in silence.

"You must be chilled as I am, Xanthos," Matina said. "Come in, and we'll light a fire. It will help warm us."

Inside the house, Matina lit a lamp. Xanthos ignited some kindling in the fireplace. The flames flared, and Xanthos sat on the floor before the hearth. Matina sat beside him. Beyond the perimeter of firelight, he glimpsed the haunting presence of the polished boots.

For several moments, they sat in silence, and then slowly, shyly, Matina reached across the space that divided them and took his hand. He felt her fingers trembling.

"I know as Stelios left that you will be leaving soon," she said, her voice echoing in a whisper from the shadowed corners of the room. "I am afraid, as I was afraid with Stelios, that you may not return and that I will never see you again."

He was overwhelmed by what her words revealed of her feelings. In that moment, he felt the two of them secluded in some haven, isolated from the life of the village. Beguiled by her lovely face glowing in the light of the fire, he raised her hand to his lips and gently kissed her fingers. He heard her shaken breath, and she shifted closer. He moved nearer to her, and then they kissed. His lips hadn't kissed a woman since his beloved Chryseis. Now he savored the sweetness of such intimacy once again.

Emboldened by the kiss, he reached out and touched Matina, caressing her arm. He stroked her leg, feeling the firmness of flesh beneath her frock. A tightness in his chest made it difficult for him to breath. Even as he mustered the boldness to caress her, part of him stood aside, spectator as well as participant, watching in amazement at timid, irresolute Xanthos in the role of lover.

Suddenly she pulled away and rose to her feet. For an anxious moment, he feared her feelings about betraying her dead husband meant she was rejecting him. He braced himself to hear her tell him to leave. But without speaking, she turned and walked toward the alcove that held the wooden-postered bed. For what seemed to Xanthos another endless passage of time, the only sound in the house was the rustling of wind through the eaves and the crackling of logs in the fire. Into that stillness, he heard her call his name.

He rose and stood uncertainly for a moment before the fire. Then he walked slowly toward the shadowed alcove. He was startled to see her figure under a coverlet in the bed. In the faint reflection of light from the fire, her face was pale, the garland of her hair dark against the whiteness of the pillow.

"Come to bed, Xanthos," she said, her voice strangely quiet, almost toneless.

He fumbled at his clothing, removing his shirt, pulling off his shoes and stockings, tugging down his trousers. He lacked the courage to remove his underclothing. As he approached the bed, she drew the covers aside. He slipped beneath them, conscious of his body suddenly shivering and cold. She shifted closer, her thigh pressing his thigh, her toes touching his ankle.

"You must think me bold and shameless," she whispered.

"No!" the word came burning from his lips. "Oh no, Matina . . . "
He felt the pounding of his pulse. "I love you . . . "

They did not move for several moments. She fumbled beneath
the covers and found his hand. She drew it slowly toward her, and
he felt it graze the bare flesh of her thigh. She drew his hand higher,
and when his fingers touched the soft mound of her breast, she let
out her breath with a sigh.

An eruption of anxiety caused his shoulders and arms to tremble.
He drew on his memory of valor in battle to sustain him.

As if she understood his nervousness and sought to reassure him,
with her other hand she gently stroked his temple and his cheek,
caressed the slope of his shoulder and throat. He felt as if she were
trying to familiarize herself with his flesh and bone. As their bodies pressed against one another, she uttered a sound that began as a
drawing in of her breath and then became a mournful sigh. He felt
a chilling awareness of her dead husband's presence looming like a
shadow above them.

While he struggled for a way to console her, Matina's voice carried
softly through the darkness.

"Don't feel sad for me, Xanthos," she said. "Or that I come into
your arms as a mourner. In my heart, I believe that whatever happens
to us comes from God. He chose to take my Stelios from me. Now,
I must believe he has chosen to bring you to me. He gave me death,
and now he gives me life."

He felt the magic of the moment, his heart bursting to express
his emotion. All he could do was whisper her name, "Matina. . . .
Matina."

She seemed to flow toward the parts of his body that longed for her.
He caressed her breasts, kissed the softness of her throat, tasted her
breath. Where her fingers caressed him, he felt amazingly revitalized.
He inhaled the scent of her hair, a faint aroma of soap, the dampness
of a light sweat that rose from her body. His fingers felt a small mole
on her breast, a tiny blemish that made her beauty mortal. Violet
shadows rose from the hollows of her eyes.

What amazed him as they made love was the violence of his desire,
a passion not merely to enter Matina but to consume her. He heard

her cry out, a cry of joy and fulfillment that filled him with gratefulness because he had pleased her. After they came to rest, he still felt the pounding of their hearts.

The harmony of emotion that followed the joining of their bodies made him understand how meager and joyless his life had been to that moment. Banal days and threadbare nights stumbling into months and faltering into years. The blurred faces of men he had looked upon and the babbling voices of men he had heard. He considered the journeys he had made, the rituals of eating, drinking, and sleeping. Pages of his journal filled with his scribbles.

Lying beside Matina, sweat drying in a fine film on his body, he comprehended what had been absent in his life to that moment was love . . . the melding of a man and woman who might have once existed as a single body and a solitary soul now miraculously reunited.

Her lips were close to his ear, her breath warm against his cheek.

"I love you, Xanthos . . . Xanthos, my beloved."

He savored her words, repeated them under his breath, absorbed them into his heart.

"I love you, Matina . . . my dearest."

He knew those words of love had been uttered by men and women multitudinous times before, but in that instant he heard them echoing in his ears as if they were being spoken on the Earth for the very first time.

Soon afterwards, Matina fell asleep in his arms, but he resisted sleep. He did not wish to relinquish the joy and intimacy of the moment, remembering each caress, each whispered expression of love that had passed between them. He savored their union, the soft and yielding core of her body when he entered her.

He held up his hand and saw his fingers outlined in the faint glow of the fire, as if it were no longer his own hand but that of someone reborn, the hand of a lover fulfilled by having loved and been loved.

Into that moment of joy and fulfillment, like a chilling wind, he recalled the somber admonition of the poet.

> We live in the middle of things
> which have all been destined to die.
> Mortal have you been born,

to mortals have you given birth.
Reckon on everything.
Experience everything.
Yet, do not forget that nothing
of what you embrace and hold
will remain eternal.

He dozed briefly and woke with a start. Knowing he had to leave
Matina's house before daylight, he rose quietly from the bed and
fumbled into his clothing. He bent and tenderly kissed Matina's cheek
and heard her sleepy voice whisper a final endearment.

He slipped from the house, walking as stealthily as a prowler the
short distance to the house of Elias and Anna. In a corner of the sky,
the first faint glow of dawn appeared over the peak of the mountain.

In the silent, sleeping house, he undressed again, wondering if
Anna or Elias had heard him enter, and then he slipped into bed. He
marveled at how, despite his weariness, his body felt transformed.

Finally, as a brighter dawn made its foray into the shadowed corners
of the room, Xanthos, the scribe, reborn now as Xanthos, the lover,
felt his body drifting into a contented and harmonious sleep.

Even as he yearned with all his soul and heart to remain with Matina, he made preparations to leave the village as he had planned.
Meanwhile, Matina and he shared each night remaining before his
departure, making love as they had loved the first time. Xanthos was
astonished at the wellspring of desire and virility Matina unleashed
in him. He was also conscious that she was so much younger than he
was, twenty-eight to his forty-five. Yet, he consoled himself because
he never felt his passion to be less intense than her own.

On several occasions, they discussed betrothal and marriage.

"There will be many villagers who think our marriage a betrayal
of my dead husband," Matina said. "But I don't care."

"Let them think what they will," Xanthos said. "We needn't stay
here but can live elsewhere. I'll take you back to Zante. You'll find
the island lovely and tranquil."

There wasn't any way to conceal his jubilation from Anna and Elias,
who savored his joy, winking and smirking, shaking his head and
rolling his eyes like a jester. Anna seemed pleased for both Matina

and Xanthos, as well, but she expressed her concern to Xanthos that a villager might glimpse him entering and leaving Matina's house.

"You had best be cautious about visiting her at night," Anna said gravely. "When the villagers find a morsel of scandal to feed upon, they become voracious as vultures. You'll be leaving and free from their malicious gossip, but Matina will have to remain." She paused. "You know there are fools who believe a widow should never find happiness but mourn forever."

"I'll return as soon as the war allows, and we'll marry then," Xanthos said. "That should put the gossip to rest."

Knowing they would soon be separated, even the nights with Matina weren't enough to satisfy their desire. During the day, they took walks up the mountain, making love in secluded, flower-strewn groves.

In the evening, Matina came to the house for supper, and the four of them were unrestrained in their laughter and joy.

Xanthos found everything about Matina an enhancement of her beauty, whether it was smudges of flour on her cheeks and on her apron, a trace of butter on her fingers, the stain of wine on her lips. He spoke of those feelings to Elias.

"Smells and smudges of flour, indeed," Elias scoffed. "Those are a lover's blunted senses of sight and hearing. Wait until after you are married, and the daily monotony begins. You'll still love her, but the blemishes and smells will lose their mystery."

"You never mentioned monotony when you were so eager to get yourself home," Xanthos scolded him.

"That is the weakness of men," Elias sighed. "When our dream is achieved, we become human once again."

Xanthos ignored his friend's admonitions. He adored Matina and thought of her every moment they were separated. What little time he spent alone those last few days were not spent making entries in his journal but writing ardent love poems to Matina instead. He had never before so clearly understood the power a woman had to take total possession of a man.

After dinner when Matina returned to her house and after Anna and Elias had gone to bed, Xanthos would make his stealthy journey to Matina's house. She'd have left the door unlocked, and when he entered the house warm with the fire burning in the hearth, she'd be waiting.

Knowing how it pleased him, she would have unbraided her hair, and it tumbled dark and loose across her shoulders. He fondled it with his fingers, feeling the fine texture of the strands. They sat for a while before the fire and then walked into the alcove to undress. Their nightly ritual of lovemaking would begin.

They loved and slept for a while and woke and loved again. In the intervals, he heard the wailing of the wind, a bough scraping across the roof of the house, the bark of a dog. He felt the immensity of the sky above them, the curve of the earth. With the same meticulous attention to detail he had used to record the events of the revolution, he analyzed and pondered the facets of love, the power of passion that drew two people together in their pairing, nourishing love that vanquished loneliness.

Yet, never far from their joy, because of his readings in history and the tragic destiny of men, he was reminded of the mystery that ensnared humans in their brief span of time on Earth, the dark unknown each life is bonded by, the vagaries of life and death. Those were enigmas he had always pondered, and now he considered the place of love within those polarities.

In those moments when Matina slept and he lay sleepless beside her, he thought about the battle at the Mills of Lerna and his comrades who had fought beside him. He remembered the long trenches they had dug in which to bury the dead. They'd tossed in the shattered bodies, misshapen corpses with dangling entrails, limbs, and faces shot apart or slashed away. Each of those dead soldiers must have had a woman he loved who loved him and would never see him again. If Xanthos had been among those killed in that battle, he would never have known the joy he was experiencing now.

When they weren't making love, Matina and Xanthos spent hours talking, sharing experiences of their lives, recalling emotions and longings that dated from childhood. Matina spoke of loving Stelios and he told her of Chryseis, his student on Zante.

Several times Matina recalled the first night she and Xanthos had made love.

"I know I will never overcome a feeling of shame at my brazenness that night inviting you into my bed," she said ruefully. "I suppose I will also feel, God help me, that in some way, it was a betrayal of

Stelios. But, my darling, I do not regret it. If I had not been so bold, I would have missed all these hours of joy and love."

He confessed that if she hadn't been the one to encourage him, he doubted whether he would have had the courage to make the first move.

One morning, they visited Matina's father-in-law, the father of Stelios and Anna. Since the death of his wife, he lived alone in a small house at the outskirts of the village. He was a white-haired, hawk-featured old man with bushy black eyebrows shadowing the stern glint in his eyes. Xanthos felt the old man's hostility, and resentment sweep across him in virulent waves. He understood that Theokovis Vrouvas saw him as a despised intruder, violating the sacred memory of his son.

When Matina asked timidly for his blessing, the old man stared at her in scornful fury and turned away. On their walk back to her house, Xanthos saw Matina's cheeks moist with her tears. He made an effort to console her.

"I expected he would reject us," Matina said in resignation, "but still in my heart, I dared hope he might show some mercy."

On Sunday morning, the day before Xanthos planned to depart, they attended services in the village church. The liturgy was conducted by the village priest, Father Basil, a tall, ungainly cleric in his middle sixties. He had a thick, unkempt beard littered with crumbs of food. When he stood before the altar in his threadbare vestments, the years of bending to speak to his shorter parishioners had created a permanent slump so even when he stood fully erect, he always seemed to be bent over.

Father Basil's sermon that final Sunday dwelt on the sin of adultery. His words cut through the small church like the slash of a scythe across a field of wheat.

"As a jewel of gold in a swine's snout," Father Basil cried hoarsely, "so is a fair woman who is without discretion. Lust not after her beauty in thine heart; neither let her take thee with her eyelids. The way of transgressors is hard, and only fools make a mock at sin."

When they walked forward to join other parishioners in taking communion, as Father Basil thrust the small, golden spoon with the sacramental wine into his lips, it seemed to Xanthos the burning eyes of the priest held censure and accusation.

After the liturgy, when Matina and he left the church, as if aware they were the culprits of the priest's sermon, villagers stared at them with hostility and condemnation.

"The old fool has never married and has no conception of love!" Anna said angrily. "Sermons such as those today just feed the gossip of petty souls."

"I won't permit Matina to suffer any hostility or harm," Xanthos said.

"We'll look after her," Anna said firmly, and Elias nodded in fervent agreement. Still, Xanthos felt compelled to revisit the priest.

He waited impatiently in the nave while the priest listened to several villagers who lingered to speak to him. When his turn came, Xanthos confronted the tall, stooped cleric before the shadowed sanctuary of the church still bearing the scents of incense and candles.

"I am leaving in the morning to rejoin General Kolokotronis," Xanthos spoke quietly. "When I return, the widow Matina Vrouvas and I plan to marry. While I am gone, she will be under the care of my friends Elias and Anna Karnezis." He paused, a vein of iron entering his voice. "I ask, Father, that she remain under your protection, as well. If any harm comes to her from any of the villagers, if they malign or slander her in any way, they will answer to me. They will also incur the enmity of my patron, General Kolokotronis, whom I have asked to be my best man, my *koumbaros*."

The priest stared at him, blinked, and pursed his lips as if he were biting into a lemon.

"God be with you, my son," he said gravely. "May you return safely when our beloved land has been liberated. As for your marriage, it would be a matchless honor to have our great General Kolokotronis visit our small, poor village."

As he walked out of the church, Xanthos felt a twinge of remorse at having used the venerable name of Kolokotronis to impress and intimidate the priest. But when he considered protecting Matina, he would have dared much more than that bald-faced lie.

Early the following morning, streamers of dawn fringing the darkness of the night sky, Xanthos prepared to leave. His horse was saddled, the bags lashed to its flanks laden with food and flasks of water Anna and Matina had packed for his journey.

He embraced Anna and Elias fondly in farewell.

"Come back to us safely, Xanthos." Anna's voice was husky with emotion.

"He'll be back!" Elias cried. "If he came safely through the battle at the Mills of Lerna, he'll survive whatever lies ahead!"

Afterwards, Anna and Elias left Xanthos and Matina alone. The words of love he had rehearsed in preparation for that moment seemed suddenly pallid and useless. Nor did Matina seem to feel any need to speak. They had spent so many hours sharing the experiences and emotions of their lives, so many hours loving, that their parting did not require words. They embraced a final time, and then Xanthos swung up into his saddle. He looked down at Matina's face, memorizing her loveliness to sustain him in the weeks and months ahead. Then he tugged at his horse's reins and rode from the village at a slow gait.

At a curve in the road, he allowed himself the heartache of glancing back. Her figure grown smaller, Matina stood watching him. He waved, and she raised her hand in a final, fleeting gesture of farewell.

Leaving Matina and his friends was unlike any departure he had ever experienced. He rode from the village that morning possessed of an uncommon exhilaration of spirit. As the ordeal of battle taught him the fragile and transitory nature of man on earth, finding Matina helped him comprehend the ways in which love mended the torn edges of existence. He envisioned a day when he'd return to the village, and Matina and he would marry. God willing, they would bear children, sons and daughters to deliver them from the vanquishment of their own death.

Meanwhile, he rode through the unveiling of a day more splendid than any he could ever remember. As if he were seeing dawn breaking for the first time, he watched the shadows of the Earth's eastern rim vanishing. The ravens of night fled, carrying on their black wings the last beams of a crescent moon. When the corona of the sun became visible, the sky blazed with fire and the mountain burst into life.

Around him, beauty and vitality abounded. Birds cackled in the cliffs, and wild pigeons soared up the sheer surfaces of rock. Tall eucalyptus trees cast their cooling shade across slopes that glowed with hyacinth, mimosa, and bougainvillea. Patches of heather, thyme, and sage flourished, filling the air with their spicy scents. Beneath the hoofs of his horse, trembling stalks of asphodel tossed their spores into the air. In the distance, leafy grape fields glistened in the pellucid light. Throughout the history of the Hellenic world, life and nature were woven together as sacred entities blessed by the gods. The people honored the deities by dedicating the oak to Zeus, the laurel to Apollo, the olive tree to Athena, the myrtle to Aphrodite.

The magnificence of the day and his own euphoria filled Xanthos with a conviction about the indestructibility of their land. Their nation had existed in bondage for centuries, but its people, sturdy as the thick spears of wheat that grew even in poor and barren soil, survived to pursue freedom.

Perhaps Prometheus carrying fire from the gods to Earth and Theseus entering the spider maze of the labyrinth to slay the Minotaur belonged in the realm of myth, but the reality went beyond myth. This land had produced warrior-kings, poets, and philosophers, created the golden age of Pericles, built temples of unparalleled symmetry, and sculpted statues so breathtaking that looking upon them, men and women felt their eyes overwhelmed. And all through each of these epochs and achievements, the resolve to live as free men and women had never wavered. The mighty epics of Homer and the dramas of Aeschylus, Sophocles, and Euripides, from the land battles at Marathon and Thermopylae, the great sea battle at Salamis—all depicted and honored the victory of men over tyrants, the supremacy of freedom over slavery.

In that prescient moment, he renewed his vow to do whatever lay in his power, whether by pen or sword, to help once again liberate their ancient, sacred, and imperishable land. Toward that end, he drew once more on Thucydides: "But the bravest are surely those who have the clearest vision of what is before them, glory and danger alike, and yet notwithstanding, go out to meet it."

Riding lightly in his saddle, a humble scribe who had become warrior, lover, and diviner of the future, Xanthos rode confidently and fearlessly to join the army of Kolokotronis.

FINIS

EPILOGUE

🌿The Greek War of Independence lasted almost ten years. For most of that time, the fighting was limited to the Peloponnesus, a few mountainous regions of northern Greece and Crete, and to the engagements of the Greek fleet at sea. But the brutality and ferocity of the struggle matched that of any global conflict. That the Greeks were not always in agreement on the course of the war was proven by the two civil wars that were fought during the revolution, and that, once, three assemblies convened at the same time in different parts of Greece, each one claiming to have been lawfully granted the authority to represent the people.

If any single element united the Greeks during the ten years, it was their suffering. The community of Kydonies was destroyed in 1821, men massacred and women and children sold into slavery in the thriving markets of the Ottoman Empire. The island of Chios suffered the same fate in 1822 (to become the subject of Delacroix's painting *Massacre at Chios*), the island of Psara in 1824; and there were massacres of thousands of Cretans that same year and the fall and massacre of the Greeks at Missolonghi in 1826 (where Lord Byron, lover of the Greek spirit, had died of disease in 1824). In 1825, the dreaded Ibrahim Pasha, son of Mohammed Ali of Egypt and vassal and ally to the sultan, invaded the Peloponnesus with a strong force of Egyptians and for the next five years burned and devastated that land. But the Greeks made a few cruel entries of their own, notably the massacre of Turks at Tripolitza.

When it seemed that Ibrahim Pasha would reconquer those final areas of Greece still remaining free, a muddled or deliberate mis-interpretation of orders from the admiralty by an English admiral named Sir Edward Codrington, who was sympathetic to the Greeks, produced at Navarino in October of 1827 one of the great sea battles in history, when a fleet of English, French, and Russian ships sank a fleet of almost eighty Egyptian and Turkish warships. By this irredeemable defeat, the Turks were denied any ultimate victory, although Ibrahim Pasha continued to ravage the land for several more years.

When the Egyptians and Turks were finally driven from the Peloponnesus, the Greeks suffered a devastating famine, widespread disease, and additional warfare because of rampant jealousy among leaders of the various factions. The Greeks also endured the humiliation of having the Great Powers so apportion her boundaries that only 800,000 Greeks lived within the new free Greece while 2,500,000 still dwelt in unliberated territories. Among the areas excluded from the Greek state were the Ionian Islands, Thessaly, Macedonia, western Thrace, a part of Epirus, and the eastern Aegean islands. Also excluded was the island of Crete. By that culpable decision, Cretans obtained only the freedom to fight and die for an additional seventy-five years before they gained their independence. Finally, to exercise some control over the volatile Greeks, the Great Powers installed a foreign king, Otto, son of King Ludwig of Bavaria, to rule the new Greek state.

For any novelist or historian writing of Greece, the province of what is fictional or mythic and that of what is factual are often inextricably meshed. The sense of place and of time is so immersed in a vision and memory of the past that all events are somehow obscured in what the humanist-scientist Loren Eiseley has called the "necromantic centuries."

One heroic fact about that small, mountainous, and tragic country comes stunningly clear. From the time of the Persian invasions, through centuries of Roman and Ottoman rule, through two world wars, two Balkan wars, an Italian invasion, and German occupation in World War II among the most brutal imposed on any conquered land in history, Greece has managed to endure and survive. Even in recent times, after World War II, she suffered famine, a fearful civil war, and a series of military coups from which she emerged, free once more.

Perhaps an answer to the method of that survival is provided by the poet and novelist Nikos Kazantzakis, the greatest of the modern Greeks: "The Greek Race has always been, and still is, the race which possesses the great and dangerous prerogative of performing miracles. Just like the powerful, long enduring races, the Greek race may reach the depth of the chasm, and exactly there, at the most critical instant, where the weaker are destroyed, it fashions the miracle. It mobilizes all of its qualities and in one stroke soars up, without intermediate pause, to the summit of salvation. This abrupt surge, toward the heights, unexpected by logic, is called, 'miracle.'"

GLOSSARY

AGA	Turkish military chief
AGORA	Marketplace
ARCHON	Greek of the upper class (also PRIMATE)
ARMATOLOS (pl. ARMATOLI)	Greek militiaman retained by Turks to protect the roads against the klepht bands
BEY	Turkish dignitary, ruler
BISMILLAH	"In the name of Allah" Turkish battle cry
BRULOT	Fire ship
CAIQUE	Small fishing boat
CAPITAN-PASHA	Lord High Admiral of the Turkish fleet
CAPOTE	Greek peasant's cape
CHAROS	Another name for Death, the ferryman of Death (also CHARON)
CHIBOUK	Long-stemmed pipe
DERVISH	Moslem monk, sometimes practicing whirling and howling as a religious act
FUSTANTELLA	White, pleated kilt worn by Greek peasants
GIAGIA	Grandmother
GIASOU	Hello, how are you?
GLENDI	Feast, celebration
INFIDEL	Derogatory term for anyone not practicing the Moslem faith
JANIZARY (pl. JANIZARIES)	Turkish mercenaries conscripted at first from Christian families by taking the elder son
KAFENEION	Coffeehouse-tavern
KHARAJ	Head-tax required of every non-Moslem subject of the Sultan to avoid beheading

KLEPHT	Greek guerrilla fighter living in the mountains
KOUMBAROS	Best man, godfather of one's child
MANTINADES	Rhymed, song-poems
MOREA	Another name for the Peloponnesus, the heartland of Greece
MULLAH	Turkish priest, teacher
MUSSULMAN	Turk (also, MUSLIM, OTTOMAN)
PALIKAR	Warrior
PARNASSUS	Mountain in central Greece
PASHA	Turkish ruler of a province or pashalik
PAXIMADI (pl. PAXIMADIA)	Dark-brown snacks of twice-baked bread, the staple of shepherds
PHANARIOT	Greek from the Phanar or Lighthouse section of Constantinople
RAYAH	Human cattle
RHYMADORI	Balladeer, folk singer
SERAGLIO	Turkish palace, sometimes harem quarters
SERASKER	Turkish commander (also KAIMAKAM, VOIVODE)
STREMA	About a quarter acre of land
SUBLIME PORTE	Seat of Turkish Government, palace of Sultan Mahmud II
SULTAN	Ruler of the Turkish Empire; in 1821, Sultan Mahmud II
TAYGETUS	Mountain of the Mani
TURKOCRETANS	Cretan apostates who accepted Moslem faith
VIZIER	Turkish administrator
VRAKES	Cretan, baggy breeches
YATAGHAN	Long, curved sword

Harry Mark Petrakis is the author of twenty-one books, including *A Dream of Kings*, which was made into a major motion picture. He has held appointments at Ohio University as McGuffy Visiting Lecturer and at San Francisco State University as Kazantzakis Professor in Modern Greek Studies. He was twice nominated for the National Book Award in Fiction, won the O. Henry Award, and received awards from Friends of American Writers, Friends of Literature, and the Society of Midland Authors.